D0858417

Our Lady of Pain

a novel by Elena Forbes

ALSO BY ELENA FORBES

Die With Me

Our Lady of Pain

a novel by Elena Forbes

MACADAM CAGE

MacAdam/Cage
155 Sansome, Suite 550
San Francisco, CA 94104
www.MacAdamCage.com

First published in Great Britain in 2008 by Quercus

Library of Congress Cataloging-in-Publication Data

Forbes,Elena.
Our lady of pain / by Elena Forbes.
p. cm.
ISBN 978-1-59692-316-4
1. Murder—Fiction. 2. Young women—Fiction. 3. Serial murder investigation—
Fiction. 4. Police—England—London—Fiction.
5. London (England)—Fiction. I. Title.
PR6106.O67O97 2008
823'.92—dc22
2008029584

For George

Prologue

It was seven in the morning but so dark it might have been midnight. Snowflakes whirled like moths in the orange glow of the streetlamps, blurring the skeletal outline of the trees, settling on the thick crust that already covered the ground. The gates to Holland Park had been unlocked only a few minutes before and she stopped just inside, jogging up and down on the spot and stretching her legs as she gazed around, her breath a pale cloud blown away on the air. There was nobody in sight, the only sign of life the keeper's fresh tracks which disappeared from the gate in the direction of his office, its lights a dim blur in the distance. Squinting, she thought she saw his retreating shape but she couldn't be sure.

The park lay before her, open and inviting. On one side, playing fields led away down the hill towards Kensington High Street. On the other, the black tips of the trees that marked the edge of the woods were just visible behind the walls of Holland House. The landscape was almost unrecognisable, outlines softened, features obliterated under a uniform sea of bluish white, strangely luminous under the dark sky. Marvelling at the transformation, she started to run slowly down the long, broad avenue, feeling the scrunch of the deep, powdery snow underfoot. The music from her earphones filled her head, a bass riff pumping, the song spinning round and round. Needles of ice stung her face and the cold penetrated through her trainers and clothing. But she didn't care. Elated, still adrift on the tide of alcohol from the night before, she felt as though she could fly. She was out of control but it had been worth it.

She passed the ornamental gates of Holland House, the jagged ruins just behind, and turned up through the formal gardens, picking her way around the frosted patterns of low hedging which framed the empty flowerbeds. She climbed the steps to the North Lawn and ran towards the woods. The smell of bacon wafted momentarily on the air from the youth hostel just behind and she felt a stab of hunger. Only another ten minutes or so and she would be done; she would reward herself with a full English breakfast in one of the cafés along Holland Park Avenue.

Once in the woods, the track narrowed and the trees arched high above her, forming a tunnel. The few lamps were widely spaced, casting pools of weak light on the path below, which illuminated the trunks of the trees and the bushes immediately around. Beyond, in the thick undergrowth, everything was black. She lengthened her pace and drove herself faster now, down the hill. The freezing air made her lungs ache and her breath came in short, almost painful bursts. She felt tired already, each stride an effort. Almost at the bottom, she tripped and fell hard on the ground. Winded, gasping, laughing at her clumsiness, she rolled over onto her back and lay there, gazing up at the murky sky, letting the flurry of fat, feather-like flakes melt on her skin. Her earphones had fallen off and she noticed how still everything was, how the snow seemed to deaden any sound. Apart from her own breathing, all she could hear was the distant call of a bird high up in the trees and the muffled drone of cars on the periphery of the park.

After a moment, she pushed herself up into a sitting position and stretched out her calves, flexing her feet backwards and forwards to get rid of any stiffness. She brushed away the thick dusting of snow from her hair and clothes and gathered up her earphones. About to stand up, she noticed that one of her laces had come undone. As she bent forwards to retie it, she heard the sharp crack of a branch close behind. Then someone softly spoke her name.

'You work for a murder squad?' Sarah asked, arching her dark eyebrows, as if the idea was extraordinary. 'What's it like? I mean…what you have to deal with, what you see…God, it must be awful.' She gestured vaguely in the air with her hands as the words tumbled breathlessly from her lips.

Mark Tartaglia leaned back heavily in his chair, choosing his words carefully. 'What can I say? It is awful, but someone has to do it.'

They were sitting together at one end of the refectory table in his sister Nicoletta's kitchen in Islington. He took a gulp of wine, his eyes focussing fleetingly on the dark wood dresser that ran along one wall. As tall as the ceiling, it dwarfed everything else in the room. It had once belonged to his grandmother, salvaged many years before from his family's first grocery shop in Edinburgh. Symptomatic of the rest of the house, the shelves were drowning under a sea of china, oddments, children's pottery and artwork. Family photographs were dotted everywhere, including one of himself taken at Christmas, bleary-eyed, wine glass in one hand, cracker in the other, and wearing a stupid pink paper hat.

At the other end of the room, amid a cloud of steam and a theatrical clattering of pots, pans and crockery, Nicoletta was busy putting the final touches to the main course. She was wearing a simple navy blue and white wrap-around dress that clung to her body and emphasised her wiry thinness, a little too much, he thought. Her long, straight black hair was coiled up and loosely clipped on top of her head and, as she talked and moved around, nodding and waving her hands in the air, she looked as though she were conducting an orchestra. Her husband, John, stood at her side taking orders, pale head shiny with perspiration, sleeves rolled up, and an incongruous pink flowery apron protecting his front.

As with most Sundays, they had all been to Mass together that morning, along with their cousins Gianni and Elisa, who were now seated at the other end of the table, attempting to teach Nicoletta and John's children, Carlo and Anna, how to play I Spy. Carlo, aged four, sat on Gianni's lap, Gianni helping him with the words, while Anna, nearly six, sat beside Elisa. Their laughter and high-pitched voices reverberated off the low ceiling, piercing sharply through the thickness in Tartaglia's head. Usually he was delighted to be around them, but he hadn't been sleeping well and had drunk too much the night before in an effort to anaesthetise himself into a state of unconsciousness.

'Do you only investigate murders?' Sarah asked, after a moment.

Struggling to focus, Tartaglia looked back at her. 'Can't hear myself think over that racket. What were you saying?'

Sarah coloured. 'I'm sorry. I asked if you only dealt with murders. I really didn't mean to sound so surprised. It's just that I spend my days with text books and students while you...you...'

'It's OK,' he interrupted, before she went any further. 'I'm used to it. I usually try and keep quiet about what I do for a living, at least when I meet someone for the first time, but you caught me off guard.'

'Sorry again.' She smiled tentatively. 'Is it like on TV? Like *The Bill* or *Frost*?'

'No. It's actually quite different. We're not attached to a police station. We don't even have cells or interview rooms or anyone in uniform. We just work in a normal office and, as you say, murder's all we investigate.'

'I see. So you're like a crack team?'

'We're specialists, if that's what you mean.'

'It sounds incredibly interesting, really it does.'

She still seemed embarrassed, as if she had said something rude. Not wanting to make her feel awkward, he was about to mutter some sort of vague palliative when Nicoletta rushed over to the table, carrying a dish of buttered spinach.

'Mark's a detective inspector,' she said, dropping it down on a mat in front of them. She shook her hands vigorously and blew hard on her fingertips for a second. 'He's been involved in some very interesting cases. You should ask him to tell you about it.'

Sarah gave a wan smile.

'Are you sure I can't help?' Tartaglia asked, half getting up from his chair.

'Thanks, but everything's under control,' Nicoletta said briskly, before wheeling around and returning to the stove.

Usually when he went to lunch with Nicoletta and John, everybody mucked in. That's what family lunches were all about, she always said, and he usually did more than his fair share of the washing up. But this time was different. She had him practically chained to his chair, his cousins deliberately placed out of range, forcing him to give Sarah his full attention. With his fortieth birthday looming in a few years, Nicoletta wasn't content to leave anything to chance, especially not what she viewed as his generally lackadaisical approach to romance.

However, he could hardly blame Sarah, who was hopefully unaware of the setup. Compared to the motley array of Nicoletta's female friends who had been trotted out for him over the years, she was actually quite attractive, with nice, hazel eyes and a shapely figure. If she hadn't been a friend of his sister's, if he had met her somewhere else, he might have made more of an effort. But he didn't feel in the mood and he had no intention of letting Nicoletta pull his strings.

Noticing that Sarah had finished her wine, he reached across and poured the last inch in the bottle into her glass, carefully avoiding the thick, inky dregs at the bottom.

She smiled. 'Thanks. The wine's lovely. Is it Italian?'

Checking the label, he nodded. 'From Sicily. Merlot apparently. I'd better get us some more.'

Grateful for an excuse to stretch his legs, he got up from the table with the empty bottle. He glanced briefly through the misted windows at the snow-covered back garden beyond. It was extraordinary to have so much snow in February, but then nothing about the weather was a surprise any longer. Even in the warm fug of the kitchen, just looking at it made him shiver. He hated winter, February particularly, the bitterest, blackest month of all, when it seemed that spring would never come again.

He went over to the kitchen area where John was busy straining some vegetables at the sink while Nicoletta transferred a roast from an oven dish to a carving board. Tartaglia leaned over her shoulder and inhaled the pungent aroma of truffle, porcini mushrooms and garlic. The smell was familiar, the recipe as usual one of their mother's.

'Veal?'

'Veal. Go and sit down.' Not even looking at him, she shooed him away impatiently with her hands, a gesture also reminiscent of their mother.

'Here, you'd better take this with you,' John said with a sympathetic smile, exchanging the empty bottle for a new one that was already uncorked. 'What do you think of it?'

'Very nice.'

'It's from a small producer just outside Palermo. Your dad's just started to import it into the UK and he sent us a case for Christmas.'

'Wish he was as generous with me. Thinks I can't tell the difference between plonk and decent stuff.'

'You can't. Now go and sit down,' Nicoletta hissed, elbowing her way past her brother with a stack of clean plates.

Tartaglia retreated back to the far end of the table, skirting around his nephew and niece, who had started to squabble for some reason.

'What were we saying?' he asked, sitting down again next to Sarah, trying to block out the noise.

She watched as he refilled their glasses. 'Why do you think people are so obsessed with serial killers? It's all so incredibly gruesome and horrifying, yet the TV and bookshops are full of it.'

Tartaglia nodded thoughtfully. It was a question he had often asked himself. 'I suppose people like to scare themselves. The serial killer is just the modern-day bogeyman, the real-life stuff of nightmares. The fact that some of them are never caught just adds to the myth. Thank God they're rare, at least in this country. Most of the murders we investigate are a lot more mundane.'

'Still, it must be extraordinary. I mean, murder's hopefully something none of us will ever come across in our lifetime. Don't you find it odd?'

He shrugged. 'Odd' wasn't the word he would have chosen.

'I find the stuff in the papers bad enough, particularly when it's about children. But you're face to face with it every day. I'm surprised you can sleep at night.'

'Sometimes I don't.'

Sarah looked at him inquiringly over the top of her glass and he could see that she was hoping for more of an answer. But what was he supposed to say? Did she really want to hear how some cases preyed on his mind so that he couldn't sleep, how some images were impossible to eradicate? If he were honest, he had never become hardened to murder, never managed to make himself entirely immune to the dirtiness and darkness of what he saw, or the personal tragedies and fall-out from every killing. But he had no desire to start analysing it over the lunch table with someone he barely knew.

'It's difficult to put into words,' he said, hoping to change the subject, although he wasn't sure what else they had to talk about. They had already exhausted the topic of her job as a lecturer, like Nicoletta, in the Modern Languages department at University College London, and nothing else had come up naturally in conversation.

She looked at him quizzically. 'Well, considering everything, you look pretty normal to me.'

He took a sip of wine. 'Thanks—if that's meant as a compliment.'

'It is. You know, if we were playing "What's My Line", I would never have guessed what you do for a living.'

'I don't look like a policeman? Now I'm disappointed. It's the only job I've ever had, apart from working in my parents' shop in the school holidays.'

She shook her head, smiling. 'You definitely aren't how I imagine a policeman, not a real one anyway. You're too, well…' She hesitated, looking a little embarrassed. 'On TV they're too good to be true, aren't they? And they always solve the crime.'

He nodded. 'Unfortunately, real life's not like that.'

There was a sharp scream from the other end of the table, followed by the sound of breaking glass. He looked over and saw Carlo and Anna being forcibly held apart by Gianni, while Elisa rushed to the sink to get a cloth to clear up the mess.

'Anna, Carlo, if you don't behave, you'll go to your rooms,' Nicoletta said, with a cursory glance in their direction as she swept over to the table, bearing large white platters of steaming polenta and sliced veal, topped with a layer of mushrooms. She placed them down carefully so as not to spill the juices and wiped her palms hurriedly on the front of her apron.

'Do tell Sarah about some of your cases,' she added to Mark, tucking in a few stray wisps of hair behind her ears before striding away again to the stove. 'Tell her about that bridegroom one,' she shouted from across the room.

He stared at her, amazed that she should mention the case by name, but she looked away, occupied with something else. The case was too recent, too raw a subject, and one which was contributing to his current sleeplessness, although she wasn't to know that. He and his colleague Sam Donovan had nearly lost their lives trying to catch the serial killer known as The Bridegroom. It was the closest he had ever come to dying. The sense of horror at what might have been still affected him, the sequence of events replaying in his mind over and over again in the small hours of the night.

'I expect the last thing Mark wants to do is to talk shop on a Sunday,' John said, arriving at the table with a huge jug of water and a fistful of serving spoons. 'The rugby's on later. Can you stay?'

Tartaglia was about to reply when he felt the vibration of his phone in his pocket. Taking it out, he saw Detective Chief Inspector Carolyn Steele's name flash on the caller ID and got up hurriedly from the table, almost glad of the interruption.

'Work, I'm afraid,' he said to Sarah with an apologetic shrug, and rushed past Nicoletta, who was on her way back to the table with more food.

'Hey, Marco,' she shouted after him. 'You're not going, are you?'

He ignored her and went outside into the hall, closing the door firmly with his foot before he flipped open the phone.

'Where are you?' Steele asked, her voice quiet and crisp against the background of voices coming from the kitchen behind him.

'At my sister's. In Islington. About to have lunch.'

'Good,' Steele said, as if she hadn't heard the final sentence. 'That's not too far away. I want you over at Holland Park immediately. We have a suspicious death. Sam's there now with the crime- scene manager. The rendezvous point's in the main car park, on Abbotsbury Road, in between Kensington High Street and Holland Park Avenue.'

*

The Ducati slithered to a halt on the icy ground, front wheel nosing deep into a bank of shovelled snow. Tartaglia killed the engine and lights and dismounted, noting, as he removed his helmet, how dark it was even though it was still early afternoon. The whole of Holland Park had been sealed off and the car park had been cleared; the only remaining vehicles belonged to members of the police or forensic services.

He spotted DS Sam Donovan in a far corner. She was talking into her phone, standing beside a small semi-circle of uniformed police from the local station who were gathered around the open back of a van. One of them was distributing plastic cups and a thermos of something hot was making its way down the line. Judging from the colour of what was being poured, it looked like tomato soup.

As he walked towards her, Donovan gave him a small wave and, after a few more words, snapped her phone shut.

'You got here quickly,' she said, picking her way gingerly through the snow towards him.

Her short brown hair stood in spiky tufts in the cold air and her eyes were watering, a smear of mascara under one of them. She was wrapped up in a short, black and white checked coat that looked quite unsuitable for the weather, with a bright orange and red patterned scarf wound round her neck.

'There wasn't much traffic. Everyone's having lunch, I suppose.'

He followed her up a steep, slippery flight of steps into the park, noting that she was wearing a skirt for a change, and quite a short skirt at that, barely longer than her coat, although he couldn't see much of her slim legs as they were encased in a pair of enormous Wellingtons.

'So, what have we got?' he asked at the top, wondering why she was dressed up on a Sunday.

'Victim's female, late twenties or early thirties. She's been stripped naked. No ID as yet and cause of death unclear. They're searching the area for any clothing or personal belongings but nothing's turned up so far. CID are checking with MISSPER right now.'

'Who's the CSM today?'

'It's Nina Turner. I've just been speaking to her.'

'Good,' he replied. Nina was married to one of the other DIs in the Barnes office where he worked and was generally very thorough. 'Where is she?' He hadn't noticed her in the car park.

'She's gone off to sort out the dog teams but she'll meet you at the crime scene in ten minutes. We'd better get a move on as it's a bit of a hike.'

They passed the Belvedere Restaurant and cut across the back lawn towards the woods. The last time he had been to Holland Park had been in the summer a couple of years back, when he had gone with Nicoletta, John and a group of friends to the open-air opera. It had been Verdi or Donizetti, something lyrical and Italian. He remembered the strident sound of the park's peacocks shrieking from time to time over the music and how hot it had been, sweating in his jacket and tie under the airless, tented canopy. Looking around now, the place was unrecognisable and he wished he had more time to stop and enjoy the spectacle.

It had been blowing a blizzard for days and the ground and every horizontal surface were covered in a thick white crust, several feet deep in places. Much of it was undisturbed, although a number of human tracks carved through the snow on much the same path as they were taking, with what looked like the tracks of dogs curving off every so often into the distance. Although it had snowed heavily overnight, the park had been open for business that morning and he wondered how much ground had been disturbed and contaminated before the whole thing was closed off.

'Christ, it's cold,' Donovan said, tucking her chin further down into the folds of her scarf. 'I hate winter.'

'Me too. Who found the body?'

'Some kids, playing hide-and-seek this morning.' She spoke breathily, as she struggled to match his pace. 'I expect they got the fright of their lives, poor things. Dr Browne's examining the body now.'

'Arabella? What sort of mood is she in?'

She smiled. 'It's Sunday and she's missed lunch.'

'She's not the only one,' he said with feeling.

She looked over at him inquiringly.

'I was at Nicoletta's,' he added, finding it necessary to explain for some reason. 'We had barely started.'

She gave him a look of sympathy. 'Poor you. She's a fantastic cook, I remember. Was she matchmaking again?'

'Of course.'

'And?'

'Nothing,' he said emphatically, which brought another smile to her lips. 'It was one of her friends from work. A woman called Sarah. Perfectly nice...'

'But not your type?'

'No. I was actually pleased to get Steele's call.'

They tramped through the deep snow in silence and entered the woods. He wondered if she was thinking of the time when he had taken her to Nicoletta's for lunch a few months before to cheer her up after the Bridegroom case. Perhaps the association was enough to awaken unpleasant memories and he looked over at her, but nothing registered in her expression.

The woodland on either side of the track was dense, with a mixture of rhododendrons, tall hollies and bare deciduous trees that created a canopy of branches over their heads. Tartaglia thought how incredibly rural and quiet it all was, with not a road or house in sight.

Apart from the wooden fencing on either side of the path, they might easily have been somewhere in the country, instead of central London. Numerous fallen trees dotted the area, brought down in the recent storms. Some still lay where they had fallen; others had already been partially cut up into logs. One, which looked as if it must have been well over a hundred feet tall, with a huge, ivy-clad circumference, had smashed through the wooden fencing that ran along one side of the path, its massive, frosted roots exposed to the air, like a giant hand.

The ground was uneven and they hadn't gone more than a few yards when Donovan stumbled and slipped, her foot coming out of one of the boots. He reached out just in time to stop her falling.

'Thanks,' she said, shaking the snow off her red-stockinged foot before putting it back into the Wellington and walking on. 'My feet have turned to ice. I can hardly feel them, let alone get a grip in these boots.'

'They're about the only practical thing about your get-up,' he said, wondering again where she had been.

She laughed. 'I borrowed them from one of the uniforms. I didn't have time to go home and it was either that or ruin a brand-new pair of boots.'

A gust of wind blew a shower of ice particles into Tartaglia's face from one of the overhead branches and he suddenly felt very cold, in spite of his heavy-duty leathers and boots. He heard the distant whirr of a helicopter somewhere above and he and Donovan glanced up at the sky. Although it had stopped snowing, it looked ominously dark and he remembered that the weather report had promised fresh snow.

'It's amazing how quickly the vultures appear,' she said, as the helicopter noise grew louder.

'Somebody's been hot on their mobile to the news desk, as usual. I hope there's nothing for them to see.'

'All well under cover, according to Nina. Don't worry.'

A minute later he saw the flicker of electric light through the thick branches ahead and heard the murmur of voices. They followed the track around into a wide clearing where several other paths came together, like the spokes of a wheel. A few wooden benches were dotted around as if this were a favourite place to sit, although he couldn't imagine why as it was all so gloomy, with no view except of the trees. Here again the tracks were well trampled in the middle, although the banks of snow at the edges were high and untouched. A couple of uniforms from the local station stood huddled together just in front of the inner cordon, stamping their feet for warmth. Beyond, several blue-suited SOCOs were moving along slowly on their hands and knees in the snow, combing the ground.

'The body's in there,' Donovan said, stopping just in front of the cordon tape which stretched across the path and pointing towards a large, fenced-off area of woodland about twenty feet away. He could just make out the top of the forensic tent behind some thick undergrowth.

'How the hell do I get in?'

'There's a gap just along there to the right. Nina should be here any minute now. If you don't need me, I'll go back to the car park and see how we're progressing with the ID. I'll call you if there's any news.'

Tartaglia signed in with the uniformed gatekeeper and put on protective clothing, gloves and overshoes before ducking under the tape. He walked around the perimeter of fencing, following the boarded walkway put down over the snow by the SOCOs to protect the track, until he came to the gap in the fence. He paused for a moment, gazing into the dense wooded area beyond. Even at this time of day it was dark in there, and nothing much was visible from the public path. Short of jumping over the high fence, the gap seemed to be the only way into the enclosure beyond. The hole had been inexpertly patched with chicken wire, with several broken wooden staves poking up through the mesh like bones. Judging from the tufts of hair caught on

some of the points, it was a passage much used by dogs and other animals. He stepped carefully over the low barrier and started to pick
his way through the deep snow, struggling to find sure footing
amongst the hidden layers of bracken and fallen branches.

The small forensic tent was tucked away in the middle of the enclosure behind a thicket of holly. Someone was moving about inside,
silhouetted against the bright light of the lamps. As he lifted the flap,
he was confronted by the broad rear view of Dr Browne, kneeling over
something on the ground, a man with a camera standing beside her.

'I want some final close-ups from this angle,' Browne barked at
the photographer, pointing with a gloved hand. 'And the other side
too before we turn her over. Then I want some more shots of her
hands and feet before I bag them up.'

The photographer moved in closer and started snapping away. As
each flash lit up the area, it penetrated Tartaglia's head like a blade,
leaving an echo of brilliance dancing in front of his eyes.

'Afternoon, Dr Browne,' he said, blinking several times, trying to
focus, although with Browne and the photographer blocking his view
there was nothing much to see.

Browne jerked round and peered up at Tartaglia through half-
moon spectacles, just visible between the hood of her suit and mask.

'Glad you could finally make it,' she said gruffly.

'Was I that long?'

'When you're stuck out here in the bloody cold, a minute seems
an hour.' The photographer was still snapping away and she turned to
him. 'Give us a minute will you, John? Inspector Tartaglia wants to
feast his eyes on our wood nymph and there's not enough room in
here to swing a cat.'

'OK,' John said cheerily, putting his camera down. 'Give me a
shout when you're ready.' He stepped out of the tent.

'You've certainly got an interesting one here,' Browne said,

wheezing as she struggled to her feet. 'Which is some small consolation for spoiling my Sunday lunch. Take a look.'

She shifted aside. Under the dazzling glare of the electric lamp,
Tartaglia saw the naked body of a young woman. She was kneeling
down in the snow, head bent right over touching the ground, her face
almost entirely hidden beneath a tangle of pale blonde hair which
spread out stiffly in front of her like waterweed. He followed the delicate outline of her shoulders, the smooth curves of her back, her hips
and buttocks, which were glistening and luminous under the light.
Her legs and arms were folded beneath her and disappeared into the
snow. For a moment he pictured a partially carved statue emerging
from a block of marble, so pale that it was difficult to see where the
snow ended and flesh began. He felt cold just to look at her.

As he adjusted his eyes to the light, he could just make out faint
patches of pinky-red livor mortis along her neck, shoulders and back,
just visible beneath the sparkling carapace of ice.

'So she's been moved,' he muttered, looking over at Browne. 'Was
this how you found her?'

'More or less. From what I've been able to see, there are some
areas of lividity along the back of her legs and arms too, so she was
lying flat on her back for several hours after death, although she was
moved into the current position before the lividity became completely
fixed.'

'Any idea when she was moved?'

'In these temperatures it's difficult to tell. Judging from the colour
of the hypostasis, she's been kept at a low ambient temperature either
here or somewhere else. As you know, it's impossible to be precise,
but I'd hazard a guess that she was shifted anything between twelve
to thirty-six hours after death. And it gets even more curious, as you'll
see if you take a closer look.' She raised her thick brows for emphasis.

Intrigued, he moved forwards and knelt down beside the unknown woman, carefully brushing aside some of her hair and examining what he could of her face. Her forehead rested on her hands and her eyes were open and stared vacantly at the ground, eyelashes and brows frosted white. She looked maybe in her late twenties or thirties, although it was always difficult to tell.

'Oh Christ,' he said, as he moved aside some more of her hair. Her hands were tightly bound at the wrists with duct tape and clasped as if in prayer.

'Her knees and ankles are also taped together,' Browne said. 'Although you won't be able to see properly until we get her out of here.'

He nodded automatically, still focussing on the woman's hands. Her nails were manicured but unpainted and she wore no rings, or any form of jewellery, although that meant nothing.

'Any idea about cause of death?' he asked, getting to his feet, still looking at the woman. Something about the pose immediately struck him as symbolic, although he couldn't think what it reminded him of. The image locked in his mind as he wondered who she was, whether she had a husband or family or friends who were missing her.

Browne grunted and folded her arms across her bulk. 'Not obvious yet, other than that she clearly didn't do this to herself.'

'You surprise me. So no visible signs of injury?'

'There's some minor bruising to her face and a few deep scratches around her mouth. From what I can see, it's possible she was sexually assaulted. Once we turn her over, I'll take swabs. But a full exam will have to wait until I get her back to the mortuary. It also makes more sense to fingerprint the tape on her arms and legs back there and I can't examine her properly until I remove it. We'll catch our deaths if we stay here much longer.'

'You'll check the tape for traces of saliva?'

'Of course,' Browne said, emphatically. 'I can't see anyone bothering with a pair of scissors out here. We'll look for tooth marks on the tape as well, just in case.'

'Assuming she's been out in the open all this time, I suppose there's no way of telling if she died here or if she was dumped?'

Brown shook her head. 'The snow under her is about a foot deep, and when we got here, she had another six inches or so on top of her which was fresh and untouched. I'd say most of the more recent stuff's probably accounted for by what fell in the night.'

'So, she's been here at least twenty-four hours?'

'At least. She's also got traces of leaf mould in her hair. The only place where the ground is exposed is under some of those thick holly bushes outside. Maybe that's where she was lying before. I've sent someone out to take samples.'

'It's not easy getting into the enclosure, even in daylight. And there's nothing in here for anybody to see. Are there any signs that she was dragged or pulled along at all?'

'Apart from what I've already mentioned, the body's unmarked. She either got here under her own steam which, I agree with you, seems unlikely, or she was carried in, dead or alive.'

Tartaglia nodded. 'Which means we're looking for somebody capable of lifting a grown woman of...' He looked down at the body in the snow, trying to gauge her size fully stretched out. '...Medium height, slim build. Probably about eight to eight and a half stone, I'd say.' Browne nodded in agreement. 'Not a simple thing,' Tartaglia continued, 'given the fence and the uneven ground. Any thoughts on time of death?'

Browne frowned. 'You know what I usually say—'

'Yes. I know. When was she last seen? When was the body found?' Like most pathologists he had come across, Browne was notoriously reluctant to estimate times of death. 'Can't we do a bit better than that today, Doctor?'

Browne took a deep, wheezy breath and placed her hands on her ample hips. 'Well, as I'm in a charitable mood...it started snowing on

Thursday, so we're definitely looking at sometime within the last three days.'

'That's a great help.'

'Don't interrupt. I was going to say that in my view we're looking at less than that. She's at ambient temperature and rigor's only coming on now, although it's pretty weak because of the cold. Unless she's been kept in a freezer, which the lab will tell us, my guess is that she's been dead for no more than a couple of days. I know you boys like chapter and verse, but that's the best you'll get out of me until the post-mortem this evening, and that may well not tell us anything.'

'Thank you,' he said, with an appreciative smile, which Browne returned with a curt nod of her head. 'Call me when you want me for the post-mortem. Anything else?'

'Yes. Speaking of verse, you'll be interested in this.' With another wheeze, she bent down and picked up an evidence bag, which was lying on the ground beside her case with a number of other bags and medical implements.

She thrust it at Tartaglia. 'Someone's got a vivid imagination.'

Through the clear plastic he saw a creased sheet of white paper with some printed words centred in the middle of the page:

Cold eyelids that hide like a jewel
Hard eyes that grow soft for an hour;
The heavy white limbs, and the cruel
Red mouth like a venomous flower;
When these are gone by with their glories,
What shall rest of thee then, what remain,
O mystic and sombre Dolores,
Our Lady of Pain?

'It fell out of her mouth when I was examining her,' Browne said. 'Seems an odd place to find a piece of bad poetry, don't you think?'

'Yes. It's certainly very theatrical.'

'*CSI* has a lot to answer for, if you want my opinion.'

Tartaglia nodded, still looking at the sheet, trying to make sense of the strange images. Was it some sort of a joke or did it actually mean something in terms of the dead woman before him? The ringing of his phone interrupted his train of thought. He found Donovan at the other end.

'We've got a result back from MISSPER,' she said. 'It looks like we have an ID on the victim. Her name's Rachel Tenison. She was an art dealer and she was last seen at work in the West End on Thursday, late afternoon. Her business partner reported her missing on Friday when she failed to turn up for an important meeting at lunchtime. The age and physical description fit perfectly and she lives only a few minutes from the park.'

2

Just before seven that evening, Tartaglia found himself outside the old-fashioned, redbrick mansion block on Campden Hill where Rachel Tenison had lived. He had come straight from the post-mortem, leaving it in full swing when Nina Turner had called to say she was ready for him to view the victim's flat. Although they still had no official ID on the victim, photographs on her passport and driving licence confirmed her identity and her flat was now being treated as a potential crime scene. The stretch of pavement and road immediately outside the building had been cordoned off and traffic diverted elsewhere. He pushed his way through the small crowd of local residents and reporters who had gathered in front of the tape, and was signed in by a local uniformed officer. He crossed the road and went up the steps and in through the large mahogany front door. Lit by an enormous brass chandelier, the lobby was dazzlingly bright after the darkness outside and smelled strongly of something pleasantly chemical;— metal polish or furniture wax, he wasn't sure which. The floor and stairs were thickly carpeted in a muted tone of blue and the glossy off-white walls looked newly painted, brasswork everywhere shining.

Donovan was waiting for him just inside, already kitted out in the full forensic gear. A dressing area had been set up at the back of the hall and she waited while he quickly helped himself to protective clothing.

'The flat's on the fifth floor,' she said once he was ready, and led him towards an ancient-looking cage lift that nestled in the stairwell. 'After Rachel Tenison was reported missing on Friday afternoon, a couple of uniforms from the local station came over here that evening to follow up on the report.'

'That was quick,' he replied, wrenching back the gate and stepping inside. People were reported missing in London all the time, but there was a whole host of reasons why someone might take off and forget to tell anyone where they were going. Usually there was nothing sinister behind it and they eventually reappeared without anything having been amiss.

He slammed the gate shut and Donovan pressed the button for the fifth floor. 'I guess that's Kensington for you,' she said, pressing again after nothing happened. 'Plus the business partner knew which strings to pull. Anyway, the porter let them into the flat, but there was no sign of a break-in and nothing looked amiss, so they left it at that.'

The lift sprang to life with a jolt and slowly started to progress upwards.

'Well, the timing fits perfectly with what I managed to squeeze out of Dr Browne,' Tartaglia said, wishing he had taken the stairs. The last time he had been in a similar lift he had been stuck between floors for well over an hour. 'If she was killed in the park, that means she was there roughly two days. Given the location and all the snow, I'm surprised she was found so quickly. You say there's no evidence of a struggle or anything suspicious having gone on in the flat?'

'No. Nothing.'

'What about CCTV footage?'

'There's a camera on the front door but it's only activated if someone presses one of the bells and it doesn't film anyone going out of the building. The fire doors can only be opened from the inside and there aren't any cameras on them. Wightman's checking with the council as we speak to see what's around in the streets.'

'They'll be few and far between in this neck of the woods.'

It was an expensive, residential part of town, tucked away from the shops and bars of Notting Hill Gate and Kensington High Street. Car crime, petty burglaries and the odd drug-related mugging were the usual fare in this sort of district. However much the victims complained about inadequate police protection, resources were stretched and councils were loath to spend money littering the streets with cameras just to protect residents' personal property.

The lift came to a juddering halt at the fifth floor and, before it could change its mind, Tartaglia yanked open the door, nearly jamming his fingers. He let Donovan out in front of him and followed her along the corridor that led off the main landing. Donovan stopped outside a panelled wooden door and knocked. After a moment it was opened by the tall, slim figure of Nina Turner, the crime-scene manager, dressed in forensic suit and overshoes. Her long dark hair was entirely covered by the hood of her suit and all he could see of her face above the mask was a pair of well-defined dark brows, framing almond-shaped brown eyes.

'We're making good progress,' she said in a muffled voice, ushering them into the warm flat. 'We've done the light-source exam and taken photographs of some finger marks that came up, but so far there's nothing particularly interesting. We've also taken random swabs as discussed earlier and have just started powdering the surfaces you wanted done.'

'Good.' He glanced down at the small, marble-topped console table by the door. An empty blue and white china bowl sat in the middle. Alongside was a folded copy of *The Independent* and a neat pile of unopened post.

'It's all from Friday,' Nina said. 'Nothing personal, just bills and circulars, but we'll take it away, just in case.'

'Any idea who brought it up here?'

'There's a note on the kitchen table from someone called Leonora. It says she did four and a half hours of cleaning on Friday.

I'm assuming she collected the post from downstairs and, from what I can see, she made a thorough job up here. Acres of beige carpet everywhere and not a mark or speck of dust to be seen. The woman deserves a medal.'

'We must get hold of her. Do we have an address book or PDA for the victim?'

Nina shook her head. 'We found a handbag by the door, with the victim's purse. There's about a hundred pounds in cash and a full complement of credit cards, driving licence, et cetera, along with the usual bits and pieces we ladies carry around. But there's no BlackBerry or mobile or anything like that. We haven't come across a computer in the flat, although there's wiring for one and a printer in the spare bedroom.'

'There's no sign of a break-in?' Donovan asked.

Nina shook her head. 'The victim's keys are also missing, so maybe someone let themselves in. But if anyone's been in here, there's no sign of it that I can see.'

'Maybe she left her stuff at the office, for some reason,' Donovan said.

'Speak to Nick,' Tartaglia replied. 'We'll need to get hold of her business partner and see whether he knows anything about it.'

Donovan nodded and started searching in the pocket of her suit for her phone.

'There were a couple of dirty mugs and some glasses in the dishwasher,' Nina said, starting to walk with him along the corridor. 'Do you want them all printed? They're the only things the cleaner doesn't seem to have scrubbed or polished within an inch of their life.'

'Yes. Anything else?'

'Nothing out of the ordinary so far. You sure you want to look around?'

'You know me. I want to get a sense of her, what her life was like.'

He followed Nina into the living room, where a short, female

SOCO was busy dusting the door handle for fingerprints. It was a large room, with three tall windows stretching almost floor to ceiling, each with a small wrought-iron balcony outside. He walked over to one of the windows and stared out at the dark, cloudy sky. It was snowing hard again, dense flurries blowing past the window and adding to the already thick layer on the balcony. No doubt there was still a crowd of hardy reporters on the pavement below, but he couldn't see them. Looking down the hill between the houses, he watched the cars moving slowly in the distance along High Street Kensington, lamps sparkling through the misty air like a chain of fairy lights. He thought of Rachel Tenison as he had first glimpsed her that afternoon in the park, so white and delicate, kneeling down in the snow, like a beautiful flower unfurling.

After a moment, he turned around. The room was sparsely furnished with a mixture of antique and modern pieces. The curtains were neutral, the walls a similar shade and, apart from the back wall which was taken up with floor-to-ceiling bookshelves, there was no colour anywhere. A large, dark landscape, painted in oils, hung over the mantelpiece in a heavy gilt frame and provided the only decoration. 'Bland' was the word that came to mind. The room looked like an expensive hotel suite, rather than somebody's home. He walked over to the bookcase, which was also plain and functional in style. It was filled with an unremarkable mixture of classics, modern fiction of the type usually found in the bestseller charts, and a smattering of biographies along with a large section on Art History. The only notable thing was the fact that the books were ordered into sections according to category and in alphabetical order. It was how he liked to keep his own books at home, but he rarely came across anyone else of a similar mind.

A collection of silver-framed photographs sat on a table behind one of the sofas, the only items of a personal nature anywhere in the

room. Most of the pictures looked at least a decade or so old, judging
from the clothes and hairstyles. In one of them he thought he recognised the dead woman, perhaps in her late teens or early twenties,
and he was struck by how very pretty she had been, something he
hadn't been at all aware of in the park, although death had the effect
of reducing everyone to a commonplace waxwork. She was standing
beside a tall, serious-looking man with dark hair. He looked older and
his arm was wrapped around her almost protectively, while she looked
up at him, smiling.

'Does she have a partner?' he asked, looking around at Nina, who
was standing just behind him.

'Not according to the porter who lives downstairs. He says she
lives on her own and I haven't found anyone else's clothing or stuff,
so far as I can see. Do you want to take a look at her bedroom?'

'Yes. Maybe it will tell me a bit more about her. I'm getting nothing from this room.'

He followed her back into the hall, where Donovan was still on
the phone, and along the corridor to the bedroom at the far end. As he
walked in, he saw himself and Nina reflected in a row of mirrored
cupboards, which stretched along the entire facing wall. Behind them
was a huge, carved-wood four-poster bed, richly hung with curtains of
deep red. He turned around, surprised to see something so dramatic
in this flat. The bed was made, the linen crisp and white, a pale gold
throw draped over the end. Sitting on the floor at the end of the bed
was a handsome old-fashioned trunk, covered in weathered black
leather and intricately studded with rows of tarnished brass nails.
Apart from the bed, it was the only thing of character in the whole
room and it stuck out like a sore thumb. Wondering what was inside,
he bent down to open it, but either it was locked or the lid was
jammed shut.

'Haven't come across a key, so far,' Nina said.

'Well, try not to force it open unless you have to,' he said, still looking at it, curious to know why it was kept in such a prominent position and why it was locked. 'It's a lovely thing.'

Apart from a small armchair and a couple of bedside tables and lamps, there was no other furniture in the room. A couple of books sat on one of the bedside tables, along with an alarm clock, but what struck him most was the absence of clothes or shoes, or any of the usual day-to-day clutter and mess of life. He had never seen a room so tidy.

'It's weird,' he said to Nina. 'This place doesn't look lived in, does it? It could almost be a theatre set, although somebody would have made a better job of dressing it.'

Nina nodded. 'We'll bag up the bedclothes and stuff, but according to the note in the kitchen, the sheets went off to the laundry on Friday.'

'That's bad luck,' he said, walking over to a door in the far corner of the room.

He switched on the light and glanced into the small en-suite bathroom. White towels were carefully folded on a rack and the few jars and bottles on show were lined up in a neat row on the limestone counter, with a couple of large bottles of perfume and a dish of soap on the glass shelf above. It was similarly clinical, with none of the usual feminine clutter and paraphernalia. Catching sight of himself in the mirror, he noticed the circles under his eyes and the fact that he had forgotten to shave that morning. Too bad, he thought with a sigh, switching off the light and ducking out again. It was Sunday, after all.

Nina was waiting for him just outside.

'People say *I'm* obsessive,' he said, 'but this is taking things to an extreme. I've never known a woman's bedroom and bathroom like this. Where's all the stuff you women consider so essential, all the things you can't live without...?' He paused, thinking of the armies of bottles, potions and strange, unfamiliar medicines and tonics that had invaded his bathroom from time to time in the past.

'That's a cliché,' Nina said sharply. 'Not every woman's messy.'

'Well, this isn't normal, and it says a lot about Rachel Tenison. What about her clothes?'

'I've only had a quick look so far, but it's all expensive, although quite plain and tasteful, nothing glitzy. As you can imagine, the shelves and drawers are as tidy as a shop display. Everything's colour coordinated, can you believe. We'll go through everything properly once we finish the powdering.'

He exhaled with frustration. He was starting to find the anonymity of the flat and its lack of a human presence disturbing. There was no personality. Nothing. What sort of woman would live like this? He couldn't get a picture of her at all.

He rubbed his chin, gave the room a final cursory glance and decided it was time to move on. 'You'd better show me the rest of the flat, for what it's worth.'

As they came out of the bedroom, a tall, lanky SOCO padded down the corridor towards them, a large satchel and a camera slung over his shoulder.

'I've almost finished,' he said in a muffled voice to Nina. 'Just got the bedroom to do next.'

'Good. When you're done, can you help Jan with the powdering? Where's Dave?'

'In the study, boxing up the files and the answer machine.'

He squeezed past them and Nina led Tartaglia back down the corridor and into a room at the other end. Apart from a single bed tucked away in a corner by the window, its principal use appeared to be as an office, with a simple modern desk, a chair and a filing cabinet. As they entered, a SOCO shuffled out backwards from under the desk with a long length of cable in his hands.

'What have you got?' Nina asked.

'Nine messages going back to last Friday,' the man said, getting to his feet and pulling the wire free, which he then wrapped around a small answer machine. 'Three hang-ups, four calls from a woman called Selina, wondering where she is, and one from a woman called Liz saying she's running late but will be over shortly. I've listed them with the times.' He passed Tartaglia a sheet of paper from the desk. 'You'll get a full transcript once I get back to the office.'

'Thank you,' Tartaglia said, folding the sheet and tucking it away in his pocket.

He heard what sounded like the flat's front-door buzzer in the background.

'I'll go and see who that is,' Nina said.

Leaving the SOCO to unravel the tangle of wires beneath the desk, Tartaglia walked over to the window and looked out. The gaggle of reporters were still on the pavement down below, huddled together in front of the tape. In the distance, he could see the dark tops of the trees in Holland Park. What had she been doing there, he wondered. Or had she been taken there after death?

He turned around, about to go, when he noticed a set of six large, framed, grainy black-and-white photographs that took up most of the back wall. Each image was of a naked man, wearing a mask. With some the mask covered the entire face, with others just the upper half. The men were muscular, almost overdeveloped, and were posed against a variety of interiors, the images slick, atmospheric and designed to titillate. Intrigued, he walked up to them and studied them more closely. Each print was signed and numbered in the corner, clearly part of a limited edition, and he wondered how much something like that cost. A small fortune, no doubt. The general feel reminded him of a Herb Ritts postcard of a well-hung man on a motorbike, which a girlfriend had once sent him as a joke. The biker was supposed to be him, although the bike was a Harley instead of a Ducati, not that she knew the difference. While the pictures could hardly be described as hardcore, they were the first sign of personality in the otherwise anodyne flat and they made a strange tableau. Even stranger was the fact that they were stuck away behind the door of the study, almost hiding, although if Rachel Tenison had been sitting at her desk with the door closed, she would have been able to enjoy them. It made him think of the Kubrick film *Eyes Wide Shut*. He was just wondering what it had meant to her and what sort of woman would choose such images, when Nina put her head around the door.

'You'd better come, Mark,' she said. 'There's a lady downstairs. She says she's come to see Rachel Tenison. Says she was supposed to be having dinner with her. She was quite insistent, so they let her through. Sam Donovan's gone down to see her.'

He found the woman sitting at the foot of the thick-carpeted stairs in the lobby. Her head was bowed and she was crying softly. She was wrapped up in a long, black overcoat that enveloped most of her legs and fanned out over the couple of steps above, like a skirt. Her hands were clasped tightly over her face and all he could see was a pale triangle of forehead beneath a mess of long, fair hair.

Donovan was sitting beside her, an arm around her shoulders. 'The porter's gone to get her a glass of something strong,' she said, looking up at him. 'Her name's Liz Volpe. She's a good friend of Rachel Tenison's. Apparently they were supposed to be having dinner together tonight.'

'We're going to need to talk to her,' he said quietly, against the sound of muffled sobbing. 'I'll go see if we can use the porter's flat.'

They were soon grouped around the porter's small gas fire in his basement sitting room. The door was shut, the porter no doubt lurking somewhere outside, hoping to catch a thread of what was happening. The cramped space was uncomfortably warm and

Tartaglia stood by the window, which he had forced open a few inches to let in some air. Donovan sat next to Liz Volpe on the sofa, a box of tissues between them. A large measure of Bell's had worked its magic and the colour had started to return to Liz Volpe's cheeks.

'She was my closest friend,' she murmured, almost to herself, wiping her face with a hand and shaking her head slowly. 'I just can't believe it.'

It was the first time he heard her speak clearly. Her voice was low and a little husky, as if she had a cold. 'You mentioned that, apart from a stepbrother, she had no immediate family,' Donovan said, and waited for her response. Still apparently lost in her own world, Liz didn't appear to hear.

'We'll need to contact the brother as a priority,' Tartaglia said.

After a moment, Liz nodded. 'Patrick. Patrick Tenison. The MP.' She gulped at the air like a fish out of water.

'Do you have his number?' he asked, recognising the name and stifling a sigh. A body in Holland Park was newsworthy in its own right, but the involvement of an MP in a murder investigation spelled extra, unhelpful media attention. He couldn't picture the man's face, but from what he remembered Tenison held some sort of office in the shadow cabinet.

Liz bent over and fumbled in a large, over-filled black handbag that lay at her feet on the floor. Pieces of papers, keys and various items of make-up and loose change spilled out onto the carpet as she searched. 'My address book…it's in here. Somewhere.' She waved her hand vaguely at the bag and sat back with a heavy sigh, as if the effort were too much for her. Hunched deep into the sofa again, she bowed her head and folded her arms tightly across her chest.

'I'll find it,' Donovan said, gathering up the bag and its contents and starting to rummage through it on her lap.

'Look, I know now isn't a good time, after what you've just learned,'

Tartaglia said, wishing he didn't have to trouble her. 'But we're going to have to ask you a couple of questions.' There was no reaction and after a moment he continued: 'Do you have any idea what Miss Tenison might have been doing in Holland Park?'

Again, he wasn't sure if she had heard. He was about to rephrase the question when she nodded slowly again. 'Liked jogging…running …every morning, before work…used to go running together… since we were kids…was going to go this morning…but the snow… decided not to.' Her face was half-hidden behind a curtain of hair and she spoke so softly he could barely hear her and missed some of what she said. But he got the general picture.

'You were supposed to see her for dinner this evening?'

She nodded slowly.

'When did you last speak to her?'

She leaned back and gazed up at the ceiling, as if trying to find the answer. Tears filled her eyes again and she closed them, rubbing her wet face with her hands and finally cupping her hands over her eyes. 'Last week. Thursday, I think. Yes, Thursday.'

'And before that?'

'Not for a while,' she mumbled. 'I've been away.'

'Look, I'll leave you alone now. Sergeant Donovan can see you home, but we'll need to speak to you again, in more depth, first thing tomorrow morning. Please can you give Sergeant Donovan your contact details.' He still wasn't sure that he was getting through. He knelt down so that he was on her level and said, 'In the meantime, I'm sorry to have to ask you this, but can you think of anybody who might have wanted to harm Miss Tenison?'

Her hands slid from her face and she looked up at him, shocked, as if he had said something incredible. Against the hot pink of her skin, her eyes were an extraordinary blue.

'Can you think of anyone?' he repeated, when she didn't reply.

'No,' she whispered and hid her face in her hands again.

Straightening, he took a business card out of his pocket and put it on the coffee table in front of her. 'Call me on this number if you think of anything, otherwise I, or one of my team, will see you tomorrow.'

As he walked out of the room and closed the door behind him, his mobile rang. It was Dr Browne at the other end; she had just finished the post-mortem. Turning his back on the porter, who was hovering hopefully in the tiny hallway, mug of tea in hand, Tartaglia listened carefully for a moment.

'Right. I'll be over straight away.' He flipped his phone shut and strode out of the flat before the porter had a chance to ask him anything.

3

He found Dr Browne, still in her gown, stooped over a vending machine in the basement corridor of the mortuary.

'Damn thing keeps giving me white when I want black,' Browne said without looking up, as she punched several buttons impatiently, setting the machine buzzing into action. Tartaglia noticed a number of discarded plastic cups of milky coffee on the table beside it.

Wagner's *Siegfried* blared out along the corridor from the open door of Browne's office a few paces away. Tartaglia liked opera, particularly Italian opera, but he found Wagner impenetrable, particularly *Siegfried*. It reminded him of an opera-singer girlfriend who had made him sit through the whole of the *Ring* cycle before she would go to bed with him. Typical that the music appealed to Browne.

'Damn,' Browne barked, burning her fingers as she struggled to extract an over-full cup from the machine. 'Want a coffee?'

'No thanks.'

Browne took a sip and puckered her lips. 'Don't blame you, it's foul. Wouldn't normally bother with this muck but my filter machine's broken. Let's go into my office.'

She made a sweeping gesture and strode along the corridor, shoes squeaking on the linoleum, with Tartaglia following in her wake. She led him into a small, windowless room, one wall of which was lined with shelves stuffed with medical-reference books and papers. The only decoration was a glossy wall calendar hanging over a filing cabinet. February's photograph showed a hearty-looking venison stew with parmesan mashed potato, accompanied by the recipe, and having had little to eat since breakfast, Tartaglia found the sight mouth-watering.

The remains of vinegary-smelling fish and chips lay on a greasy spread of paper on top of a pile of files on the desk. With a grunt that was almost a growl, Browne heaved herself down into a large arm-chair behind her desk and fumbled in a drawer for the remote, which she used to mute the music. Waving Tartaglia to sit opposite, she stuffed a couple of large, limp chips into her mouth, then gathered up the remains in the paper and dumped the package in the bin.

'As I mentioned on the phone,' she said, giving her mouth and fingers a perfunctory wipe on a crumpled paper napkin before tossing it away, 'cause of death was asphyxiation.'

'Was she strangled?'

Browne leaned back in her chair and started to swivel slowly from side to side, clasping her hands loosely across her stomach. 'The hyoid bone is fractured but there's no superficial pattern of injury, so I would rule out manual strangulation. It could have been caused by a heavy blow, but my guess, based on some other things we found, is that she was held in some sort of a forearm lock.'

'From behind…'

The pathologist nodded. 'There are abrasions under the victim's chin caused by some sort of sharp object.'

'Something on the killer's clothing?'

'Quite possibly.'

'Or a watch or item of jewellery.'

Browne grunted again and compressed her small, pink lips. 'Could be, or something like a metal button or cuff link, perhaps. There are also deep scratch injuries on her face which look like defence wounds.'

'So the killer's behind her,' he said, trying to visualise the scene, 'forearm around her neck in some sort of a control hold. As she struggles to free herself, she scratches her own face.'

'That's about the measure of it.' Browne shrugged, still swivelling.

'We've taken samples from underneath her nails.'

'Let's just hope she scratched whoever it was.' A man was more likely to use an arm lock to subdue a victim, but it didn't take much strength to kill somebody that way; it required only sufficient sustained pressure and the ability to keep holding on to the victim. 'Was she sexually assaulted?'

'Ante-mortem bruising to the thighs and vaginal area would suggest it, certainly, although it's always difficult to be a hundred per cent sure, as you well know. There are also bruises on her neck and breasts and the inside of her thighs consistent with her being bitten or sucked. We've swabbed for saliva but the marks are not clear enough to see a proper dental pattern. What's odd is that all of the bruising occurred at least a couple of hours before death, if not longer.'

He frowned. 'You're sure the interval's as large as that?'

Browne stopped swivelling and folded her arms. 'Most definitely. The bruising is too well developed.'

'So, the assault and the killing may or may not be linked.'

'It's not clear.'

Tartaglia rubbed his chin, trying to make sense of it. 'But what are the odds of being raped, and then killed, by two different people in the space of a few hours?' he said, almost to himself. 'It must have been the same person—or perhaps she wasn't raped.'

Browne shrugged as though it was none of her concern. 'As I said, it's not clear. However, one thing I can tell you is she reeked of booze when I opened her up. The toxicology report will confirm the precise amount but I'd say she was well over the drink-drive limit at the time of death.'

'So, she's pissed, has rough sex, consensually or not. Fast-forward a couple of hours or so and she's killed and left lying somewhere on her back. Then later, the killer returns and moves the body into the position we found her in.'

'That's about the sum of it.'

'Was she dead when she was tied up?'

Browne peered at him thoughtfully over her glasses. 'That's not straightforward either. There are restraint marks on the inside of her arms where she was held down, as well as chafe marks and swelling around her ankles and wrists consistent with her having been secured in some fashion. They weren't caused by the duct tape but by something more abrasive. Again, allowing for the development of the bruising and swelling, this was all several hours before death.'

'Could it have been some kind of rope?'

'No. Something harder and sharper. I'd hazard a guess that she was handcuffed.'

'Which goes along with the idea of rape.'

Browne nodded. 'The lack of swelling immediately around the tape at the wrists and ankles would suggest that she was either dead or very close to death when the tape was used.'

Still puzzled, he thought back again to Rachel Tenison's flat. 'There weren't any signs of a struggle or assault at her flat. Maybe she was killed somewhere else, then trussed up with the duct tape and dumped sometime later in the park, although how the hell you lug a body into the middle of the park without being seen beats me. And why go to the trouble?'

Browne gave him a level stare. 'I wouldn't like to speculate.'

Short of any immediate insight as to what might have happened, he was about to ask her to give it a try anyway, when his phone rang. It was Donovan.

'I've managed to get hold of the stepbrother, Patrick Tenison,' she said. 'He was on his way back to London from his constituency, where he lives. He says he'll meet you at his flat in an hour.'

Patrick Tenison's flat was on the top floor of a tall, converted nineteenth-century building in Westminster, close to the Houses of Parliament. Tenison buzzed Tartaglia in and was waiting for him in the doorway of his flat as Tartaglia climbed out of the lift. Casually dressed in brown cords and an open-necked checked shirt, he was tall and well built, with a broad face and very short dark hair. Tartaglia recognised him immediately as an older version of the man in the photograph in Rachel Tenison's flat.

He held out his hand to Tartaglia. 'Please come in, Inspector. Is it snowing again?' He glanced at Tartaglia's wet leather jacket and helmet as he ushered him into the cramped hallway beyond.

'Just started as I was leaving. It's coming down quite heavily now.'

'You can hang your things up there to dry, if you want.' Tenison pointed to a set of pegs by the front door. 'Doesn't matter if they drip on the floor. The carpet needs replacing, if only the landlord would get around to it.'

Tartaglia put his helmet on the floor and unzipped his jacket. Removing a pen and notebook from the pocket, he gave the jacket a shake and hung it up. He followed Tenison into a small, low-ceilinged sitting room at the back. In a corner of the room, a tray of drinks stood on a small table which Tenison was mixing himself a large brandy and soda.

'Can I get you something?' Tenison's voice was flat, without energy.

'I'm fine, thank you.' Tartaglia sat down in an armchair and gazed around at the cramped interior.

The room was furnished with dull prints, reproduction furniture and plain, oatmeal-coloured carpet. It looked like a cheap corporate let and not somewhere that Tenison spent much time, judging by the lack of any books or personal belongings. A pair of small windows was set into the eaves, and through the open blinds Tartaglia could see the glittering lights and outlines of the buildings along the Thames as well as the London Eye.

'Can you tell me what happened?' Tenison asked, coming over to Tartaglia with his glass and lowering himself into one of the armchairs opposite. 'The police who came to my house…they said her death is suspicious, that she was strangled. They said she was found in Holland Park.' He spoke quietly, enunciating each word precisely as if trying to control his speech. He put the glass to his lips and drained it in three gulps.

'That's right,' Tartaglia replied guardedly. 'Do you have any idea what she might have been doing there? It's only a stone's throw from where she lived, so I wondered…'

'She used to go running there most mornings. She loved the park. It's why she bought that flat.'

It corroborated what Liz Volpe had said and Tartaglia made a note. 'She'd go running even in bad weather?'

'Particularly in bad weather. She liked to have the park to herself.' Tenison put down his empty glass and rubbed his eyes. 'You know, it's funny. I always warned her about running alone. I told her it was dangerous, but she paid no attention to me.' He looked up, his brown eyes searching Tartaglia's face. 'What happened?'

'I'm sorry, but I can't give you any more details at the moment.'

'You must be able to tell me something.' Tenison was still staring at him. 'Was she…was she assaulted? Was it sexual?'

'I really can't tell you anything further now,' Tartaglia said firmly. Tenison's desire to know more was only natural, but the less he, or anyone else close to Rachel Tenison, knew about the details, the better. Everyone in her immediate circle of family and friends was under suspicion, until alibis could be confirmed.

'I see,' Tenison said, frowning as though he didn't appreciate the lack of clarity. 'Do you have any idea who did it?'

'It's far too early to tell, Mr Tenison. It's one of the reasons I'm here. Am I right in thinking that you're Miss Tenison's next of kin?'

Tenison gave a slight nod. 'I'm actually her stepbrother. My father married her mother when Rachel was three and Rachel took our
family name.'

'Are they still alive?'

He shook his head. 'They were both killed in a car crash when
Rachel was twelve. I was living with my mother at the time. She offered Rachel a home as there was nowhere else for her to go.' Tenison
spoke dispassionately, as though he was a third-party observer, but
everyone dealt with shock in different ways. Tartaglia had the impression that his detached manner was just a mechanism for keeping
himself in check.

'Nowhere? What about Rachel's father?'

'She never knew him. He walked out on Rachel's mother just after
Rachel was born and that was the last they heard of him. He never got
in touch. He could be dead too, for all I know.'

Coming from a large and extended close-knit family, all of whom
would have welcomed him with open arms in similar circumstances,
Tartaglia was moved by the thought of a twelve-year-old girl left completely on her own in the world apart from a stepbrother and his
mother. Again he thought of Rachel Tenison as he had found her, so
fragile and broken, and felt a pang of intense sadness along with a
sudden, irrational desire to protect her, even in death.

'We will need you to identify her body,' he said, his eyes still on
Tenison's leaden face.

Tenison nodded. 'Whatever I can do to help.'

'Can you think of any reason at all why someone might have
wanted to kill your sister, Mr Tenison?'

Tenison closed his eyes for a second, then shook his head with a
sniff. 'Rachel was a very special, very talented woman,' he said with
sudden feeling. 'She had no enemies. Everyone who knew her loved
her.'

'What about her friends? Is there anyone she was particularly close to?'

'You should speak to Liz. Liz Volpe. She has known Rachel the longest. They went to the same school, from the time Rachel came to live with us.'

'Anyone else?'

Tenison sighed. 'Most of Rachel's other female friends are married and have families. Their lives went in different directions and a couple moved out of London. Rachel was a godmother to a few of their children, but I get the impression she didn't see them that often.'

'So who did she see? I presume she didn't stay at home all the time.'

'Rachel put most of her energies into her work, Inspector. Her business was like a marriage or a surrogate child, if you like. It didn't leave much time for anything else.'

'She was successful?'

'Very.'

'I hope you won't mind my asking, but from what I've seen, Miss Tenison seems to have been a wealthy woman.'

'She inherited some money and property from her mother, all of which she ploughed into the business. She worked incredibly hard and the business has done well. They're now one of the top dealers in Old Master paintings in London.'

'Do you know the name of her solicitor?'

Tenison looked puzzled. 'You think somebody did this for money?'

'At this stage, we have no idea. You know the cliché—we have to look at every angle.'

Tenison nodded slowly. 'Crowther and Phillips, in Lincoln's Inn Fields, but I can save you the trouble of speaking to them. I'm Rachel's executor. Apart from a few small charitable bequests, she left her shares in the business to Richard Greville, her business partner. Her flat and most of the contents, bar family stuff, go to Liz Volpe. The rest of her assets are to be placed in trust for my two children, James and Lorna.'

'She left nothing to you?' he asked, surprised, as he jotted down the details.

'That was the way I wanted it.' Tenison compressed his lips as though he had no desire to discuss it further.

'Did any of the beneficiaries know about the contents of Miss Tenison's will?'

'Look, Inspector,' he said emphatically, leaning forwards, elbows on his knees. 'None of them would kill Rachel for the money.'

'Please answer the question, Mr Tenison. I have to check everything, tick all the boxes.'

Tenison sighed and leaned back again into the sofa. 'All right. For what it's worth, I'm pretty sure they don't know. Rachel was a very private person and she would keep that sort of thing to herself. Anyway, why would she tell them? It wasn't as if she thought she was going to die. It was supposed to be just a sensible precaution. Neither of us dreamt it would ever come to this.'

'When was the will drawn up?'

'A couple of years ago. The chap at Crowther and Phillips will be able to tell you precisely when.'

Tartaglia made a note to get someone to check. 'Would you describe your relationship with Miss Tenison as close?'

The question seemed to surprise Tenison and he took a moment to answer. 'Yes, we were close. Very close.' With a sigh, he got to his feet and walked over to the window, gazing sightlessly outside. He seemed physically drained, as though the stuffing had been knocked out of him. On such a big, powerful-looking man, the impression was striking. 'I have no other brothers or sisters and neither did she,' he said. 'I'm seven years older, but there was a real bond between us which grew over the years, although we never really lived in the same house together for long. I've always felt very protective of her. She was such a pretty, fragile little thing when she came to us. She would barely speak or offer an opinion and she hated leaving the house, as though something terrible might happen. It used to drive my mother mad.'

'But you cared about each other?' Tartaglia asked quietly.

'Yes. Very much so. I…' Tenison's voice tailed away and he rubbed his face vigorously with his hands.

'You saw quite a lot of each other?'

With a snort, Tenison turned around to face Tartaglia. 'We had several mutual friends. She introduced me to my wife, Emma. They were at university together.'

'Where is your wife, Mr Tenison?'

'In Hampshire. We have a house in my constituency. She lives there full-time with our children. I only come up to London for work.'

'She was there last Friday?'

'As far as I know. Is that when you think—'

'Again, we're not sure yet. Miss Tenison was reported missing Friday afternoon by someone in her office. The last time they saw her was around six o'clock Thursday evening. We will obviously try and establish her movements afterwards, but given what you've told me about her habit of running in the park in the morning, it seems we're looking at her being attacked on Friday. Can you please tell me what your movements were that day.'

Tenison looked at him astounded. 'Me?'

'These are just routine things we have to ask everybody we speak to.'

He gave a weary sigh. 'Of course. I'm sorry. I suppose you have to check, don't you? Friday? Well, I was here—on my own, obviously— until about eight. I then caught a train down to Hampshire and I was in meetings for most of the day. I've been out of London until now.'

Tartaglia made a note. Once they had a more precise idea of the chronology of events and an estimate for time of death, they would check everything thoroughly. 'Going back to the issue of motive, did Miss Tenison ever discuss her relationships with you?'

'What, with men?'

'Yes.'

'Not really.'

'But she had relationships?'

'Nothing serious that I'm aware of, certainly not recently.'

'Forgive me, Mr Tenison, but your sister was in her thirties and she was an attractive woman. There must have been somebody at some point in her life. She must have had lovers.'

Tenison stared at him without speaking.

'It's very important,' Tartaglia added.

'OK, Inspector. I take your point.' He came back to the sofa and flopped down, legs stretched out in front of him. 'Have you spoken to Richard Greville?'

'Her business partner? He's been contacted but he's abroad.'

'They had a long affair, if you can call it that. Richard used to be her boss at Christie's. They got along so well, so to speak, that they left to set up the business together.'

'But it's over?'

'Yes. From what I know, it finished a while ago.'

'Was it a serious relationship?'

'At one point, I think so. Problem was, Richard was already married.'

'He wouldn't leave his wife?'

'No. Anyway, I'm not sure Rachel would have wanted him to.'

'What do you mean by that?'

Tenison frowned, as though he had said something out of turn. 'I think she was happy with the way things were, that's all.'

Tartaglia felt there was more behind Tenison's words, but now was not the time to probe. 'And Richard Greville?'

Tenison shrugged. 'Who knows. I doubt Rachel was his first affair, or his last. He's been married to Molly for twenty years or so and he's quite dependent on her, in a funny sort of way. She gives him the security and bolstering he needs so that he can play around. Rachel would never have done that for him.'

'Who broke off the relationship?'

'Rachel, I imagine, although there were no fireworks, as far as I'm aware. The affair had just run its course.'

'Was Greville bitter about it?'

'Not that I know of.'

Tenison made it sound so straightforward and simple, but in Tartaglia's experience relationships were rarely so cut and dried, nor did they usually end happily on both sides. Either Tenison was naïve or he wasn't giving him the full story.

'Did Greville's wife know what was going on with your sister?'

Tenison took a deep breath, as though he found discussing such things unpleasant. 'Some people can't see the nose on their face, but Molly's quite sharp. I'm sure she guessed, although Richard was probably stupid enough, and vain enough, to think he had her fooled. But I don't see her killing Rachel, if that's where you're heading with this.'

'Why's that?'

'What would be the point? The affair was over.' His tone was curt and dismissive.

Tartaglia studied Tenison for a moment. He wondered if his reaction was prudish or merely disapproving. Objectively, he was a good-looking man but there was something flaccid and a little prim about the set of his features that spelled weakness.

'You're sure about that?'

'Positive.'

'I get the impression you don't like Richard Greville very much.'

Tenison shrugged. 'I don't. And I didn't like Rachel getting involved with him, either in business or romantically. But you can't tell people, particularly not someone like Rachel. You have to let them make their own mistakes and hope they learn from them.'

Tenison picked up his glass and got up to refill it, as though he wanted to change the subject.

'So, who has she been seeing since then?' Tartaglia asked, not willing to let it go.

'I really have no idea. I'm sorry,' Tenison said stiffly, over his shoulder, as he mixed his drink.

'She didn't mention anyone to you?'

'Why would she? I wasn't her keeper, and as her brother, I'm probably the last person to know.'

It was a fair point. Thinking about his own love life, or lack of one, Tartaglia nodded. He was hardly likely to unburden himself to Nicoletta; far from it, in fact. Although women were generally more confiding by nature.

Again, he asked Tenison, 'But you are sure the relationship with Richard Greville was over?'

'Absolutely positive,' Tenison said, returning to the sofa with a half-full glass and sitting down heavily again. 'I know Rachel. She wouldn't have gone back to Richard, even if he begged her on bended knee and offered her the world.'

Surprised at the strength of Tenison's tone, Tartaglia was struck by the intense look in his eyes. 'Maybe she didn't tell you.'

Tenison shook his head forcefully. 'I knew my sister better than anyone, Inspector. With Rachel, there was no going back.'

It was well past midnight by the time Tartaglia arrived home in Shepherd's Bush. Apart from a ginger cat loping across the road, everything was still, all the windows dark, everybody in bed long ago.

He killed the engine and pushed the Ducati up over the icy pavement and into the front garden, careful not to let the gate clang behind him. He parked the bike out of sight behind the high hedge, activated its alarm and covered it with the sheet of plastic that he kept behind the dustbins. His flat was the ground floor of a house in the middle of a small criss-cross of quiet residential streets, close to Hammersmith Broadway. He liked the area, with its wealth of shops and inexpensive restaurants up on the main road, and a couple of good pubs only a few minutes' walk away. Convenience was everything when you lived on your own and worked the hours he did.

The solidly built, late Victorian terraced houses were set back from the street behind low walls and strips of front garden. There was something reassuring about their simple redbrick façades and comfortable proportions, with large bay windows on two storeys and attic gables above. Somebody in his family had once said, 'Georgian for beauty, Victorian for comfort,' and he often thought how true that was. Most of the houses in the street had been converted into flats, some owned by the council or local housing trusts, the rest in private hands, with a few still remaining as undivided family homes. Cherry trees lined both sides of the road, their branches now bare and frosted with snow. But in just a few weeks they would be laden with pink blossoms, adding a touch of magic to the street.

He opened the front door and, from the small communal hallway, let himself into his flat, straight into the sitting room. He switched on the light and drew the old wooden shutters across the window, blocking out the orange glare of the streetlamp immediately outside. They were the original shutters, and when he had first moved into the flat it had taken him days to prise off the layers of paint and get them to work. He had also resurrected as many of the other original features as he was able, taking up the ancient patterned brown carpet, sanding and varnishing the hardwood flooring, stripping the mantelpiece down to its original white marble. He had also unblocked the fireplace, although, when he had first tried to light a fire in the grate, the room had filled with smoke—the chimney hadn't been swept for decades.

The central heating had gone off a couple of hours before and the room was cold, with an almost icy chill in the air. He went quickly to the boiler cupboard in the hall and pressed the over-ride button, before going back into the sitting room and removing his jacket. As he undid his tie, he played back the only message on the answer machine. It was from Nicoletta, questioning why he had had to leave so abruptly and asking what he thought of her friend Sarah. It all seemed days ago instead of hours. Perhaps he should have made more of an effort with Sarah. There were moments like this when, tired and alone late at night, he ached for company and for the physical presence and warmth of a woman. But a friend of Nicoletta's was not the answer.

He listened to Nicoletta's voice for a moment, its tone of weary recrimination almost drowned out by the babble of children's voices. When he had had enough, he pressed Delete without listening to the rest. Why did she have to take everything so personally? He felt the familiar jolt of irritation, marvelling at how she seemed incapable of understanding the nature of his job or why family lunch shouldn't take precedence over a new murder investigation. Thinking of lunch made him realise suddenly just how hungry he was: he'd survived for most of the day on little more than coffee and a handful of cigarettes. He knew he should get some sleep before the briefing at seven a.m.— it was going to be another long day—but he had to eat something before going to bed.

He went into the kitchen, opened the cupboards and fridge and took out a small bag of new potatoes, eggs and some parmesan. He saw from the label that the potatoes came from Cyprus, where no doubt spring had already arrived. He washed them quickly and boiled them in their skins before slicing them and frying them in olive oil until they were golden at the edges. As he whisked the eggs and added them to the pan with the grated parmesan, images of the day's events floated through his mind.

He was hopeful after everything Dr Browne had said that the lab would come up with something interesting, possibly even a DNA match. But that was all going to take a while. Meanwhile, establishing a timeline was vital. After what he had heard, it seemed likely that Rachel Tenison had gone running in the park as usual on the Friday morning and possibly met her killer there. But with the assault, if that was what it was, and the killing happening several hours apart, it wasn't straightforward.

When the frittata was nearly done, he browned the top under the grill, then transferred it to a plate, cutting it into wedges and adding salt and pepper and some more parmesan, followed by a large dollop of tomato ketchup. His mother would have thrown up her arms in horror. Tomato ketchup? Marco, how *can* you? He could practically hear her voice and picture the expression of disgust that went with it. Smiling at the thought, he took his food and a bottle of beer into the sitting room and ate with the plate on his lap.

He finished his meal quickly, put down his plate and stretched his legs out in front of him, resting his heels lightly on the edge of the coffee table. He lit a cigarette, enjoying the surprising stillness of the hour in the centre of London; only a few weeks ago he had heard a fox barking outside. His mind drifted back to the case. Stranger-killings were generally opportunistic, haphazard events, with all the usual hallmarks of a chaotic, sick mind. But the way Rachel Tenison's body had been tied up, almost ritualistically, required careful preparation. Then there was that strange poem. Whatever the killer had meant by it, it was clearly premeditated.

They still had no idea if she had been killed in her flat, or in the park or, indeed, somewhere else, although the more he thought about it, the more the park seemed the most logical place. Removing her clothing made sense. It was the easiest way of destroying forensic evidence, as anyone who had watched *CSI* a couple of times would know. Again, it showed that the killer was thinking in an organised fashion. But why truss her up like that after death and arrange her in that strange symbolic pose? And why the poem? What message was the killer trying to send? The monochrome image of the naked and bound Rachel Tenison kneeling down in the snow flashed through his memory again. He just couldn't get rid of it. It was odd how, even unbidden, such things imprinted themselves on the mind. He wondered what sort of woman she had been, recalling her strangely impersonal flat: the blandness, the orderliness, the large, scarlet-curtained bed and the weird photographs. She was an enigma and she intrigued him.

With no easy answers within his grasp and his eyelids starting to feel leaden, he stubbed out his cigarette and forced himself to find his bed, pausing only to remove his clothing before crawling naked under the covers.

4

It was just past seven in the morning. Donovan manoeuvred her blue VW Golf into a space in the small outdoor car park at the back of the murder squad's offices in Barnes and switched off the ignition. As she climbed out, she noticed how dark the sky was, but at least the snow had stopped for the moment. She was late. Her head still foggy from sleep, she had struggled to wake when the alarm buzzed at six. From where she lived in Hammersmith, it was only a ten-minute drive to Barnes, across the Thames via Hammersmith Bridge. In the summer she would often cycle to work, taking the road that skirted the leafy playing fields of St Paul's Boys' School and ran along the river all the way to Barnes. But in winter, all that mattered was to get to the office as quickly as possible.

The low-built early-seventies office block was situated halfway along Station Road, which connected the Green, with its picturesque duck pond and cluster of eighteenth-century houses, to the wilderness of Barnes Common. The brick building was an eyesore in a much sought-after part of town, only a few miles from the centre of London yet with the feel of an old-fashioned village, bounded by the river. The locals were a well-heeled mix of doctors, dentists, lawyers and media types, along with a number of well-known actors, and it was an odd location for two of the Metropolitan Police's murder squads, particularly given the fact that they were rarely ever called upon to investigate a homicide in their own backyard.

A freezing wind gusted around Donovan as she climbed out of the car, whipping the tail of her scarf into her face and stinging her eyes. She slung her heavy bag over her shoulder, gathered her coat tightly round her and rushed through the back door and up the stairs to the first floor.

The morning debrief had just started in the large, open-plan office at the front of the building. The room was crowded and she eased herself onto a desk near the back, beside Nick Minderedes, his thick black hair still wet from the shower, who sat cradling a steaming mug of coffee in his hands. Tartaglia stood at the front of the room, the board behind him already showing a map of the Holland Park area, along with photographs of the victim. Their boss, DCI Carolyn Steele, sat beside him, dressed in her usual uniform of plain dark trouser suit, today's version with a hint of a pin-stripe, plus crisp white shirt. She looked fresh, as though she had managed a full night's sleep, her short, dark hair sleek as usual, her face impassive as she listened to Detective Constable Karen Feeney reporting the findings from several interviews conducted the previous night.

'The park-keeper saw her come into the park just after the gates opened on Friday morning,' Feeney was saying. 'He was sure she was on her own. He said he used to see her most mornings. Apparently, she was often there waiting when he came to open the gates. She always took the same route, he said, which goes right past where her body was found.'

'Did he see anyone else around?' Tartaglia asked.

'No, Sir. But he said it was so cold, he didn't hang around.'

'Well, at least we have our starting point and it's looking more likely that she was killed in the park and left there.' He looked over at Detective Constable Dave Wightman, who was standing at the front of the group, notebook in hand. 'OK, Dave, tell us what you've got.'

Short and thickset, with fair hair, glasses and a boyish face, Wightman was the newest recruit to the team. 'Nothing from local CCTV, so far, Sir,' he said. 'There are no cameras in the immediate vicinity, but we've taken everything from the surrounding area just in case and we're going through it all now.'

'What about the door camera?'

'It's triggered every time someone rings one of the bells, but there's no way of knowing which bell is activating the camera. The footage just shows a continual stream of people coming to the door.'

'How many flats in the building?' Steele asked, in her quiet, flat-toned voice.

'Over forty, Ma'am. It will take a while to eliminate each of the callers.'

'If you need help, you'd better call on the locals,' Tartaglia said. 'Have you tracked down the cleaner?'

Wightman nodded. 'She's a Filipino, lives on one of the council estates in Notting Hill. She was out playing Mah-Jong all night and I've only just managed to speak to her now. She said she cleaned for Rachel Tenison on Tuesdays and Fridays and has worked for her for just over two years. Last Friday she arrived as usual around ten o'-clock. When she let herself in, Miss Tenison's handbag was in the hall, which she said was odd, and the flat was unlocked and the alarm was off, which also wasn't normal. She thought Miss Tenison was at home until she realised there was nobody there.'

'Maybe Rachel Tenison didn't bother with the alarm when she went out for a run. If so, it means she never returned to the flat after the run.'

'The cleaner didn't say, Sir. Miss Tenison was never at home when she came in to clean. They usually spoke on the phone or left each other notes.'

'Was anything else out of the ordinary?' Steele asked.

'She thought not, Ma'am.'

'So, what sort of state did she find the flat in?' Tartaglia asked. 'Was it a mess, was it tidy, untidy?'

'Said it was quite tidy, or at least I think that's what she said.' Wightman consulted his notes then added, 'Nothing that aroused any suspicion, at any rate.'

'Had the bed been slept in?'

'Yes.'

'But nothing unusual?'

'No, Sir. She said she cleared away some glasses and a couple of empty wine bottles.'

'Where were they?'

Wightman again checked his notes. 'In the sitting room. She said it looked as though Rachel Tenison had had guests. She said she put four or five glasses in the dishwasher but she didn't set it off because it was more or less empty. She said Miss Tenison liked to fill it up before switching it on. Something about saving electricity.'

'The glasses have gone off to the lab,' Tartaglia said, addressing the room. 'At least we now know when they were used.'

'Perhaps some of the glasses were there since before Thursday night,' Steele said.

Tartaglia shook his head. 'From what I've seen, Rachel Tenison doesn't seem like the sort of person to leave dirty glasses lying around for days.'

Wightman nodded. 'The cleaner said she liked things nice and tidy, that there was never much of a mess to clear up, unlike some of her other jobs. Said it was a pleasure to work for her.'

Tartaglia rubbed his chin thoughtfully. 'So, let's assume the glasses were from Thursday night. Rachel Tenison went out running early Friday morning. She probably intended to clear them away when she got back. What about her running clothes? Did you ask the maid if she found them in the flat?'

'There was a basket of dirty clothes, which she washed, but they were all dry. It was snowing heavily Friday morning. If Rachel Tenison had been out running, her clothes would have still been sopping at ten o'clock.'

'Yes. So it's looking more and more as though Rachel Tenison never went back to the flat to change. Thank God the dishwasher was nearly empty and we have the glasses. At the moment they're the only things we have to go on.' He looked over at Nina Turner, who had just come into the room. 'What's the latest from the park?'

'No sign of her clothing or personal possessions yet, but hopefully something will turn up today.'

She was looking even thinner and more angular than usual in a plain grey trouser suit and blue shirt that highlighted her olive skin. Her long dark hair was tied back in a ponytail and she was fully made up even at that early hour of the morning, something that Donovan wasn't sure whether to admire or despise.

'How long do you expect to keep the park closed?' Steele asked.

'Another couple of days,' Nina replied, with a glance in Tartaglia's direction. 'Progress is slow with all the snow. At least we now know where she entered the park and which route she is likely to have taken. We had the dog teams in yesterday, and they'll be back again today. We'll keep looking, but to be honest, apart from her clothing and personal things, I don't hold out much hope. Assuming she was killed on Friday, the park was open for business for two whole days before we sealed it off.'

'What about the victim's flat?' Tartaglia asked.

'We finished the powdering last night and removed a number of prints which have gone off to the lab.'

'And her things?'

'We'll be going through everything today. When we're finished, we'll start on the luminol spraying.'

Tartaglia looked over at Minderedes. 'What have you got, Nick?'

Minderedes slid slowly off the desk, mug in hand, and cleared his throat. 'Uniform are trying to trace any runners or dog walkers who might have been in the park that morning, but so far the few that have come forward all say they were there later. Nobody saw anything amiss.'

'You've told CID to run background checks on all of them?'

Minderedes nodded.

'So her body was either well hidden by then, probably in the thicket where she was found, or it had been taken somewhere else, although that seems unlikely.'

'Maybe she met her killer in the park and went off with them somewhere, where she was killed,' Minderedes said. 'The killer then came back and dumped her body in the park later.'

Steele shook her head. 'Possible, but unlikely. If the killer came across her in the park, why take her away somewhere and then bring the body back? We're talking central London here, not some deserted woodland. That park is crawling with people during the day. It's too risky.'

'I agree,' Tartaglia replied. 'And as we now know, her body was found very close to her usual running route. Let's stick with the most obvious explanation for the moment, unless something new comes to light.'

'But she was assaulted several hours before she died,' Karen Feeney said, from her desk at the front. 'How does that tie in?'

Tartaglia nodded. 'All we know is that she had sex with somebody a few hours before she was killed—very rough sex, by the sounds of it. She also had quite deep abrasions on her wrists and ankles where she had been secured. But it might have been consensual. We know nothing yet about her personality or background.'

'So what do you think happened?' Steele asked. 'Some sort of sex game gone wrong, perhaps?'

'Quite possibly, although the killer may not be the person she had sex with. Rachel Tenison went running most mornings, so maybe someone's been watching her or maybe it's somebody she already knows.'

'Was she gay or bi-sexual?'

'Not according to her brother, but obviously it's something we must check as we go along. A woman could easily kill another woman with an arm lock, if she knew what she was doing. We mustn't rule out a woman having done this, although as you all know the statistics are against a woman committing this sort of crime, particularly given the potential sexual motivation.'

'But why use an arm lock?' Feeney asked. 'Surely, the killer would come at her from the front and strangle her with his hands.'

'It's possible the victim tried to get away,' he said. 'Maybe the killer only intended to subdue her. It's easy to go too far, for things to get out of control in the heat of the moment. Anyway, as the victim struggles to free herself, something the killer's wearing—maybe a watch or a bracelet or something sharp like that—cuts into her, under her chin. All of this could have taken a matter of minutes, at the most. At some later point, the body was moved. Hyperstasis indicates that she was lying flat on her back for several hours before she was tied up again. Maybe the killer was disturbed and had to go back later to finish the job, to make a spectacle of her. The killer strips her naked, ties her up with duct tape and puts a poem in her mouth, then arranges the body in a kneeling position, almost sacrificial. You've all seen the photos by now.'

'She looks like she's praying,' Feeney said.

'Begging for mercy, more like,' Minderedes added.

Tartaglia nodded. 'It's a deliberate message of some kind, although it's open to interpretation.'

'We were really lucky to find her so quickly,' Donovan said, thinking back to the overgrown enclosure in the woods. 'She could have been there weeks, if not months. The kids who discovered her were only able to get inside because part of the fence had come down and there had been no time to repair it.'

'That's right,' Tartaglia replied. 'We have to assume that we weren't meant to find her so quickly. We're looking at a killer who's organised and thinking clearly, not someone in a panic. That's as much as we can tell at the moment. In the meantime, we must concentrate on the victim profile and find out who Rachel Tenison saw on the Thursday night after she left work. Have you got hold of a copy of her diary yet, Nick?'

Minderedes shook his head. 'The business partner—Richard Greville—was out of the country. I got hold of him late last night. He'll be back at the gallery this morning.'

'I'd like you and Sam to pay him a visit. We'll need access to her business phone records and files, plus details, if he has them, of her mobile phone. You know the score. Who's dealing with her landline records?'

'I am,' Wightman said. 'We should have the printout later today.'

Tartaglia looked over in Donovan's direction. 'Sam, can you follow up on the poem? Unless the killer's just trying to mislead us, it was put there for a reason. I want the rest of you to concentrate on the park, names and addresses and a full check on anyone who goes there regularly and anyone seen hanging around since the park's been closed off. Given the circumstances, we can't rule out a stranger killing. In the meantime, Karen and I have an appointment at nine with Rachel Tenison's friend, Liz Volpe.'

'What about the press, Sir?' asked DS Sharon Fuller, the office manager, who was sitting just behind Donovan. 'Will you be releasing the victim's identity today?'

'Yes. As soon as her stepbrother formally IDs her. It should be public knowledge by lunchtime.'

'There will be a formal press briefing later this morning, ahead of the lunchtime news,' Steele said. 'Superintendent Cornish will be handling it. But if you get anyone ringing up, refer them to the press office or pass them on to me.'

'There's going to be a lot of media attention,' Tartaglia added. 'Rachel Tenison was a well-known West End art dealer and her stepbrother's in the Shadow Cabinet. You can imagine the headlines. I can't stress enough how important it is that the crime-scene details are kept out of the public domain. Everything, and I mean everything, must be kept under wraps. Understood?'

5

Just after nine that morning, Tartaglia and DC Karen Feeney stood outside the address Liz Volpe had given them in Notting Hill. The white-painted Victorian house was imposing, with ornate cornicing, arched balconies and a large classical portico above the front door. It stood at the end of a terrace of similar houses, straddling the corner of two roads and backing onto a broad expanse of railed communal gardens that sloped gently up the hill behind, towards Notting Hill Gate.

Tartaglia rang the bell marked Volpe, and within seconds, her voice crackled over the intercom. He announced himself and Feeney.

'I'm right at the top,' Liz said. Her voice sounded sleepy, as though she had only just woken up.

He heard the click of the receiver, followed by the buzzer, and quickly pushed open the heavy, dark green door.

With Feeney labouring behind him, he climbed the broad, curving staircase until he reached the top-floor landing, where he waited for Feeney to catch him up. There was only one door and it had been left ajar. There was no sign of Liz Volpe and they went inside, entering into a broad hallway that seemed to be used as a dining area, with a table and some foldaway chairs parked to one side. Weak grey light filtered in from a skylight above, illuminating a clumsily painted mural of a Mediterranean view on the back wall.

Within moments, Liz appeared in the corridor behind them. Dressed in faded jeans and trainers, she was pulling on an enormous charcoal grey cardigan over a tight black T-shirt and had the dishevelled, disorientated look of someone who had only just got out of bed.

'I'm sorry to have kept you,' she said in a low, husky voice, tugging her thick, dark blonde hair free of the neck of the cardigan. Her face was pale, her eyes red and swollen.

'This is Detective Constable Feeney,' Tartaglia replied.

Liz stretched out her hand in greeting, giving them both a tense smile. Her fingers were cold and were quickly withdrawn to her side. 'Let's go and sit down.'

As she led the way along the corridor and into the sitting room at the end, she moved slowly, almost shambling, as if she were still half-asleep or in a trance. She was a lot taller than he had noticed the previous night, almost his height, thin and athletic-looking.

The room they entered was large, on the corner of the building, with a high ceiling and windows on two sides set into the sloping eaves. Liz switched on the lights and gestured them towards a comfortable-looking sofa by the fireplace, placing herself opposite in a high-backed, brown leather armchair, legs together, hands folded stiffly in her lap, the wooden coffee table like a barrier between them.

Sitting down, Tartaglia glanced around, taking in the faded green walls, the overflowing, rickety bookshelves and the scuffed wooden floor, which was covered in a variety of dusty ethnic rugs. A flat of that size, in that area, must be worth a fortune, but the furnishings might easily have come from a junk shop. There was also nothing feminine about the place, no ornaments or pictures, other than a large, weathered old print of a racehorse in a heavy black frame over the mantelpiece.

'Have you lived here long, Miss Volpe?' he asked, as Feeney sat down beside him and began rummaging in her oversized handbag for a notebook and pen.

Liz shook her head. 'It's my brother's. I'm just staying here temporarily while he's away. While I sort myself out. I've been living abroad, you see.'

As he returned her gaze, he realised that he hadn't really looked at her properly the night before. All hunched up in her long black overcoat on the stairs or the porter's sofa, with her long fair hair hanging over her face, there hadn't been a lot to notice, and it was as though he was seeing her for the first time now. Her eyes were large and blue. Her face was more handsome than pretty, with a broad nose and a full, generous mouth, but the overall effect, with her height and hair, was striking.

'I'm sorry to bother you again so soon, but I need to ask you some questions. It's very important that we find out as much as we can about Rachel Tenison's background.'

'I understand,' she said quietly, glancing down at her hands. 'What do you want to know?'

He noticed that her long fingers were bare, nails cut functionally short.

'Had you been friends for long?'

She met his gaze. 'Over twenty years. We were at school together.'

'So you know the family well?'

'I know her brother Patrick, but I never met Rachel's parents. They died before she came to my school.'

'So, you must have been close.'

'I suppose so, yes.'

He picked up the hesitation in her voice. 'You don't seem sure.'

She sighed. 'We've known each other for a long time. We had a lot of shared experiences, if that's what you mean by "close". We cared very much about one another, but we didn't live in each other's pockets like some girls do. I'm not like that and nor was Rachel.' Her reply rolled off the tongue a little too quickly, as if she had rehearsed it all beforehand.

'What was she like?' he asked, observing her closely.

She frowned as if she didn't see the point of the question. 'Quiet, always a bit of a loner. The whole teen thing of boys and make-up and parties…well, it wasn't her cup of tea at all. An old head on young shoulders, if you know what I mean. Rachel preferred to have her head stuck in a book than talk about pop music and normal stuff like that.'

'But you weren't put off?'

'We both discovered, more or less at the same time, that we loved history of art and as we got to know one another better, we became good friends.'

'And you stayed friends?'

Liz took a deep breath and nodded. 'We went to university together and then carried on seeing each other in London when we started work.'

'So when did you last speak to her?'

She paused and bit her lip, looking away towards the window. 'Last week. I told you.'

'When exactly?'

'Thursday. I called her…said I was back in London for a few weeks. We arranged to meet for dinner last night, as you know.'

'And there was nothing in your conversation to give you any cause for concern?'

Again the hesitation as her eyes met his. 'Absolutely not.'

'When did you last see Miss Tenison before that?'

'About ten weeks ago.'

'Why so long?'

'Perhaps I should explain. I'm also in the art world, but I'm an academic. I've been working on a research project for a private foundation in the US. I've been based there for the past year, but it brings me to Europe quite a lot, which is why I'm here now. I saw Rachel when I was last over.'

She pulled out a crumpled paper tissue from her sleeve and blew her nose.

'What did you talk about?'

A flicker of unease crossed her face and she shifted in her chair, looking down momentarily at the tissue, which she was scrunching into a tight ball. 'Nothing in particular, just mutual friends and work. The project was coming to an end and I wasn't sure what I was going to do...wasn't sure if I wanted to return to the UK.'

'Did she talk about her personal life at all?'

'Not really.'

'What? She said nothing at all?'

'Nothing that sticks in my memory.' Her tone was overly sharp and impatient. She was trying to hurry over things for some reason and Tartaglia's curiosity was aroused.

'But you say she was a good friend?'

'Yes. Why do you keep asking?'

'I'm just trying to get a picture of her, that's all,' he said simply, hoping to allay whatever fears she had. 'Didn't she have any weaknesses, any passions, any problems?'

'Of course,' she said with a sigh. 'I feel I'm not doing her justice. I suppose when you know somebody well, it's difficult to describe. I don't want to sum her up with a few cheap one-liners.'

Even though he sympathised, he felt she was trying to distract him from the real issue. 'But you must have had some clue what was going on in her life.'

She hesitated. 'Perhaps I'm not explaining things well.' She shifted awkwardly in her seat as if she was uncomfortable and removed a cushion from behind her back, dropping it on the floor. 'Ah, that's better,' she sighed. 'Where were we?'

'I said that you must have had some clue what was going on in Miss Tenison's life.'

'Yes, well, I've been away for a while. Rachel was also very closed. It was sometimes difficult to tell what was going on inside, even for me.'

'She found friendships difficult?'

She nodded slowly. 'She could be awkward, even with people she knew well. I guess it's not surprising, after what happened in her childhood.'

'Apart from you, who else did she see?'

'She tended to stick with people she had known for a long time, people she felt comfortable with. There's Patrick, of course, and his wife, Emma, and their two children. And her business partner, Richard, and his wife…' Her voice tailed away as if she was thinking of something else. Again her eyes fixed on the space beyond the window. 'Most of her energy went into the business. She was very driven.'

He thought he glimpsed an inner bitterness but he wasn't sure. Perhaps she had felt neglected. She looked away and he saw tears forming in her eyes.

'Tell me about her business partner, Richard Greville. I understand that they had a relationship.'

She looked up, surprised. Surprised that he knew or surprised that he was asking, he wasn't sure. 'That's over.'

'Are you sure?'

'Yes. It finished before I went off to the States the first time and that was just over a year ago.'

'You're quite sure it ended? Maybe she just didn't tell you.'

She shifted in her seat again and crossed her legs. 'No, I'm sure I'm right. I could tell things had changed. Call it woman's intuition, although nothing was ever said.'

'Who broke it off?' Feeney asked, looking up from her notepad.

'She did, from what I know, but I think they both realised it was for the best. He's married. In the end I think the business was more important to both of them than whatever sexual thing they had going.'

'Do you think he harboured a grudge?' Tartaglia asked.

Liz raised her brows. 'Richard? He's not the type. And before you ask me, I certainly don't see him killing Rachel in a fit of jealousy.'

'Jealousy? What would Richard Greville have to be jealous about? Was there someone else? From the photos I've seen, she was an attractive woman.'

'It's just a figure of speech,' she said quickly. 'Richard's not the jealous type.'

'But there was somebody else. Is that what you're saying?'

She touched her lips briefly with her fingers. Once more Tartaglia was aware of a hesitation that seemed to signify concealment.

'I don't know,' she said. 'I think Rachel was seeing somebody, but I'm not sure.'

'Do you have a name?'

She shook her head. 'It was just something she said. A throwaway remark, that's all. I really can't remember anything else and I may have got it wrong.'

'You're sure about this?'

'No, I'm not sure. It's just an impression. That's all.'

'It's very important that we talk to anybody she has seen, let alone had a relationship with, in the last few months. You can't remember anything else?'

Her look was challenging. 'No. I told you. Why do you keep asking?'

Even as she spoke, he knew there was something missing, something she wasn't saying. He didn't know her at all, but he could feel it. It was nothing new, it happened all the time in interviews, the self-editing, the filtering, either deliberate or unconscious. It was his job to weed it out and get to the truth. But he felt somehow that with Liz Volpe it wasn't going to be easy and his curiosity deepened.

'What about before Richard Greville?'

'She'd had the odd relationship, but nothing special, nothing serious.'

'I'll need their names and details if you have them. We'll need to check on everybody.'

She shrugged. 'If I can remember, certainly. But this was a while ago and, as I said, there was nobody special.'

'But Richard Greville was?'

'Certainly more special than anyone else before.'

He nodded, although he felt far from satisfied. He couldn't force her to talk but he was determined to find out one way or another. He decided to try a different tack. 'How would you describe her? I gather she didn't find relationships easy?'

She seemed to consider the question then shook her head. 'No. She was shy and shyness makes people awkward, cuts them off. Rachel just found it difficult to form emotional ties. It's a defence mechanism. I think, beneath it all, she was frightened of exposing her-self, of getting hurt.'

'It's early days but it's likely she was killed by a man and proba-bly someone she knew,' he said forcefully, catching her eye. 'Come on, you were her best friend. You really expect me to believe she told you nothing about what was going on in her life?'

She flushed. The knuckles of her hands were white as she clenched her fingers in her lap. 'Perhaps there was nothing to tell.'

Running his fingers through his hair, he leaned towards her, try-ing to bridge the gap between them. 'Nothing to tell? Look, maybe you're trying to protect your friend out of some sort of misguided loy-alty, but she must have had a life outside work and, if you were as close as you say you were, you must have known about it. Even if they don't live in each other's pockets, women talk. They can't help con-fiding in their friends. Whether you were in the US or London, there's the phone and the email. We'll be checking the records to see what was really going on.'

Tight-lipped, Liz held his gaze, but she didn't reply. He could see the pain and stubborn defensiveness in her eyes, and there was no point in going any further for the moment. He had to let her calm down first. Maybe then she would be more prepared to open up.

He stood up and Feeney followed suit. 'Thank you. I'll be in touch if there's anything else. One last question. For formality's sake, could you tell us what your movements were last Friday morning.'

She looked startled, as if she wasn't expecting the question. 'I was here. In this flat. Surely you don't think I—'

'It's just a formality. Please answer the question.'

'I flew in from New York first thing on Thursday.'

'So, Friday morning, you were on your own?'

There was a marginal hesitation before she replied. 'Yes. Of course.'

A blast of cold air hit Tartaglia and Feeney as they let themselves out of the building. Tartaglia shivered as he looked up at the leaden sky. More snow was definitely on the way. He turned up his collar against the wind and shoved his hands deep in the pockets of his overcoat.

'So, what do you think?' Feeney asked, as she trailed behind him through the snow and grit on the pavement. Her bushy red hair was tied back as usual, this time in some sort of a half-plait, half-ponytail concoction. Even though it was still early in the day, it was already starting to unravel, frizzy tendrils escaping like snakes all around her broad, plump face. 'I most definitely got the impression we weren't being given the full story,' she continued in her soft lilting voice, not waiting for his response.

Tartaglia stopped at the edge of the pavement while a line of cars and vans passed them and struggled slowly up the hill. 'She's holding back, I agree. But it could be for a variety of reasons.'

Feeney shook her head vigorously. 'That bit about not having a clue about her best friend's love life—well, it's a load of shite, if you want my opinion. Just ask any woman. Doesn't matter if she's been abroad.' She hurriedly smoothed a woolly, pink-gloved hand over the top of her head as she looked questioningly at him.

'I'm sure you're right, but now was not the time to push.'

'Shall we get her into an interview room and make it formal? Maybe then she'd be a bit more willing to cooperate.'

Tartaglia shook his head. 'Not just yet. If there was something material, I think she would have told us. Whatever else she said, or didn't say, I got the impression that she genuinely cared about Rachel Tenison.'

'But why tell such a bare-faced lie? Does she think we're idiots?'

There was a gap in the traffic and he led the way through the greying slush, across the road to where their car was parked.

He understood and sympathised with Feeney's frustration and impatience, but you couldn't make someone talk if they didn't want to, and pressure could be counter-productive. After what had happened, it was natural that Liz Volpe wasn't thinking straight. They needed to give her a little time, leave things to sink in properly first. And if that didn't work, they could always try the heavy approach later.

Once at the car, he turned to Feeney. 'I think she's holding back because she's a private person and loyal to her friend,' he said. 'I saw the expression on her face as I kept pressing. She sees it as muckraking and she doesn't yet understand why it's relevant. It's all happened so quickly, she's in shock and she's being defensive. It's only natural. And she doesn't trust us.'

Feeney didn't reply, although he could see from the set of her thin-lipped mouth that she didn't agree.

'We'll get it out of her one way or another, don't you worry,' he added firmly, opening the passenger door and climbing in.

From behind the curtain, Liz watched Tartaglia cross the road, his stride thrusting and purposeful, as if impatient to get on with things. His hands were jammed deep in his pockets and he held his head high, shoulders back. For some reason she thought of Kipling's 'The Cat That Walked by Himself'. The funny little red-haired constable struggled to keep up with him, her oversized mackintosh flapping behind her as she picked her way hesitantly through the snow. What an odd pair they made. They stopped by an ordinary dark blue car, exchanged a few words, then climbed in, the constable taking the driving seat.

Although in some ways the interview had not been as bad as she had been expecting, it had still left a nasty taste. She resented the probing and the pushing—almost as if she herself was on trial. And some things were none of their business. She was certain Tartaglia had guessed that she was hiding something, although there was no way he could know what it was. But the more she thought about it, the more uncomfortable she felt. She was sure she hadn't seen the last of him.

She watched their car move slowly from its space and then accelerate away up the hill. Once they were safely out of sight, she perched on the arm of the sofa, picked up the phone and dialled a number. After a moment, she heard him answer.

'They've just gone,' she said. 'You wanted me to call you.'

'How was it?'

'Could have been worse, I suppose.'

'Did they give you the third degree?'

She hesitated. 'I think I got off quite lightly. God, I've got such a hangover. I drank myself to sleep last night. And I had such terrible, terrible dreams...all about Rachel.'

'You should have let me come over.'

'No. That wouldn't have been a good idea.'

She realised that her tone had been a little sharp and there was a pause at the other end before he spoke again. 'So, what sort of things did they ask?' His tone was casual, trying to disguise his interest, and it almost made her smile to find him so boyishly transparent for a change.

'They wanted to know about my friendship with Rachel, what she was like, who might have wanted to kill her. You know the type of thing. What could I say? I did my best in the circumstances.'

She tried to make it all sound matter-of-fact and she heard him exhale, possibly with relief, at the other end. She paused, thinking back again to the exchanges with Tartaglia, the way he had looked at her questioningly, trying to read between the lines of what she was saying. That wouldn't be the end of it, she was sure.

'And what did you say?' he asked, now more insistent.

'Just general things, nothing specific.'

'You didn't tell them anything?' She heard the worry in his voice.

'Of course not.'

'You're sure?'

'Of course I'm sure. I know what I said.'

'Good.' Another pause, then: 'Shall I come round later?'

Tartaglia's sharp, dark eyes loomed in her mind, as though he was still watching her. Even though rationally she knew it was a foolish idea—he had far better things to do than keep an eye on everybody who had known Rachel—she still felt wary.

'Please let me come over,' he said, before she had a chance to reply.

'No. I don't think that's wise.'

'Now you're being melodramatic.'

'Perhaps.' She closed her eyes and pressed her fingers against her temples, as if to block out the image of Tartaglia's handsome face. 'But still, I don't think it's a good idea. Anyway, I've got a foul headache that won't go away.'

'I can make you better,' he said, softly.

She opened her eyes and stared unfocussed at the street below. The centre of the road had been heavily gritted and was a wet, grey slick, with mounds of dirty-looking snow piled up high along the edges and on the sides of the pavement. A bus had come around the corner and had stopped in the middle of the road, unable to pass because of a double-parked car. Traffic was backed up all the way along from the lights at Elgin Crescent and she heard the impatient hooting of horns.

With Rachel's death, something material had changed. She couldn't put it into words, and certainly not to him, but she felt deeply uneasy. She wanted to close her eyes, bury her head in his arms and forget the outside world for a while. But that wasn't the solution, as she well knew; life wasn't that simple anymore.

'Please let me come over,' he said. 'I want to be with you.'

'No. Not tonight. I told you I need some time on my own.'

6

'Is that a Raphael?' Sam Donovan asked, gazing at the large, ornately framed canvas that hung behind Richard Greville's desk.

A weak smile flickered over Greville's gaunt face. 'Very good, Sergeant, but I'm afraid I must disappoint you. It's a copy, although a very good one, probably painted only a few decades after Raphael's death. We occasionally deal in his drawings upstairs but the oils rarely come up for auction and when they do, they fetch many, many millions. This one, however, came my way a long time ago and I bought it for a song. So I can afford to have it all to myself, wasting away down here, and I'm rather fond of it. It's really rather well done.'

They were in the basement office of the Greville Tenison gallery in Dover Street, Mayfair. The dark red, windowless room smelled strongly of cigar smoke and was lined with books, the only natural light coming from a small lantern skylight in one corner. Greville looked to be in his mid to late fifties, tall and thin, with a mop of lank sandy hair that flopped over his forehead. Dressed casually in a pink oxford shirt, unbuttoned at the neck, and fawn trousers, he was slumped behind his desk in a velvet-cushioned armchair, his face out of range of the dim orbit of light cast by the small brass reading lamp. It was only mid-morning, but he cradled a cut-glass tumbler of whisky in his hand, stroking the pattern with his long, pale fingers from time to time, as if for comfort.

They had spent the first few minutes discussing his art business in general terms, as Donovan felt Greville appeared to need a gentle preamble before she attempted to question him directly about Rachel

Tenison. As they talked, she could hear footsteps on the wooden floor above and the distant murmur of conversation drifting down from the ground floor gallery, where Minderedes was busy interviewing Selina, Greville's pretty, blonde assistant.

'How long have you known Rachel Tenison, Mr Greville?' Donovan asked, glancing at her watch and deciding it was time to move on to specifics.

Greville sighed, screwing up his small blue eyes for a second as if even the mention of her name was painful. 'Over ten years. She worked for me first at Christie's, then we decided to go into business together.' He spoke slowly and deliberately as if every word was an effort.

'Was it an equal partnership? I mean...' Donovan tried to pick her words carefully.

'We owned the gallery fifty-fifty. But what you really mean is, what was a woman like Rachel doing going into business with an old sod like me? It's a fair question. I suppose in those days I had all the contacts and the knowledge and she had the money. But she learned quickly. Soon she had a whole fistful of clients. She was a class act, no doubt about it.' There was no apparent bitterness as he spoke, only a wistful sadness.

'So the relationship between you worked well, you would say?'

He nodded. 'We were complementary. I don't know what will happen now...now she's...gone.'

'You reported her missing on Friday. What gave you cause for alarm?'

'Rachel had a meeting with a client, a very important client. He's an American from Texas who buys a lot through the gallery, and we often bid for him at auctions. She was supposed to see him at his hotel and discuss some things that were coming up for auction. She was then taking him out to lunch and going with him and his wife to the ballet on Friday evening.'

'All that just for a client?'

'It's perfectly normal in our world. We develop close relationships with our collectors and give them the Rolls Royce treatment when they're in town. It's what brings in the pounds, or in Mr Gunn's case, millions of dollars, all with a nice, healthy commission. Anyway, when Rachel didn't fetch up at Claridge's, I immediately knew something was wrong and I got Selina to phone the police.'

'You didn't phone yourself?'

'I was in Geneva seeing another one of our collectors. That's where I've been until this morning. It was easier to get Selina to call. Apparently it took a while before she spoke to the right person.'

'So you were in Geneva on Friday?'

'That's right. I flew out first thing that morning. I was in the middle of a meeting when Selina called to say that Rachel hadn't come in and she couldn't reach her by phone.'

'You didn't think Miss Tenison was ill?'

Greville shook his head. 'Rachel was never ill. Never. And if she had been, she would have called in. She was like that. As you can imagine, I was really worried.'

'But you carried on with your meetings?'

Greville banged his glass down hard on the desk. 'What else was I supposed to do? The bloody clients wanted to see me. And of course I had no idea what had happened. I heard nothing until later that evening, just before I went to bed, when I picked up a voicemail on my mobile. Someone from the local station said that they had taken a look around her flat—no doubt cursory—and that nothing appeared to be amiss.' He paused before adding, 'I then called the station myself. They seemed to think it was none of my bloody business if Rachel had decided not to come in to work, that no doubt there was some sort of personal reason why she hadn't turned up. I knew something was wrong but they just wouldn't bloody listen. Told me to call again if she hadn't turned up on Monday. Sort of implied I should mind my own business.'

He took another slug of whisky and Donovan waited for him to continue. She understood his feeling of impotence and why, in the light of what had happened, he felt bitter. But there had been no justification to send out search parties, particularly after Rachel Tenison's flat had been checked and nothing suspicious found. Even if they had searched the park sooner, by the time the first call from Greville's office was logged, Rachel Tenison was already dead.

'I called several times after that on Saturday and on Sunday,' he added forcefully, as if feeling the need to justify that he had done all he could. 'But I couldn't get hold of the person who had left the message. Kept getting a bloody answer machine and everyone who knew anything about it seemed to have gone home. Then somebody telephoned me last night and told me Rachel was dead. That her body had been found in Holland Park.' He put down his glass and rubbed his face with his hands, shaking his head as if he still couldn't believe what had happened. 'I somehow feel I should have been here, in London. Perhaps I should have flown back sooner....''

'If it's any consolation, we believe Miss Tenison was killed early on Friday morning.' He stared at her blankly and she repeated herself: 'Even if you had got more of a response from the local station, there was nothing that you or anyone else could have done, I assure you.'

He nodded slowly, grimacing, and drained his glass as if disgusted with the whole process. 'Don't normally drink like this,' he said, putting the glass down firmly on the desk in front of him. 'Certainly not in the morning. But I haven't slept. Don't think I'll get much work done today. I'll probably close the gallery and go home after you've gone. Need to get my mind around what's happened. Work out what's to be done, how I'm going to tell the clients.'

His grief and shock seemed genuine and she wished she didn't have to trouble him further. 'Can you think of any reason why somebody might have wanted to kill Miss Tenison?' she asked, after a moment.

He looked up at her and blinked. 'No. Everybody adored her. That's how she was. Rachel could charm absolutely anyone.'

'There's nothing you know of, in her work or personal life, that might have threatened her in any way?'

'No. Nothing.' He frowned. 'Surely it's simple. There's some bloody nutter on the loose, some sick maniac let out of jail or hospital because the government won't pay to keep them locked up where they belong.'

'We're considering all possibilities, Mr Greville,' Donovan said, not wishing to be drawn into a political discussion, although she sympathised. 'And one of them is that she was killed by someone she knew.'

He shook his head vigorously. 'Why would anyone who knew Rachel want to kill her? It doesn't make sense.'

'What about one of her clients? As you say, the relationships sound quite close. Couldn't one of them have crossed the line?'

'No. Nobody I can think of, at any rate. Of course, some of them probably found her attractive. It's part of life and she was a very pretty girl. But Rachel was incredibly careful about things like that, never went too far, always kept firm boundaries. The clients knew that and respected her for it. She was always completely professional.'

'What about her personal life?' She caught his eye, wondering if he would bring up his relationship with Rachel Tenison voluntarily.

Greville looked surprised. 'You think this was a crime of passion?' He rubbed his chin thoughtfully for a moment before saying, 'Can't think of anything recent. There was a fellow at Christie's who used to follow her around a bit like a lost lamb, but I don't think she was at all interested. No idea what happened to him, and he was so wet you could wring him out...he's hardly the type...Anyway, it wasn't anything meaningful, if that's what you're looking for. She used to have lunch with the occasional friend but that's all.'

'Was there anyone else?'

'I remember a journalist, some chap she was at university with. He came into the gallery a few times recently—I think he was doing a piece about Nazi looted art—but there was nobody important that I was aware of, nobody who would feel strongly enough to—'

'It's impossible to tell, Mr Greville, what people feel, what they show, what they keep hidden. I'll need all the names you can think of.'

Greville sighed, as if it was all an enormous effort. 'The chap at Christie's…he was called Rupert something…in British Pictures, I seem to remember. Maybe he's still there. The journalist's name was Jonathan, but you'd better ask Selina. She knows more about this sort of thing and she's mistress of the diary.'

'And what about you, Mr Greville?' She held his gaze. 'I understand you had a relationship with Miss Tenison.'

He stared at her, pursing his thin, dry lips and sucking in his breath sharply. 'I really don't think that's any of your business.'

'Everything is our business. Please can you tell me about it.'

He knotted his hands and looked away. 'There's nothing much to tell, really.'

'But it went on for several years, I understand.'

'Yes. But it was over many moons ago and, as I said, it's really none of your business.'

He spoke dismissively, as though what had happened was something unimportant, but his eyes were watering and his face was flushed. He refused to look at her.

'I'm sorry, Mr Greville, but I really do need to know more. Did she end it or did you?'

He felt in his trouser pocket and pulled out a large, creased blue-checked cotton handkerchief and blew his nose loudly. 'She was the one who ended it,' he said, stuffing the handkerchief forcefully back into the pocket with a sniff.

'Were you unhappy about it?'

He shook his head, bewildered. 'It didn't make sense. There was nobody else, you see, nobody else.'

'You're sure?' she asked, wondering if Greville was being naïve.

'Yes,' he said, looking affronted. 'There was no reason for it. I gave her what she wanted. She was safe with me.'

It was such an odd remark, Donovan lost her train of thought for a moment. 'What do you mean by safe? Safe from what?'

Greville sighed deeply and gazed into the distance. 'What I meant was, some people like danger, like to put themselves in the way of temptation and trouble. I was a safe haven for Rachel, what she needed.'

'You're saying Miss Tenison liked danger?'

'I'm saying she needed looking after. She was fragile. A delicate creature. Like a precious, beautiful flower. I took care of her.' A brief smile of affection illuminated the sadness of his pale, worn features.

'Like a father figure?'

Greville knitted his brow as though he didn't like the term. 'I suppose I could give you all the obvious kitchen psychology crap about her background, but it's not really relevant, is it? My lovely, lovely girl is dead.'

Holding Donovan's eye almost challengingly, he reached behind him and fumbled until he found the catch to the cupboard. He yanked it open and retrieved a bottle of Famous Grouse. It was about a third full and he poured a good inch or so into his glass.

'Did your wife know about your relationship?'

'No, she did not,' he said firmly, struggling to screw the cap back on as though his fingers were stiff and putting the bottle down on the desk in front of him. 'And I want it to stay that way, do you hear?' He sank back into the chair and took a gulp of whisky.

'If you've told us the truth, Mr Greville, and your wife does the same, and your alibis check out, there's no reason for her to know anything about what went on between you and Rachel Tenison.'

An expression of relief passed over his face and he smacked his lips. 'Good. As I said, it was all in the past. There's no point upsetting her now.'

'It would be helpful if you could give us a DNA and fingerprint sample so that we can eliminate you from anything found in Miss Tenison's flat.'

'Fine by me.' He gave a vague wave of his hand.

'We'll also need to check where you were on Friday.'

'Be my guest. I've nothing to hide. Speak to BA. They'll confirm that I was on the first flight out to Geneva on Friday, crack of bloody dawn.'

'Thank you. We shall.' Feeling that she had probably got as much as was useful out of Greville for the moment, Donovan stood up, took a card out of her bag and pushed it across the desk. 'If anything springs to mind, however trivial, please give me a call.'

He nodded. 'Of course. Liaise with Selina about the files and Rachel's diary, will you? Whatever access you need is fine, but speak to her. She deals with all the admin crap.'

Donovan walked out of his office, half closing the door behind her. As she turned to go up the stairs, she caught sight of Greville's long, pale face framed in the narrow gap. For a moment, he stared down at the desk in front of him, as if lost in thought, then he bowed his head and put his face in his hands. His shoulders started to heave and it looked as though he was crying, although there was no audible sound. From what she could tell, he had told the truth and her heart went out to him.

Upstairs she found Minderedes perched on the corner of Selina's desk.

'Time to go,' she said briskly. 'Got everything we need?'

'Yes.' Minderedes slid off the desk and started to walk with her towards the door. They were almost out in the street when he looked back at Selina, made the shape of a phone around his ear and mouthed the words 'call me'. Donovan said nothing and went out into the street ahead of him, letting the glass door slam behind her. If he wanted to behave like an idiot, it was his lookout.

It was freezing cold, the sky threatening again, and she pulled her coat even more tightly round herself. There was still some snow on the ground but it was turning into slush and her feet felt wet even after the short walk from the car to the gallery.

'Don't know about you,' she said sharply, as Minderedes emerged through the door, grinning, 'but I need a coffee and something to eat. There's still time on the meter, if we're quick.'

'Yeah. Could murder something hot.'

They crossed the road to a small café on the opposite side and bought pastries and coffee, taking them to the counter in the window where they stood looking out at the street and the Greville Tenison gallery. Even though it was nearly lunchtime, there were few passers-by and hardly any traffic, most people kept away or inside because of the cold. Within minutes she saw Richard Greville come out, dressed in a long dark coat and brown hat. He walked away along the road and turned down Hay Hill towards Berkeley Square.

'Greville was on a six-fifty flight to Geneva last Friday morning,' Minderedes said, in between bites of a large cinnamon Danish, a second still waiting untouched on his plate. 'The flight landed about nine-thirty local time, then he had meetings with a couple of clients which took up most of the day. He spent the weekend with some other clients near Basle.'

'What about Mrs Greville?'

'She apparently stayed in London. I've got the home address and I'll go round and see her later.' He crammed in another mouthful of pastry. Elbow on the counter, beige mac carefully folded over his arm, he picked at any fallen scraps of pastry or nuts as if it pained him to see anything go to waste. How he remained so skinny was a mystery.

Donovan took a small bite of her croissant, wishing that she didn't feel quite so hungry. 'You'll double check with the airline to make sure he actually took it?'

'Of course. But if so, he's out of the frame.' Minderedes raised his thick brows and grinned at his attempt at a pun, brushing away a light dusting of icing sugar that had fallen on his tie.

'What about Selina? Does she have an alibi?'

'At home. Her flatmate can corroborate. You really think the killer could be a woman?'

Donovan took a gulp of the unpleasantly milky cappuccino. 'Can't rule it out, although as we all know, it takes a lot of strength to shift a body. I just don't see a woman using an arm lock unless she's been in the armed forces or had some sort of martial arts training. What about the missing laptop and phone?'

'Still missing. Apparently, she kept the laptop at home and rarely used it for work. I've got a note of her personal email address, although any emails she's already downloaded onto the laptop won't be kept by the service provider. At least her work computer's backed up on the office network. As far as Selina knows, her BlackBerry was her only mobile phone, but it only links in to the work email.'

'So, it looks as though they've been taken. What about her diary? Is that on the network?'

Minderedes nodded. 'I've got a printout and Selina's emailing the full version along with the client list. Most of the clients live overseas, so hopefully it will be pretty easy to eliminate them.'

'How about the American she was due to see on Friday?'

'He's still in town. I'll go over to his hotel once we're done. Selina says it's only a couple of minutes' walk from here.'

'So what did *Selina* have to say about Greville?' she said pointedly.

Minderedes used a paper napkin to wipe a trace of milky foam from his lips, folding it carefully and putting it down by his plate. 'She's only been there a couple of months but she said he and Rachel Tenison got on like the proverbial house on fire.'

'We'll need to speak to whoever worked there before.'

'All under control,' he said, patting his breast pocket with a tight smile. 'I've got the woman's name and the phone number of the agency. Anyway, according to Selina, the gallery's doing really well. I'll check with the bookkeeper and the accountant, and the bank of course, but it all sounds hunky-dory. Not a whiff of anything smelly there.'

'What about Rachel Tenison's private life?'

'According to Selina, she didn't have much of one or, at least, if she had anything personal going on she didn't shout about it at work or scribble it all over her diary. Her work's her life, you know the line.'

'What about Thursday?'

After biting the corner off his second pastry, Minderedes took a folded sheaf of papers out of his pocket and leafed through until he found the right page. 'Thursday, here we are. Not a lot going on, apparently. They were getting stock ready for Maastricht.'

'Maastricht?'

'It's some sort of big art fair in Holland. Anyway, the carrier delivered some canvases back from the framers in the afternoon and Rachel Tenison cut out around six, after they'd gone. Said she was meeting someone for a drink.'

'Who?'

'In the diary it's down as "JB—drink". He showed her the page, then folded the papers away in his pocket. 'Doesn't even say where they were meeting. Selina said that sort of shorthand entry was normal, even for business contacts. Said she got to know who most of them were if it was to do with work, but JB doesn't ring a bell.'

'So, it's personal. What a way to run an office.'

'Selina said Greville's even worse; it's impossible to keep track of him. He can't work a computer and keeps a written diary in his pocket, which she has to take off him from time to time to enter into the system so she knows what's going on.'

'Sounds very Stone Age, but I suppose if it's just the two of them they can just about make it work. What about the phone records?'

'Copies are on their way.'

'So, what else did Selina have to say? You two seemed to be getting on really well, from what I could see.'

Minderedes gave her another smile. 'Nice little girl, Selina. Very helpful. But not really my type.'

'You don't have a type,' she said, with a derisory snort.

Minderedes shrugged. 'Whatever. She'll have the files ready if we want them but she says she can't believe any of the clients would kill Rachel Tenison.'

Donovan put down her cup and studied him for a moment. Slick Nick. That was his nickname around the office and he seemed quite pleased with it. It certainly summed him up, with his bleached teeth, sun-bed tan and fine gold chain around the neck, but he was nothing more than a well-seasoned alley cat and it amazed her how many women were taken in. She supposed it was all a matter of confidence, in his blood from birth. Not for the first time, she found herself wishing that life would deal him a few hard knocks—anything to bring him down a peg or two, although people like him always seemed to be Teflon-coated. She envied him his lack of self-doubt. How easy life must be if you always thought you were right.

'You're going to take her out, aren't you?' she asked. Although he didn't reply, she noted the stubborn tensing of his mouth as he drained his coffee. 'Don't bother to lie.' She just wanted to hear him say it, watching the colour rise to his sallow cheeks as he avoided her eye. 'Can't you play it straight, for once? Can't you interview a woman without trying to get into her knickers?'

He slammed down his cup, making the spoon jingle in the saucer, and glared at her. 'What's it to do with you? I'm allowed a life, aren't I?'

'If it's female and it moves, shag it. That's your motto.'

'For fuck's sake, she's over sixteen. She can make up her own mind. Anyway, with the hours we work, how the hell am I supposed to meet anyone who isn't a sodding, pain in the arse, uptight police-woman? Tell me that.'

'You seem to manage pretty well, from what I've seen. You know what Mark will say, if he finds out, don't you?'

At the mention of Tartaglia's name, Minderedes bridled. 'Going to tell him, are you? Whisper in his little ear, all cosy cosy, just the two of you? That's what you'd really like, isn't it?'

'That's a load of crap and you know it,' she said vehemently, want-ing to slap his face.

'Anyway, what about him and that red-haired pathologist? Fiona...what's her name? She cuts up the bodies and he gets his end away. Very nice.'

'Christ, you're twisted. Anyway, that's history, not that it's any of your business.'

'Nor is it any of *his* fucking business what I get up to in *my* own time.'

'Yes it is, if it's to do with an ongoing case.'

'Selina's not a material witness, right? And you're a fine one to talk. What about you and—' He stopped short, mouth half-open and stared at her horrified for a second, before clamping his mouth shut and fixing his gaze out the window as if there was something very in-teresting to see on the other side of the road. His embarrassment was the only thing that stopped her from punching him.

He was referring to the man known as Tom, a serial killer who had murdered several young girls, who had put both her and Tartgalia's lives in jeopardy. Nobody at work dared mention to her face what had happened. But she knew they all talked about it behind her back, hushing their voices sometimes, cutting conversations short when she came into the room. Christ, how naïve they were, especially for a bunch of detectives. Did they really imagine she had no idea what they were talking about? But there was no point in having it out with Minderedes. He wasn't worth the breath. Anyway, he was just echoing what they all thought. The best thing was to try and ignore it, not give him the satisfaction of a reaction.

Suddenly, she became aware that the café had become very quiet. She turned around to see several faces looking at her. Wondering how much they had overheard, she scooped up her bag and turned to Minderedes.

'I'm going to try and trace the poem,' she said in as flat and business-like a tone as she could muster. 'Call me when you've spoken to the client.'

Without giving him the chance to say anything, she strode out of the café into the cold street.

7

It was late afternoon and already dark when Wightman dropped Tartaglia in front of La Girolle, a restaurant in the backwaters of Kensington, and sped off around the corner in search of a parking place. Rachel Tenison's name and photograph had been released to the press earlier that morning, with an appeal for help in tracing her final movements, and calls had started to come in with possible sightings and information. One in particular sounded interesting. The manager of La Girolle had called in to say that Rachel Tenison had dined there with an unknown man on Thursday evening, the night before she was murdered, and as the location was close to where she had lived Tartaglia decided to follow it up himself.

Waiting for Wightman, he took shelter from the cold wind underneath the restaurant's wide, black awning, admiring the huge lead tubs of designer topiary that were chained and padlocked to the railings to prevent theft. A few minutes later, Wightman came thudding down the pavement, just as Tartaglia heard the sound of his phone. 'Go and find the manager,' he said to Wightman, flipping open the phone. 'I'll join you in a minute.'

It was the CSM, Nina Turner. 'We're done here now,' she said, 'but you told me to call if I found anything interesting in the flat.'

'Spit it out.' He was freezing cold and impatient to cut to the chase.

'To be honest, I'd rather you came and took a look yourself,' she said, a little hesitantly. 'I really don't think I can do it justice over the phone. Sharon said you were just down the road.'

'OK,' he replied, a little mystified. 'I'll be over as soon as I'm done here.'

He snapped the phone shut and went into the restaurant, wondering what it was that couldn't be described over a phone. The interior was dimly lit, and expensively furnished with suede-covered bucket chairs and banquettes all in shades of brown. Looking closer, he noticed that the walls were clad in leather. A tall, thin waiter was busy smoothing a starched white cloth over one of the tables at the front, while another bustled around with a tray of small square vases containing white rosebuds and placed one in the centre of each table. Wightman was at the back, perched on a stool at the black and chrome bar, a tall glass of something in front of him. Knowing Wightman it would be a Diet Coke. It was all he ever drank.

As Tartaglia went to join him, a short, bald man in a well-cut dark navy suit and vivid mauve tie glided through the swing doors.

'I am Henri Charles,' he said in a thick French accent, extending a plump hand to Tartaglia, accompanied by the faint, lemony smell of cologne. He had a trim, carefully sculpted black beard, which added definition to an otherwise weak chin, and gave him a saturnine appearance.

'Please take a seat, Inspector. May I offer you a drink?'

'Glass of fizzy water would be nice,' Tartaglia said, suddenly thirsty, and sat down on a stool next to Wightman.

'I've explained to Mr Charles why we're here,' Wightman said to Tartaglia, as Charles spooned ice and a slice of lime into a tall glass and filled it with a small bottle of Perrier from a cupboard below. 'He was the one who made the call. He was on duty the night Miss Tenison had dinner here.'

Charles passed Tartaglia his drink. 'Yes. I recognise her from the photograph in the newspaper.'

'You're sure it was last Thursday night?' Tartaglia asked, taking a large sip.

He arched his thick dark brows. 'Of course. Let me fetch the book so you can see yourself.'

Charles emerged from behind the counter and crossed the room to the small reception desk at the front of the restaurant where he retrieved a large, leather-bound book. Coming back, he inserted himself between Tartaglia and Wightman and slapped the book down on the counter in front of them. He started to leaf through the pages.

'Here it is, last Thursday, as I say.' He ran a stubby finger along the many entries until he came to the name of Tenison.

'Can I see the phone number?' Wightman asked. Charles turned the book towards him and Wightman made a note.

'It says the booking was for eight-thirty,' Tartaglia said. 'What time did they arrive?'

'They were late…maybe about twenty minutes.'

'Can you describe him?'

Charles flicked a minute speck from the sleeve of his jacket. 'He look like a businessman, or at least that is my impression.'

'What do you mean by that?'

Charles shrugged. 'He was wearing a suit and tie. He look like he came straight from work. Most people around here dress more casual when they go out.'

'Aside from his clothes, can you describe him?'

'I did not see him particularly well. He was facing the window.'

'Where was this?'

'Table number seven, over there in the corner.' Charles turned and pointed to a small table by the window. It was set apart from the rest of the tables in a recess of its own.

'Did they ask for that particular table?'

Charles puckered his fleshy lips. 'They request somewhere quiet when they make the reservation. It's written here.' He tapped the page in front of them.

'Did you speak to either of them when they arrived?'

'I mark off the reservation in the book, as you can see, and then show the lady to the table. When the man came in, he went straight over to join her.'

'Did you speak to him?'

'No.'

Tartaglia glanced over again at table seven. If Rachel Tenison's companion had been sitting with his back to the room, his face wouldn't have been easily visible to any of the other tables.

He turned back to Charles. 'But you saw Miss Tenison clearly?'

'Most definitely. She faces into the room. Almost immediately after the man arrive, he leave the table and he goes outside. I see him walking up and down, up and down, talking into a mobile phone.'

'But it was freezing,' Wightman said, surprised.

'We do not permit them to be used in this restaurant,' Charles said firmly.

'Who took their orders?' Tartaglia asked.

'I did, but the man was outside. The young lady, she order for him. Then I sent over the sommelier so she can choose the wine.'

'And you're quite sure the lady was Miss Tenison?'

'No doubt,' he said with a smile, running his hand over the fine stubble on the top of his head. 'She is beautiful and I do not forget a face.'

'Had you ever seen Miss Tenison's companion before?'

Charles shook his head.

'Did they stay a long time?'

'No. Not long. That is also why I remember. They have the starters and then the main course. I'm not sure if they even finish. They have some type of…of disagreement.'

'You heard them arguing?'

'No. The restaurant is full and it is very noisy. I remember the lady get up and ask me for her coat. She look upset, angry maybe. I ask her if anything is the matter with the food and she says no, then she leave. I remember seeing the man sitting by himself at the table, maybe he waits for her to come back. As I said, we were very busy and next time I look over, maybe five minutes later, he is gone.'

'What time was this?'

'Ten, maybe ten-thirty. I don't keep my eye on the clock.'

'How did they pay?' Wightman asked.

'He left cash on the table. He was in so much haste I don't think he even ask for the bill but the cash was more than enough.'

'Did you get any feel for their relationship at all?' Tartaglia asked. 'Were they lovers, would you say?'

Charles grimaced. 'Impossible to know. Maybe he hold her hand.' He nodded slowly. 'Yes, maybe he hold her hand. That is my impression.'

'What else do you recall about him? Was he tall or short? Fat or thin? Young or old?'

'Tallish maybe, but he is mostly sitting when I see him. Like you, he's not fat.' This said with a quick glance at Tartaglia's waistline. 'Maybe your age, maybe older. Sometimes it is difficult to know.'

'Anything else you remember?'

'I have the impression he had dark hair. Short but thick. Not like me.' He patted the top of his shiny head.

'How dark? Do you mean black?'

Charles put his head to one side and studied Tartaglia. 'You have the Latin hair, the real black. His is not like that, from what I remember. I would say brown, dark brown perhaps. It all look the same in this light.'

All cats are dark at night, Tartaglia thought. But if nothing else, the general description ruled out Richard Greville. 'Was the man English?'

Charles shrugged. 'I'm sorry, but what is English these days? I'm a Gascon; I can't tell you that. It's like asking an Englishman to...' he paused, his hand fluttering back and forth as if he were trying to pluck the words from the air, '...to know the difference between a truffle and a lump of coal.'

Wightman dropped Tartaglia outside Rachel Tenison's apartment block and drove off in the direction of Barnes. The building was still cordoned off and Tartaglia went through the process of being signed in again, ignoring the group of reporters who were still hanging around on the pavement outside, along with a news crew who seemed to be filming live. This time he went straight up the stairs to the fifth floor, not wanting to chance the lift on his own.

Nina Turner met him at the door, still in her forensic suit and mask. 'Sorry to be so mysterious, but I thought you'd better take a look before it all goes off to the lab. Photographs wouldn't do it justice.'

'You're killing me. What is it?' he said, striding alongside her down the passage towards the bedroom.

'It was all in that trunk you liked.'

'You found the key?'

'Yes. No damage done, you'll be pleased to hear.'

The bed had been completely stripped of its linen and hangings and the room now looked even more bare and empty and colourless. The box sat on a plastic sheet on the floor in its original position, lid closed. Not wearing gloves, he waited for Nina to open it.

She bent down and lifted the lid. What he saw made his pulse quicken. Inside was a collection of steel handcuffs, manacles, leather straps and gags, along with a number of masks, similar to the ones in the photographs in the study. Some were half-face, some full-face. Even without someone behind them, they were sinister. When people's homes were searched, the most extraordinary and unexpected things often came to light, but he hadn't envisaged finding anything like this here.

He stared down at the box, wondering. A woman who wanted to be tied up—wasn't that every man's fantasy? Although he had never, so far, been with a woman who liked that sort of thing, he had to admit the thought was arousing. He had imagined Rachel Tenison as successful and driven, certainly not submissive in this way, and he was fascinated. He was glimpsing a secret world, her secret world, inside a locked box. He looked up for a second and saw himself reflected in the mirrors, with the bed just behind. The image of her—white as snow, kneeling down, her head bowed and hands clasped—flitted into his mind.

O mystic and sombre Dolores, Our Lady of Pain.

Had it all been some sort of violent sex game gone wrong? Was that the significance of the poem?

Moving aside some of the masks, Nina pulled out a full-face gimp mask made of studded black leather, with a zip at the mouth.

'Do you suppose it's made to measure?' She held it up delicately between the tips of her gloved fingers.

'I wonder,' he said, wishing that it could give up its secrets. He stared so hard at the mask and its empty slit eyes that his vision began to swim. What sort of man had she liked? Was it meant for a particular man and if so, who and where was he? He looked around at Nina. 'Did you find anything else? Anything of a heavier S&M nature? Anything that looks at all professional?'

'No. Nothing like the gear we found in that flat off the Edgware Road.' She dropped the mask into the box and closed the lid. 'There was some rather interesting underwear and rubber stuff at the top of one of the cupboards, but I'd say this lot's purely recreational, for home use. Just a big girl's dressing up box, really, although for a girl with very different tastes to mine.'

8

'A girl with very different tastes.' Nina Turner's words stuck in Tartaglia's mind as he walked back down the stairs. It was one tiny but important mosaic in a picture that was only just starting to form, each piece more fascinating than the last. He knew so little about Rachel Tenison but he wanted to know so much more.

As he pushed open the front door of the building, a gust of freezing air hit him in the face. Bracing himself, screwing his eyes almost shut, he went down the steps and made his way to the outer cordon, where he was once more signed out. It had just started to snow again, although unconvincingly, tiny particles of ice fluttering on the air like leftover confetti. Head down, he skirted around the small, stalwart band of reporters still gathered outside, and began walking down the hill towards the tube station. He let the dark of the evening close around him, losing himself in the to-and-fro of the people on the pavement, marvelling at the kaleidoscope of lights in the distance from the passing traffic along Kensington High Street, blurred by the misty air. But the image of the trunk in Rachel Tenison's bedroom, and its contents, was uppermost in his mind.

He had called Donovan from Rachel's flat and asked her to speak to Richard Greville immediately about the contents of the trunk to see if it meant anything to him. However, the description of the man seen with Rachel in La Girolle didn't fit Greville who, in any case, had a cast-iron alibi for the Friday morning. But even if Greville was into that sort of thing, even if he could give some added colour to the picture they were building of Rachel Tenison, it was nothing more than useful background knowledge. Everything pointed to there being somebody else.

Marching along, stamping hard on the icy pavement for warmth and with the sheer frustration of it all, he thought back to the interview with Liz Volpe that morning, picturing her blank, unfocussed stare, hearing her flat-toned, husky voice. 'I've been away. I'm out of touch,' was the limp excuse she had volunteered. But it just didn't ring true. As he knew only too well, in the age of phone and email and BlackBerrys and the like, it was impossible to be out of touch. Physical separation meant nothing to family, friends or the office. If they wanted to get hold of you they would, whether you liked it or not. He had the impression that Liz had been trying to distract him from something, something that she didn't want to talk about. His gut instinct nagged at him, telling him that, at the very least, he was being given an edited version, which left him with a burning, insistent curiosity to know what had been left out and why.

Liz Volpe put her glass of red wine down by the side of the bath and turned off the taps. It was deep enough now, almost up to the plughole. She twisted her hair quickly into a knot and clipped it up on top of her head. Shrugging off her brother's old towelling dressing gown onto the tiled floor, she tested the water with her toe. Steam was rising from the surface and the water was piping hot, just the way she liked it, foamy and pleasant-smelling from something she had found at the back of the bathroom cupboard.

She stepped in and lowered herself slowly into the tub, closing her eyes as she slid down until the water was around her neck, just touching her chin. It felt good after the bone-chilling cold outside and she stayed with her eyes closed for several minutes, trying to forget where she was. Her thoughts turned back to the job interview she had had earlier that day for a curatorship at one of the London museums, replaying in her mind the conversations and the general attitude and body language of the various people she had met. Even then, while talking about herself and why she was coming back to London, she had found it difficult to concentrate. She was sure she had come across badly. It was impossible to be normal, to block out the thoughts and images of Rachel. She could still hear her voice so clearly, and what she had said just wouldn't go away.

Just as she opened her eyes and stretched for her wine, the phone started ringing in the hall. She listened, hearing first her brother's terse recorded message cutting in after a few rings, followed by Jonathan's deep, gravelly voice.

'Are you there, Lizzie darling? Pick up, will you? Lizzie...hello? It's me.' The words were a little slurred. There was a pause and she thought he had hung up. Then he said, more serious this time: 'Pick up the phone, Liz. I know you're there. I walked past your door only five minutes ago and the lights were on. Look, I need to see you. I need to talk. What's happened to Rachel, well, it's doing my head in, is what it is. I feel terrible. Call me, will you? I'm going round to the Electric for a drink. I *really* need to see you. Please.' The please offered as an afterthought. Again a pause, as though he was still waiting for her to answer, followed by the click as he hung up.

She sighed and took a large sip of wine, gazing at her toes which were peeping up through the white snowy foam at the other end. The dark nail varnish was starting to chip at the edges and they looked strangely detached from the rest of her, which sort of summed up how she felt. After the initial shock, just numbness, coupled with guilt—although by rights it should have been Rachel feeling guilty. But no matter how much she tried to convince herself of that, it made no difference. Rachel didn't know the meaning of the word. Anyway, Rachel was dead.

There were still moments when it didn't seem real, as though she would wake up and find that it had all been a bad dream. Again she wondered at her own lack of emotion, finding Jonathan's reaction equally surprising. Why should *he* be so churned up? She was curious now to know what he wanted. Perhaps she should call him back. It would be good to get out for a while, have a few drinks and try and forget about things, if only she could keep him off the subject of Rachel.

She pulled out the plug and stood up. As she climbed out, she heard the sound of the doorbell. Irritated that he had just assumed she was in and available, she picked up the dressing gown from the floor, slipped it on, and went to answer the intercom, prepared to give him a piece of her mind.

'What is it you want?' she shouted into the mouthpiece.

'It's DI Tartaglia. May I come up and speak to you?'

She closed her eyes for a second, wishing suddenly that it had been Jonathan after all. 'I'm sorry. I thought you were someone else. I was in the middle of having a bath.' She hoped he would take the hint and go away.

'I'm sorry, but I need to speak to you. It can't wait.' His tone was insistent and she could tell he wasn't going to let it go.

'OK,' she said, with what she hoped was an audible sigh. 'You'd better come up, then. I'll go and put some clothes on.'

Liz had left the door to the flat open again and Tartaglia closed it loudly behind him, so that she would know he was there. Assuming she was in her bedroom, he went along the corridor and into the sitting room. The lights were on, but the room was cold as though the heating was turned off. He had been there several minutes and was studying the print of the racehorse over the fireplace for want of anything else to do, when she appeared in the doorway behind him, arms tightly folded. She was wearing the same baggy grey cardigan and jeans from that morning and was barefoot, her toenails painted a dark purple, almost black. Her face was flushed and bare of make-up.

'I'm sorry to call round unexpectedly,' he said, 'but there are some things I need to ask you.'

She nodded. 'I've been out all day and the heating's turned off in here. Let's go into the kitchen. It should be warmer.'

He followed her back along the hall to the kitchen, which was next to the front door. He took off his jacket and sat down at the table, waiting for her to join him.

'Sorry it's such a mess,' she said, hurriedly moving aside some newspapers and clearing away what looked like the remains of her breakfast from the table. Still the same vague way of moving, as if she wasn't quite sure of what she was doing, as if her thoughts were elsewhere and she was just going through the motions.

She turned around to face him, sweeping some strands of hair off her face with her hand. 'Would you like a glass of wine? I'm having one.' He sensed her tension and wondered why she was nervous.

'Yes, please.' He could certainly use a drink and maybe if she had one too, she would relax a little.

She poured out two large glasses of red wine, emptying the remains of an open bottle on the counter, then joined him at the table, placing herself opposite him.

'Do you mind if I have a cigarette?' he asked.

'Be my guest. May I have one too?' She took the Marlboro red he offered her, adding, 'I don't usually smoke nowadays,' as if it were important. She stood up again, rummaged in a cupboard then came back to the table carrying a saucer. 'My brother hates smoking, so there are no ashtrays.'

Surprised that her brother was so fussy, given the general state of the flat, he leaned across and lit her cigarette, then his own. She took a deep drag and coughed.

'I'd forgotten how strong these are,' she said, and cleared her throat. 'So, what do you want to ask me?'

He relaxed back in the chair and looked at her for a moment, noting the tiredness in her face, wondering where to start. For a moment the image of the masks and handcuffs in Rachel Tenison's trunk flashed before him again, but he would ask her about that later.

'You knew Miss Tenison better than anyone. If you were in my shoes, where would you start looking?'

'I've no idea.'

She answered a little too quickly and he didn't believe her. 'Look, there's a strong possibility the crime was sexually motivated and that Miss Tenison knew her killer. But the only relationship we know of was with Richard Greville, which apparently finished a year ago.'

'That's right.' She gave him a wary look as she sipped her wine. 'I thought we went over all that this morning.'

'Was she gay, or bi-sexual maybe?' Even though Patrick Tenison had said not, he had to check again. A brother might not know everything about his sister.

'No. Absolutely not. That much I can tell you.'

'You want to find out who killed your friend?' His voice was challenging.

Her eyes widened. 'Of course I do.'

'Then help me. I'm struggling to form a picture of her.' He paused for a moment, letting the silence stretch as he inhaled some smoke, beginning to feel calmer. 'OK, let's start with Richard Greville. Explain to me the dynamics of their relationship. He was much older. Didn't she like men of her own age?'

Liz grimaced. 'Usually, yes. But with Richard it was different. I personally never understood the attraction—Richard's not my cup of tea I mean, nothing to do with his age. But I suppose it's that old chestnut. Rachel was looking for a father figure and Richard fitted the bill.'

'Did it make her happy?'

She appeared surprised at the question. 'I don't know,' she said, reflectively, meeting his gaze for a moment with an air of frankness that he found instantly appealing. 'In a funny way, Rachel liked the fact that Richard was under her spell, but I think once she had him there, the attraction sort of wore off. I got the impression that she took him a bit for granted.'

'But I thought the relationship went on for several years.'

'I doubt if it would have lasted that long without the business. Richard was the anchor in Rachel's life in more senses than one.'

'It didn't bother her that he was married?'

'Morally you mean?'

'In any way you like.'

Tipping the ash from her cigarette, she again looked him straight in the eye. 'I don't think it bothered her in the slightest, either morally or in the sense that she had to share him with someone else. She knew he was hers. He would have left his wife at the drop of a hat if only Rachel had asked, but she didn't want that.'

'She told you all this?'

She shook her head. 'This is me just reading between the lines, which I had to do a lot of the time with Rachel. She wasn't someone who ever poured out her feelings, believe me.'

'But she told you about her relationship with Richard Greville.'

'She didn't actually tell me. I found out by accident...' She paused and gave a hesitant smile. It was the first time he had seen her smile and it brightened her whole face. He noticed that she had a small gap between her front teeth and he thought she looked really lovely.

'Please go on.'

She shook her head and sighed. 'Well...it was sometime after they had set up the business. It was early evening and I happened to be in the West End for some reason, so I stopped by to see if Rachel was still at the gallery. She usually worked late and I thought she might like to go out for a drink. I couldn't see anyone around but there was a light on in the back and the door wasn't properly shut. I pushed it open and wandered in. I still didn't see anyone so I started to go downstairs. I found them, or heard them, screwing down in his office. Perhaps it was her office, I can't remember.'

'They left the door upstairs unlocked?'

She shrugged. 'Maybe it was accidental, or maybe what had happened between them had been spur of the moment. Although, maybe the idea that someone could just walk in and find them added to the thrill. Some people like that sort of thing.'

She spoke dismissively, as if it was all part of another world, and for a moment he found himself wondering what sort of thing *she* liked.

'You told her you knew what was going on?'

'Yes. I confronted her with it the next day—I don't like being lied to, even though it wasn't really my business. She then explained that she and Richard were having an affair, or something along those lines. She was quite matter-of-fact about it, like someone telling you what they've had for lunch. She said it was early days and she would have told me about it eventually, which I'm sure she would have done but, well, it wasn't her way to discuss such things.'

He picked up a hint of bitterness in her tone, which he found curious, and he wondered if for some reason she had been jealous. Women's relationships with one another were baffling. Friends one minute, sworn enemies the next, they could be so close, so intense; it left no room for anyone else. He had often felt shut out. But perhaps there were some women who found such intimacy claustrophobic. Perhaps that was what Liz Volpe was trying to say. But he felt there was something else behind her words, which he couldn't for the moment fathom.

He put down his glass and stubbed out his cigarette, leaning forwards, holding her gaze, sure that there was something more. 'Please go on.'

Liz shrugged. 'It's nothing really. I just got the impression that I had somehow spoiled her fun by finding out.' Blowing a final plume of smoke into the air, she mashed her cigarette hard on the saucer. 'Maybe now you'll believe me when I tell you I have no idea if she was seeing somebody before she died.'

'OK,' he said, although he still wasn't convinced. 'We now know a little more about Rachel's movements on the Thursday night after she left work. She met somebody for a drink with the initials JB. Do they mean anything to you, by any chance?'

'JB?' She raised her eyebrows and gave him a strange look, which he didn't understand, then shook her head.

'Later, she was seen having dinner in a local restaurant with a man, probably the same one. You really have no idea who it was?'

'No. Why should I?'

'Miss Tenison had sex with someone later that night, possibly the same person she saw for a drink and then dinner. The sex was violent, abusive...'

'Jesus,' she exhaled, putting her hands to her mouth. 'Poor Rachel.'

'We're not sure if it was consensual or if she was raped.'

She stared at him. 'What do you mean, you're not sure?'

'Forensically, it's almost impossible to tell the difference between rough sex and some cases of rape.' He paused, noting the shock on her face.

'You're saying it may have been consensual?'

'Your friend liked rough sex. Did you know that?'

She shook her head slowly. 'You're making this up.'

'We found some stuff in her flat. Seems she was into bondage. She liked being tied up.'

'Rachel? You're joking.'

Again he was sure her reaction was genuine. 'You know nothing of this?'

She flushed and banged her fist on the table. 'Why the hell would she tell me that sort of thing? There are limits, you know. Although perhaps you don't believe that.'

'But you've seen the photographs in her flat. The ones of the men in masks.'

'Yes,' she replied, more quietly, as if it was starting to sink in. 'But photographs are one thing, it doesn't mean…' She bit her lip and looked away.

'Didn't you think they were a bit weird?'

'I didn't make the connection.'

Her attention seemed to be elsewhere and he wondered what was going through her mind. She seemed close to tears and he wondered if it was simply shock, or something more. But he couldn't stop there.

'Getting back to what happened, whether it was rape or not, the sequence of events points to her being killed last Friday between seven and nine in the morning. So, whoever she had sex with was one of the last people to see her alive. He may also be her killer. When we spoke this morning you said you had the impression she was seeing some-body. I need to know more about it.'

'I think I need another drink first,' she said, getting up from the chair and going over to the counter where she took a bottle of wine from the rack. 'I was thinking about it earlier, trying to remember ex-actly what it was Rachel said.' Cradling the bottle and still looking upset, she leaned back on the counter and gazed vaguely into the mid-dle of the room. 'We'd had a couple of glasses of wine at her flat and then we walked around the corner to get a bite to eat. We were just chatting about this and that, about people we knew. Nothing impor-tant, really. Then her phone buzzed. She had it sitting on the table in front of her and she picked it up. It was a text message and I remem-ber wondering what was so important that she needed to look at it immediately. It was almost as though she'd been expecting it. She read

it quickly, then excused herself from the table. I noticed that she took
the phone with her. When she came back a few minutes later, her
whole mood was different.'

Liz picked up a corkscrew and pulled out the cork, then came back
to the table.

'You think she'd called whoever it was?' he asked, as she topped
up their glasses and sat down.

She took a gulp of wine as if very thirsty, then shook her head. 'I
have no idea. But something had definitely happened. She looked really tense, almost angry. I asked her if she was OK and she said yes,
but I didn't believe her and I kept pressing her about it until finally she
said, "It's just some stupid man, that's all. But I don't want to go into
it." Something along those lines.'

'She was referring to a lover?'

'I guess so, although maybe she meant Richard. Maybe they'd had
a row. Although if it was Richard, she'd mention him by name,
wouldn't she?'

'Did she say anything else?'

'No. That was it. I would have pressed her about it, but some people she knew came over and asked if they could join us for a drink
and we moved on to other things. Anyway, perhaps I've read too much
into what she said.'

'Surely she mentioned the man's name? I mean, you must have
spoken after that evening?'

'We didn't speak after that evening,' she said emphatically. 'That
was the last time I saw her.'

'Can't you give me a name?'

Her expression hardened and her fingers tightened around the
stem of her glass. She pressed her lips together stubbornly and shook
her head. 'I don't *have* a name.'

Her face had turned quite pink, but he still hadn't finished. 'There's another thing that puzzles me. Why didn't you speak after that? Or at least email one another.'

'Because we didn't,' she almost shouted.

He realised he had touched a nerve. 'Did you quarrel? Is that why you're out of touch?'

'No.' She stared at him with fierce, round, watery eyes.

'It's never a good idea to lie, but this is a murder investigation.'

'I know what it bloody is and I'm not lying.'

He still didn't believe her but there was no point pushing further. If he wasn't careful, she would show him the door. 'OK, let's try something else. Some lines of poetry were found on her body. I know it's a long shot, but I was wondering if they might ring a bell. Maybe they meant something to Rachel.'

He reached into a pocket of his coat and passed her a folded photocopied sheet. She opened it and glanced down the page, mouthing some of the words as she quickly read.

Then she frowned and looked up at him. 'You say this was found on her body?'

'Yes. Do you know it?'

'I've never seen it before, but it's horrible. I wish you hadn't shown me…' Tears were running down her cheeks and she stood up, scraping her chair back. She turned away and hugged herself tightly, shoulders shaking. 'I wish I hadn't seen it…' She let the paper float to the floor.

'I'm sorry.'

She shook her head and leaned forwards against the counter, clutching at her stomach as if about to be sick and started to cry in great, gulping sobs. Not knowing what to do, he got up and walked over to her, and gently touched her shoulder. She half turned towards him and, without thinking, he put his arms around her and pulled her into him like a child, waiting for her to calm down. Standing there, holding her, he realised he hadn't been this close to a woman in months. The touch, the warmth, the unexpected intimacy, was stirring, and for a moment he closed his eyes, enjoying the feel of her and the lovely smell of her hair. With a jolt he remembered who he was and why he was there. Not trusting himself, he let go of her abruptly and stepped back. Christ, what the hell had he done? A moment's stupid impulse and she could have him on a disciplinary charge. He must be out of his mind.

She opened her eyes and looked at him questioningly. Wiping her face with the back of her hand, she tugged a tissue from her sleeve. She dabbed at her eyes and blew her nose loudly.

'I'm really very sorry indeed,' he said. 'I should never have shown it to you. I just needed to know if it meant anything.'

'It's not just the poem,' she said quietly, her hands limp at her sides. 'It's everything. It's such a shock. I still can't believe what's happened.'

'I'm also sorry to keep pressing you, but I have to find out all I can. You do understand, don't you?'

She nodded, blowing her nose a second time.

'Are you going to be all right?'

'Yes, I'll be fine. Thanks.' She tossed the tissue in the bin by the sink and smoothed down the edge of her cardigan, her voice back to normal as though it had all been just a passing squall.

9

A couple of hours later, the distant keening of a saxophone above strings and drums greeted Tartaglia as he pushed open the door of the Bull's Head. Situated at the end of Barnes village high street overlooking the Thames, only a short walk from the office, it was one of his favourite haunts. It had once been a Victorian coaching inn and its main room was unusually large and open plan, with the bar sitting in the centre like a hub. He loved the atmosphere, particularly in winter, when the pub's unpretentious bare brick walls and comfortable, unfussy furnishings were enveloped in a warm, welcoming fug. The room was almost empty, apart from a few locals who were dotted around quietly sipping their drinks. The pub was famous for its nightly sessions of jazz and most people were still in the back room listening to whatever was on that night's musical menu.

His eyes were watering from the cold and it took a moment before he saw Donovan tucked away in one of the alcoves off the main room.

'What kept you?' she asked a little irritably, looking up as he walked over. An almost empty half-pint glass and the remains of what looked like lasagne sat on the table in front of her.

'I stopped by the office for a minute but Steele caught me on my way out.' He unzipped his heavy leather jacket and dumped it down with his rucksack on the bench beside her. 'Fussing about the press as usual. "This case is high profile. You know the score. We need to come up with something fast." He mimicked Steele's precise, clipped way of talking. 'She wants an instant solution. Thinks I can pull a bloody rabbit out of a hat.'

Donovan sniffed and offered him a glimmer of a smile. 'Well, if anyone can magic up a rabbit, you will, Mark.'

'Thanks for the vote of confidence. I wish the Witch of Endor felt the same. The fact that we have an MP as the next-of-kin is making her particularly edgy, never mind the fact that he hasn't a whisker of an alibi for the Friday morning. That counts for nothing. How's the lasagne?'

'It was cannelloni and it was delicious, thanks, but I'm afraid I had the last portion. You'd better hurry if you want something to eat. There wasn't much left when I went up.'

'Can I get you another drink?'

She shook her head 'I'm fine. I'm so tired, if I have another it'll finish me off.'

He went over to the bar where a couple of regulars were perched, deep in conversation about what sounded like the rugby.

'Evening Silvia,' he said, to the landlady, who was tidying up behind the counter. 'Pint of Young's and something to eat. What've you got left?' The small blackboard above the bar was practically scrubbed clean.

'Not much, I'm afraid,' she said, giving him a warm smile. 'Had a whole crowd in this evening to listen to Humphrey Lyttelton and they've practically cleaned me out. But I can do you shepherd's pie and salad if you don't mind waiting a few minutes.' She started pumping the beer.

'That'll be great.'

'Long day?'

'In spades.'

'I'll bring your food over when it's ready,' she said with a look of sympathy, sliding the full glass towards him and wiping her hands briskly on her white apron.

He paid and carried his pint back to Donovan and sat down opposite her.

'At least we now know for sure that Greville was on the plane,' he said, taking a large draught of bitter.

'And some neighbour can confirm seeing Mrs Greville outside her house just after eight-thirty in the morning. She was apparently still in her nightie and was arguing loudly with a traffic warden who was about to ticket her car on a yellow line. They only live in Islington, so she could have definitely made it to Holland Park and back, but apart from the timing there's nothing else to put her in the frame. Also, if jealousy was the motive, why kill Rachel Tenison when it seems like the affair had fizzled out some time ago?'

'What about the S&M stuff in Rachel's bedroom?'

'When I saw Greville this evening, he claimed to know nothing about it. It will be interesting to see if his DNA turns up on any of the stuff, but for the moment I'm inclined to believe him. Also, for what it's worth, he said that the physical side of his relationship with Rachel Tenison had tailed off long before it actually ended.'

'So he really was a surrogate father figure after all,' he said, as Silvia came over with his food and cleared away Donovan's plate.

'So it seems.'

He unravelled his knife and fork from the paper napkin and, as he started on the shepherd's pie, there was a strange, musical tinkling from somewhere close by. He looked questioningly at Donovan.

She shook her head. 'Yours, I think.'

Tartaglia put down his fork and reached into his pocket for his phone. The screen showed a new message:

Wn r u goin 2 kum an c me u bugger. Luv trev.

'It's Trevor. He's taken up texting as a hobby.'

Trevor Clarke was their former DCI and someone of whom they were both very fond. He had been badly injured in an accident on his motorbike and had been in hospital for nearly a month before being allowed home. Carolyn Steele had been brought in to take over, but in Tartaglia's eyes she could never replace Clarke.

'Typical,' he said, showing Donovan the message. 'Practically the only word he's bothered to spell properly is bugger.'

'How is he?' she asked as he snapped the phone shut and turned back to the shepherd's pie.

'Making slow progress,' he said, between mouthfuls. 'At least he has Sally Anne to look after him. Poor Trevor, he'd probably kill for some of this.' He waved his fork towards the plate. 'She's put him on some sort of special macrobiotic diet and made him give up the booze and the fags.'

'I'll bet he loves that,' Donovan said, smiling.

'I owe him a visit, although I don't know when I'll get the time.'

'I'm sure he, of all people, will understand.'

'I suppose so,' said Tartaglia, although he knew Clarke didn't understand at all. He wanted to be kept in touch with every minute detail of any new case, as if what was going on in the office were his only lifeline. He still talked as though one day he would be fit and able to stride back in through the door and take charge again as normal. It saddened Tartaglia to hear him talk that way, and he wished with all his heart that it were true and that everything could be again as before. But it was never going to happen and underneath he suspected that Clarke understood the reality of his situation.

'How did you get on with the poem?' Tartaglia scraped up the last mouthful of pie and tried to put the thought of Clarke, with all his wasted energy and wisdom, out of his mind.

'I Googled it and it came up right away. It's by Swinburne. He was into S&M big time, so maybe that's how it ties in. I spoke to my dad about it and he's going to put me in touch with a Swinburne expert he knows at Birkbeck College. I thought it would be interesting to get some more background stuff. If nothing else, it might give us more of a clue as to why it was put on the body.'

'Good idea. I showed it to Liz Volpe, Rachel Tenison's friend, this evening, but it meant nothing to her.'

She looked at him questioningly. 'Is she a suspect, do you think?'

He put down his fork and met her gaze. 'Not at the moment, although she has no alibi for the Friday morning. There's something odd about the two women's relationship but unless we can turn up something more tangible, I can see no real motive.'

'She inherits a flat on Campden Hill. People have killed for a lot less.'

'Yes. But think of the stuff found in that flat, think of the poem and the medical evidence. It's all about sex. The way the body was bound and exhibited after death was also sexual and ritualistic.'

'You think it's someone she knew?'

'You know what Trevor would say: try the likely before you consider the fantastic. According to everyone we've spoken to so far, Rachel Tenison wasn't gay. So, it's likely to be a man and likely to be someone she knew. The laptop and phone are both missing. Dave has been onto the ISP but they don't store copies of emails once they've been downloaded. The same goes for texts. Somebody—I'm assuming the killer—knew this and took them to hide their identity. It means the killer wasn't a stranger.'

'Going back to Liz Volpe, Karen told me you both had the feeling she was hiding something.'

He sighed and rubbed his face with his hands, feeling suddenly very tired. 'Yeah. I just don't know what.'

'Is she protecting someone?' Donovan asked.

'Possibly, although I don't know who,' he said vaguely, thinking back to the conversation earlier, some of Liz's words replaying in his mind. He thought of her slouched across the table from him, legs crossed, cigarette between her fingers, with her large eyes and mane of hair. He remembered the touch of her, the feel of her, the warmth and smell…he stopped himself. He had been too long without a woman. 'I just don't get it,' he added, after a moment, hoping that Donovan had no idea what he had been thinking. 'I believe she really cared about Rachel Tenison. You saw her reaction when she heard what had happened. Right?'

Donovan nodded. 'She genuinely seemed to be in shock.'

'It's difficult to fake something like that, but some of the things she said don't add up. She said she thought Rachel was seeing someone, mentioned a text she received while they were having dinner. But that was all. She didn't know who it was and didn't ask. She said they didn't speak or communicate again, and that was over two months ago. It just doesn't make sense.'

'No, it doesn't,' Donovan said. 'Maybe she's worried that if we start unpicking things, something else is going to come out.'

'Of course, but what? Surely she wants to find her friend's killer? But she refused to give me the name of any man Rachel might have been seeing.'

'You think she knew what was going on?'

'That's what my gut's telling me. At first I put it all down to her being in shock and not thinking straight, not wanting to dish the dirt on her friend, whatever it is. But she's had time now to think things over. When I pressed her again this evening, she trotted out the same old thing: she was away; she had no idea what was going on; she doesn't know of any man. And she doesn't know anything about the S&M stuff we found in the flat.'

'It could be true.'

He shook his head. 'Do you honestly believe that?'

'We're not all Bridget Jones, you know,' she said, a little sharply. 'We don't all wear our hearts on our sleeves and confess our inner-most feelings at the drop of a hat.'

'I didn't mean that,' he said quickly, wondering why she was being so unusually sensitive. 'I'm just going on my instinct, that's all. Rachel Tenison must have confided in somebody, surely, and who better than her closest friend?'

'I guess it's all a matter of degree. Some people are just more closed than others.'

'Now you're sounding like Liz Volpe. I just find it strange that she was so out of touch with what was happening in Rachel Tenison's life that she can't even give me a name.'

Donovan paused for a moment before replying. 'Maybe they weren't as close as she has made out.'

'Then why is Liz Volpe one of the two main beneficiaries of Rachel Tenison's will? Why leave her the flat, if they weren't close?'

Donovan shrugged. 'Maybe there really isn't some dark secret or some mystery man. It's not a crime, you know, to be single.'

'Of course it's not,' he said with feeling. 'But what about the handcuffs and the masks? She wouldn't have much fun with them on her own. And the pre-mortem wounds on her body, they were hardly self-inflicted.'

'OK. Point taken. But if I were into being handcuffed and screwed by a man in a mask—which I hasten to add I am not—I think I'd keep it to myself. I certainly wouldn't tell my sister Clare, and she's probably closest of anyone to me.'

'But Clare would still know you had some bloke around.'

'I suppose so. As we live together, I don't have much choice in the matter. But maybe if I lived on my own, I wouldn't be so open. Anyway, some men, some women, are best kept on the side.'

'Meaning?' he asked, a little surprised, wondering if she was thinking of someone in particular.

She shifted in her seat and folded her arms as though she felt uncomfortable going any further.

'You were saying,' he prompted her, now curious.

'Well, surely you've had relationships that were all about sex, where the last thing you'd want to do is to introduce that person to your family and friends. Also some people are just plain secretive; it's a thrill not having everything out in the open, isn't it? I'm sure that's half the reason why people have affairs. They like all that cloak and dagger stuff. Makes it all so much more exciting.'

He remembered what Liz had said about the affair with Richard Greville: 'I got the impression that I had spoiled her fun by finding out.' He thought of the locked box in Rachel Tenison's flat, the text message at the restaurant table and the oblique reference to a man. Perhaps being secretive was a part of Rachel's nature; perhaps, as Donovan said, it also turned her on.

'You really think Rachel Tenison had a secret life of some sort? I mean, why bother? She lived on her own. She had nobody checking up on her.'

Donovan sighed. 'That's not the point, though, is it? It's a shame Greville knew so little about what she did outside the gallery. He probably saw more of her than anyone else; but then he's a man and he's been involved with her. She would keep certain things from him.'

'What about the gallery assistant—the one that was there up until a few months ago? There must have been phone calls, messages, the sort of thing a woman would pick up on.'

'Nick's dealing with it,' Donovan said. 'Gallery assistants seem to be his speciality at the moment.'

The sudden sharpness in her tone made him look at her more closely. The large grey eyes and small, neat features were impassive but he knew there was something more.

'Everything OK?'

She glanced away and nodded, picking up her glass and tipping the last sip into her mouth.

'Come on, Sam. What's up?'

She put down the glass and shrugged. 'He's just such a fucking wanker, that's all.'

'Who? Nick?' He thought for a moment, sifting through the limited possibilities. Knowing Minderedes, it was likely to be one thing, or a variation on the theme. 'You and Nick? Surely—'

She looked up, blazing, and folded her arms tightly across her chest. 'Of course not! I wouldn't touch the toe-rag if he were the last man alive! I'd rather *die.*'

'Then what's wrong?' he asked, amazed at the force of her reaction. Minderedes could be an annoying sod at the best of times, particularly where women were concerned, but Donovan rarely seemed to be bothered by him.

She said nothing, compressing her lips tightly, her eyes suddenly watering.

'Sam, please tell me. What's he done? You *can* tell me, you know. Whatever it is.'

The doors to the back room burst open, the jazz session over, and people started streaming into the bar. Donovan muttered something, which Tartaglia failed to hear. She bowed her head and he noticed tears streaming down her cheeks, saw one land on the back of her hand. Amazed, still wondering what on earth was wrong, he got up and went to her. Moving his jacket to one side, he slid onto the bench next to her and put his arm around her, shielding her with his shoulder from the rest of the room.

'Hey. This isn't like you,' he said, handing her his unused napkin. 'What the hell's the matter?' He had never seen her like this before, never normally seen her anything other than confident and upbeat, except in the dark days that had followed the Bridegroom case, when he had glimpsed another side. Then she had retreated into herself, closed off and untouchable, refusing any offers of help or counselling.

But that phase had seemed to have passed.

'Do you *want* to talk about it?' he asked, leaning in close to her so that he was almost whispering.

After a moment, she nodded. She blew her nose and leaned her head lightly against his arm. It suddenly struck him how extraordinary it was to have two women crying on his shoulder in one evening, and for a second he was reminded again of Liz Volpe in a way that made him feel quite uncomfortable.

'So, what is it?' He gave Donovan's arm a little squeeze of encouragement. 'Spit it out.'

She exhaled sharply. 'He was chasing after Greville's gallery assistant, that's all.'

'And that upset you?' he asked, dumbfounded.

'No,' she said firmly, shifting in her seat as though uncomfortable and blowing her nose again. 'I told you, I don't care a flying fuck about that prick. It's what he said when I told him he shouldn't behave like that. He…he…' She puckered her lips and shook her head.

'What, then?'

She took a deep breath. 'Well, he said I was a fine one to talk. *Me,*' she added with emphasis, turning and looking up at him. 'I nearly hit him.'

Tartaglia still found himself struggling to understand what she meant. Then it came to him. 'You mean about…?'

'About Tom. Yes.' She stopped him before he could say the killer's real name, as if using his code name was easier to take. Stunned at Minderedes's lack of sensitivity, extraordinary even by his standards, for a moment Tartaglia was carried back to that time three months before. What had happened still hung over both of them like a dark, poisonous cloud. In a quiet moment, Donovan had once confided in him how she dreaded being on her own, dreaded going to sleep, fearing the dreams, the nightmares that would come. It had rocked her self-confidence. Rightly or wrongly, she blamed herself for everything that had happened and nothing that he, or anyone else could say or do could make it better.

'I screwed up big time, didn't I?' she said, suddenly turning her small, taut face towards him again, like a child demanding an answer. 'It's what they all think, isn't it? It's what they're all saying. Behind my back.'

'No. No, it's not,' he said softly, shaking his head. Nobody would dare say such a thing within his earshot and he couldn't believe that any of them actually thought it either. He pulled her closer to him and ruffled her short, spiky hair with his hand. 'You're wrong, Sam. Nobody thinks that. Please believe me.' But as she looked away he could tell that she wasn't convinced and he didn't know what else to say.

'They don't understand,' she mumbled, starting to cry again. 'They have no idea.'

Her body was rigid with anger and as she pressed her head tight into his arm, he could feel the wet of her tears on his sleeve. 'No,' he said, after a moment. 'They can't understand. They weren't there. But you know I do. And I don't blame you for anything.'

Outside, Donovan got into her car and watched Tartaglia start up his motorbike and drive away. She let the engine idle, waiting for the heater to kick in, and sat in silence, staring through the misty window at the curving slick of the river and the dark outlines of the trees on the other side of the bank. What a fool she was, what a sopping wet, pathetic little fool. How could she have let herself go like that? What must Tartaglia be thinking of her? She hated the fact that she seemed to cry so easily these days. She felt so stupid letting herself down, even though she knew he of all people wouldn't see it as weakness. But everything had suddenly seemed to press down on her until she could no longer hold it in. Minderedes's words had gashed things open again and she felt so angry, yet powerless to do anything about it. Try as she might to suppress the horror of what had happened, the memories and the guilt were ever-present. Whatever Tartaglia said, however much he seemed to understand, nothing could make it go away.

Again she thought of Tom—he was never far from her thoughts, his shadow falling on her wherever she went. She couldn't think of him by his real name. He was just Tom. The chameleon. The beast. The vampire. Somehow he had taken on mythic proportions.

She remembered how she had been completely taken in by him, how she had actually once found him so attractive. The thought made her shiver. She could still see him sitting there next to her on the sofa, so very close, head slightly tilted to one side, studying her as if she were a butterfly in a killing jar fluttering its wings for the last time. The way he had looked at her in those final moments, and his voice, were indelibly burnt on her mind, the tone hardening, sharp and almost angry just before she lost consciousness: *The answer was staring you in the face all the time and you haven't got a fucking clue.*

It was all her fault. Everything was her fault. She should have known.

As for Tartaglia, the momentary physical closeness, coupled with his kindness, had stirred her up. Thank God he had never realised how she felt, how sometimes it made her ache just to look at him. She had thought she'd come to terms with it, blocking it all out, forcing herself to stop thinking about him in that way until it had become second nature. There never could be anything between them but friendship and a part of her was happy with that. If only she could get a grip and prove herself to him, somehow redeem herself in his eyes, maybe she could put things right again.

Cursing herself for being so feeble, she blotted her tears with the edge of her jumper and turned on the radio. They were playing Fergie's 'Big Girls Don't Cry' from her debut album. As she put the car into gear and drove off, turning left away from the river and down the quiet High Street, she listened to the lyrics and found herself smiling at the irony. Big Girls Don't Cry. It said it all, really.

10

'Shall I be Mum?' Detective Superintendent Carolyn Steele asked Tartaglia, presiding like a conjuror over the tray, complete with teapot, cups, sugar bowl, milk jug and a plate piled high with plain chocolate digestive biscuits.

Mum? He stifled a smile. With her short, broad-shouldered, athletic body and severe mannish trouser suit, there was nothing mumsy, or remotely cuddly and comfortable about her.

'How do you take yours?'

'White, no sugar, thanks.'

It was day three of the investigation. She had been up in Hendon for a meeting with her superiors and had missed the early morning debrief. She poured out the strong brew, passed Tartaglia his cup, then added milk and two sugars for herself. She passed him the plate of biscuits and he took one to show willing. As she helped herself to another, her phone rang and she grabbed it, cradling it against her ear with her shoulder as she dunked her biscuit in her tea. A male voice was just audible at the other end.

Tuning out the few terse snatches of conversation from Steele's side, Tartaglia glanced out of the window behind her at the row of small Victorian houses across the street. It had started to thaw overnight and water was dripping from the roof into the street below, little streams running down the window. The sky was ominously dark and it looked as if the heavens were about to open. Looking over at Steele, he wondered who was at the other end. Superintendent Cornish maybe, or someone else up in Hendon. Definitely someone senior, judging by Steele's deferential tone.

Sitting there, waiting for her to finish, it was hard to remember that only three months before this had been Trevor Clarke's office. So much had changed in that time and the room itself was almost unrecognisable. The filthy Venetian blinds had been removed, the windows cleaned, and the air smelled fresh, no longer infused with the usual mixture of stale smoke, chicken pot noodle and cheap aftershave. Even the old battered desk had been rejuvenated, its surface more or less clear, pens in a leather holder, files neatly stacked to one side.

He noticed a large black and white photograph of Rachel Tenison sitting in the in-tray. He had no idea where Steele had got it from or what it was doing there, although he assumed that it was for press use and probably provided by Patrick Tenison. He reached over and picked it up. It looked like a professional studio shot and a good one at that, much clearer and more revealing than the few family snaps he had seen. Pale blonde hair framed her heart-shaped face and her lips were slightly parted as though she was about to speak. There was a sweet, girlish prettiness about her broad forehead and small, rounded features, but the way she held her head, looking directly at the camera with an upward tilt of her chin, was challenging. And there was a light in her eyes, a mischievous sparkle, as if she was flirting with the photographer, which he found instantly beguiling. For a moment his thoughts turned back to her barely furnished bedroom with its huge bed, its mirrors and the locked trunk, and again he wondered what she had really been like.

Steele slammed the phone down in its cradle. 'That was the Kensington and Chelsea Borough Commander again. Poor man's being plagued by a posse of retired majors, maiden aunts and nannies complaining about Holland Park being shut. He's desperate for us to release the crime scene.'

He put down his cup and saucer with a rattle. 'Christ! A

woman's been murdered and all they can think about is walking their bloody dogs.'

'Only to be expected, really,' Steele said dryly, with a dismissive wave of her hand. Tartaglia wasn't sure if she was writing off mankind in general or just the well-heeled inhabitants of Kensington. 'Any idea when we can reopen it?' she added, putting the last piece of biscuit into her mouth.

'Should be today. Forensics have more or less finished. There's no sign anywhere of Rachel Tenison's clothing and there was too much foot traffic on the path near where her body was found to pick up anything significant. Now the snow's melting, there's probably not much point in keeping it closed.'

Steele yawned and helped herself to another biscuit. 'Good. I'll let him know. But that wasn't why I wanted to see you. There's something that needs looking into.' She took a small bite of the biscuit, chewing it carefully and thoroughly before continuing: 'I had a journalist on the phone this morning, asking if we thought there might be a link with the Catherine Watson case.'

Tartaglia gave her a blank look. 'Catherine Watson? Doesn't ring a bell.'

'No, it probably doesn't. It was about a year or so ago and it was handled up in Hendon. I don't remember the exact details, other than that the woman, a teacher I think, was found murdered in her flat. It was very close to where I live, only a few streets away, which is why it particularly sticks in my memory. I remember worrying at the time that we had some nutter loose in the area, although luckily there was no repeat.'

'Which journalist are we talking about?'

'Jason Mortimer, so it's worth taking seriously.'

'He thinks he's got a story?' Tartaglia asked thoughtfully. Mortimer was a heavyweight crime reporter on one of the dailies and the mention of his name had usually been enough to make even Trevor Clarke, who had little time or respect for the press, sit up and take notice.

'I get the impression he's just fishing, but we obviously need to find out one way or another if there's any substance to it before he digs up something more concrete and splashes it all over his rag.' She gave a little involuntary twitch, as if stung by something, possibly imagining the headlines.

'Did Mortimer tell you why he thought there might be a link?'

'No. He was quite cagey, which could mean anything. If he's had a tip-off, he's not divulging. But what I do remember is that Catherine Watson had been tied up and tortured before she died. It was really quite horrific and the details were not in the public domain. Why Jason's picked up on it I don't know, and he's not saying. But given it's him, it's worth seeing if there are any similarities with the Holland Park murder. The files are coming over later this afternoon.'

'Did they catch whoever did it?'

She shook her head. 'DCI Alan Gifford was the SIO. My team was in the next-door office and I remember it all going on. In the end, they drew a blank. The review team went over it all quite thoroughly, but as far as I'm aware it was never solved.'

'Have you spoken to DCI Gifford?'

'Can't. Gifford's dead. He retired about six months ago—I went to his leaving do—and within a couple of weeks he keeled over from a heart attack, poor guy. But speak to Simon Turner next door. He was Gifford's DI, before he moved to Barnes.'

Simon Turner now worked for DCI John Wakeley, who headed up the other murder investigation team based in Barnes. Turner's office was across the divide, on the other side of the building, but there was no sign of him. A young female detective, who Tartaglia assumed was a new recruit, was sitting just outside Turner's office eating a sandwich at her desk. She told him that Turner was tied up all day at the Old Bailey, giving evidence in a murder trial. Tartaglia took a note of Turner's mobile number and left a message asking him to call.

Back in his own office, he had barely sat down when Feeney appeared in the doorway.

'I think I've found the bloke Rachel Tenison had a drink with the night before she died,' she said, looking pleased with herself. 'There are only three entries in her contact list with the initials JB and I've spoken with two of them and ruled them out. The only one left is somebody called Jonathan Bourne. I've tried his number twice but the phone seems to be permanently engaged. He lives in Notting Hill. I thought I'd go over there now.'

'Greville mentioned that she had a friend called Jonathan. I think I'll come with you.' He was already on his feet.

11

An icy drizzle had set in by the time they left Barnes Green. Feeney was a fast and efficient driver and Tartaglia could see the frustration building as she was forced to manoeuvre her way, stopping and starting, in and out of the heavy traffic. Tartaglia sat in the passenger seat, watching the windscreen wipers move rhythmically back and forth, brushing away the sleet. By the time they got to Notting Hill it was nearly two-thirty. Jonathan Bourne lived in a converted former post office, just off the Portobello Road. The building was several storeys high and had been divided into a number of flats. Feeney pressed the buzzer for Bourne's flat but there was no response. As they waited, a plump woman in a long, dark coat and flat-heeled boots opened the front door to the block and came out.

'Do you know which floor Jonathan Bourne is on?' Feeney asked. 'He's not answering the bell.'

'That's probably because he can't hear it,' she said with a grimace. 'He's on second and he's definitely in. Got his music on full volume, as usual. I live below him, more's the pity. Can't get to sleep a lot of the time but nobody seems to want to do anything about it. Council are bloody useless.' She assumed a disgusted expression as she pushed past them and turned up the street.

The lift was out of order and they took the stairs. As they reached the second floor and heaved open the fire door, a blast of music came at them down the corridor like a gust of hot air. 'Johnny Come Home' by Fine Young Cannibals, something Tartaglia hadn't heard for a good ten years.

Bourne's flat was at the end. Tartaglia pressed the bell outside, then knocked, but getting no response, he started to pound on the door with his fist.

'Police. Open up,' he shouted.

He continued to hammer. A few moments later, the door opened and a tall, pale-faced man, with a dishevelled mop of thick, reddish-brown hair, peered out. He was naked, except for a small green towel, clasped around his middle.

'What the fuck do you want?' the man shouted over the music.

Feeney held up her warrant card. 'Police. Are you Jonathan Bourne?'

'Hang on a sec.' The man disappeared behind the door. Within seconds the volume was turned down and he reappeared.

'What do you want?' he said, holding the door ajar. 'I'm busy.' His speech was a little slurred.

'I'm Detective Inspector Tartaglia and this is Detective Constable Feeney,' Tartaglia said. 'We need to speak to you.'

Bourne squinted at the warrant card. 'Can't you come back another time?'

'No. We need a word with you now.'

'Look, it's not convenient.'

'We can either do it here, or you can come with us to the local station. Your choice.'

'Can't it wait? I'm in the middle of things. You know.' Bourne raised his brows meaningfully and jerked his head towards the room behind him.

'No, it can't wait, Mr Bourne. But I'd rather you went and put some clothes on first. And turn off the music.'

Bourne fixed him with a bleary stare. 'Is it the noise? Have the fucking neighbours been complaining again? Because if so—'

'No Mr Bourne,' Tartaglia interrupted. 'It's not about the noise. It's about Rachel Tenison.'

Bourne looked surprised. 'Rachel? Ah, silly me. Should have thought of that.' He frowned. ''Course, you said you were detectives, didn't you. You'd better give me a minute.'

He left the door open and Tartaglia and Feeney followed him into a large, open-plan room with two tall windows overlooking the street. Bourne padded across the floor, switched off the music, then stooped to collect a trail of discarded clothing before disappearing through a door in the far corner of the room into what Tartaglia assumed was the bedroom. Bourne slammed the door behind him. Moments later a toilet flushed and they heard muffled voices through the partition wall.

Waiting for Bourne to re-emerge, Tartaglia gazed around. A small modern kitchen area was tucked to one side of the front door, divided from the rest of the room by a breakfast bar piled high with empty wine bottles, dirty plates and glasses. The rest of the room looked like a cross between one of the bric-a-brac shops they had passed in the Portobello Road and a taxidermist's workshop, with a couple of stag's heads on the wall above the door and domed glass cases full of stuffed birds dotted about on tables. In one corner, a pair of mangy-looking stuffed monkeys clambered up a wooden branch that had been turned into a lamp and, on the desk beside it, a human skull wearing a purple fez served as a paperweight.

A strong, familiar smell hung in the air. Walking across the room, Feeney just behind him, Tartaglia saw the telephone handset lying on the floor by the window, next to a pile of cushions, along with a half-full bottle of wine, two unfinished glasses and a pub ashtray with the remains of a joint.

'Someone's been having themselves a little party,' Feeney said, folding her arms disapprovingly. 'And at this hour of the day too.'

Tartaglia stifled a smile. In Feeney's well-ordered life there was a correct time and place for everything and he imagined that drinking and the like was strictly reserved for after dark.

Within minutes a scrawny, weary-eyed blonde emerged, dressed in a pair of tight jeans, heavy boots and a leather motorbike jacket. She walked unsteadily past Tartaglia and Feeney as if they were invisible, collected a crash helmet from behind a chair and made her way out the front door. Shortly after, Bourne reappeared wrapped in a flowing red velvet dressing gown.

'Shall we?' he said, waving his hand vaguely towards the sitting area.

Without waiting, he flopped down heavily in the middle of the sofa, leaving Tartaglia and Feeney to take the two ancient-looking armchairs opposite. Although Tartaglia couldn't picture Bourne in a suit, or any particular clothes for that matter, his auburn hair might easily appear dark brown in the dim light of La Girolle. He wondered if Henri Charles would recognise him.

'You know that Rachel Tenison has been murdered?' Tartaglia asked, as Bourne lounged back against the cushions and crossed one long, pale leg over the other.

'Yeah, I heard,' Bourne replied, rubbing his eyes. 'So what is it you want?'

'We're trying to trace Miss Tenison's movements after she left work last Thursday. I understand you saw her that night.'

'That's right. We met up for a drink.'

'Where was this?'

'Her place.'

'Her flat, you mean?'

Bourne yawned. 'Where else?'

'I just want to be clear, Mr Bourne. The two of you were friends then?'

'Yeah. I've known Rachel—knew Rachel—from university.'

'So it was a social visit?'

'Not really. I'm a journalist. I'm doing a piece for one of the Sunday magazines. It's about Nazi-looted art and the Simon Wiesenthal Foundation. Her gallery's been involved in the recovery of a particular painting and I needed to talk to her about it.' As he spoke, he fiddled with the long, tasselled belt of his dressing gown.

'What time did you get there?'

'About seven. Had a couple of glasses of wine, had a bit of a chat, then I left.'

'What time was that?'

'Bit before eight.'

Feeney frowned. 'That was a pretty quick drink.'

Bourne glanced wearily over at Feeney. 'What's quick? I was there about an hour. Anyway, she said she had to meet someone for dinner.'

'Who was that?' Tartaglia asked.

Bourne frowned. 'How the hell should I know?'

'She didn't mention anyone by name?'

'No. None of my business, was it?'

'So you left?'

'Yeah. When she saw what time it was, she practically poured my glass of wine down my throat and booted me out the door. Said she was going to be late.'

'And you have no idea where she went after that?'

''Course not. I came back here. Had some work to finish off.'

'Can anyone confirm that?'

'Give me a break. I live on my own.' He spread his hands wide as if it should be obvious.

'Why didn't you come forward with this information?'

Bourne shrugged. 'Why should I? I've got nothing to say.'

'As I said, it's very important we trace her movements leading up to when she was killed. It's been in all the papers and on TV. Surely you were aware of that?'

'I just had a drink with her, for Christ's sake. It's not a crime, is it?'

Maybe it was the drink or the dope, but Bourne was being overly defensive and Tartaglia sensed he was hiding something.

'You say you were friends, Mr Bourne.'

'That's right.'

'More than friends, perhaps?'

Bourne gave Tartaglia a quizzical look. 'What, me and Rachel? You must be bloody joking.'

'Why's that so incredible?'

Bourne shook his head despairingly. 'Rachel's not my type. Wasn't, I should say.'

'What do you mean?' Feeney cut in.

Bourne sighed as though it were obvious. 'No chemistry, you know. Just one of those things. You either have it with a woman, or you haven't. I'm particularly fussy, as it happens.'

'Did you have dinner with Miss Tenison afterwards?' Tartaglia asked, thinking back to the scraggy little blonde he had just seen leaving Bourne's flat. Rachel Tenison had been a lot better looking, although looks weren't everything.

'No. It was just a drink.'

'You didn't stay the night?'

Bourne rolled his eyes as though he had never heard anything so ridiculous. 'Jesus. Why can't you guys listen? I told you. It was just a drink, so stop trying to jerk my chain.'

He was sweating and Tartaglia wondered if it was just the heat of the room, the dope, or simple nerves. Whatever it was, he was sure Bourne was lying.

'Could you tell us where you were Friday morning?'

Bourne looked blank. 'Friday?'

'Yes. Between seven and nine.'

'Here. Told you, I came back here after seeing Rachel. You trying to catch me out, or something?'

'Just checking Mr Bourne. You live on your own, so I suppose nobody can confirm that you were actually here.'

Bourne gave him a glassy-eyed stare but said nothing.

'As you had a drink with Rachel Tenison at her flat, it would be helpful if we could take your fingerprints. That way we can eliminate them from the others we've found.'

Bourne's mouth hardened as if he didn't like the idea. 'I'll think about it.'

'It really shouldn't take much of your time, Mr Bourne. DC Feeney here can arrange it. I understand there's a fingerprint machine at Notting Hill station. We can also take a DNA swab at the same time.'

Bourne jerked his head forwards. 'What, am I a fucking suspect?'

'We just want to eliminate you from our enquiries.'

'Yeah, yeah, that old cliché. I can see where this is going. Can't you be more inventive?'

'You obviously want Miss Tenison's murderer to be found?'

'What do you think?' He glared at Tartaglia for a moment before tossing back his head. 'Look, of course I want Rachel's murderer found. But I didn't kill her and I have no intention of giving you a swab and having my DNA find its way onto the national database. I know my rights. You lot think DNA's the magic bullet, don't you?' He pointed an accusatory finger at Tartaglia.

'No...'

'Well, I can give you chapter and verse on what's wrong with it. I've done a piece on it for one of the Sunday supplements...went into all the cock-ups...how the statistics are misleading, how easy it is for third party transfer, how basically it's not what it's cracked up to be.' He checked the points off vaguely on his fingers as he spoke. 'So, if you want my DNA, you'll have to arrest me first. And you've got no grounds for that, have you? Now stop wasting my time and leave me in peace.'

Pulling his dressing gown around him, he got unsteadily to his feet and started towards the front door. Having no other choice, Tartaglia and Feeney followed suit.

'No, you're right, Mr Bourne,' Tartaglia said. 'At the moment, we haven't got enough to arrest you. Thank you for your time. If you think of anything else, please give us a call.' He put his card on the kitchen counter.

'Sure, but don't hold your breath.' As Bourne held open the door for them he looked Tartaglia blearily in the eye and flashed a wide, toothpaste smile. 'By the way, I've got a good one for you. How does a nutter find his way out of the woods?'

Tartaglia frowned. 'Is this a joke, Mr Bourne?'

'Yeah. Just up your street. He follows the psycho path.' He was still grinning at his own humour as he slammed the door behind them.

'Jesus wept,' Feeney said, stony-faced, as she followed Tartaglia down the corridor. 'What an arrogant prick. He thinks he's God's gift, doesn't he?'

'He certainly does,' Tartaglia replied, starting down the stairs. 'Unfortunately he's also right. We're nowhere near having enough to arrest him and that's the only way we'll get his prints and DNA off him. In the meantime, I want a thorough background check on Jonathan Bourne. I'm sure he's hiding something and I want to know what it is.'

As they walked out of the building into the drizzling rain and started down Portobello Road, Tartaglia's mobile began to ring. He stopped to shelter in a doorway and, flipping it open, found DS Sharon Fuller at the other end.

'I've just had Patrick Tenison on the phone,' she said. 'He wants you to call him. He was quite insistent. He wants to know if there's any progress.'

'OK,' he said reluctantly, imagining how Tenison would think it his due. Appeasement without information was what was required. Tenison might be next of kin, but he had no alibi for the time of his sister's murder, although so far there was no clear motive to mark him as a possible suspect. 'On second thoughts, ask Carolyn Steele to call him back. She's very good at the old soft-soap. Is there anything else?'

'Yes. I've just taken a message from a Dr Huw Williams. That's apparently spelt the Welsh way. He was very particular about it on the phone. Anyway, he says he was Rachel Tenison's psycho-something-or-other. His rooms are in Harley Street and he can see you at 4:00 p.m. He said he has some information we might find useful.'

12

'Please take a seat. Dr Williams will be with you in a minute.'

The short, grey-haired receptionist closed the door behind her, leaving Tartaglia alone in the waiting-room.

He took off his wet jacket and hung it on the coat stand in the corner next to the window. The sky was already dark and there was little to see other than the outline of a tall crane and the backs of the buildings beyond, all of which appeared to be offices. The room was expensively, if unimaginatively, furnished, with a collection of comfortable-looking sofas and chairs and old-fashioned prints of London views on the walls. The smell of fresh coffee drew his attention to a tray on a table under the window, laid with thermos jug, cups and saucers, milk and sugar. He unscrewed the lid of the jug and poured himself a full cup. He had only had a sandwich for lunch and he was already starting to feel hungry, his energy beginning to flag. He added a little milk, then turned, cup in hand, to examine the rows of glossy magazines laid out neatly on the centre table. He was about to sit down with a copy of *GQ* when the door swung open and a heavily-built man with thick, curly brown hair, strode into the room.

'Inspector? I'm Huw Williams.' He held out a powerful hand. Wearing a well-cut dark suit and pale yellow shirt without a tie, he looked to be in his late forties and not at all like the grey-bearded, bespectacled stereotype of a shrink Tartaglia had been expecting.

'Let's go into my room so we won't be disturbed,' Williams said with a business-like smile. 'Bring your coffee with you if you like.'

Williams's office was at the front of the building. The blinds were drawn and the lighting low, giving the room a cosy feel in spite of the lofty ceiling. A large, old-fashioned desk occupied one corner and at the other end of the room, a pair of low-slung chrome and black leather chairs faced one other, next to a daybed. A small, round white Formica table was placed in the space between the two chairs and highlighted from above by a spotlight. It was all carefully staged and reminded Tartaglia of a TV chat show set.

Williams gestured Tartaglia towards one of the chairs and sat down in the other, his back to the shuttered windows.

'It's good of you to contact us, Dr Williams,' Tartaglia said, taking his seat.

'I would have called sooner but I've just got back from a trip. I had a shock when I saw the papers this morning.' Williams's face was shadowed and Tartaglia found it difficult to read his expression, although his deep, resonant voice was somehow accentuated by the lack of light.

'I understand that Rachel Tenison was your patient.'

'That's correct, until August last year. My background's in medicine and psychiatry but I now practice as an analyst. I saw Rachel pretty regularly for about nine months and I was very sad to learn of her death, particularly given the circumstances.' Williams paused and cleared his throat as if he didn't know what to say next.

'I understand you have some information which may be useful to the investigation.'

Williams placed his elbows on the arms of his chair and steepled his fingers under his chin. 'Criminal psychology isn't my field but I imagine it's just as useful to profile the victim as it is the killer.'

'Yes,' Tartaglia said, taking a mouthful of coffee and putting the cup and saucer down on the table. 'The problem is, I'm finding it difficult fleshing out a picture of Miss Tenison. I feel there's a lot missing. Can you start by telling me why she came to see you?'

Williams took a deep breath. 'Like most of my patients, Rachel was experiencing problems in her life. As you probably know, she lost her immediate family in an accident when she was very young. Rightly or wrongly, she saw this as the root cause of her general un-happiness.'

'How often did she come to see you?'

'Usually once a week.'

'That's roughly thirty-six hours,' Tartaglia said, doing a quick mental calculation. 'You must know a great deal about her.' For a sec-ond, his mind turned to Liz, wondering if she even knew of Williams's existence. 'I'm particularly interested in her personal relationships, men in her life, you know the sort of thing. There's a good chance the killer was someone she knew. There's also potentially a sexual moti-vation to the crime.'

Williams nodded slowly. 'I understand, but it's not that simple. Patients come to see me with a wide range of problems; they're hav-ing difficulties at work, say, or in their marriage. Over time, the real underlying issues emerge, but not always. With Rachel, I barely glimpsed beneath the surface.'

'Surely something came out about her private life,' Tartaglia said impatiently, hoping this wasn't going to be a waste of time.

'Of course. She talked about her stepbrother, Patrick, and his family. They seemed very close. Issues with her business partner, Richard, came up on a pretty regular basis but they were quite petty and probably not of interest to you.'

'Did she mention the fact that she and Richard Greville had had a long-standing affair?'

Williams smiled. 'No. There was no mention of it, which doesn't surprise me. Rachel was not someone who liked to talk about emo-tional issues.'

'But the affair finished at least a year ago, according to people we've spoken to. Why would she mind talking about it?'

'Even if the affair was over, she wouldn't want to risk delving into it. She was quite closed, self-contained if you like, and very controlled. She was also highly intelligent, and I realised early on that our sessions were conducted on her terms, not mine.'

'But she must have thought you could help her in some way.'

Williams made a movement with his hands to signal agreement.

'Do you deal with sexual problems?'

'Quite often. I'm not a sexual therapist but naturally I come across sexual problems in my work. Usually, they are symptoms of other underlying problems.'

'From what we know, Miss Tenison was into S&M. She liked being tied up. I can't go into the details of her murder, which haven't been released to the public, but there were elements of it in the way the killer presented her body. We're trying to figure out how it all links in. Is there anything you can tell me which might help?'

Williams nodded slowly. 'With regard to Rachel specifically, I had started to guess that there was something she wanted to keep hidden from me. In one of our sessions I caught a glimpse of it. She described a dream she had had and it became clear she had a fantasy about being raped.'

'Raped?'

'You sound surprised, but it's actually quite a common female fantasy. It's all about dominance and submission, not rape in the real sense of the word.'

Tartaglia thought of the photograph of Rachel Tenison he had taken from Steele's office and the look in her eyes, paradoxically innocent yet mischievous. 'How does somebody get into this sort of thing?'

'Usually someone else will initiate it, suggest they try something new, someone who may be older or more experienced or in a position of power in the relationship. They then discover that they like it and it develops from there. Often they end up taking things a stage further or in a different direction.'

With a sudden flash of intuition, Tartaglia wondered if Richard Greville had been the initiator. It explained a lot of things about the dynamics of their curious relationship and why Rachel Tenison had finally thrown him over. She had moved on. 'Going back to what you were saying about her having a rape fantasy,' he said. 'Why pretend it was just a dream? Why hide what was really going on from you?'

Williams smiled. 'Oh, it's quite common in people with sexual perversions.'

'Really?'

'I'll give you an example. A colleague of mine had a patient who came to see him twice a week for nearly two years. You'd imagine he'd know the man pretty well, wouldn't you? Well, it wasn't until the man was found dead at the bottom of a friend's swimming pool, having drowned himself apparently by mistake, that my colleague discovered that the man practised autoerotic asphyxiation.'

'I thought they usually tried to hang themselves or put bags over their heads.'

'Drowning has the same effect. It's all about cutting off the air supply. Anyway, the long and the short of it was, the poor man had been happily tying weights to his feet and half-drowning himself for years, until one day it all went wrong and he dropped the scissors, or whatever he normally used to cut himself free. My point is, in all that time, he never once mentioned his habit to his analyst.'

'That's extraordinary.'

Williams shrugged. 'People with sexual perversions tend to be devious. You have to see them as just another type of addict, hooked on their own particular drug. Why would they want to mention it to someone like me, who might suggest they stop?'

'Then why come and see you in the first place?'

'Because they're depressed or unhappy about something else. They don't see their habit as the problem; they think they can control it. It's all carefully compartmentalised and a lot of them manage to lead perfectly normal lives on the surface.'

'How the hell can their family and friends not have any inkling?' Tartaglia said, thinking of Liz.

'Sometimes they do, but usually not. As I said, this type of person is devious. On the surface, there's nothing to hint at what is locked away beneath.'

Tartaglia rubbed his lips thoughtfully, wondering if after all Liz had been telling the truth. 'Is there anything else I should know?'

Williams leaned forward in his chair, hands clasped in front of him, the spotlight just catching the top of his head. 'Ethically this is a very tricky situation, but given what's happened, there is something which may have a direct bearing on your investigation and it ties in with what we have just been discussing. It's the reason I rang you. I'll go and get my case notes.'

He got up from the chair and went out of the room, returning after a few minutes with a thick yellow file. He sat down again, put on a pair of reading glasses, and started leafing slowly through the dense typewritten sheets.

'I make notes during each session, then dictate these reports immediately afterwards, with my observations. That way they're usually more or less verbatim. Ah, yes, here it is, July 24th.' He glanced down the page and turned over the next sheet. 'We spent much of the session talking about Rachel's relationship with her stepfather. He was very repressive, a bully by all accounts, although she would never admit it. She was finding the whole thing quite difficult so I let her sit for a while in silence. About five minutes passed, then she said, completely out of the blue, "I went to a bar last night and I picked up a man. We ended up going back to my place together and having sex."'

Williams peered up at Tartaglia over the rim of his glasses. 'This is the first time she had ever mentioned a sexual experience.'

Tartaglia frowned, trying to stifle his excitement. 'Do you think she was telling the truth or just trying to get a reaction out of you?' If Rachel Tenison really was in the habit of picking up men in bars, the field of possibilities had opened wide.

'Both, I'd say. She knew as well as I did that this was something totally new in terms of our discussions.'

'What happened next?'

'I asked her if the experience had been enjoyable and she replied that it was "good". I then asked her if she had ever done it before and she said "no".'

'But she was lying?'

'I'm certain of it, but I let it go.'

'Why lie to you? Why bother to mention it in the first place, if she didn't want to talk about it honestly?'

'Because she was playing a game. She wanted to arouse my interest.' Williams looked back at his notes. '"Tell me about what you did before you went to the bar," I then asked. She said she came home and was about to pour herself a drink when she realised she fancied a cocktail and that she wanted somebody to make it for her. She said she knew a place close to where she lived, with a barman called Victor who made great martinis. She said he knew just the way she liked them. Then she described slowly and in a lot of detail how she got changed, right down to the perfume and the colour of her lipstick. The preparation was careful, deliberate and ritualistic, which also suggested that this was an habitual practice.' Williams looked up at Tartaglia again and added, 'It was also clear she was trying to titillate me.'

Williams's face was expressionless, as if it meant nothing to him personally. Tartaglia pictured her, slender and pretty, with her lovely cloud of pale blonde hair and a provocative look in her eye. What was it like, just the two of them face to face in that dark room? It was an intimate situation, door closed, blinds down, removed from the out-side world. He imagined her there, hour after hour, talking about herself, sitting just where he was now, Williams opposite. So close. Had Williams wanted to do more than just listen? Were psychoana-lysts open to normal male responses? Or did they have some mechanism for blocking them off? It was interesting that Williams had never once referred to the fact that Rachel had been an attractive woman. He spoke of her as intelligent, controlled, self-contained, but not attractive, let alone beautiful, as if such a quality didn't register on his radar. Professional ethics aside, surely Williams couldn't be obliv-ious to what was in front of him?

'It was illuminating,' Williams continued, deadpan. 'I wrote down almost word for word her account of going into the bar. Would you like me to read it?'

'Please.'

'This is what she said.' He cleared his throat. "I felt a buzz as I walked in. The lights were dim and the music was good and loud. The room was already pretty full and most of the tables were taken. Sev-eral people were sitting along the bar and I found an empty stool near the end and ordered a vodka martini. There was a huge mirror over the bar and I could see the whole room reflected in it. I was listening to the music, just sipping my drink, when I saw a man standing a lit-tle further along the counter. He must have just come in, as I hadn't noticed him before. He was good-looking, in his twenties, olive-skinned and well built, with wavy black hair. I watched him for a few minutes and he seemed to be on his own. He joked a little with one of the barmen as though he knew him, although I had never seen him be-fore, and he bought a beer. He downed almost all of it in one and I thought he must be very thirsty. He was wearing jeans, and a tight T-shirt that showed off his muscular arms and he had a tattoo of a dragon on one of them. I wondered if he was into martial arts.

"He looked my way and I caught his eye in the mirror and he smiled. He had nice, even, white teeth and a lovely mouth. He raised his glass to me and I smiled back, then turned away to my drink. But he didn't take his eyes off me. I could see him out of the corner of my eye. He was challenging me to look round, seeing if I was up for it. I turned my head ever so slightly towards him across the bar and, for a moment, we just held each other's gaze. Then I smiled again, gave him a little nod and got up. I left some money on the bar for my drink and walked out. I didn't turn around but I knew he would follow."

Even though Williams's voice was deep and masculine, Tartaglia felt as though she was talking directly to him. He pictured her sitting at the bar, her hair framing her face, looking into the mirror, catching his eye and smiling. For a moment, he imagined himself smiling back, watched her slide slowly off her stool and walk out of the bar without a backward glance, knowing that he would follow.

'That was all,' Williams said, looking up. 'But it gives you the general picture.'

'You said these were her words,' he said, a little bewildered. 'How can you remember so accurately? Did you tape it?'

'No. I'm blessed with perfect recall, something which I find very useful in my profession.'

'You're lucky,' Tartaglia said, thinking of his father who had a similar type of memory. Sadly, he hadn't inherited it. 'Did she talk about what happened after?' He imagined the darkened anonymous bedroom with its huge bed and the black studded trunk at the end.

Williams shook his head. 'She wouldn't go any further and I didn't press her.'

'She meant it as a tease?'

'Maybe, but she didn't realise what she had given away in return. A whole new layer had opened up. I had glimpsed inside the box, the hidden life, and had confirmation of something I had suspected for a while. I hoped in time we might explore it further. But she only came for a couple more sessions and she refused to talk about anything other than her parents.'

'When was your last session?'

Williams checked his notes. 'August 10th. She then sent a cheque and a polite letter thanking me for my help and saying that she felt much better. It was another lie, of course. The real reason was that I had got too close.'

Thoughts buzzing, Tartaglia rubbed his face with his hands and got to his feet. Williams followed suit.

'Did she mention the name of the bar?'

'No. But based on her description of what happened, it will be somewhere close to where she lives. Within easy walking distance.' He escorted Tartaglia into the small hallway.

'We'll need copies of all your notes,' Tartaglia said, handing Williams his business card. Their eyes met and again he found himself wondering what Williams had really thought and felt about Rachel Tenison.

Williams inclined his head. 'I'll get my secretary to bike them over to you later today.'

Tartaglia stopped by the door and turned back to face Williams. 'Do you think she was aware of the risks in what she was doing?'

'I'm sure she was completely aware, Inspector. That's what it was all about. And the danger would have heightened the thrill.'

Thundering down the stairs two at a time, Tartaglia thought of the contrast between what the world saw of Rachel Tenison, what her family and friends knew of her, and what lay beneath. Hers was a secret form of rebellion against the straitjacket of what was expected, a resistance to ties and commitment. He couldn't blame her and for the first time he felt a glimmer of understanding as well as sympathy. He had had more than his fair share of one-night stands in the past and he knew how addictive it could be. It was something he tried not to dwell on, something he struggled to put out of his mind some nights when he lay awake and alone in bed. Sometimes he was tempted to pull on his clothes again and go to one of the bars near his flat and try his luck. But what then? There was no lasting satisfaction, only the emptiness that had been there in the first place. And yet as he pictured her face again, her words flowing over and over through his mind, a part of him wished he had known her, even just for one night. He thought of the poem and its strange imagery. Our Lady of Pain. Not Dolores. Rachel.

Outside, it was still raining heavily and the traffic was backed up all the way along Harley Street. It took him a minute before he spotted Feeney, car idling on a yellow line further down the road. He climbed into the passenger seat and told her the gist of what Williams had said. 'I want you, and whoever's available, to check out all the bars within walking distance of her flat. We're looking for a barman called Victor. Get some help from the locals. Somebody, somewhere must have seen her.'

'What about you?'

'I'm going back to the office. I need to look at the Catherine Watson files. If there is a link, maybe we can shortcut the whole process.'

As he climbed out of the car, he heard his mobile ringing and ducked into a doorway to answer it.

'I'm in St James's,' Donovan said a little breathily. He could hear the thud of her footsteps on pavement, traffic in the background. 'I've just been seeing some of the people Rachel Tenison used to work with at Christie's.'

'Anything interesting?'

'No, not really. Nothing recent anyway.'

He told her about what Williams had said.

'Do you want me to go and give Karen a hand?' she asked, when he had finished.

'No,' he said, checking his watch and realising with annoyance that Turner still hadn't returned his call, even though the court session must have already ended. He explained to Donovan what Steele had told him that morning about the Catherine Watson case. 'I want you to help me review it. Find Simon Turner, wherever he is, and get his input. He's the only one at hand who knows the case.'

13

'Nice to see you, Sam.' Simon Turner greeted Donovan with his easy, lop-sided smile. 'It's been a while since we had a jar together. Almost thought you'd been avoiding me.'

'Just busy, that's all,' Donovan said, although it wasn't exactly true. She hadn't felt much like socialising with any of her work colleagues lately, even Turner, whom she liked more than most.

He sat sprawled in a dim corner of the White Hart, an almost empty glass in one huge hand, a cigarette clamped in the other, looking like a throwback to the Vikings with his brutally short, white-blond hair and strange pale eyes. She set down her bag on a chair and peeled off her coat. She had had quite a bother getting hold of him, leaving two lengthy messages before he had finally returned her call and agreed upon a place to meet. She wondered how long he had been sitting there.

'I'll get us some drinks,' she said, scooping up her purse from her bag. 'It's a whisky isn't it?'

He stubbed out the butt of his cigarette in an already full ashtray. 'Mmm. Glenmorangie, please. Make it a double if you're buying, and plenty of ice, no water. It's been one shit of a day. And a couple of packs of peanuts while you're at it. I'm bloody starving. Here, take this,' he said, suddenly delving deep in his pocket and fishing out a crumpled twenty pound note. 'Can't make a lady pay, can I? Even if you are here on business.'

'It's OK. You can get the next round. I'm sure we'll be having more than one.'

He shrugged good-humouredly and stuffed the note away.

She went up to the panelled bar, eventually managing to attract the attention of a sullen-faced barmaid with a tousled beehive of dyed black hair. She ordered a glass of house white for herself and whisky and nuts for Turner. The counter was in need of a good wipe, and she was careful where she rested her hands while she waited. It certainly wasn't the sort of place she would normally choose for a drink, and she assumed Turner had selected it purely on location, as it was only a few blocks down the road from the Old Bailey.

With its dingy furnishings and swirly-patterned carpet, it was one of a dying breed of London boozers, a mock Victorian relic, circa 1980. The room wasn't particularly full but the air reeked of stale beer and cigarettes, the imminent smoking ban failing to make any impact so far. Personally, she preferred the modern look that was sweeping through the city, pubs like the White Hart cleared out and transformed with candles, velvet, bare floors and comfy sofas. They were all more or less interchangeable, but at least they were pleasant to be in, although few had the character and genuine atmosphere of the Bull's Head in Barnes.

She paid, getting little more than a curt nod from the barmaid, and brought their order back to the table.

'So why was it such a bad day?' she asked, sitting down opposite Turner.

He flexed his muscular shoulders as if they were stiff and tore open a pack of nuts, pouring himself a large handful, which he tossed into his mouth. 'One of the key witnesses has gone AWOL,' he mumbled, chewing vigorously. 'And on top of it all, the judge kept us late because he can't sit tomorrow. He's on holiday, so screw the rest of us. At least I'll have the chance to catch up on some paperwork.' He grimaced, then chased the nuts with a large slug of whisky.

He had taken off his jacket and rolled up his sleeves and he tugged abstractedly at the knot of his tie. Once undone, he yanked the plain blue tail of silk free of his collar and tossed it onto the table as if he never wanted to have anything more to do with it again. He looked unusually tired, his large, pale face gaunt, shoulders sagging, another cigarette already between his fingers.

'How are things with Nina?' Donovan asked, noticing that he wasn't wearing his wedding ring.

A shadow crossed his face and he took a long drag on his cigarette, puffing out a series of perfect rings before answering. 'She's bloody left me, that's what. Walked out and gone to stay with some friend or other while we work out what to do with the flat.'

'Oh, Simon, I am sorry,' Donovan said, trying to sound it, but not in the least surprised.

They had always seemed an ill-matched couple, Turner so relaxed and easygoing, Nina prickly, serious and driven. Never one to let herself go, she didn't have much of a sense of humour and Donovan had never really warmed to her. She didn't know all the details, except that Turner had once indiscreetly let slip that his relationship with Nina had evolved from a drunken one night stand when they were both working up in Hendon. But when Turner had transferred down to Barnes, he had been on his own and that was when Donovan had got to know him. Then after a few months Nina had started appearing in the pub after work and Donovan gathered things had started up again. Next thing she knew, Nina was pregnant and they were heading down the aisle. Then there had been some problem and Nina had lost the baby.

He frowned. 'Have you seen her at all?'

'Briefly. She was the CSM on the new case we're working, but you know how it is. We didn't get a chance to talk. I didn't realise anything was wrong. What happened?'

He sighed heavily. 'All my fault really. Wasn't giving her the proper time and attention, apparently. Wasn't there for her when she needed me.'

She assumed he was referring to Nina's miscarriage. 'You think she'll come back?'

He shook his head. 'Seems she's got some new bloke. Can't blame her. I mean, who in their right mind would put up with what we do, eh?' He shrugged, as if it were all par for the course. 'Anyway, you didn't come here to listen to me droning on about my sodding personal life. You said you wanted to know about the Catherine Watson case. Let's get it over with, then we can let our hair down. So what can I tell you?'

She gave him a brief outline of the Holland Park murder, then explained about the press tip-off. Turner listened thoughtfully, working his way through another cigarette and the remains of the whisky.

When she had finished he got slowly to his feet and stretched his arms and shoulders. 'On second thoughts, maybe I need another drink. Can I get you one too?' Loomingly tall, he gazed down at her as he fumbled in his pocket for his money.

'Why not?' she said, noticing that her glass was almost empty. She had already decided that she wasn't going back to the office that evening. 'Although I'd rather have a glass of red. The white was like vinegar.'

He lumbered over towards the bar and leaned heavily on the counter as if exhausted while he waited to be served. From the back, she noticed that his trousers were even more baggy and shapeless than usual and he looked as though he had lost quite a bit of weight. She liked the way he didn't seem to care a toss about his appearance, wearing his suits as if they were to be lived in and used. She wondered what Turner was really feeling about Nina. It was difficult to tell. His whole manner was of someone who didn't mind much about anything, who took most things in life carelessly in his stride as if his focus was elsewhere. A bit of a dreamer, was what her granny would have said.

The black-haired barmaid came over after a moment. The sour look gone, her face suddenly animated, she and Turner talked like old friends as she measured out his whisky and then the wine. At one point, he said something that caused the girl to toss her head and give him a full, brilliant smile before sliding him the drinks. Turner returned the smile with interest, put a note on the counter, then waved her away as she made as if to give him change. Whatever else was going on in his life, at least his old charm hadn't deserted him.

'You got her to smile. I certainly couldn't,' Donovan said irritably, as he brought the glasses back to the table and flopped down on the bench with a loud grunt.

Turner shrugged as if it was unimportant and took a slug of whisky. He lit a cigarette and leaned forward. 'OK. Let's get down to business. The stuff about a link's interesting—we never solved the case, as you know. But from what you've told me so far, I'm not getting the vibes.'

'You don't see any similarities?'

'Yeah, there are some, enough for someone on the outside to be asking the question. But I'm not sure yet. I'd have to take a much closer look.'

'Tell me about the Watson case, then.'

He pulled hard on the cigarette before replying. 'Catherine Watson was murdered almost a year ago to this day. She was a university lecturer in her late thirties, taught English, if I remember right. She was single, by all accounts a nice, intelligent, decent woman, much loved by her family and friends, almost a saint if you believe some of them. Kind to small animals and children sort of thing. She lived in a ground-floor flat up near Cricklewood tube, did extra coaching in her spare time to make ends meet, had the odd relationship, but nothing long-lasting or meaningful. A bit of a loser on the romantic front, is how I'd sum her up. You know the saying "Always the bridesmaid, never the bride"? Well, that was Catherine. I read her diary. I read her letters. Whatever her friends said about her independent spirit, about her being fulfilled on her own, from what I could see, she was sad and lonely.'

'Then the week before she died, she's on the phone telling her married sister up in Manchester that she thinks she's in love with someone. The sister, who's heard it all before, listens politely but doesn't ask any questions. Before you ask, we never found out his name or if he even existed. He might have been a figment of Watson's imagination. Anyway, Saturday night comes, Watson lets somebody into her flat and the next morning, bingo, she's dead. The door had been left ajar and her neighbour finds her. She'd been stripped naked, bound, gagged and sexually assaulted, then strangled with a pair of her own tights. Unfortunately, whoever did it used a condom and removed the evidence from the scene.'

He paused to stub out his cigarette and take some whisky, swirling the ice around in the glass before continuing: 'It was my first case as a DI and I remember it vividly.'

'Did you have any suspects?'

'Sure. The neighbour who found her, for starters. Name's Malcolm Broadbent. He was a very odd bloke, lived alone on the floor above. Had quite a soft spot for her, by all accounts. Used to wash her car, carry her shopping in, do odd jobs around the house for her if she wanted. And he kept an overly close eye on her comings and goings, or so one of her former lovers said.'

'But you had nothing on him?'

He ran a big hand through his tufted blonde hair and shook his head. 'No. His prints and DNA were all over the crime scene. But as I said, he often visited Catherine Watson's flat. To make things worse, he tried to revive her when he found her, thought she was still alive.'

'And she wasn't?'

'Dead as a dodo. Had been for hours.'

'How could he think she was still alive?'

'Broadbent said she moaned when he picked her up. But it was just a lie, like most things he told us. Anyway, he was screaming blue murder, wailing like a banshee, asking for someone to come and help him. He made so much noise, he had all the occupants of the house and neighbours tramping in and rubber-necking, nobody thinking it might be a good idea to keep them out. Then someone dialled 999 and a full emergency crew stormed the flat to try and revive her. At least then some bright spark spotted that she was starting to stiffen up like a board and must therefore be dead. Someone from the local station arrived on the scene and sent the lot of them packing. But the damage had been done. The crime scene was totally fucked, from a forensic point of view.'

'You think Broadbent trashed it deliberately?'

'Well, it certainly looked suspicious.'

'You arrested him?'

'Yeah, several times in fact. He had no alibi for that night, but as he lived alone and rarely went out, that wasn't unusual. We searched his flat, found a whole load of porn. We also found photographs of Catherine Watson, and some other women who we never managed to ID, taken with a telephoto lens.'

'He was peeping?'

'Not really. They were just ordinary women, walking along the street, chatting with friends, shopping, you know, everyday stuff, nothing kinky. What was interesting was they all looked a bit like Catherine Watson, same physical type. He watched them from a distance and snapped away, said it was an exercise for a photography course, although we couldn't find any evidence of his doing one. The man lied through his teeth about a lot of things. But taking photos in public places isn't against the law and you can't hang a man for his fantasies. The SIO, Alan Gifford, was convinced he was our man, absolutely rock hard sure. But in the end, we had to let him go. Apart from Broadbent's general weirdness, we had no real evidence, certainly nothing that would stand up in court.'

'You said there was another suspect.'

'Yeah. Michael Jennings. He was one of Watson's students, flunked his year-end exams for some reason and she was helping him with some extra tuition.'

'He went to her flat?'

'No. They only ever met at the college. But a witness saw a man matching Jennings's description walking along Watson's street at roughly eight o'clock that evening. Said he saw him go into Watson's house, although there were several people going into the house that night as the bunch of Kiwis on the top floor were having a party. Problem was, the witness was a local junkie and not a hundred per cent reliable. He failed to pick Jennings out of a line-up and we had bugger all else to place him at the scene. In the end, we were forced to let it drop.'

'Were those the only two suspects?'

Turner nodded. 'We interviewed her family, friends and former lovers, as well as all her work colleagues and students. We took over six hundred calls following the *Crimewatch* appeal and checked out every single one, however dodgy. We trawled through the sex offenders' register, followed up on anyone, of any age and background, with a conviction for rape or attempted rape living either in that part of London or close to where Catherine Watson worked. But no new leads came to light. It was Alan Gifford's last case before he popped his clogs. I think it finished him off.'

'What do you mean?'

Turner gave her a weary look. 'You know what they say, don't

you? Never let a case get under your skin, never get emotionally involved. Well, Alan forgot all of that. It was like he was on a crusade,
the only bloody knight in shining armour Catherine Watson ever had.
He was tired most of the time, on some sort of medication, I discovered later. He'd just been through a really messy divorce and he was
ill, though he didn't know it then. That sort of stuff can mess with
your mind and screw up your judgement, big time. He probably knew
it would be his last big case before he took retirement, probably
wanted to go out with a bang. Anyway, he let himself get right in deep,
became obsessed with finding Catherine Watson's killer, almost had a
personal vendetta going against Broadbent, as if he was the only man
left to defend her honour. And he failed her, like all the rest.'

Donovan had been sipping her wine as he talked and she finished
the final mouthful, thinking through everything he had told her, wondering what Tartaglia would make of it. 'Did you think it was Broadbent?'
she asked, after a moment. 'Did you agree with Alan Gifford?'

Turner shrugged. 'I wasn't as sure, if I'm honest. But then I didn't
have Alan's experience. I agreed with him that the killer was likely to
be someone known to Catherine Watson. There were no similar at-
tacks either in the area or anywhere else in London at the time. Even
though the press started getting their knickers in a twist about a serial
killer on the loose, it was a load of rubbish. To me it was simple.
Catherine Watson was a cautious, careful woman. She had good security on her door, proper locks and bolts, almost overkill, like she was
worried about such things. She wouldn't have let someone into her
flat unless she trusted them. There was a theory that there might have
been more than one person with her. The bloke who lived below in
the basement thought he heard several people walking around. But
the floorboards are creaky and there was the music playing loud. We
never got very far with it as an idea.'

'You said she was lonely. Do you think she picked up men for sex?'

Donovan asked, wondering about a possible link with Rachel Tenison.

'If she did, we found no trace of it. From what I know of Catherine, she wasn't the type to go cruising bars, if that's what you mean. I got the impression she was a romantic, looking for Mr Right. She was just bad at picking them.'

'What about her boyfriends?'

'We did a thorough background search on all of them, going back several years. But we couldn't put any of them in the frame. In the end, we kept coming back to the same thing: if it wasn't Broadbent or, possibly, as a long shot, Jennings…who the hell else could it be?'

14

Tartaglia went into the sitting room and closed the shutters. The boxes containing the Catherine Watson case files were sitting by the front door where Wightman had dropped them off earlier. He bent down and dug around inside until he found what he wanted, then crossed the room to the sofa and sat down. Starting with the photographs of the crime scene, he leafed through until he came to the images of the dead Catherine Watson. She was lying on her back, face up. In some shots covered by a blanket, in others, the blanket had been removed and she lay exposed and naked. Close-ups showed the extent of her injuries: bruising and cuts around her mouth, where it looked as though she had been hit; deep ligature marks at her wrists, ankles and neck where she had been tightly bound at some point while still alive, although there was no sign of the materials used to do this. He was used to seeing such images, but they never failed to affect him, particularly when a child or a woman was the victim. As he gazed at her white, vacant face, noticing the smudges and tear trails of mascara around her eyes, he said a silent prayer for her.

He lit a cigarette, wondering what, if anything, she had had in common with Rachel Tenison. The nature of some of her injuries was the only thing so far to suggest any connection, and there wasn't a clear and direct parallel. Then he turned his attention to the postmortem report. It suggested that handcuffs and possibly rope or cord had been used to secure her while alive. Shallow cut-marks were found on her breasts and abdomen, consistent with a sharp blade, and she had been raped, sodomised, and strangled with some form of ligature. Traces of cotton wool had been found in her mouth, pre-sumably used as part of the gag. Taking out the exhibits file, he found a note saying that several short lengths of cord, a wad of cotton wool and a pair of flesh-coloured women's tights had been recovered from the scene. There was a further note to say that an open packet con-taining an identical type of cotton wool had been found in the cupboard in Watson's bathroom.

He put them down and opened the manila folder containing the closing report, which summarised the case. Catherine Watson had last been seen at five-thirty on the Saturday evening when she had gone into a local shop to buy various items of food. A till receipt recovered from the kitchen bin listed milk, bread, cream, bacon, parmesan, eggs, spaghetti, strawberries, a bag of salad and a tub of Green & Black's vanilla ice-cream, along with a bottle of Australian cabernet sauvi-gnon and candles. Looking at the items, it occurred to him that she had been planning on preparing a spaghetti carbonara, and the wine and candles suggested she was making a special effort for someone. Had she been excited, looking forward to that evening? Had she trusted the wrong person and invited in her killer? It was a poignant thought.

Catherine Watson's body had been discovered by a neighbour, Malcolm Broadbent, at around nine o'clock on Sunday morning and the emergency services had arrived at nine-sixteen, a doctor pro-nouncing her dead at nine-twenty-two. According to the report from the pathologist who had attended the scene, she had been dead for at least six hours, which put the estimated time of death in the early hours of the morning.

Reading further, it had been assumed that she had never gone to bed that night: the bed was still made and her nightdress neatly folded under her pillow. Most importantly, there were no signs of a break-in. The back door, which led to the garden, with access down a small passageway to the main road, was firmly locked and bolted and it seemed likely that she had let the killer in through the front door. There were no reports of shouting or screams or anything unusual, apart from the fact that the occupant of the basement flat said Catherine Watson had been playing music unusually loud and late that night. But as it was Saturday night, and the tenants on the top floor were holding a party and making a lot of noise too, nobody had bothered to ask her to turn it down. Her neighbour in the flat below thought he heard music and footsteps until well after one o'clock in the morning, but there had been a lot of coming and going on the staircase related to the party on the top floor and he wasn't a hundred per cent positive that it had all come from her flat. According to the report, based on the nature of her injuries and the witness statements, the killer had taken his time and tortured her over a period of several hours.

Tartaglia turned the series of events over in his mind, thinking back to what was known about Rachel Tenison's final movements. If Jonathan Bourne had been telling the truth, which was a big if, she too had had a mystery caller. The assault on Catherine Watson had been considerably more violent, but in her case what had happened was unlikely to have been consensual. Perhaps the greater the resistance, the greater the violence used, as was often the case with rape.

Inside one of the folders he found the crime scene footage taken by one of the forensic team, neatly labelled with date, time and Catherine Watson's address. He switched on the TV and slid the DVD into the player. The initial images showed a wide, busy suburban street, with rows of tall houses on either side. A bus and several cars sped past, along with several passers-by, one stopping and grinning inanely at the camera over the crime scene tape before being waved on by a uniformed officer. A moment later, the camera zoomed in on the shabby exterior of the house where Catherine Watson had lived. Moving forwards, it focussed first on the tall hedge and wooden gate that marked the boundary with the pavement, then lingered on the paved front garden behind, with its collection of rubbish bins. Then up a flight of steps and in through the open front door, panning the dark communal hall before switching to the door on the left, the entrance to the ground floor flat.

The door opened immediately into a large sitting room with white walls. Weak winter sunlight flooded in through a large bay window, bleaching the frayed brown carpet; motes of dust danced in the shafts of light. The camera took in the limp, floral-patterned curtains and tired furnishings, the cheap paper shade on the ceiling light, the full-to-bursting rows of books on either side of the marble fireplace. Framed photographs of a couple of young children sat on the mantel shelf, along with a plant in a ceramic container and a pair of white china candlesticks. The candles were burned down to stumps, solid rivulets of crimson wax flowing over the sides and onto the shelf of the chimneypiece. Were they the ones Catherine Watson had bought earlier in the day?

A couple of large floor cushions formed a seat in the bay window, a pen, some sheets of paper and a couple of books on the floor beside them, where Watson must have been sitting working or reading in the sunshine. According to the report, her body had been found in the sitting room, but as the camera panned the interior, Tartaglia saw no signs of a struggle.

The footage that followed revealed a small dark hallway, followed by a small shower room and an L-shaped kitchen in what appeared to be an extension at the back. Judging by the array of cookbooks and tidy rows of kilner jars on the shelves, Catherine Watson had liked to cook. Again, everything seemed to be in its place. The camera lingering briefly on windows and a back door, showing that they were closed, their locks un-tampered with, then travelled a little shakily back down the hall into the bedroom.

The curtains were open and no extra light was needed to see Watson's naked body. She lay in the middle of the double bed, arms at her sides, as if asleep. As the camera zoomed in on the deep, dark marks at her ankles, wrists and neck, Tartaglia wondered again about the significance of the open curtains and the candles.

He decided he had seen enough for the moment and stopped the disc. He pulled out some more photographs and found a three-quarter-length shot of Watson taken when alive. It was a sunny summer's day and she was leaning against the stone pillar of some sort of classical-style building, arms folded in a relaxed fashion, smiling. He couldn't tell if she was tall or short, but she had a decent figure and nice legs, even if the baggy skirt and blouse she was wearing did her no favours. She had shoulder-length, wavy brown hair and a broad, pleasantly fleshy face, with a wide mouth. She wore little or no make-up from what he could tell. Her expression seemed to radiate an easy warmth and kindness and he pictured her as the sort of woman people would go to with their problems, although maybe he was reading too much into the image. From a purely physical point of view, he couldn't see any resemblance between Catherine and Rachel.

With more questions than answers, he suddenly realised he was hungry and looked at his watch. The rest of the files would have to wait until later.

He picked up his phone and dialled Donovan's mobile. She answered almost immediately.

'I'm at home,' he said. 'Have you found Turner?'

'He's with me now. We've been having a drink. He's been telling me about the Watson case. We were just about to go and get a Chinese.'

'Well, make it a take-out and order something for me too,' he said impatiently. 'And some beers while you're at it. I want you both over here now. I need to talk to him.'

'Broadbent opened the curtains in both rooms, from what we could tell,' Turner said, lazily.

He gave a wide yawn, scattering cigarette ash with one hand as he spoke, a fresh tumbler of whisky clasped at a dangerous angle in the other. Surrounded by the debris of plates and discarded food cartons, he lay at Donovan's feet in a cloud of smoke, spread-eagled like a pasha on the floor, head and shoulders propped up on a pile of cushions.

Tartaglia had opened the window a few inches to clear the air and Donovan could feel the cold, damp draught on her shoulders. The soft pattering of rain was lulling her to sleep and she stretched in the depths of her chair, flexing her legs and fighting off the urge to put her feet up on Tartaglia's expensive-looking glass coffee table. She felt incredibly tired, happy just to listen and let the two of them do the talking. She sensed Tartaglia's growing impatience, but there was no hurrying Turner. He had polished off several inches of Tartaglia's Glenfiddich and was threatening to finish the rest, the many whiskies of the evening finally beginning to take their toll even on a man of his size. He usually held his drink better than most but Donovan had never seen him tank back so much before, certainly never seen him half-cut the way he was now. Nor had she ever seen him chain-smoke his way through so many cigarettes. God only knew what he would smell like in the morning.

'What about the body?' Tartaglia asked.

'Broadbent moved it. Said she was in the sitting room when he found her. Took her into the bedroom. Un-gagged her. Cut off the tape that was binding her. Laid her out on the bed with a blanket over her.'

'Why did he do that?' Tartaglia asked.

Turner shrugged. 'Said he thought she was still alive.'

'Going back to the Saturday night, she went shopping for food in the afternoon. It says on the till receipt that she bought a bottle of wine and candles...'

'Yeah. Looked like she had a date.'

'According to the post-mortem report, her stomach was empty apart from the wine.'

Turner nodded. 'Check the files. You'll see a note of what was found in the bin. A whole load of cooked food, some sort of pasta from memory—certainly enough for two, nothing eaten. The empty wine bottle was there. Somebody cleared everything away. Washed the dishes.'

'That's the sort of guest I like,' Tartaglia said, looking at Turner. But it was water off a duck's back. 'So, she had a date. You never found out who it was with.'

'Her diary was blank for that evening,' Turner said wearily. 'Blank for most evenings, poor, sad cow.'

'You checked her email?'

''Course. And her phone. But nothing gave.'

'So it must have been a verbal arrangement. Maybe she bumped into someone and asked them over.'

Turner nodded again. 'Maybe. 'Course, we checked her movements in the days before she died but never turned up anything.'

'What was she wearing?' Donovan asked.

'Never found the clothes.'

'She was wearing make-up, according to the report,' Tartaglia said. 'Sounds like she had made an effort for someone.'

Turner shrugged again and took another sip of whisky.

A moment's silence followed, before Tartaglia spoke again. 'There's no point wasting any more time on this. The Watson case is cold. You and Gifford did all you could by the sounds of it, and the re-view team failed to turn up anything new. The only point is how this relates to Rachel Tenison.'

'Can't help you there,' Turner said, eyes half closed.

There was another long pause. Tartaglia stretched his legs out in front of him, arms behind his head, and stared vacantly into the centre of the room. Donovan wondered what he was thinking. He looked tired, still in his work clothes, a dense shadow of stubble on his face, his wavy black hair a little dishevelled. He was clearly disappointed that there wasn't an immediately clear link between the two cases, but life was never that easy.

After a moment Tartaglia slapped his thighs and got to his feet. 'Think we're done for the night. Don't you?'

He caught Donovan's eye as he bent down and started to clear up the debris on the floor. She rose to help him, leaving Turner still glued to his cushions.

Tartaglia collected up the plates and was about to go to the kitchen when he looked over at Turner. 'Do you have any idea what position Catherine Watson was in when she was originally found?'

'You mean by Broadbent?'

'Yes.'

'We did a reconstruction. Should be some photos in there.' He waved vaguely at the box of files sitting by the door, sending another tube of ash onto the floor. 'We had him go over it many times, tried to catch him out, but he stuck to the story...'bout the only thing he did stick to. Never changed the details one jot.' He stared down at his glass, seemed surprised that it was empty, and reached for the bottle beside him.

'OK. I'll look at it later. But did the injuries to her body match what he described?'

'Yeah.' Turner exhaled loudly and frowned. 'Maybe he was telling the truth about that bit.'

Donovan followed Tartaglia into the kitchen at the back and dumped the cartons and bags on the black granite counter. The space was clean and modern, all stainless steel and wood, with a pale floor and a round glass table in one corner. It was certainly stylish, but she found it quite cold and clinical, preferring something more homely and rustic like the kitchen she shared with her sister Claire. She glanced out of the window but it was so dark outside and the window so misted with rain, she couldn't see anything of the small back garden.

'What the hell's the matter with him?' Tartaglia said, jerking his head in the direction of the sitting room as he started to rinse the plates and cutlery in the sink.

'He told me earlier this evening that he and Nina have split up.' She dropped the empties into the bin. They had eaten almost everything, apart from some rice and chicken in yellow bean sauce. It was too good to throw away and she left the cartons on the counter in case Tartaglia wanted to keep them.

'She looked perfectly normal to me the other day, what I could see of her.'

'She's the one who's left him. Apparently, she's found someone else.'

'Why am I not surprised?' he said, loading the plates and cutlery into the dishwasher. 'And he'll have problems in spades if he keeps this lark up. Wakeley will have him out on his ear if he catches a whiff of alcohol on his breath. You know what he's like.'

'I'm sure Simon's not drinking during the day.'

Tartaglia gave her a sceptical look and wiped his hands on a tea towel. 'Going out and getting rat-arsed isn't going to solve anything.'

Donovan folded her arms and leaned back against the counter. He could be so black and white at times, as if he never made mistakes, as if he never let his emotions get the better of him. But she knew better.

'He still loves her, for Christ's sake. He's hurting. Aren't you in the least bit sympathetic?'

Tartaglia grabbed a cloth from the sink. 'Of course I am,' he said, moving her aside and wiping the counter. 'But getting pissed isn't going to bring Nina back, if that's what he wants.'

'I don't know what he wants but he's so down. Think how awful it must be going back to that flat on his own, with Nina not there, with all the memories.'

Tartaglia rinsed the cloth and hung it over the tap to dry. 'I imagine it's hell, but only he can sort this out.'

He gave her a pointed look. She wondered if he thought she was interfering or if he meant something else. She felt the colour rise to her cheeks. She may have half-fancied Turner in the past but Tartaglia wasn't to know that. Anyway, she had more than enough sense to steer clear of Turner in his current state. What he needed was sympathy and understanding until he found his feet again, although Tartaglia clearly didn't see it that way. Things had always been a little awkward between him and Turner, although she had no idea why. She wondered if it was professional rivalry—both strong-headed men of roughly the same age, experience and rank—or perhaps it was simply because they were chalk and cheese.

There was a loud clatter from the kitchen door and a scrawny, pale grey Siamese cat appeared through a flap in the bottom panel. It uttered a strange raucous sound and made a beeline for Tartaglia, rubbing itself up against one of his legs as it looked up at him expectantly.

'In a minute, Henry,' Tartaglia said, as if used to it.

'Didn't know you had a cat.' Donovan bent down to stroke it but the cat ignored her, its eyes pinned on Tartaglia.

'I don't. He belongs to the lady upstairs, but he likes to spread himself around.'

'But you have a cat flap.'

'It was put in by the previous owner,' Tartaglia said, moving to the counter and tipping what was left of the chicken in yellow bean sauce onto a plate. 'I just haven't got around to changing it.'

He added the remains of the fried rice and put the dish down on the floor. Henry tucked into it immediately as though he ate Chinese every day.

'Right, we're done.' Tartaglia dumped the cartons in the bin and switched off the light. 'Let's get Simon into a taxi.'

They found Turner curled up on the floor in a foetal position fast asleep amongst the cushions, cuddling one tightly in his arms. His mouth was open and he was snoring.

'I'd better go,' Donovan said, picking up her bag and coat as Tartaglia rescued Turner's glass and the stub of a cigarette from his fingers. 'What shall we do with him?'

Tartaglia sighed. 'Suppose we'd better leave him where he is. Nothing's going to wake him in that state. If he's stiff in the morning, it's his own bloody fault.'

He saw Donovan safely to her car, then came back inside and tidied up as best he could around Turner. Relieved that the floors were wooden and that Turner had somehow missed the rug with his ash, he collected the glasses and ashtray and took them into the kitchen, along with the remains of the bottle of Glenfiddich. He fetched a couple of blankets from the cupboard in the hall and as he draped them over Turner's comatose form, Henry curled himself into a tight knot next to Turner's chest, as though he belonged there. Amused at Henry's perennial fickleness, Tartaglia gazed down at Turner for a moment. Love made fools of even the most rational of people, including himself, and maybe he had been a little insensitive—Donovan certainly thought so.

He sensed Turner's desperation and he felt for him. But the man was also a bloody idiot. Was it fair to have married Nina? Had he really loved her? Or was it yet another of Turner's whims, one of his ill-thought-out, knee-jerk responses to whatever life threw at him? As for Nina, Tartaglia remembered an evening with her not that long before she married Turner, when she had told him about the problems she and Turner were having. Fuelled by wine and the lateness of the hour, she had let down her guard and he had glimpsed the insecurity and neediness beneath. Turner was hardly the man to make her happy, although he hadn't said so for fear of hurting her. He hoped they would be able to work it out between them, but he gave it slim odds.

As he thought of the two of them together with all their wasted emotions and doomed relationship, unaccountably he felt a pang of longing as sharp as the blade of a knife. He looked up at the mantelpiece where he had temporarily placed the black-and-white photograph of Rachel, retrieved from Steele's office. She stared down at him and he closed his eyes, picturing her as she had once been, warm, teasing, vibrant and full of laughter. He heard her telling Williams about what had happened that night. He imagined her in her dark, mirrored bedroom, taking off her work clothes and getting dressed again to go out, brushing her silky hair, putting on her make-up and perfume and walking down to the bar. He saw her sitting on the stool and ordering herself a martini. As she sipped her drink, she looked into the large mirror, met his gaze and smiled.

He opened his eyes and shook his head at his foolishness. He would never know her. She was lost to him. What he needed was a real flesh-and-blood woman, warm, tangible and responsive, not a ghost.

He was about to switch off the light and go to bed when he remembered what he and Turner had been talking about. He helped himself to the last cigarette from Turner's pack on the floor and sat back down on the sofa with the box containing the crime scene files. He flicked through the divisions until he found a slim folder marked 'Crime Scene Reconstruction'. As he opened it and pulled out a stack of A4 photographs, the first image, the symbolism of the pose now all too familiar to him, made him gasp.

The model representing Catherine Watson was crouched down on her knees, naked, head bent forwards, hair pooling over her face. Her mouth was gagged with a pair of beige tights, which were tied tightly around her head. Her legs were trussed at the knees and ankles with duct tape, and her hands bound in front of her, clasped as if in prayer.

15

'DI Turner is being seconded to the investigation,' Steele said, from behind the wide, tidy barrier of her desk. 'Naturally, I'll need you to update him on the state of play. He can use Gary's desk until he comes back.'

For a moment Tartaglia said nothing, refusing to look at Turner who was standing next to him, hands in his pockets, staring out of the window.

It was late afternoon and three days had gone by since Turner had spent the night at Tartaglia's flat. Since then, Tartaglia hadn't seen him or heard from him and had almost managed to put him out of his mind. No amount of telling Steele that Turner was a loose cannon and that he didn't need his involvement would make any difference. They were short-staffed at a senior level and it hadn't taken long for Steele to cook up a deal with her boss, Detective Superintendent Cornish, to persuade DCI Wakeham to spare Turner temporarily. The prospect of clearing up two high profile murder investigations for the price of one meant Cornish was prepared to sanction almost anything.

'How's this going to work?' Tartaglia asked, flatly.

'You and your team will continue to focus on the Holland Park murder as before,' Steele said briskly. 'That's still our priority. Solve one and maybe we'll bag the other.'

'What about the press? Are you going to speak to Jason Mortimer?'

'Not for the moment. As far as the press is concerned, the Catherine Watson case is still officially closed. That goes for Mortimer too.

However, DI Turner will be unofficially reviewing it in the light of what's happened in Holland Park. Given the similarities, there has to be a link somewhere. He will also be following up on the whereabouts of Malcolm Broadbent and Michael Jennings.'

She rose to her feet and smoothed down the front of her jacket, meeting over. There was no point saying anything and Tartaglia left the room followed closely by Turner.

'Hey Mark,' Turner called after him in the corridor. 'Look, I'm sorry. It wasn't my idea, you know.'

'Fine.'

Turner gave him a baleful look, hands still deep in his pockets as if they were glued to the place. 'Honestly, Mark. Please believe me. This is the last thing I need at the moment.'

He gave Turner a curt nod of agreement. Reluctantly, he had to admit that it made sense, if only Turner could keep himself under control. 'Just don't go getting in the way. I've got enough to deal with without having to worry about you.'

'Aye, aye, Sir,' Turner said, with a glimmer of a smile, and followed Tartaglia into the open plan office where everyone available was already assembled for an impromptu meeting.

With the image of the drunken Turner asleep on his floor still fresh in his mind, Tartaglia took up his position at the front, Turner next to him, and explained Turner's presence. By now, they all knew about the Catherine Watson case and Turner's involvement, and the news that he was being seconded to the team was greeted with only moderate surprise.

'The main thing to remember,' Tartaglia said in summary, 'is that nothing has changed from our point of view. I want the names of everyone to do with the Watson case cross-checked against anyone known to Rachel Tenison, but we will continue to put all our efforts into finding whoever killed Rachel. If we turn up Catherine Watson's killer in the process, then so much the better. But that's not our focus. DI Turner will be dealing exclusively with that side of things.'

'Do you think the two cases are linked, Sir?' Minderedes asked, from the back of the room.

'It's possible,' Tartaglia replied. 'Although it's also possible that we have a copycat on our hands. Hopefully, with DI Turner on board, it will all become clear quite soon, one way or another.'

'But I thought the way they were tied up was identical,' Minderedes added.

'Yes, but how many people saw the reconstruction photographs? Impossible to tell. According to DI Turner, DCI Gifford was pretty open with the press and gave some of them access to a lot of the crime scene stuff. Although it was strictly off-the-record, there was a lot of leakage. Anybody in quite a wide circle might have known about the way Broadbent found the body. Again, that's a line of enquiry DI Turner will be following.'

He glanced over at Turner, who was swaying slightly, eyes half closed. His suit was crumpled as if he hadn't changed it that morning and he also hadn't bothered to shave. Standing next to him in Steele's office, Tartaglia had caught the sourness of sweat and cigarette smoke from his clothes. Turner needed to get a grip on things if he was to be of any help, but there were no signs of him pulling himself together. Maybe it explained why Wakeham had been so happy to get shot of him for a while; perhaps Wakeham thought it would help take Turner's mind off things and that there was little damage he could do nosing about in an old investigation.

'As far as the Holland Park case goes,' he continued, 'all access to photographs and anything to do with the crime scene is on a need-to-know basis only. If in doubt, if someone's pestering you, refer them to me or DCI Steele. We can keep Jason Mortimer quiet for the moment, but the last thing I want is some other bright spark of a journalist spotting the possible link and blasting it all over the papers. I'm sure Catherine Watson's family wouldn't thank us for that either. Is that clear?' Everyone in the room, except Turner, nodded. 'Now, what's the news on the bars?'

'We've been to every watering hole in a mile radius of her flat,' Feeney said. 'A couple of the barmen thought they recognised her, but weren't a hundred per cent sure. She may just look familiar because of the photos and stuff in the papers. We only found one place she went to on a regular basis. It sounds like the one the shrink described, because they had a barman called Viktor. That's spelled with a 'K'. Apparently, he's from somewhere in Eastern Europe. According to the person I talked to, he and Miss Tenison had quite a thing going for a short while, although someone else said Viktor made it up. Apparently he liked to exaggerate about his conquests.'

'Have you spoken to him?'

She shook her head. 'He's not working there any longer and nobody knows where he's gone. Seems he fell out with one of the other barmen a couple of weeks ago over a discrepancy in the takings and did a bunk. I may have a lead through someone else who knows him, but we're going to have to go carefully. It sounds as though he's here illegally and if he knows we're after him he may go to ground.'

'Well, keep on it,' Tartaglia said. 'This Viktor sounds like our best bet at the moment.' He looked around the room. 'Anyone else?'

'Yes, sir,' Minderedes said, raising his hand. 'I spoke to the partner at Crowther and Phillips who dealt with Rachel Tenison's affairs. He says she came in to see him just over two months ago and asked him to draft a new will. What's interesting is it removed Patrick Tenison as executor and cut out Liz Volpe completely. He sent it to her for signature but never heard anything back. He spoke to her once and she said she was thinking it over and would get back to him. But she never did, so the old will stands.'

'Did he know why she wanted to make a new will?'

'No.'

'Did he say whether or not he thought Patrick Tenison and Liz Volpe knew about the changes?'

'He didn't know that, either. He seemed to think it wasn't for him to question his client's change of mind.'

'So who would have got the flat in the new will?'

'Everything, bar the business, went to Tenison's nephew and niece, and her sister-in-law, Emma, was to be appointed executor.'

'How odd,' Tartaglia said thoughtfully. 'I wonder why she decided to change it. It certainly gives Liz Volpe a financial motive for murder, although I don't see how she would know enough about the Watson murder to try and link the two.'

There was silence for a moment, then Donovan spoke. 'It possibly explains one thing. It sounds as though Rachel Tenison and Liz Volpe had a falling-out for some reason. Which is why they haven't been in touch.' She was perched on a desk next to Karen Feeney, chewing on a pencil and swinging her legs backwards and forwards. 'I mean, why else would you cut your best friend out of your will? It wasn't as if she had anyone else to leave her money to. Though it doesn't explain why they were supposed to be meeting up on Sunday—unless Liz Volpe was lying about that.'

'It was in her diary, ' Wightman said.

'Well, we need to get to the bottom of it,' Tartaglia replied, wondering if any of it was relevant to the case. Liz Volpe may have lied about a number of things but he still didn't see her as a murderer. 'Perhaps the dinner was some sort of attempt at a reconciliation. We'll need to talk to her again. How are you getting on with the phone records, Dave?'

Wightman cleared his throat. 'There are three pay-as-you-go numbers that keep coming up regularly in the last three months, on both her landline and her mobile. We're trying to trace them but we're not having much luck so far. One of the phones made three short calls to her the night she died.'

'How short?'

'No more than thirty seconds.'

'Probably got the answer machine message. There were several hung-up calls that night.'

'We've got onto the supplier to see if we can pinpoint the location where the calls were made and we should hear back later today. She also called Jonathan Bourne's home phone from her landline on the night she died. It was just after eleven o'clock and they spoke for a couple of minutes. He claims it was something to do with the story he was writing.'

'So, he was home by eleven o'clock,' Tartaglia said. 'He only lives down the road, so it doesn't mean much. But why would she be ringing him at that hour?'

'Perhaps she wanted to apologise for storming out of the restaurant,' Wightman said. 'Except the restaurant manager failed to ID him.'

'He's still not off the hook. It's like the black hole of Calcutta in that place and the manager said he didn't get a good view of the man. How are you getting on with the background research, Karen?'

Feeney shifted in her seat and gave him a tight smile. 'One interesting thing's come up. Jonathan Bourne did a twelve-month stint as a junior on the crime desk of his current paper. It was several years ago, long before the Watson murder, but he may still have his contacts.'

'Now that is interesting. At the moment, we have nothing to link Bourne to Catherine Watson, but we must keep trying. Any news from forensics on those glasses?' he asked, turning to Donovan.

'The report's just come in. As you know, five glasses were recovered from the dishwasher, all of which the maid found lying around the flat that morning. Three wine glasses and two small tumblers. All of them had the maid's prints on them, which confirms that they were the ones that she put into the dishwasher. The victim's prints and DNA were on one of the wine glasses and one of the tumblers, unidentified male A's prints and DNA on both a wine glass and a tumbler, unidentified male B's prints and DNA on another wine glass. There were traces of white wine in the wine glasses, possibly from the same or a similar bottle, and vodka and cranberry juice in both of the tumblers.'

Tartaglia nodded. 'How confusing. Sounds like she had another visitor. Bourne said he only had a glass of wine with her. Without knowing which set of prints belongs to him, it's almost impossible to tell what's going on. Let's try him again and explain the situation. Maybe he'll be prepared to cooperate if he thinks it'll get him off the hook.'

Wightman shook his head. 'He wouldn't yesterday. He made a big deal about it and started giving me all that human rights crap.'

'Lean on him. We need to know which prints are his. According to Bourne, he left the flat before she did. He said she was in a hurry to get rid of him. Say for a moment that he's actually telling the truth, he leaves her flat at about eight. The restaurant booking was for eight-thirty but she arrived twenty minutes late, the man just after her. It would take about ten to fifteen minutes to walk it, but if she was driving, or in a taxi, the journey would be five minutes at the most. That's well over half an hour to play with.'

There was a knock at the door and Sharon Fuller looked in. 'Sorry to interrupt, Sir. But I've just taken a call from one of Rachel Tenison's neighbours. He says he saw someone coming out of Rachel Tenison's flat last Friday night.'

'Friday? Is he sure?'

'So he says. He lives just along the corridor.'

'Why didn't he come forward before?'

'He's been away on business since Monday and only came back this morning.'

'There was no sign of a break-in when we were there on Sunday night, although her laptop and phone haven't turned up. Who else had keys to the flat?'

'Just her brother and the cleaner,' Donovan said.

'Well, double-check where they were Friday night. It sounds as though that's when the phone and laptop were taken.' He thought back to the way the flat had been when they found it. Everything had been tidy, in its place, no evidence at all of anyone searching through things. 'If it isn't either of them, it means the killer took Rachel Tenison's keys off her body. We need to find out if anything else is missing.'

16

Hands in the pockets of her coat, feet planted slightly apart in her warm, thick-soled boots, Liz Volpe stood for a moment in the corridor outside Rachel's flat, gazing at the new steel door that guarded the entrance. Wondering what had been done with the lovely old wooden one, she felt a sense of unease. At least everything else still looked familiar; the carpet, the wallpaper, even the large, unexplained scuffmark to the left of Rachel's door, and the eternal smell of cleaning polish. But she was dreading going inside; so many memories trapped within its four walls, along with the unpleasant echoes of what had happened there three months before. She could still hear Rachel's voice, those cruel words, replaying in her mind.

Taking a few deep breaths, she raised her fist to knock. She had barely heard the rap of her knuckles on the metal when the door flew open, revealing Tartaglia.

'There you are,' he said, as though he knew she had been standing there a while. He stepped back to allow her inside. 'I'm sorry to drag you here, but as my constable explained on the phone, someone was seen coming out of Miss Tenison's flat. We need to find out if anything's missing.'

'How on earth did they get through all of that?' Liz asked, looking at the door.

'This was installed on Sunday. The intruder was seen last Friday night.'

'You're sure it was this flat? They all look the same from the outside.'

'It's definitely this one,' DS Sam Donovan said, emerging behind them from the sitting room and giving Liz a warm smile. 'I've just in-terviewed the man who saw the intruder. He lives just along the corridor and he was a hundred per cent positive.'

She was pretty, Liz thought, with small, regular features, lovely skin and large, clear grey eyes, although she went out of her way to hide her femininity with her painfully short hair and androgynous clothes. Today she was wearing a bright purple shirt, black trousers and braces, with a pair of Doc Martens. Her coat and bag were thrown over her arm and she appeared to be on her way out.

'What did he look like?' Liz asked.

'According to the witness, slim, somewhere between five feet eight and six feet tall,' Donovan replied. 'He was wearing baggy jeans, train-ers and some sort of an anorak with a hood pulled up over his head. The neighbour didn't see his face clearly.'

'The witness is doing an e-fit now, although I doubt it will be much use,' Tartaglia said, looking at her in a way that made her feel uncomfortable, as though he expected her to know who the intruder might be. As she turned away, she saw her tired, pale face in the hall mirror. If only she could get a decent night of sleep, but she kept wak-ing and when she did sleep, her dreams were full of Rachel.

'I'd better be off, Mark,' Donovan said to Tartaglia. 'Where will you be later?'

He checked his watch. 'Back at Barnes in about an hour, I guess. Then home. Call me when you're done.'

'Will do,' she replied, struggling with the main lock on the door, which appeared to be stiff. Tartaglia stepped forward, grasped the knob and forced it to turn.

There was an easy familiarity between them, as though they were friends rather than superior and subordinate. Perhaps the police were less formal than she had imagined, or maybe murder squad detectives were more collegiate and less hierarchical. Even so, they appeared close and she found herself wondering about the nature of their relationship.

As the door closed behind Donovan, Tartaglia looked around at Liz. 'Do you feel ready to take a look around?'

'As ready as I'll ever be,' she said, taking a deep breath to calm her nerves. He had no idea just how difficult it was for her going back there again.

'As I said, I want you to concentrate on looking for anything that might be missing or different from what you're used to. Our people have been all over the flat earlier this week and we've taken away some of Miss Tenison's personal items and papers for analysis, but we try to put things back as we find them. If you see anything out of place, let me know and I'll make a note of it.'

While he was speaking, her eyes fell on the blue and white bowl that sat on the small console table by the door. It was where Rachel used to keep her keys. But it was empty.

'Her keys are missing,' he said, as though reading her thoughts. 'As are her mobile phone and laptop.'

'You think they were taken by the man on Friday night?'

'It looks that way.'

'Was it an ordinary burglary?'

'No. It's more likely that whoever killed her wanted to eradicate any trail of contact.'

'Is that why you think the killer's someone she knew? Someone she was in contact with?'

'It's part of the reason, yes.'

'But if she was killed Friday morning, why would anyone take the risk of coming here later? And why leave it until that evening? From what you told me, Richard had already reported her missing.'

'It's not clear.'

As he seemed unwilling to be drawn into any form of discussion, she turned away and walked into the sitting room.

Everything looked tidy as usual, everything in its familiar place, as if the room were still in use. It was so strange being there and she felt like an intruder. The curtains were drawn back and a tall vase of flowers in a mixture of reds and oranges sat on top of the small chest of drawers between the two windows. The scent was strong and they still looked fresh, although they must have been left over from the week before. She hoped that somebody would think to throw them away before they started to rot. The only signs of disturbance were the very visible smears of dark grey powder that marked many of the surfaces.

'We've taken prints, where possible,' Tartaglia said, from the doorway, 'although there wasn't much to find. Unfortunately, Miss Tenison's cleaner seems to have been good at her job.'

Still looking around the room, Liz felt dazed. She had never really liked Rachel's choice of décor and furnishings, which she found dull and old beyond her years. Rachel had inherited some of the furniture, but she had failed to put her own stamp or personality on anything. It was as though she was trying to conform to a stereotype that might have pleased her dead parents. Liz thought of the conversation that had taken place in that room the last time she was there, Rachel on the sofa, feet up in front of the fire, nursing her glass of wine, she in the large armchair by the window. She could almost see Rachel sitting there now, picture her sharp-eyed expression as she let slip the words that had destroyed everything.

Trying to close off the memory, Liz walked over to the table behind the sofa. Drawing a squiggly line with her finger in the fine film of powder, she glanced at the ranks of familiar, silver-framed photographs. They had been there as long as she could remember: pictures of Rachel's mother and father, her grandmother, her brother Patrick, along with a picture of herself and Rachel together in school uniform. She picked it up and gazed at it, wondering why Rachel had kept it on show for all those years, why it was still there now. They both seemed so young; hair scraped back, faces still soft and unformed, white, gangly legs sticking out beneath the horrible grey pleated skirts. Even then she dwarfed Rachel in height.

She thought of the time they had first met twenty years before. Sister Margaret, headmistress of St Anne's, had walked into the classroom in the middle of a lesson one morning, trailing a small, pale-faced girl behind her. She could still picture Rachel, a scrawny little waif, with huge, dark-shadowed eyes. Shifting awkwardly from one foot to another, she looked like a nervous pony, with her funny, ragged mane of pale blonde hair held back by an Alice band. Only later, did Liz discover that Rachel had chopped off her hair with her stepmother's kitchen scissors the night before coming to school.

'Is anything wrong?' Tartaglia had come over to where she was standing.

She put the photograph down, still looking at it. 'No. Nothing. It's just very odd being here, that's all.'

He gave her a nod of sympathy. 'Is everything as you remember it?'

'More or less.' She was on the point of turning away, wishing he would leave her alone, when she noticed a gap at the back of the photographs.

She frowned, trying to think back. 'There's a photo missing. It was definitely there last time I came to the flat. I particularly remember it because it was new and I hadn't seen it before. Rachel rarely ever changed the photos.'

'Can you describe it?'

'It was of Rachel, a really good close-up, taken at one of the gallery parties last year, I think. She was talking to someone, although they weren't in the picture, and laughing, looking lovely. Richard had it blown up and framed and gave it to her as a birthday present. He may have a copy somewhere. The frame was particularly nice, I seem to remember. Richard's good at that sort of thing.'

'Why did she put it at the back?'

'Who knows? I suppose she didn't want anyone to think she was vain.'

'Vain?' He looked at her curiously. 'And was she?'

Vain? Self-obsessed? Insecure? What was the difference? Rachel had certainly been very aware of the power of her looks. But Tartaglia was being deliberately provocative and Liz had no desire to answer him. The way he was staring at her was also provocative, almost intimate. For a moment, she saw him as a man, rather than a policeman, and it struck her again just how handsome he was. Then she reminded herself why she was there and what it was he actually wanted. She owed him no explanation of Rachel's character—or of what had happened between them.

'Was she vain?' he persisted. 'You can say what you think. It's just the two of us here, off the record, and I won't put it in my report. What was she really like?'

'She wasn't exactly vain. But that's not what you're asking, is it?'

He put his hands in his pockets and shrugged good-humouredly. 'I'm still trying to flesh her out in my mind. I also want to understand the dynamics of your relationship. Did the two of you quarrel? Is that what this is all about?'

'I've told you everything you need to know,' she said, and turned away. Before he had the chance to ask her anything else, she walked out of the room and into the corridor. She felt like leaving, but he was right behind her. His phone started ringing.

'Can you take a look in her bedroom, please?' he asked, as he fumbled in his pocket for it. 'I'll catch up with you in a minute.'

Rachel's bedroom was the last place she wanted to see but she had no choice. Hoping that he would be held up on the phone for a while, she went along the corridor and hesitantly pushed open the door.

She wasn't sure what she had been expecting to find, but the vision that had been filling her head for so long, of a darkened, intoxicating room and two people together in that huge, richly coloured bed, was nothing like the reality that greeted her. The overhead lights were harshly bright and the bed had been stripped of all its hangings and bedclothes and reduced to a pathetic bare wood frame and mattress. She breathed a sigh of relief and stood for a moment in the centre of the room gazing around.

The old trunk, which had belonged to Rachel's grandfather, had gone from its place at the end of the bed and she wondered if the police had taken it for some reason. She made a mental note to ask Tartaglia. She walked over to one of the cupboard doors, which was open, and looked inside. She saw the dark, familiar ranks of Rachel's clothes, her shoes lined up neatly in racks beneath. It was as though Rachel had never left, as though she might return at any minute to get changed. Her familiar sweet perfume lingered in the air, no doubt coming from the clothes, and Liz closed the door quickly to get rid of it.

The sight of her own washed-out, un-made-up face in the mirrored panel of the door made her turn away and she went over to the bedside table and switched on the lamp. Feeling suddenly very tired, she sat down on the edge of the mattress, waiting for Tartaglia. Unlike her own bedside table, which always seemed to be crammed with an endless amount of stuff, Rachel's was almost clear, apart from an electric alarm clock, which ticked loudly in the quiet of the room, and a couple of books. On top was a glossy biography of Bess of Hardwick; underneath it, Irène Némirovsky's *Suite Française*. The biography looked new and unread, but when she opened *Suite Française*, the pages fell open in the middle, a postcard with a picture of a renaissance Madonna marking the place. She turned it over. Scrawled in large, backwards-sloping writing, in heavy black ink, were the words:

This reminds me of you. I see your face everywhere
and I can't stop thinking about you. Why won't you
answer my calls? I must see you. Please, please call
me. I love you.

It took her a moment to decipher the extraordinary handwriting,
made even more difficult by a semi-circle smudge right in the middle
of the card where someone, no doubt Rachel, had put down a wet glass
or mug. The message was signed with a single cross, with no date or
signature. The card was from the National Gallery, the postmark
Paddington, dated about six weeks before.

'What's that you've got?'

The sound of Tartaglia's voice behind her made her start and she
turned around. She hadn't heard him come into the bedroom and
wondered how long he had been standing there.

He came over to where she was sitting and she passed him the
card. 'This was in one of the books on Rachel's bedside table. Your
people must have missed it.'

He gave a cursory glance at the front then turned it over and read
what was written on the back. His expression hardened. 'Is this Miss
Tenison's writing?'

'Definitely not. And before you ask, I don't know who wrote it
and I've never seen it before.'

17

'I'm intrigued to know why you're interested in this particular poem, Sergeant Donovan,' Professor Kate Spicer said, her round, brown eyes alive with curiosity as she played with the string of pearls around her neck. 'My secretary tells me you're investigating a murder.' She emphasised the word murder with apparent relish, speaking in a clipped, light Australian accent.

'I'm afraid I can't tell you very much about it,' Donovan replied. 'But the poem is a possible clue in the case. We're trying to understand the psychology or significance of it, if there is any.'

Mugs of steaming hot, milky coffee on the floor, photocopies of the poem on their laps, they were sitting together on the small grubby green sofa in Professor Spicer's book-lined office on the second floor of number 30 Russell Square. The large, eighteenth-century building in the heart of Bloomsbury was home to Birkbeck College's School of English and Humanities. In spite of the building's clean, classical lines, the interior was a rabbit warren of staircases and cheap partitions that gave no hint of its former glory.

Dressed in a well-cut navy wool trouser suit, Spicer looked to be in her late forties or early fifties and was almost as short as Donovan, although considerably rounder, with a helmet of tight, curly brown hair, which framed an open, pleasant face. Donovan hadn't set foot in any academic establishment since leaving university, but she felt instantly transported back in time to her tutor's shabby quarters. Even the smell was the same: a mix of stale cigarette smoke, instant coffee and dusty books.

'You said it's a clue. Is it about the identity of the murderer, do you think?' Spicer asked, inclining her head a little and crossing her legs, flashing a pair of very high-heeled fuchsia shoes, which made Donovan smile. Spicer's room might be almost identical to her old tutor's, but she was far removed from the frayed academic who had been Donovan's tutor.

'Yes, or possibly the victim. We're just not sure. It may also be a red herring.'

'Well, let's see what we can do to help,' Spicer said, with a business-like toss of her head. 'The poem's full name is *Dolores, Notre-Dame des Sept Douleurs*. It's a reference to the Virgin Mary, of course, and we can go into the full meaning and symbolism in a minute, if you like. How much do you know about Charles Algernon Swinburne?' She pronounced each word distinctly, as if it was important to give him his full name.

'Not a great deal, I'm afraid. He never cropped up in any of the courses I did.'

'Then let me give you a quick overview first. As you probably know, he was a contemporary of the Pre-Raphaelites and quite a radical character in his youth. He was bi-sexual, alcoholic and heavily into the pleasures of flagellation which, like a lot of young men in his day, he discovered at school. He was seen by many of his peers as depraved. His work has been out of fashion for a long while, but sometimes he has the touch of genius, at least in my view. This is undoubtedly one of his finest poems. Sadly, he went badly off the boil as he got older, but don't we all?' She gave a dismissive shrug.

'When was the poem written?'

'It was originally published in a collection of poetry in 1866 and created quite a furore as the main themes are masochism, flagellation and paganism. You can just imagine how that was received in some circles.' Professor Spicer tapped the pages with her glossy red fingernails for emphasis. 'But *Dolores* was so popular, it was reprinted all on its own, which says a lot for the Victorians, I think. Of course, it doesn't have the impact today that it would have had in Swinburne's time.'

'Who is Dolores?'

'She's a beautiful, cruel and libidinous pagan goddess. She has absolutely no compassion or humanity.' Spicer put on a pair of tortoiseshell reading glasses, which were hanging on a beaded chain around her neck, and scanned the pages. 'Listen to this,' she said, raising one hand. 'He says: *Ah beautiful passionate body, That never has ached with a heart*, and he describes her as "Our Lady of Torture" and "Deadly Dolores", but of course he's relishing his pain, absolutely wallowing in it. Look at lines 180 and 181: *Pain melted in tears and was pleasure, Death tingled with blood and was life.* That should give you the flavour.' She glanced up at Donovan over her glasses, with a smile.

'It certainly does,' Donovan said, wondering how it related to Rachel Tenison.

'There's another bit I want you to hear.' Spicer quickly flicked through the pages until she found the place. 'Here it is:

By the ravenous teeth that have smitten
Through the kisses that blossom and bud,
By the lips intertwisted and bitten
Till the foam has a savour of blood,
By the pulse as it rises and falters,
By the hands as they slacken and strain,
I adjure thee, respond from thine altars,
Our Lady of Pain.'

Spicer looked up at Donovan again and clasped her hands enthusiastically. 'Now, isn't that quite wonderful? It has a whiff of the real Black Mass—recalls the Marquis de Sade, of course.'

'It's certainly very striking.'

'Yes, but ignoring all of that sensationalistic stuff, it's essentially a love poem.'

'A love poem? I haven't read it right through but it doesn't seem very romantic to me.'

'Ah, but it is, in Swinburne's own particular way. Take these lines:

In the daytime thy voice shall go through him,
In his dreams he shall feel thee and ache;
Thou shalt kindle by night and subdue him
Asleep and awake.

That's rather nice, don't you think?'

Wondering if she had missed the point, Donovan gazed down at the photocopied pages, scanning the lines again and noting how the words "blood" and "death" and "sacrifice" ran through them as a leit-motif. 'Well, it all seems pretty twisted to me,' she said, after a moment.

Spicer smiled. 'Each to his own, surely. Forget your preconceptions, Sergeant. However abnormal it all appears, if you're looking for the essence of the poem and what it means in the context of your murder, I tell you it is truly about love.'

Not knowing how she was going to explain that interpretation to Tartaglia, Donovan said: 'You mentioned that Swinburne's out of fashion now. Is he still studied at university? I'm wondering how somebody might have come across the poem.'

'Anyone who's doing nineteenth-century English literature would know of it, certainly. It's very much of its time and I certainly include references to Swinburne and *Dolores* in my lectures. There's also a wider audience to consider. The name and general characteristics of the Lady of Pain were borrowed by the Dungeons and Dragons role-playing game, although of course the poem doesn't come into any of that.' Professor Spicer folded her hands on her lap and leaned forwards towards Donovan. 'Are you absolutely sure you can't tell me anything more, Sergeant Donovan? I'm going to die of curiosity, otherwise.'

Donovan smiled, wishing she could explain, but the poem was one of many things that had to be kept out of the public domain. 'It's probably not giving too much away if I say that the poem was sent to a woman, who's now dead, and we don't know who sent it.' It was distorting the truth a little but she wanted to appear helpful.

'Well, I don't need you to tell me that the sender's male, do I? Is he the killer, do you think?'

Donovan smiled. 'I can't say any more. I'm sorry.'

Spicer put a finger to her lips, looking thoughtful. 'Of course, he's totally obsessed, poor chap. Do you know Keats's *La Belle Dame Sans Merci*?'

'Vaguely.'

'Well, in just the same way, Dolores knows no mercy. Was your victim a bit of a *femme fatale*?'

'More of a mystery.'

'Mystery. There you go. That's part of the allure. Pity the man that falls in love with her.' Spicer sat back against the soggy cushion of the sofa with a happy sigh, as if she'd solved the puzzle.

'Hang on a minute. If we come back to the poem and the reason why someone might have sent it, what sort of message is he trying to give? There's no anger or bitterness. As you say, the man's really into his pain.'

'That's Swinburne for you.' Spicer reached down to the floor and picked up her mug, sipping at it thoughtfully. 'But even in the modern context, the same must hold true. I think whoever sent it is telling her that he loves her, in spite of whatever she's put him through. Human nature is perverse, Sergeant. Just think how many people you know who fall for the wrong person—even though they know it's the wrong bloody person. Doesn't matter how much advice you give them, the more the silly creatures get hurt, the more they keep going back for more. It's as though they want the pain. Of course, I'm just reading between the lines here and using my imagination. But if he's your murderer, maybe, finally, he's had enough. The poor little worm turns.'

Liz settled back into the depths of the large, leather armchair with her glass of wine, tucking her stockinged feet up underneath her. 'If Rachel was killed on the Friday morning, what was she doing the night before? You said she had a drink with someone. Have you found out who it is?'

'We're gradually piecing it together,' Tartaglia replied noncommittally from the sofa opposite. 'Do you mind if I have a cigarette?'

'Feel free.'

He took the pack from his pocket and lit up. They were in the sitting room at Liz's brother's flat. They had been right through Rachel Tenison's apartment, but Liz had spotted nothing else of interest, apart from the missing photograph and the postcard. Sensing that she was finding the whole situation difficult, he had suggested that they go somewhere else to talk. He had further questions to ask, but rather than take her to an interview room in a police station, which would probably make her clam up, he had accepted her invitation of a drink.

'Why won't you tell me what you've found?' she asked. 'You want me to help, don't you?' Her tone was accusatory and her eyes were fixed on him, as if somehow she could force him to talk.

He drew on his cigarette, and decided that if he gave a little, it might encourage her to open up. 'OK,' he said. 'I'll try and be a bit more open with you. What we know is that between seven and eight on Thursday evening, she had a drink in her flat with someone called Jonathan Bourne.'

'Jonathan?'

'You know him?'

'Yes. Yes, I do.'

'Hang on a minute. I told you a few days ago that she had a drink with someone with the initials JB. Why didn't you say anything?'

She looked at him blankly. 'I don't remember that.'

He didn't believe her. Thinking back to her reaction that particular morning, he knew that the initials had meant something to her. 'Come on. You can do better than that.'

She shrugged as if it was unimportant. 'Honestly, I don't remember. Anyway, loads of people have the initials JB.'

'What, loads of people you know?'

'But Jonathan's the last person...'

'What are you saying?'

She put down her glass. 'Well, he and Rachel didn't get on. It all goes back to when we all shared a house together at university. He's very messy, used to make a lot of noise, use up everybody's stuff and not replace it. You know the sort of thing and no doubt you've worked out by now what Rachel was like. He really used to wind her up and they had terrible rows. I was always stuck in the middle, trying to keep the peace.'

'He's still a friend of yours?'

'Yes. A good friend.' She paused. 'Do you know why they were having a drink? Was it something to do with work?'

'That's what he said.'

'Well then.' She folded her arms, as if that was the end of the matter. 'Look, Inspector. Jonathan's no more of a murderer than I am, or perhaps you have me down as a suspect too.'

'If you were a suspect, we wouldn't be having a cosy chat like this.'

She smiled. 'OK. Sorry. But you can't condemn Jonathan for having a drink with Rachel. She wasn't killed until the next morning.'

He inhaled some more smoke, still looking at her, still feeling that

she was trying to convince herself as much as him. 'After meeting
Jonathan Bourne, Miss Tenison was seen having dinner with a man
in a restaurant in Kensington. Jonathan Bourne says it wasn't him,
but we're not sure if he's telling the truth.'

'Why would he lie about that?' she said flatly.

He noted her lack of surprise or curiosity, as though she had an
idea who the man was.

'Look, I've been open with you. Now I need you to come clean
with me. I want the truth and I'd prefer to hear it from you here,
rather than down at the local nick. But it's your choice.' Avoiding his
eye, she reached for her wine again. 'You know that you're mentioned
as a beneficiary in Rachel Tenison's will?'

'Yes. Patrick Tenison told me.'

'Do you know she decided to change her will a couple of months
ago? That she wasn't going to leave you anything?'

She choked, cupping her hand over her mouth. 'No. He didn't tell
me that, but it doesn't surprise me.' She cleared her throat, swallowing heavily, and put down her glass again. 'I suppose I'd better come
clean. As you rightly suspected, we had a quarrel.'

'What happened?' he said, irritated that she didn't appear in the
least bothered at having said nothing about it before.

She gave a heavy sigh and rubbed her eyes, then ran her fingers
back through her hair, scraping it back so forcefully off her pale face
that she looked almost deranged for a second. 'I'm sorry. I don't like
thinking about it,' she said, standing up and walking away towards
the window. She stared down at the street below.

'I need to know,' he said.

She turned around to face him and folded her arms again. 'Do you
remember my telling you about the dinner I had with Rachel a couple
of months ago, the last time I saw her?'

'I remember.'

'Well, it was after that dinner. Back at her flat. I started to tell her about some problems I'd been having with someone I'd been seeing. He was married. I wasn't sure what to do and wanted some advice, but she just brushed me off quite brutally, and I'll never forget what she said.'

'Go on.'

'"Why can't you bloody well find someone of your own for a change?" That's what she said.'

'That's a very strange remark. What did she mean by it?'

Liz shrugged. 'Maybe she was empathising with his wife. Anyway, she then told me that the man was using me, that he didn't care about me at all.'

'How would she know that? Was he someone she knew?'

Liz shook her head and looked away. 'I tried to make light of it, but it was as if I'd slapped her. And the way she looked at me. God, it was frightening. I'd never seen her so angry before. She told me I was irresponsible and frivolous and didn't care about the damage I caused. I still remember her words. "You're just playing at it, like a kid with a new toy. You don't care about anyone but yourself. You don't know what it is to really want someone, to really love them."' Liz grimaced. 'It was as if I was cheap and heartless.'

'This was all because of this man?' he asked, puzzled.

'That's right.'

He thought of Rachel Tenison, of her fragile, delicate beauty, wondering why she had cared so much. For someone who was apparently so controlled and emotionally shut down, as well as sexually promiscuous, it was an extraordinary reaction, particularly with a woman who was supposed to be such a close friend. Bitterness and jealousy were the words that came to mind, yet they seemed so out of character with the little he knew of Rachel. 'Are you sure there's not something you're not telling me?'

She looked away as though she didn't like the question. 'That's all she said.'

'Well, she sounds very angry about something, as if it was personal. Could she have been thinking of her relationship with Richard Greville? You weren't…'

'Certainly not,' she said, looking affronted. 'I've never had anything to do with Richard in that way.' With one last glance out of the window, she drew the curtains tightly across and turned back to face him. 'Anyway, I didn't want to hear any more, so I left. As I told you, it was the last time I saw or spoke to her. That's why there were no calls or emails between us.'

It still didn't make sense, as though she was only giving him half the story. 'What happened after that?'

She put her hands to her head. 'Jesus. Why can't you leave it alone?'

'Because I need to understand everything. Tell me what happened.'

She marched over to the coffee table and poured herself a fresh glass of wine. 'If you must know, I got a letter from her about a month later. I recognised her handwriting on the envelope but I was still angry so I tore it up and threw it away without reading it.'

'Why didn't you mention all this before?'

'Why? Because it's painful thinking about it,' she said, eyes blazing. 'Also, what happened between me and Rachel has absolutely nothing to do with her murder. And it's nobody's business but mine.' She took a gulp of wine.

'What was she like?' he asked after a moment, feeling as though he had completely lost his bearings. 'What was she *really* like?'

'What are any of us like? How can we define it?'

'But you knew her. I didn't.'

'Count yourself lucky,' she replied, with a sudden sharpness of tone that took him by surprise. 'Look, I've got a splitting headache and I've had enough of these questions.'

He stared at her for a moment, noting how tired and pale she looked, then nodded and got to his feet. He couldn't force her to speak to him. 'Tell me one thing. You had no further contact with her after that?'

'That's right. Not until she rang me and said we needed to talk. She must have heard that I was coming over again. We agreed to meet and you know the rest.'

'There's nothing else?' he asked, searching her face vainly for some sort of intimation of the truth.

She shook her head, but he still didn't believe her.

Liz saw him to the door and closed it firmly behind him. As she heard the sound of his footsteps retreating down the stairs, she leaned back against the wall and hugged herself.

Christ, what a balls-up. She knew she hadn't sounded at all convincing, but Tartaglia had caught her unawares. Going back to Rachel's flat had been unnerving and she felt suddenly exposed. She had the impression that he saw right through her, saw her weaknesses, her guilt and her lies.

Her head was aching as if it would explode and she pressed her fingers hard on her temples, trying to replay the conversation in her mind, worrying about what she might have inadvertently let slip.

She was jerked out of her thoughts by the sound of the front door buzzer. He must have come back again. More questions. How was she going to get through it?

Reluctantly, she picked up the intercom. But the voice she heard was Jonathan's.

'Liz? Let me in, will you?' he mumbled.

Although she had no desire to see him, it was a relief to hear his voice and not Tartaglia's.

She buzzed him in and, leaving the door to the flat ajar, went back into the sitting room to tidy up. Just as she emerged, hands full with the dirty glasses, ashtray and half-empty bottle, Jonathan appeared in the hall in front of her.

He slammed the door behind him. 'Why is it I get the impression you're avoiding me?' he asked, following her into the kitchen. 'You haven't returned any of my calls.'

'I'm not avoiding you. I just haven't felt like seeing anyone.'

'But I'm not anyone.'

Rather than reply, she turned her back on him, dumped the bottle on the counter, then rinsed the glasses and ashtray before putting them in the dishwasher.

'See you've been having company,' he said. 'Getting cosy with the law, are you?'

'No.'

'Funny, 'cause I recognised the bloke with the black hair who came out of here. I knew who he was straight off. It was the fucking detective who gave me such a hard time. Told you about him, didn't I?'

'You did,' she said, washing her hands. 'That's about all you told me.'

'What did he want?'

She turned to face him, shaking her hands dry and wiping them on her jeans as there was no tea towel. 'He wanted to ask me some more questions about Rachel. Did he see you?'

'I don't think so. Why does it matter?' He caught hold of her arm and pulled her towards him. 'Aren't you going to give Johnny-boy a kiss?'

She gave him a quick peck on the cheek and tried to pull away but he held on to her, nuzzling her cheek before kissing it. His stubble scratched her skin and she could smell alcohol on his breath.

'Mmm. You smell good. I like that perfume you're wearing.'

She pushed him away. 'Don't start all that again. Do you want a drink, or not?'

He leaned back against the counter and shrugged good-humouredly. 'What's the fuzz doing drinking wine with you, anyway?'

She took a clean glass out of the cupboard and passed it to him, sliding the open bottle along the counter towards him. 'Trying to find out my innermost secrets.'

'Trying to make me jealous, more like.' He poured what was left in the bottle into the glass, filling it almost to the top. 'You like to wind me up, don't you? Do you fancy him?'

She folded her arms and stared hard at him. 'He told me you had a drink with Rachel the night before she died. You never mentioned it.'

'Is that a crime?'

'No. But why didn't you tell me?'

'Darling Lizzie, there are shed-loads of things I don't tell you.' Watching her intently, he took a swig of wine. When she didn't reply, he added, 'Seriously, I didn't think it was important.'

'But the police do.'

He threw up his hands in the air, sloshing some wine on the floor. 'For Christ's sake, just because I had a quick drink with Rachel the night before she died, they now think I fucking killed her.'

'They think you had dinner with her after your drink.'

'Not you as well?' he said, thrusting his glass towards her as though it were his finger. 'Get this straight. I did not have dinner with Rachel that night, or any other night, OK?'

'Maybe not. But did you fuck her?'

He took a mouthful of wine, swilling it around in his mouth before swallowing, as though considering the matter.

'I said, did you fuck her?'

He met her stare. 'If I did, would you shop me to your policeman friend?'

'I don't know,' she said, wondering if he was joking.

'Come on, Lizzie, what's it to do with you? I'm a free agent, aren't

I? At least that's what you're always telling me, right?'

'Just answer me this, Jonathan. Did you screw Rachel that night? Just say it.'

He sighed and put down his glass. ''Course I didn't. Why would I?' He came over to where she was standing and took hold of her hands, staring down at her with bloodshot, watery eyes. 'Whatever you think, I've never had the hots for Rachel. Not really. Anyway, I wouldn't do that to you.'

She shook her head and pulled away. 'But you did before. And you both kept it secret until Rachel let the cat out of the bag by leaving her bedroom door open.'

He sighed again. 'Jesus, that was ages ago! What's this all about? What's got into you?'

As she looked at him, she pictured him and Rachel in bed together as she had found them that morning, the surprised look on his face, the triumphant look on Rachel's. She remembered how hurt she had felt, and betrayed. She wished she could trust him now, but instinct told her not to.

'What's the matter?' he asked, with genuine concern, reaching over and stroking her hair. 'What has she done to you?'

'Nothing. How can she do anything now? I'm just remembering the way she was. Not the sugar-sweet paragon that everyone is remembering now. It makes me sick. I'm talking about the real Rachel, the one who liked to pull everybody's strings, make everyone dance to her tune. Did you dance again for her, Jonathan? That's what I want to know. Were you the one in her bed that night?'

He looked at her earnestly. 'I tell you, it wasn't me. Why does it matter so much to you? Is there something you're not telling me?'

'No.'

'Then give me a break, will you?' He grabbed his glass, took another sip, then slammed it down with a grimace. 'This wine tastes like shit. Now what about something decent to drink?'

'Did you kill Rachel? That's what I want to know.'

He put his head on one side and grinned. 'No, I didn't. Did you?'

18

Rain was lashing down when Donovan left Professor Spicer's building. Having forgotten her umbrella, she ran as fast as she could, picking her way through the heavy traffic that clogged Russell Square to one of the side streets where she had left her car. She fumbled in her bag for the keys, unlocked the driver's door and jumped in. She switched on the ignition and fan and, waiting for the mist on the front window to clear, brushed as much water as she could out of her hair, gazing at the dark forms of the passers-by scurrying along the wet pavement. What she knew about Rachel Tenison's psychology fitted perfectly with the references to sadomasochism in the Swinburne poem, and what Professor Spicer had said about obsession and it being a love poem, albeit a very bizarre one, also struck a chord. But how any of it linked in with Catherine Watson's murder was less obvious.

She took out her mobile and dialled Turner's number, but there was no answer and after several rings she was diverted to voicemail. She left a message, then called Tartaglia. He picked up almost immediately. She heard loud voices and music in the background.

'Am I disturbing you?' she asked.

'No. I've just got home.'

'What's that noise?'

'It's *The Belly of the Beast*. It's a Steven Seagal film,' he added, as though she ought to have known.

'How can you *watch* that trash?'

'Listen, some of his early films are great.'

'What is it you actually like about them?'

'Well, he kicks ass and he's invincible. And he's on the side of right.'

She could hear the smile in his voice. 'Bully for him. If only real life were that simple. Just don't start growing a ponytail.'

'No chance of that,' he said with a laugh.

'Anyway, sorry to interrupt your viewing but can you turn it down for a minute? I can't hear myself speak.' He muted the sound and she filled him in on what Professor Spicer had said. 'If nothing else, the poem seems to be a clue to Rachel Tenison's character, her sexual tastes, etcetera. But there's one thing I don't get. If she and Catherine Watson were killed by the same person, why wasn't something similar found on Watson's body?'

'As far as I'm aware, there wasn't anything, but you should check with Simon. Have you spoken to him recently?'

'I can't get hold of him. He's not answering his phone.'

Tartaglia exhaled loudly. 'Well, I hope he's not getting arse-holed somewhere. He's supposed to be on call.'

'Do you still have the files on the Watson case?'

'Yes. Dave was supposed to pick them up, but he hasn't had a free moment. They're here, if you want to come over and look at them. I'm not going to bed for a while.'

Half an hour later, Donovan was sitting on the sofa in Tartaglia's flat, flicking through the exhibits file from the Watson case. Tartaglia stood by the window, smoking, and watching her. He was still in his work clothes, but had taken off his jacket and tie and rolled up his sleeves. She had given up smoking a few months back and he had opened the window to let out the smoke. Unfortunately, the icy draught just blew it straight back in and she was beginning to feel quite cold, her fingers a little stiff as she turned the pages.

The list of the items removed from Catherine Watson's flat took up more than ten tightly spaced, typewritten pages, and included the contents of her dustbin and dirty laundry basket, as well as items recovered from the area where her body had originally been found, according to Malcolm Broadbent's account. It looked as though forensics had done a thorough job in gathering up anything of possible interest although, as usual, cost constraints had meant that only the items considered to be of immediate interest had been sent off to the lab for forensic testing. Nowhere in the lengthy list was a poem mentioned.

'Maybe the poem's leading us up the garden path, at least as far as Catherine Watson is concerned,' Donovan said, when she had finished reading through. 'Although, don't you think it's a bit of a coincidence that she was an English lecturer? According to Professor Spicer, the poem's pretty obscure.'

'Did Spicer know Watson, by any chance?'

'No. Spicer's at Birkbeck, while Watson taught at UCL. It's not surprising they never came across one another. I counted nearly forty academics in the English faculty at Birkbeck College alone. Some are full-time, some are part-time and, from what I gather, there's quite a bit of turnover. I imagine UCL's the same. How did you get on with Liz Volpe?'

'We turned up something very interesting.'

She noted his use of the word 'we' and was tempted to ask if he found Liz Volpe attractive, just to see what he would say, although she was pretty sure she knew the answer. He was rarely immune to a good-looking woman, although whether he would do anything about it was another matter. Liz Volpe was not a material witness in the case, but she was sure he wouldn't take the risk.

'A photograph of Rachel Tenison is missing from the flat,' he continued. 'Same as with Catherine Watson. And there's another thing. Here, take a look at this.' He passed her a photocopied sheet which lay on the coffee table. It showed the front and back of what appeared to be a postcard. 'This was sent to Rachel only about six weeks ago.'

Donovan struggled to decipher the writing, eventually piecing it together. 'It's pretty obsessive stuff and in a funny way, it echoes the poem. Whoever wrote this is right, though. The picture does look like her,' she said, glancing up at the photograph on the mantelpiece, wondering why Tartaglia had put it there. With her broad forehead, blonde hair and large, round blue eyes, Rachel Tenison looked like an angel, or like the renaissance Madonna on the front of the postcard. It showed how deceptive appearances could be.

'Where did you find it?'

'It was in one of the books Rachel was reading, by her bed. The forensic team must have missed it somehow. The original's gone over to Questioned Documents to see what they can make of it.'

'The writing's distinctive. Was anything similar found in Catherine Watson's flat?'

He shook his head. 'I looked at the report again before you got here. All her correspondence was gone through very thoroughly at the time of the investigation. Nothing else out of the ordinary came to light, certainly nothing like that.'

He stubbed out his cigarette and slammed the window shut, drawing the wooden shutters across to block out the view of the street. 'I've just spoken to Dave,' he said, sitting down in a chair opposite her. 'One of those pay-as-you-go numbers called her home from within a quarter of a mile of her flat on the Friday night. It also comes up in the frequency analysis as one of the top thirty numbers to dial her home phone in the last three months, sometimes very late at night. The phone was bought just over four months ago.'

'Purchaser traceable?'

'No. And Rachel Tenison's home and office were the only numbers dialled, as though the phone was bought just for that purpose.'

'Someone's been very careful.'

He nodded. 'Have you managed to find the woman who was

working in the gallery three months ago? Even if Richard Greville can't remember what day of the week it is, she might know if Rachel was being bothered by someone.'

'She's moved from her previous address. We've been trying to trace her through her national insurance number but it doesn't look as if she's working at the moment. She did some temping after she left the gallery but the agency said she was planning to go off abroad for a few months of travel. Maybe she hasn't come back yet. Nick's trying to trace her parents. Greville seemed to think they live in Surrey.'

'The stuff about the poem's really interesting,' he said, after a moment. 'Where's Simon? We need to talk to him now.'

'He still hasn't called me back.'

He thumped the arm of his chair. 'Damn it. He can't just go AWOL when he feels like it and he should know that. We need his help. He's either in or out, there are no two ways about it.'

She frowned. 'He's going through hell at the moment.'

'And I sympathise, but what are we supposed to do? Wait until he pulls himself together? Two women have been murdered. It's just not good enough.'

She was forced to agree with him but said nothing. Turner was a law unto himself and there was no point leaping to his defence when she had no idea where he was or what he was up to. No doubt he was drowning his sorrows on some lonely barstool somewhere.

'You know, he should never have married Nina.'

'What's that supposed to mean?'

'Like everything, he didn't think it through.'

'She was pregnant, for God's sake.'

'It still doesn't make it the right thing to do.'

'But he loved her.'

'Maybe,' he said, doubtfully. 'But Nina's the sort of woman who needs someone secure, someone grounded, not someone who's, well…' He gave a dismissive wave of his hand.

'How do you know Nina so well?' she asked, suddenly intrigued, but added hastily, 'Don't tell me—'

'No. Nothing like that,' he replied firmly, catching her eye. 'I took her out once, that's all.'

'I didn't know.'

'Why would you? It wasn't anything, really. We just found ourselves at a loose end after work one evening. We were the last ones left in the bar and we got talking. You know how it is. Neither of us wanted to go straight home so we had a Thai from that place at the back of the Bull's Head.'

'And?'

'And nothing. She was perfectly nice, although a bit intense, that's all, and complicated. I felt sorry for her. It was clear she wasn't happy and some stuff about Simon came out. I think they had split up at that point. Maybe she thought getting married would solve everything, but it rarely does.'

'Where was Simon?'

'I don't know. Anyway, we had a perfectly nice dinner, I saw her home and that was that.'

Donovan looked away, amused at how unaware he was of how a woman might read things differently. She wondered if Nina had felt as detached about it all as he did. However, she could well understand his lack of interest. Nina wasn't his type, as she had begun to define it in her head. From what she could tell, he seemed to be attracted to women who were in some way unavailable, as if he thrived on the challenge or the uncertainty. It was the one area where his usual common sense eluded him.

'Try Simon again, will you, Sam,' he said, with a sigh.

Donovan retrieved her phone from her bag on the floor and dialled Turner's number. The phone rang, but again Turner didn't answer and she was diverted to voicemail. She left another message and hung up.

'It is Friday night, you know. Maybe he has a date.'

'In his state? I doubt it.' He frowned and shook his head in frustration. 'He's no good to us like this, you know. I really don't want to be down on him but he should never have been brought in on the case if he wasn't up to it.'

She nodded slowly. 'Why didn't you say something to Steele right at the start?'

He spread his hands. 'What could I have said? I didn't want to land the poor sod in even more hot water. Although if he screws up our investigation, I'll have his head on a plate.'

He leaned back in his chair and yawned, as though he carried the weight of the world on his shoulders. They sat in silence for a moment, then he got to his feet, as though something had just occurred to him, and went over to the collection of filing boxes by the front door. He dug around in one of them until he produced a DVD.

'What's that?'

'It's the crime scene footage from the Watson murder. I've watched it before but I want to see it again, just in case there's anything we've missed. Do you mind? You don't have to stay if you don't want to. It's pretty distressing.'

'No, I think I should see it too.'

He switched on the TV and put the DVD into the player, then sat down heavily on the sofa next to Donovan. He used the remote control to tab through external shots of a busy street, to views of the house, then to where the camera moved inside the building and into the sitting room of the flat. He let the film play.

'The sitting room's at the front,' he said, as the camera panned slowly over the room, sweeping the furnishings and lingering briefly on the details of each object and piece of furniture. Tartaglia pointed at the screen with the remote. 'This is where Broadbent claimed to have found Catherine Watson's body. As you can see, there are no signs of a struggle.'

'So what happened?'

'Several tiny spots of what turned out to be Watson's blood showed up under ultraviolet. They were on the edge of the carpet and floor, with a few specks low down on the wall beside the fireplace. They were invisible to the naked eye, which is presumably why the killer missed them and didn't try to wipe them away.'

'She was assaulted here and not in the bedroom?'

'That's right. Forensics turned up nothing in there.'

'Why were there only a few specks of blood? From what Simon told me, the attack was really vicious.'

'The theory was that the killer used some sort of ground sheet or mat to cover the area before he assaulted her, which would explain why nothing was found in the centre of the room.'

'So he came prepared?'

'It looks like it. He also took whatever he used away with him.'

'Do you think Alan Gifford and Simon did a good job?' she asked, as Tartaglia pressed Play.

'From what I can tell, yes. That was the conclusion of the review team as well. They couldn't find anything new.'

As the camera travelled along the shelves of a tall, over-filled bookcase, Donovan put her hand on Tartaglia's arm. 'Can you pause it again there? I want to look at her books. I was just wondering if maybe she taught nineteenth-century English Lit., if there's some sort of link to Swinburne.'

She squinted, trying to make out what was written along the spines, but the books were too far away.

'We can get the titles digitally enhanced.'

'Simon should be able to tell us what she was teaching,' she said, giving up, after he had stopped and started the footage several times.

'If he sobers up, you mean.'

She made no comment. There was no point arguing or saying anything else in Turner's defence.

Tartaglia started the film again and the camera panned from the bookcase to the fireplace, focussing on the mantelpiece and taking in a few family photographs, a plant, and the pair of white candlesticks covered in bright red wax, which had melted and spilled onto the mantel shelf.

'What happened there?' she asked.

'Don't you remember? She bought some candles earlier that day, along with wine and food. Judging from the amount of wax, it looks as though they were left burning all night.'

'Poor woman,' she said, with a deep sigh, picturing the unsuspecting Watson planning her evening, the wine, the dinner, the candles, getting dressed and letting in her killer. It made her shiver, thinking how close she herself had come to another, very different killer and how easy it was to be deceived by someone.

Turning back towards the window, the camera rested briefly on a couple of cushions on the floor, then swung sharply around and exited the room as though the man behind it had got bored with the view. Vague shots of a dark, narrow hallway were followed by the tiny bathroom, the kitchen, and the bedroom at the back of the flat. The camera zoomed in first on the bed, then on Catherine Watson's bleached, naked body.

'It's weird,' Donovan said, turning away. 'As you say, there are no signs anywhere of a struggle. She wasn't drugged, was she?'

'No. Nor drunk. She hadn't had more than a glass or two of wine.'

'Do you think she went along with being tied up?'

Tartaglia hit Stop and put down the remote. 'She must have done. Which means she trusted whoever it was.'

'It still isn't normal.'

'Maybe he frightened her into it, or threatened her with something if she didn't do what he wanted.'

Donovan shook her head, glancing up again at the photograph of Rachel Tenison on the mantelpiece. 'The simple explanation was that Catherine Watson was into S&M.'

'There's no history of it.'

'Then maybe she had only just acquired the taste for it. She told her sister she was in love with someone. Or maybe she just went along with what he wanted to do because she wanted to please him and she had no idea how far he intended to take it.'

He gazed at her thoughtfully for a moment, then nodded. 'I wonder if you're right. It echoes something Dr Williams said. I'm sure Richard Greville lied to us when he told us he knew nothing about Rachel Tenison's taste for S&M. My feeling is, he was probably responsible for her developing that taste. Unfortunately, it doesn't get us anywhere, and as far as Catherine Watson goes, we'll probably never know the truth. Sometimes I wish I'd never heard of the poor woman.' He got to his feet with a sigh, running his fingers through his hair. 'Do you want a drink?'

She stood up. 'No. I should be heading home.'

'Psychologically, the crimes appear so different,' he said, as though his thoughts were elsewhere. 'Maybe we should just concentrate on Rachel and let Simon, or whoever, worry about the other murder. What does it matter if some journalist threatens to publish a story linking the cases?'

Donovan put on her coat and swung her bag over her shoulder. 'If we can't make any sense out of it, how on earth will he?'

He walked over to the TV, took out the DVD and put it away in the box by the door. 'I spoke to Trevor earlier today,' he said, turning round to face her, rubbing his chin. 'He's always great to bounce stuff off and he talks more sense than anyone. I was hoping he might come up with one of his famous flashes of inspiration.'

'What did he say?' she asked guardedly. Whilst she agreed with him about Trevor Clarke's virtues, privately she thought that, at some point, Tartaglia had to give up his former mentor. Also, it would do Tartaglia no good at all if Carolyn Steele found out that Clarke was still meddling from his sick bed.

'He was fascinated to hear about all of this. He agrees the link's not entirely clear and he thinks Steele's right to keep the two separate for now. But he did have one bloody good idea. He's called in a favour or three and fixed up for me to meet Angela Harper tomorrow.'

'Angela Harper?'

'The psychological profiler on the Watson case.'

'You're joking. A profiler? Next you'll be telling me you're becoming a Muslim.'

His face cracked into a broad grin and he shook his head. 'I'm staying a Catholic for the moment, thanks. But like all Catholics, I'm open-minded.'

'Catholics? Are you kidding? They're the most bigoted—'

He waved her remark away. 'Never mind, Harper's different. She knows her stuff and she's one of the few profilers Trevor's ever had time for.'

'Well, that's certainly saying something. Are you going to tell Carolyn?'

'No, this is strictly off the record. Even if she was prepared to authorise it, and there's no real reason yet, you know how long it takes to go through the proper channels. We could be waiting weeks, if not months.'

She smiled. He could talk himself into anything if he wanted. 'You don't have to justify it to me, you know. Steele's the one you should worry about, if she finds out you've gone behind her back.'

He spread his hands. 'Look, Harper lives around the corner from Trevor and she's prepared to talk to me right away. We're meeting at his house. It's the weekend, after all. In her own private time and mine.' He spoke hurriedly, trying to downplay what he was doing.

She shook her head. There was no persuading Mark, particularly when he had Trevor Clarke behind him. 'What about Simon? You are going to tell him, aren't you?'

Tartgalia gave her a blank look. 'He's not here to tell, is he? Anyway, as you say, I can't risk word getting back to Steele. There's no point in pissing her off unnecessarily and I don't entirely trust Simon to look after my best interests.'

19

At that time of night, the roads were clear and it took Donovan little more than five minutes to drive the short distance from Tartaglia's flat in Shepherd's Bush to where she lived in Hammersmith with her sister Claire. The house was in the middle of a low-built, late-Victorian terrace, the narrow street running down to the Thames, just along from Hammersmith Bridge. Wedged between the river and the busy A4, which carved a thick groove through Hammersmith from east to west, it was a small, characterful pocket of town, with a tidy strip of park along the embankment and a couple of great pubs, offering views of the water and bridge. The only downside was the pollution and permanent drone of traffic from the A4. But it was one of the reasons Claire had originally been able to afford to buy the house and, after living there for nearly five years, Donovan barely noticed the noise any longer.

She walked up the path and let herself in through the front door. The TV blared out from the small front sitting room, where Claire was curled up on the sofa in her pyjamas and a new pink patterned dressing gown, watching the Steven Seagal film, which was still running.

'How's it going?' Claire asked, without looking up, vigorously scraping the bottom of a tub of Ben and Jerry's ice cream and putting the last spoonful into her mouth.

'Still no breakthrough, or even a glimmer of one. How about you?' Donovan took off her coat and dumped it down on a chair with her bag.

'Oh, just the usual. Although a new case came in today which might be quite interesting for a change. We've got a Russian mail order bride charged with murdering her husband, although nobody can produce the body. From what I can see, the CPS are really chancing it.'

Claire worked in a large criminal law firm, defending a whole host of clients charged with anything from parking and speeding fines to the occasional murder.

Loud screams and shouts burst from the TV and her eyes flicked for a moment back to the screen. A group of oriental-looking men were flying through the air performing incredible spin-kicks while Seagal stood in the centre, fending them off single-handedly and barely breaking sweat. He looked as though he had put on a lot of years and weight since Donovan had last seen one of his films, but the ponytail was still the same. She could watch *Kill Bill I* and *II* over and over again, but Seagal left her cold.

After Seagal had made easy mincemeat of everyone onscreen, the film cut to the commercials and Claire swung her long, pale legs off the sofa and stood up.

'You look knackered,' she said, sliding her feet into some fluffy pink slippers and stooping to give Donovan a peck on the cheek. She smelled of some sort of sweet floral soap or bath oil. Even in her bare feet, Claire was nearly a foot taller than Sam, with shoulder-length dark, curly hair which was clipped up on top of her head, the wispy ends around her neck still damp from the bath. Two years older than Donovan, she took after their father in her colouring and physique, while Donovan looked more like their mother's side of the family. Although, as their mother was just over five feet seven, nobody knew why Donovan had stopped growing so soon. Many an annoying bad joke had been made about it, as well as about the lack of any resemblance between the two girls.

'I was just going to make a cup of tea,' Claire said. 'Do you want one?'

'Why not? Though actually, I could do with something stronger.'

Donovan followed Claire down the narrow hall into the kitchen at the back. 'Is there any wine? I couldn't find any yesterday evening.'

Claire shook her head. 'I'll get some tomorrow. I've got to do a big shop and it's my turn to cook tomorrow night, if you're in. Are you working?'

'Yes. But I should be home in time for dinner. It's not as though we've got any suspects on the horizon.'

Apart from a glass of wine, Donovan wasn't sure what she fancied. She went over to the cupboard in the corner and, after rummaging around in the back, eventually pulled out a half-empty tin of drinking chocolate. 'Maybe I'll have this.'

'Not unless you want it with water,' Claire said, filling the kettle and turning it on. 'Afraid there's only a drop of milk left.'

'Damn. Suppose it'll have to be tea.' Donovan shoved the tin back in the cupboard and shut the door with a bang. 'You know, you and I need someone like Mark Tartaglia to keep house for us. I'll bet he never runs out of wine or milk or anything important.'

'You mean he has some poor woman to do it for him.'

'No. He's just like that. You should see his cupboards. He has at least three sorts of vinegar and at least as many different types of olive oil.'

'Well, I wish he lived here,' Claire said, pulling out a couple of boxes of teabags from another cupboard and examining the contents.

'He'd have a heart attack.'

'Herbal or English Breakfast? Although there's only one bag of the Breakfast and you'll have to have camomile if you want herbal.'

'I suppose you want the Breakfast. I'll have camomile, then, if there's really nothing else.'

'Thanks. I can't stand camomile. I think you must have bought it.'

'I think the cooking thing is because of his family,' Donovan said, sure that she hadn't brought the camomile into the house. 'His mother's even published an Italian cookbook.'

'They have some sort of Italian deli up in Edinburgh, I sort of re-member.'

'Yes. Although calling it a deli is a bit like calling the Ritz a motel.'

'Well, that probably explains why he didn't seem to like the spaghetti carbonara I cooked when you brought him round last time.' The kettle pinged. Claire selected a couple of mugs from the collection on the draining rack and made the tea. 'He was far too polite to say so,' she said, passing Donovan her mug, 'but I noticed he left all the bacon bits tucked under his knife and fork.'

'I'm surprised he ate that much. I remember it was like glue.'

Claire shrugged. 'Well, I'm playing safe tomorrow. You're getting Tesco's finest. I haven't got time to be creative.'

'Thank goodness for that.' Donovan removed her teabag and dropped it into the bin.

'I've got a whole load of errands to do tomorrow morning, then I'm having lunch with a girlfriend, so I'll probably get to Tesco's some time late afternoon. Let me know if you want me to get you anything.'

Donovan smiled. 'Errands' usually meant clothes shopping. 'Don't forget the wine.'

'Oh, yes.' Claire took a piece of paper from a pad by the fridge and added it to the already lengthy list. 'If you think of anything else, put it down here. And if you want to ask Mark or anyone else over for supper, give me a call.'

'Jake not around?' Jake was Claire's boyfriend. He was a criminal barrister and they had been together for about six months, although they rarely saw much of each other, both working long hours and often at weekends. Sometimes Donovan wondered what the point was, although her own job was no different in terms of the demands it made on her personal life.

'He's off seeing his parents this weekend, so it's just us.' Claire headed back to the sitting room with her mug of tea. As she opened the door, the strains of the Segal film blasted down the corridor.

Donovan decided to finish her tea in the kitchen before going upstairs to run a bath. The small, scrubbed-pine kitchen table was covered with Claire's files and papers from the case she was working on and Donovan had to move them carefully aside in order to put down her mug. As she picked up Claire's yellow legal pad and pen, about to put it on top of the pile, something tugged at her memory. She sat down and took a sip of the strong, hot tea. It was then that she remembered what it was.

She retrieved her phone from her handbag in the hall and dialled Tartaglia's number.

'I've just thought of something,' she said, when he answered. 'There were some files or books or something on the floor by the window in Catherine Watson's flat.'

'I don't remember.'

'Can you put the disc in again? Tab to the sitting room. In the corner, by the window, next to one of the large cushions. I'm sure there were some papers or something.'

'OK. Give me a minute.'

She listened as he carried the phone into the other room and she heard the Segal film in stereo, until the DVD player kicked in.

'Here we are,' he said, after a moment. 'You're right. It looks as though she was doing some work sitting in the window. I can see a pen, some papers and a couple of books on the floor beside them, although I can't read what they are. We'll have to get it blown up tomorrow.'

'Can you look in the exhibits file and see what's listed?'

'OK.'

He came back to the phone after a moment. 'Here it is: two books... ten sheets of A4 paper. That's all. Clearly nobody was very interested.' She heard the ringing of another phone in the background. 'Hang on a sec,' he said. 'It's Simon. I'll ask him if he remembers what they were.'

She couldn't hear what was said over the noise from the television, but it wasn't long before Tartaglia returned.

'He's pissed,' he said, disgustedly. 'And there's more. It's a bloody good thing he's not here in this room with me now.'

'Why?' she asked, surprised at the force of his tone. 'What did he say?'

'He didn't remember the books at all, just the papers. He said they weren't at all important and he told me we were wasting our time. When I told him we'd be the bloody judge of that and that we wanted to know what they were, this is what that gormless idiot said: "Well, it was just something she was working on," he mimicked Turner's lazy drawl. "Nothing, really. Something about a girl called Dolores."'

20

'I can't believe this meant nothing to you, that you didn't make the link.' Donovan stared at Turner incredulously, waving the sheets of paper in front of his nose, although she felt like shoving them in his face. They were photocopies of the originals recovered from Catherine Watson's flat. The ten pages of typed, double spaced A4 formed part of a chapter Watson had been writing on Swinburne and she quoted freely from the poem *Dolores* as well as discussing its meaning.

As a normal part of the processing of a crime scene, Watson's flat had been more or less stripped and its contents taken away and listed. Those items thought worthy of the expense of forensic analysis had gone off to the lab, eventually ending up in the secure storage facility there for reference if the case ever came to trial. The rest of the items, including the papers, had been sent to store elsewhere, in case they were needed at some later point. It had taken Karen Feeney and Dave Wightman all morning to locate them.

Turner grimaced and shook his head slowly, as though he couldn't believe his stupidity. 'Sam, for Christ's sake, it was over a year ago. As far as we were concerned, they were just a pile of papers Catherine Watson was working on. Why would I make the connection with your poem? Anyway, I thought you told me it was called *Lady of Pain.*'

'No I didn't,' she said angrily, looking him in the eye. She hoped he wasn't going to try and blame her for his mistake.

It was early afternoon on Saturday and the first time Turner had shown his face in the office that day. He stood beside her desk, leaning back against the wall, his large hands stuffed awkwardly in the pockets of his trousers. Everything seemed to wash over him as though his thoughts and priorities were elsewhere. He had bothered to shave for a change and was wearing a clean pale blue shirt, which picked up the colour of his eyes. If she hadn't been feeling so cross with him, she would have told him how nice he looked. Still clutching the pages, she stared at him without speaking, wondering if the stress he was under had dulled his faculties or if he was usually this vague. She couldn't imagine Tartaglia ever forgetting one single detail of a case, however old. But not everyone was like him.

Turner leaned towards her and spread his hands. 'You know, hindsight's a brilliant thing, Sam. But you've got to understand: the papers meant nothing at all in terms of the case at the time. Nothing at all. They belonged to Watson, some stuff she was working on. They had nothing to do with her killer.'

She put the papers down on the desk. Grudgingly, she had to admit that he had a point, although she wasn't sure that Tartaglia would see it that way. There was no reason for Turner or Gifford to have given the papers and books on Watson's floor a second thought. It wouldn't matter to either of them that Catherine Watson's area of speciality was nineteenth-century English literature, nor would the verses from the poem have seemed at all significant.

Turner leaned over and picked up the sheets. 'So, what have we got here?' He started to go slowly through them, wetting the tip of his thumb to help separate the pages. 'Some sort of an essay, right?'

'No. It's chapter six of what looks to me like an academic paper or book. The title, "The Decadents: A Reappraisal," is the header.'

'You sure this isn't someone's essay?'

'It's far too well written, plus it's far too long. Assuming the notes and corrections are in her writing, I'd say it's her own work she was editing.'

'We can easily match the handwriting,' he said, still leafing through.

'Looks like she didn't finish what she was doing. The corrections stop halfway through.'

'Perhaps she was interrupted or just put it down for some reason and didn't have time to go back to it.'

He rested the papers lightly on his thigh and looked at her. 'Maybe she gets a phone call, or maybe she was even doing it when the killer arrived.'

'I can't imagine sitting down to do this sort of thing if I was waiting for a hot date.'

He smiled. 'I suppose you'd be making yourself pretty?'

'Or doing the cooking,' she said sternly, annoyed that he was trying to make light of things. 'I certainly wouldn't be editing my book.'

'Well, you're not an English teacher. And Catherine Watson wasn't as pretty as you.'

'Lecturer,' she corrected him, refusing to look him in the eye. She wasn't usually pedantic but she didn't want him to think he could win her over that easily.

'Whatever. To be honest, we don't know who she was expecting that night. The candles and all the stuff she bought made us think she had a date, but we might have been wrong. Maybe she just had a mate dropping by.'

'It doesn't matter. The point is, the papers were there in the room when she was murdered and the killer must have seen them.'

He nodded slowly. 'You know two pages are missing in the middle, don't you?'

'What? Let me see.'

He passed her the papers and she flicked through them.

'Pages sixty-three and sixty-four, you'll find.'

'You're right,' she said, annoyed at not having spotted it. She sat back in her chair and closed her eyes for a moment, trying to picture the scene. 'There were two piles of paper on the floor, I seem to remember.

Maybe she put the stuff down in separate piles when she was interrupted so she could pick up later where she left off. I'll have to get some
close-up stills done from the crime scene tape.'

Turner shrugged as if it didn't matter. 'You're sending them all
off for analysis?'

'Yes. It's being rushed through.'

'That'll cost a pretty penny. What do you expect to find?'

'A fingerprint or DNA, if we're lucky.'

'You really think the killer touched them?'

'How else would he have seen the poem? It's a few pages in from
the beginning of the chapter.'

He nodded. 'Good point. Guess that's the advantage of having a
fresh pair of eyes.'

And a clear, sober mind, she wanted to say, but stopped herself.
'So, what have you been doing today, other than having a lie-in?'

Her tone came out more sharply than she had intended but he
gave her a forgiving smile.

He rubbed his hands together. 'Well, I've managed to track down
Malcolm Broadbent, for starters. If you remember, he was our number one suspect. But it looks like we can rule him out, at least for the
Holland Park murder. If his alibi stacks up, he was away visiting his
mum in Hull.'

'Which leaves the other suspect...what's his name?'

'Yes, Mike Jennings. He's moved. At the moment I haven't been
able to track him down. But I'm on the case, Sam.' He paused, gazing
at her intently with his strange, pale eyes. 'Don't worry. I know what
you think but I'm getting myself sorted. Really I am. I'm not going to
fuck things up and let you down. Honest.'

She was tempted to say that he had already done that, but she
stopped herself. He was smiling at her in a sheepish sort of way and he
reminded her of a shaggy golden retriever, thumping its tail on the car-

pet, desperate to please. More than anything, she sensed his loneliness and, in spite of her irritation, she couldn't help but feel sorry for him.

She was saved the embarrassment of finding a suitable reply by the ringing of her mobile. Claire was at the other end, in Tesco's, asking what to buy for supper.

'I can't make up my mind,' Claire said, shouting over the general background noise. 'Do you fancy lasagne or shepherd's pie or macaroni cheese?'

'Either lasagne or macaroni cheese. We had the shepherd's pie when I last cooked and it wasn't that great.'

'I'll be going,' Turner said in the background, getting to his feet.

Donovan heard Claire's voice in her ear. 'Is that Mark? Do you want to ask him along?'

'No, it's not. Actually, hang on a sec. Hey, Simon,' she called after Turner, who was on his way out the door. 'Got any plans for tonight?'

He looked round. 'Only a date with Nicole Kidman. Nothing that won't keep.'

'Well, come over and have a bite to eat at our house. My sister Claire's cooking, or rather reheating something from Tesco's. I can't promise the Domestic Goddess but it should be edible.'

'That would be nice, thanks.' He hesitated. 'If you're sure...'

'Absolutely.'

She heard Claire's voice: 'Who's that? Who's Simon? Are you two being rude about my cooking?'

'Can I bring anything?' Turner muttered.

'Just yourself and some whisky, if that's what you fancy drinking.'

'Sam, are you listening to me?' Claire shouted. 'Who's that you're with?'

'Tell you later and there'll be one extra for dinner. Don't forget to get some wine.'

Liz sipped her mug of tea and gazed out of the kitchen window at the ominous dark grey sky. She had been cooped up inside for most of the day, sorting through various boxes of things that she had stored in the spare room of her brother's flat. She had been looking for her photo albums, but God only knew where they had got to—probably still at her mother's, or at least she hoped so. Instead, she had turned up a collection of old letters and postcards, an address book, and a diary from her first year at university which she had forgotten about. Leafing through it, she was carried straight back to that time, the sparse one-line entries reminding her, like everything else, of Rachel.

She had found a suitcase of old clothing, mainly jumpers and a couple of T-shirts going back at least a decade or more. Most of it was fit only for binning, as the moths had had a field day. But one particular dress caught her eye. It was vintage 1940s, black silk patterned with small pink and red flowers. The edges were fraying, the hem was coming down and there were a couple of small holes along one of the seams, but it was still pretty and she remembered buying it for only a few pounds in the Portobello Market almost twenty years before. Jeans and T-shirts had been her daily uniform at that age and it was the only dress she had been happy to wear; looking like a stick insect, nothing suited her, as far as she was concerned.

She stood up and took it over to the mirror on the wall, holding it up against herself, wondering if she could still fit into it. But it looked incredibly short, the waist too high; she must have grown since the last time she had worn it. She folded it carefully and put it back in the suitcase. She would worry about what to do with it later. Not knowing why she had hung onto it for so long, she was struck by how much everything had changed since those days.

Sitting on the floor all that time had made her feel stiff. She needed to get out, stretch her body and feel fresh air in her lungs. Running was something she had done since her teens and she had often gone with Rachel. Every Friday, they would take their bikes to Holland Park after school, dump them at the adventure playground and race each other on foot down the tracks until, hearts bursting, they would collect their bikes and go home, always stopping in a café on the way for a milky coffee, a Mars bar and a chat. It became a weekly ritual until they both went off to university. The café had long since gone out of business and been replaced by something more glitzy and up-market, as suited the area which, in twenty years, had come up a very long way. At least the park remained more or less the same.

She hadn't been out running once since coming back to London. The weather had been so foul, with all the snow and rain, that she simply hadn't felt like it. But as she gazed out of the window, watching a woman jog slowly around the green rectangle of lawn in the communal gardens below, she decided it was time. She would go to Holland Park. Although wary after what had happened, she wanted to visit the place where Rachel had died. Somehow, she hoped it might help her find some peace. Maybe it would also bring her closer to Rachel again.

She went into her bedroom and changed into her tracksuit bottoms, T-shirt and fleece. She slipped on her running shoes, tied her hair back and picked up her iPod. It was already late and the park would soon be closing. She took the keys to her brother's car and drove the short distance up the hill to the park, leaving the car near the entrance. The notice board by the gates said that the park would close at four-thirty. She still had about twenty minutes to go, which should be ample.

Apart from a group of dog walkers gathered together on the main broad walk, chatting while their charges ran riot on the lawn below, the park was surprisingly empty for a Saturday. The sloping, muddy lawns and playing fields appeared peaceful and a light mist shrouded the dips and hollows of the grass, gathering in hazy drifts under the canopy of trees. Liz stopped by the tall, shiny black iron railings and gazed for a moment, trying to imagine how it all would have appeared the morning Rachel had died. Everything would have been white, covered by a thick blanket of snow. In the fading afternoon light, she found it hard to picture.

She walked for a few minutes, warming up, then started to jog slowly along the path beneath the south terrace, U2's 'With or Without You' pounding over her headphones. The song reminded her of university, hours spent with Rachel listening to music in her room, talking until late at night and drinking endless cups of tea and coffee.

The ruins of Holland House stood proud against the darkening sky. As she turned to look at the empty windows, wondering if, on that morning, Rachel had come this way, a sense of sadness overwhelmed her. Guilt was a terrible, insidious thing. It could eat you up. Would she ever get over it? Fighting back the tears, she pushed herself faster, past the orangery and up through the formal gardens towards the woodland area. She felt the thud of her feet on stone, then dirt and gravel, but she heard nothing over the music.

The light dimmed as she ran into the woods and it took a moment for her eyes to grow accustomed to the gloom. Dense evergreen shrubbery bordered the path on either side and the bare branches of the trees arched above her like fingers against the dark sky. She ran down the hill, following the track as it bent sharply to the left. After a minute or so, it opened up into a wide clearing, where several other paths met. A strand of blue and white police tape fluttered in the wind, one end tied to a tree. She pulled up, paused the music and removed the earphones. She wanted to hear the real sounds of the place. Tartaglia had been vague about where, exactly, Rachel's body had been found, but it had to be somewhere close by. A high picket fence ran along the track on either side, separating it from the woodland area beyond. She assumed its purpose was to stop the public trampling over the ground and disturbing the flora and fauna, although the area inside was so dark and overgrown, she couldn't imagine any human wanting to set foot in there.

She felt in the pocket of her fleece and pulled out the pack of cigarettes and lighter that Tartaglia had left behind in her flat the other evening. She had no intention of taking up smoking again but she lit one anyway, hoping it would calm her nerves. A few benches dotted the clearing. Choosing one that was sheltered by an arbour of thick holly branches, she sat down. The air was cold and damp. As she exhaled, the smoke drifted away in front of her like a ghost. Something rustled close by in the undergrowth, a bird perhaps, rooting around amongst the dry leaves on the other side of the enclosure. Scanning the area, she saw another ribbon of police tape on the other side of the fence a little way along the path in the woodland area. She was about to get up and look when there was an eruption of flapping and squawking from a group of rooks high above in one of the trees, as though they had been disturbed by something.

Peering through the branches, she saw someone jogging along one of the tracks towards her. The light was so poor, it took her a second or two to tell that it was a man. He was nearly in the clearing when he slowed to a walk and stopped. He looked tall and well built and was wearing a dark anorak, the hood pulled up over his head so that she could only make out a pale oval of face. He was carrying something bulky in his hand and walked up and down the fence for a moment, as if searching. The rooks stirred again up in the trees and he looked quickly up and down the path, as though he was checking to see if anyone was coming. His movements were furtive and she kept very still, screened by the branches of the holly tree, hoping he hadn't seen her. With a final glance in both directions, he stepped through what looked like a hole in the fence, into the enclosure beyond, and disappeared behind a thicket of evergreen.

People used the park every day and there could be a perfectly innocent explanation. Maybe he had some sort of secret assignation,
although she hadn't seen anyone else in that part of the woods. But his
behaviour was still odd and she cursed herself for having left her
phone in the car. She reached down and stubbed out her cigarette on
the side of the bench and waited. After no more than a couple of minutes, the man re-emerged from the bushes. He was empty-handed as
he jumped back through the hole in the fence and stood for a moment
on the footpath staring into the enclosure, exhaling a cloud of steam.
He wiped his forehead and mouth with the back of his hand, as
though satisfied with whatever he had done, then took off at speed
the way he had come.

As soon as he was out of sight, she got to her feet, curious to know
what he had been doing. She felt cold from sitting still for so long and
stamped her feet and stretched her arms and legs until the blood was
flowing again. She walked over to the hole in the fence and, after a moment's hesitation, stepped through the gap into the woodland area.
The ground was uneven and strewn with bracken and fallen branches.
She pushed her way through the bushes and came to a small clearing,
surrounded by tall holly trees. Something white lay in the middle of
the rough grass. She went over to it and saw that it was a bunch of
roses still in their paper wrapping. The buds were tightly furled and
they were a deep, dusky red.

21

Just after four o'clock in the afternoon, Tartaglia pressed the bell of Trevor Clarke's modern, semi-detached house in Wandsworth. Sally-Anne, Clarke's fiancée, opened the door, dressed in tight jeans, high heels and a blue tracksuit top, her long blonde hair tied back in a ponytail. She stood on tiptoe to kiss him, then let him pass. Clarke was sitting just behind her in a shiny, metallic red wheelchair.

'Great to see you, mate,' Clarke said, gliding forwards. Grinning, he clasped Tartaglia's hand, squeezing hard.

'You're looking pretty good, Trevor,' Tartaglia replied, looking him up and down. The last time he had been there, Clarke had been bedridden and painfully gaunt and pale. Although he was still thin compared to before the accident, he had filled out a little and the colour had finally returned to his long, craggy face. 'The macrobiotic diet seems to be working and I see you've got rid of that seventies moustache.'

Clarke shrugged. 'Sally-Anne insisted.'

'It tickled,' Sally-Anne said, with a giggle. 'Makes him look younger, don't you think?'

'It's a big improvement. He doesn't look like Tom Selleck anymore.'

'That's nice,' Clarke growled. 'What do you think of the chair? Lovely bit of kit, eh?'

Tartaglia studied it carefully. "Lovely" wasn't the word he would have chosen, but he assumed it did the job. 'It looks like an office chair on a box, on wheels.'

'That's the way they design them these days.'

Tartaglia shook his head. '*Design*? At least it's safer than a motor-bike.'

Clarke grinned again. 'It's nearly as fast and look, it's got all mod cons. Watch this.' At the touch of the joystick, the chair performed a variety of jerky manoeuvres. 'All I need now is satnav and I'll be back on the road and round to sort you lot out.'

'He's just like a child with a new toy,' Sally-Anne said.

'Well, it cost a bloody arm and a leg,' Clarke said, executing a pirouette. 'Might as well have some fun. Thought I'd better splash out and get the top of the range. They seem to think I might be in it for a while.'

'Stop showing off, Trevor, and let Mark pass, will you? You don't want to keep Dr Harper waiting.'

'Sorry. I was getting carried away. Let's get down to business.'

He spun around and led the way along the corridor and down a small ramp into the kitchen. Dr Angela Harper was sitting at the kitchen table, sipping something from a large mug.

'It's good of you to see me,' Tartaglia said, as she stood up and shook his hand with a cool, firm grip.

'Don't mention it. I'd do anything for Trevor here, and I'm naturally very interested to know of any developments in the Watson case.'

Her voice was pleasant and low, with a trace of a northern accent. She was wearing a charcoal grey trouser suit and was taller than he remembered. Her prematurely silver hair was cut into a neat bob, emphasising her broad, strong-boned face, and she wore no make-up apart from a slick of browny-pink lipstick.

'Let me take your things, Mark,' Sally-Anne said. 'You must be soaked. Would you like coffee or tea?

'No, I'm fine, thanks,' Tartaglia said, handing her his wet jacket and helmet.

'It's gone five,' Clarke said, zooming over to the table where he took his place at the head. 'I'm sure Mark would like something stronger.'

'Really, I'm fine Trevor. I've got to go back to the office after this.'

Tartaglia sat down opposite Angela Harper. Rain was streaming down the window behind her, but through the misted glass he could just make out the back garden with its new, neat paving and square of lawn. A couple of children's bikes stood propped against the side wall next to a large covered barbeque, and it struck him how much life had changed for Clarke since Sally-Anne had appeared on the scene nine months before.

'If you're sure I can't get you anything, I'll leave you all to it,' Sally-Anne said, bringing a tall glass of iced water over to Clarke. 'I've got some chores to do upstairs and I want to make sure the boys keep quiet while you're working.'

As she spoke, small footsteps thundered across the ceiling above. The boys were her two sons from her previous marriage, who were now living with her and Clarke.

'She gets queasy if I start talking about anything to do with work,' Clarke said apologetically, as she raced out of the room. 'Doesn't like the mention of death, let alone the gory details.' He spread his hands out flat on the table. 'Anyway, Mark, this is your show. I'll try and keep out of it. I've given Angela the gist of the Holland Park murder but you ought to run through it, in case I left something out.'

Tartaglia outlined where they had got to in the case, adding the latest piece of news about the papers and poem found in Catherine Watson's flat. Sipping her drink, Harper took in the information without speaking. It was impossible to gauge her reaction. When he had finished, she put down her mug and folded her hands neatly in front of her.

'I can see why you're puzzled. I must say, I am too.'

'The MOs are very different,' Tartaglia said. 'The poem and the way the bodies were both positioned gives us a direct link but I'm struggling to see how the same person could have committed both crimes.'

Harper nodded slowly. 'It's not immediately obvious, I agree, although the two murders do have a couple of things in common. Let's start with the Catherine Watson case, which I'm more familiar with. As you know from the files, it seems very likely that Catherine Watson knew her killer and was specifically targeted. From the evidence we have, we also know that the killer was highly organised. The planning of the assault, down to the details of the equipment he brought with him—his rape kit, if you like—would have been very important to him, probably as much as the assault itself. It's all about ritual. This is first and foremost a sexually motivated crime. I also think it mattered to him very much that she was conscious throughout the ordeal. I imagine him talking to her, describing what he's going to do. He was turned on as much by the anticipation of what was to come, of her being aware and by her reactions and fear, as by the sex itself.'

'So he's a sadistic bastard as well as a pervert?' Clarke said, with a grimace.

Harper nodded. 'The crime is certainly sadistic. I'm sure he tortured her mentally and he certainly wounded her far more than he needed to. But more than anything, it's about control and empowerment, based on the ritual humiliation and subjugation of the victim while she's still alive. As I said, her being alive and responding to him would have been very important. But unlike many sexual killers, he's not a necrophiliac. Death itself is not a turn-on.'

'Do you think it's important that Catherine Watson was a teacher?' Tartaglia asked, thinking also of Rachel Tenison as he spoke.

She smiled. 'He may have a specific grudge against teachers, but I think it's more about her role as a woman in a position of authority. Somewhere in his past he has been made to feel powerless or insignificant by a woman, or a series of women, and what he did to Catherine Watson was about reasserting himself. He controls life and he con-

trols death. Although he's essentially a rapist, not a killer and the difference is important in terms of the profile.'

Clarke bit his lip and shook his head in disbelief.

'You don't agree, Trevor?' Tartaglia asked.

'He put the poor woman through hell and she ended up dead. I
find it difficult to believe he hadn't meant to kill her.'

Harper nodded. 'I'll come on to that in a minute. The ordeal lasted
several hours, but what's interesting is that in all that time, he shows
no rage or frenzy or loss of control. He even feels secure and calm
enough afterwards to tidy up and leave the flat as though nothing's
ever happened. That's unusual and it tells us a lot about him.'

'What about the way the body was laid out?' Tartaglia asked,
thinking again of Rachel, seeing the image that was burned on his
mind of her body tied up in the snow.

'That's important too. Some sexual predators discard their victims like rubbish when they're done, but this one sees his as a trophy,
rather like a big-game hunter. He displays her in a specific way for
her to be found. He's sending a message.'

'She was hog-tied and kneeling down like she was praying,' Clarke
said, unable to contain himself. 'What sort of message is that? Is he
having a joke? Is he sticking his tongue out at us?'

'In a way, or at every woman who's made him feel small in the
past. It's the final humiliation and it's a warning. If he'd put an apple
in her mouth, I wouldn't have been at all surprised. He's saying that
she is his thing, his chattel; he can do with her what he wants.'

'He's trying to depersonalise her?' Tartaglia asked, still thinking
of Rachel Tenison and how her face was hidden.

'Yes. Although, going back to what I said before, by this point it
didn't matter to him that she was alive or dead. Death isn't the issue
here.'

'Poor woman,' Clarke muttered, and took a gulp of water.

'So you accept Malcolm Broadbent's account of how he found Catherine Watson's body?' Tartaglia asked, remembering Broadbent's statement and what Turner had said about it.

'I thought you told me Broadbent was a liar,' Clarke said to Tartaglia.

'That was Simon Turner's view.'

'Well *I* believed Broadbent,' Harper said, firmly. 'At least, I believed what he said about finding the body. He may have lied about other things, but you must remember, he was put under a lot of pressure during the interrogation. I think he would have lied about the colour of his own eyes, he was so confused and upset. In my view, his account of his behaviour at the crime-scene was psychologically consistent with his personality type.'

'What, you mean the way he fucked it up?' Clarke asked.

'I don't believe he had any idea of what he was doing, Trevor. He comes downstairs and finds the door to the ground floor flat open. He knocks, and when he gets no response he goes in and gets the shock of his life. A woman he respects and cares about, some might say even loves, is bound and gagged, kneeling stark naked on the floor for all to see. He hears her moan—'

'For Chrissake, she was dead,' Clarke protested.

'Could have been gas, Trevor,' Tartaglia said. 'The first time a body did that to me in the morgue, I nearly jumped out of my skin. Broadbent's just a layman. He wouldn't know what it was.'

Clarke nodded grudgingly. 'OK. Gas, imagination, whatever. Go on, Angela. I won't interrupt again.'

'So, Broadbent cuts off the bindings and carries her into her bedroom, lays her out on the bed and covers her with a blanket. He's screaming and shouting and calling out for help as he tries to revive her. It all makes perfect sense to me. From everything we know about him, he's a highly disorganised personality, with a below-average IQ.

He had some pretty odd habits, I grant you, but I don't think he was capable of carrying out such a methodical and controlled attack and I told DCI Gifford that at the time.'

'That didn't come out in the closing report,' Tartaglia said.

Clarke waved his hand dismissively. 'Probably because it was overseen or written by Alan Gifford.'

'You know, if they'd treated Broadbent as a witness instead of a suspect, he might have remembered something useful,' Harper said, with feeling.

'Are you saying Gifford completely disregarded your profile and advice?' Tartaglia asked, surprised.

Harper raised her eyebrows and smiled, as though it wasn't the first time it had happened. 'This is off the record.'

Tartaglia turned to Clarke. 'You knew Gifford, Trevor. What's your view?'

Clarke shrugged. 'Alan was a hard man to go against. He was a good copper, mind, but he could be blinkered. Once he'd made up his mind about something, that was that.'

'That's sort of what Simon Turner said, reading between the lines,' Tartaglia added. 'I wish he'd been more up front about it.'

'No one wants to speak ill of the dead, do they?' Clarke replied. 'Certainly not a former boss, who was a decent bloke in most respects. I'm sure in spite of Alan's blinkers, the team did a good a job.'

'As I said, I made my views known to Alan Gifford when Broadbent was arrested,' Harper said flatly, as though she didn't agree. 'I watched all of the interviews with Broadbent on videolink and nothing I saw changed my mind. He didn't match the profile and I stand by that today.'

'If he had been treated more gently, what do you think they might have got out of him?' Tartaglia asked.

'Well,' she replied, with a little nod of her head, 'Broadbent was very fond of Watson, almost to the point of obsession, I'll admit. He followed her around quite a lot when she went out, and took photos with a telephoto lens.'

'He did that with other women as well.'

'Yes. It was all pretty harmless, but he was there on the spot over several months keeping an eye on Watson. I just wonder, if Gifford and his team had taken a different line with him, whether Broadbent might have remembered something useful, that's all. Maybe he saw something when he was watching her.'

'If he did, why didn't he say so at the time?'

'Because it might not have meant anything to him and the way they interviewed him was unnecessarily aggressive and confrontational. Again, my advice was ignored. As I said, Broadbent wasn't the sharpest tool in the box and he was already in a highly emotional state because of what had happened. They should have handled him differently, much more sympathetically, if they wanted to get anything out of him.'

Tartaglia made a mental note to speak to Turner as soon as the meeting was over. It was the most interesting thing he had heard in a while and well worth pursuing. Broadbent as witness rather than suspect. They would re-interview him again as a priority, whether Turner liked it or not. 'Thanks. We'll definitely follow it up. You may like to know that Broadbent has an alibi for Rachel Tenison's murder.'

She smiled. 'I'm glad. You should tell him so. If he knows he's in the clear, you might get something out of him.'

'What about the other suspect, Michael Jennings? What was your opinion of him?'

'Oh, from what I saw of him, he was a much better fit. He's the right age group too, whereas Broadbent was too old to be starting this sort of thing up from scratch.'

'Any previous?' Clarke asked, quietly.

'No,' Tartaglia replied. 'Jennings was clean. What did Gifford think of Jennings?'

Harper sighed. 'If you want the truth, he was so set on Broadbent being the killer, I don't think he looked at Jennings as hard as he should have.'

'But they searched his flat thoroughly, twice, according to the report.'

She shrugged. 'All I can say is I was very surprised that they couldn't turn up anything on Michael Jennings. A photograph of Catherine Watson was missing, which I'm sure the killer took as a souvenir.'

'A photograph was also missing from Rachel Tenison's flat. The problem is that neither Broadbent nor Jennings come up anywhere in Rachel's life. We've shown pictures of both of them to all of her nearest and dearest but nobody recognised either of them.'

Tartaglia leaned back in his chair and glanced out of the window at the dark sky. Even though what Harper had said made good sense, there were no easy answers. He still felt miles away from any clear understanding of how the two crimes could be linked.

'Assuming the same person committed both murders,' he said, looking back at Harper. 'Don't you think it's odd there's been a gap?'

'A year's not a very long time, particularly if he's new to this sort of thing. As you know, this sort of crime's rarely a one-off, but if he's able to satisfy his urges somehow, either through his memories of the experience or in some other way, that might be enough. He doesn't actually need to kill to get what he wants.'

He turned to Clarke, who was drumming his fingers lightly on the table. 'Any thoughts, Trevor?'

'Maybe the killer's inside, or gone abroad. That's usually where the buggers are when they go off the radar screen.'

'We're trying to trace Jennings at the moment, but we're not having much luck,' Tartaglia replied, deciding that Turner needed one hell of a kick up the arse. 'Going back to the Holland Park murder, Rachel Tenison was laid out in exactly the same position as Catherine Watson.'

'Again, the murderer's making a statement,' Harper said.

'As with the poem in her mouth?'

'Yes. It's about the type of woman she was and it's also about him. He identifies with the obsessed lover, the woman's victim. Maybe he also likes linking her with his memories of Watson.'

'You said the two murders had a few things in common.'

'Superficially, yes. You have the way the bodies were displayed, which we've discussed. Both women knew their killer, a photograph of each woman was taken from where they lived and, on a deeper level, the victim profile is similar. They were roughly the same age, Rachel Tenison was thirty-five and Catherine Watson only three years older, and they were both well-educated, intelligent and successful women in their own fields. They would have been seen as powerful and authoritative and intimidating by this type of man.'

'Is this making any sense to you, Trevor?' Tartaglia asked, looking at Clarke.

Clarke shrugged. 'Maybe you have a copycat killer. Have you thought of that?'

'But why? It's not as if we're looking at a series here.'

'There's another explanation,' Harper said. 'If the same man's responsible for the Watson murder and for the Holland Park murder, it's possible he hadn't intended to kill Rachel Tenison. Maybe it was a sexual encounter that went wrong.'

Clarke shook his head, as though he didn't see it either.

'Going back to Catherine Watson, her killer probably enjoys relatively normal sexual relations with women,' Harper continued. 'They probably have no inkling of his fantasies, no idea what he's capable of.'

'You've got to be joking,' Clarke said, slapping his hand hard on the table. 'How the hell would his wife or girlfriend not know she was sleeping with a sadistic pervert? Surely a woman would know?' He looked meaningfully at Harper.

Harper laughed. 'Trevor, if I had a pound for every time someone reacted like you, I'd be rich. A lot of people keep their real sexual pro-clivities hidden away. At the extreme end, I can refer you to a number of cases where the partner of a violent rapist or sexual killer had no idea of what actually turned him on.'

Clarke waved Harper away with his hand. 'Yeah, yeah. I'll take your word for it.'

'It's all about fantasy. With some women he can play out his fan-tasies and let himself go, with others he doesn't dare to or doesn't want to. This is a man who keeps his life carefully compartmentalised.'

Tartaglia nodded; Harper's words were a strange echo of what Dr Williams had said about Rachel Tenison: 'On the surface, there's noth-ing to hint at what is locked away beneath.' It was all tying in, but what it meant, he still couldn't fathom. 'It's weird,' he said. 'You could almost be describing the Holland Park victim.'

'It really isn't uncommon,' Harper added. 'It's just a matter of de-gree. Like a lot of men with fantasies they'd rather not bring home, the killer may be using prostitutes to keep himself in check.'

'There's nowt queerer than folk, as my nan used to say,' Clarke replied, attempting a north-country accent and still looking unconvinced.

'I thought your family were all from the Elephant and Castle,' Tartaglia said.

'You don't know everything about me, Mark. Still some secrets to find out, you'll be pleased to hear.'

Tartaglia smiled and looked back at Harper. 'What I don't under-stand is why someone would suddenly do what he did to Watson. Out of the blue, with no apparent build-up to it.'

'We don't know how long the killer had the fantasies playing in his mind, how long he'd been thinking about and planning to do something like this, maybe never actually imagining he'd get the chance or go through with it. The trigger could have been something simple, maybe something that Watson herself said or something else going on in his life. Jennings's girlfriend dumped him only a few weeks before Watson's murder. Even though Jennings denied it, friends of his said he was very angry about it. Also, whoever it was may not have intended to kill Watson.'

'Might she have gone along with some of it?' Tartaglia asked, thinking back to Donovan's theory and the possibility of Watson having been in love with someone.

'Yes. Maybe one thing led to another and things got out of control.'

'But you said the killer had everything planned,' Clarke said. 'You said he came prepared.'

'Yes. But being prepared is one thing. Actually doing something is another.'

Clarke nodded slowly and took a sip of water.

'Be prepared. Now you have me imagining the Boy Scouts,' Tartaglia said.

'You're not far wrong, actually,' Harper replied. 'Rather like someone planning an expedition, he may have made a number of dry runs, tested the kit to make sure it worked, packed and unpacked it until he gets it just right. What he wears would also be important to him and he may even carry the kit around with him wherever he goes. Just having it with him, knowing it's there, will excite him and make him feel powerful. He will also dress the part in some way.'

'You're talking about role-playing,' Tartaglia said, thinking of the masks and the other contents of the trunk, the so-called dressing-up box, in Rachel Tenison's bedroom and the way Williams had described her ritual of getting dressed to go out. He wondered what her ritual in the bedroom had been, if she had different roles or fantasies that she played out according to her mood or the man she was with.

'Role-playing, definitely. Going back to the profile, one thing I found interesting and out of character was that he strangled Watson with a pair of her own tights. If he'd come meaning to kill her, he would have brought some sort of ligature with him. It suggests to me that events took him by surprise, perhaps went further than he had intended, and he was forced to improvise. It's why I'm not absolutely certain he intended to kill her.'

'What about Rachel Tenison's murder, then? You said it might have been a sexual encounter that went wrong.'

'She liked being tied up, she liked it rough,' Clarke said, before Harper had a chance to reply. 'They make the perfect couple, don't they?'

'That may very well have been what brought them together in the first place,' Harper said. 'With her, he can indulge his fantasies and he doesn't need to kill her—although what he does is all about him. I wonder if he'd actually want someone so totally into their own, well-developed fantasy world.'

'But he does kill her,' Tartaglia insisted, still feeling as though they were trying to fit a round plug into a square hole.

'Maybe, for some reason, he was pushed to it. Usually he manages to hold back his more sadistic urges, or at least contain them well enough that nobody reports him. Maybe he meets the Holland Park victim and they go back to her flat for sex. Maybe she does something to anger him or make him feel small. He's a man who likes to be in control, remember, he wants to call the shots. Perhaps she criticises him in some way, or makes him go before he's ready, or something like that. Or maybe he revealed something to her about himself that he didn't want anyone to know.'

'So, the murder was an afterthought,' Tartaglia said, thinking back to the crime-scene and all the inconsistencies that still failed to add up. What still puzzled him was the fact that the body had been moved and repositioned after death.

'Maybe.'

'That's a heck of a lot of maybes,' Clarke said, folding his arms and shaking his head again as though he didn't believe a word of it. 'I could paper the wall with them.'

'Why so sceptical?' Tartaglia asked, taking comfort from the fact that Clarke, too, remained unconvinced.

'These ruddy psychologists. They can spin gold out of the air. And by that I mean fool's gold.'

Harper smiled. 'Now you're in danger of sounding like Alan Gifford.'

Clarke grunted. 'I'm not anything like him and you know it. Seriously, Angela. A lot of what you've said makes sense, but from where I'm sitting they still look like two totally different crimes.'

Harper smiled. 'I don't disagree, Trevor. But Mark asked how the same person could be capable of both crimes. It's the only way I can make it stack up from a psychological point of view.'

'And it's not *entirely* implausible,' Tartaglia said, feeling suddenly drained by the whole discussion. 'He's killed once before. It would make sense to try and dress the second murder up like the first. He gets the idea of the poem from Catherine Watson's papers. The fact that he decides to use it shows he's arrogant. And speaking of arrogance and attention-seeking behaviour, I wonder if he had anything to do with the press tip-off.'

'Good point,' Clarke said. 'You'd better get onto Jason Mortimer right away.'

Tartaglia felt his phone vibrate in his breast pocket. Seeing Donovan's name on the caller ID, he made his excuses to Harper and

Clarke and got up from the table.

'I'm still at Trevor's,' he said, walking over to the window.

'Sorry to disturb,' she said, 'but I've just picked up a call from Liz Volpe. She's trying to reach you. Apparently, she was out running in Holland Park this afternoon and saw something very odd.' He listened as she explained what had happened. The place described sounded like the exact spot where they had found Rachel Tenison's body.

'Have you called forensics?'

'A team are on their way over to the park right now. Karen's going to collect Liz and take her down there so that she can show them where she saw the man.'

'Get Karen to take a statement and see if you can arrange for Liz to do an e-fit afterwards, while it's still fresh in her mind. How did she sound?'

'Pretty shaken. She said she wanted to see you.'

He looked at his watch. 'We're almost done here, then I was planning on heading back to the office. Tell her that I'll be over later at some point. First, I need to talk to Simon Turner.'

22

By the time Tartaglia got back to the office in Barnes, it was nearly seven in the evening and pitch black outside. The rain had stopped but the wind had picked up and the air felt cold and damp.

He parked his motorbike in a sheltered corner of the car park at the rear and walked over to the back door, the only working entrance to the building. An overweight, middle-aged man and a pretty young woman from one of the other offices stood huddled together in their overcoats just outside, neither speaking, each pulling hard on a cigarette. Sodden butts littered the wet ground where they stood, in spite of a notice and a bin placed beside the exit. It was a horrific vision of what was to come once the smoking ban came into force in the summer. Much as Tartaglia often craved a cigarette, he had managed to wean himself down to no more than five or six a day, usually enjoyed in the peace of his own home or someone else's, with a morning cup of coffee or an evening glass of wine. At least nobody could take away that freedom. But what was the pleasure in standing outside, shivering in the bitter cold, all for the sake of a smoke? You had to be desperate and he wasn't there yet.

With a brief smile of sympathy in the direction of the woman, which she warmly returned, he keyed in the access code and went inside, wishing he had time to stop and talk and wondering which floor she worked on and why he hadn't come across her before. He was halfway up the first flight of stairs when the door on the floor above flew open and Simon Turner burst onto the landing. Whistling loudly and tunelessly, Turner clattered down towards him, backpack and coat in hand.

'Simon, there you are. Can I have a word?'

Turner stopped just above him. 'What is it? I'm running late.'

'Do you know what happened to all the photographs Malcolm Broadbent took of Catherine Watson?'

'No. Why?'

'I was just wondering if Broadbent might have accidentally caught someone else on camera when he was photographing Watson, maybe someone she was with.'

'I doubt it. The shots were mostly close-ups, taken from a distance with a telephoto. A lot of the photos weren't even of Watson, just un-known women walking around in the street. There weren't any of men, if that's what you're thinking.'

'You're sure? You looked through them?'

'I didn't go through them all personally. Alan had a couple of the DCs do that.'

'But Gifford was looking for something to incriminate Broadbent, wasn't he?'

Turner chewed his lip thoughtfully. 'Evidence of the bloke's obses-sion with Catherine Watson, yes. Broadbent *was* obsessed,' he said, emphatically. 'There was no question.'

'My point is, Gifford would have told whoever was going through the photos what he was hoping to find. Maybe he didn't tell them to look for anything else.'

Turner's pale, gaunt face flushed. 'What the hell are you getting at? Is Alan on trial now?'

'You said he had a bit of a crusade going against Broadbent.'

'I don't remember saying that.'

Tartaglia shook his head. Even if Turner chose to have memory lapses, he remembered clearly what he had said. 'Maybe it was the whisky, but you certainly gave me the impression the other night that

Gifford was hell-bent on finding Broadbent guilty and he was looking for evidence to back it up. If that's the way he was handling things, he might have overlooked something else.'

'Look, it wasn't just Alan who thought Broadbent looked guilty. We all backed him.'

Tartaglia leaned against the wall and stared up at Turner, wondering why he was suddenly being so defensive. Maybe Clarke was right about Turner's loyalty to his former boss. Even so, he was sure Turner had previously been telling the truth about the way the investigation had been handled. In *vino veritas*, as the saying went, and scotch had the same effect, particularly in the sort of quantities Turner had been knocking back. But there was no point in having an argument with him now about what he might, or might not, have said when under the influence. 'So you didn't actually look through all the photos yourself?' Tartglia asked.

'Are you joking? There were thousands and thousands of bloody jpegs. I saw print-offs of the ones we kept as evidence, of course, and what was on them spoke volumes about Broadbent's character, but that's all.'

'Was it Gifford who selected which photos to keep?'

'I guess so. But it doesn't matter who did it, the photos were gone through very thoroughly, I can assure you. What's your problem?'

'I think we should look through them again, see if there's any link with the Holland Park murder. I presume copies were kept?'

Turner sighed as if it was all a waste of time. 'You'll have to check the evidence book, but unless someone kept a backup copy of his hard drive, we wouldn't have held on to more than a handful of the most interesting ones.'

'What happened to the rest of them?'

'They were all on Broadbent's computer. The computer would have been returned to him when he was released.'

'Did you remember if a copy was kept on disc?'

'No. As I said, look in the evidence book.' Turner shifted his back-pack onto his shoulder and eyed him suspiciously. 'What's making you think of this now? Is it the poem?'

'Yes,' said Tartaglia. He had no problem lying to Turner; he cer-tainly wasn't going to tell him what Angela Harper had said. Turner wasn't of a mind to listen to any doubts cast about the way the case had been handled and his first stop would be Steele's office to cause trouble.

Turner held his gaze. 'Have you been talking to anyone about the case? If so, I need to know. We don't want to get our wires crossed.'

'I haven't spoken to anyone,' Tartaglia said. It had to be a lucky guess on Turner's part, or pure cop's instinct. There was no way Turner could know about the meeting with Angela Harper. 'Look, I'm not criticising the way the case was handled—'

'Well it certainly sounds like it from where I'm standing.'

'I'm not. But the poem puts things in a different light. In spite of what common sense tells me, it seems there's a link somewhere be-tween the two cases. That means we've got to review everything again.'

'Up to you.'

'I also think we should re-interview Broadbent, this time as a pos-sible witness rather than a suspect.'

Turner stared at him as though he were mad. 'What on earth for?'

'Broadbent followed her around everywhere like a lovesick puppy. Maybe he saw something—or someone.'

'Nothing came out in any of the interviews.'

'Maybe you weren't asking the right questions. Did you show him a picture of Jennings?'

'Of course we did. Before you go trashing our investigation, Mark, I suggest you check the files. It's all in there. And the review team found nothing new.'

'I still want to see the photos.'

Turner stared at him impassively, then shrugged. 'Fine. I'll get someone round to see Broadbent right away. Let's just hope he's kept them. Now, I've got to dash.' Turner skirted around Tartaglia and started down the stairs again.

'One more thing, Simon.'

Turner turned around, frowning.

'Where are we with finding Michael Jennings?'

'We're still trying to trace him, but at the moment we've got sweet fuck all. I left a message for you. Didn't you get it?'

'I got it, but I want to know exactly who you've spoken to. You've checked with the university?'

'Of course. Jennings dropped out soon after Catherine Watson's murder. Never finished his degree.'

'What about his friends?'

'Seen or spoken to them all, or at least the ones we can find. We've been through all his known contacts.'

'Someone must know where he is.'

'We've put the word around, but so far nobody knows where he's gone, or they're not telling.'

'You've checked the prisons?'

'One of the first things we did, given the gap between the two murders. But he hasn't been inside.'

'National insurance number?'

'Not officially working or on the dole, according to the systems.'

'I don't care if he's fucking Houdini. I want him found.'

Turner's expression hardened. 'Then you'll have to ask Steele for more resources. Anyway, it's probably all a waste of time. Sam's just told me about what happened this afternoon in Holland Park with that woman...what's her name...?'

'Liz Volpe?'

'That's the one. The bloke she saw's the wrong height and build for Jennings. Jennings was only about five-eight and really weedy.'

'The man she saw may not have been the killer.'

'Right.' Turner turned to go.

'Hang on a minute,' he shouted. 'You're involved in this too, Simon.'

Turner looked up at him and shook his head. 'No, I'm not. The Holland Park murder's your case, mate. Now if it's all the same to you, I must be going.' With that he thundered down the last few stairs and out the door into the car park. The door clanged behind him.

For a moment, Tartaglia stood on the stairs gazing after him. He felt like punching the wall in frustration. Turner was rarely communicative—a lone operator, not a team player, was how Trevor had once described him. But tonight his manner had been even more abrupt and defensive than usual, almost evasive, as though he had something to hide. Maybe Donovan would know what was behind it and if it had anything to do with the case. Failing that, he would sound out Steele. She was usually up-front to the point of bluntness about most things. If Turner had been in her office complaining, or going behind Tartaglia's back for some other reason, he would soon find out.

'Why's he started up this witch hunt?' Turner said, kicking at the edge of the carpet with his toe as he stared morosely at the glass of whisky cupped in his huge hands. 'What's the point in trying to rake up the dirt now? Alan's dead.'

'I promise you that's not what Mark's doing,' Donovan replied. 'He's not like that.'

Sitting back deep in the corner of the small sofa, Turner frowned and stretched his long legs out in front of him. Donovan wondered what exactly had been said between him and Tartaglia, although she could imagine how Tartaglia might have behaved. When he wanted something, he didn't take no for an answer. It didn't matter who stood in his way. And Turner, in his current defensive state of mind, would take anything the wrong way.

Turner had arrived at her house that evening nearly half an hour late. He had been full of apologies, muttering something about getting held up at the office and wanting to go home first and take a shower. He had changed into jeans and a shirt and a dark blue jumper. The elbows were worn and the collar of his shirt was a little frayed, but he was looking good and she thought she could smell a fresh, lemony soap or aftershave when she pecked him on the cheek. It was nice that he was making an effort. He had even brought a bottle of good single malt from the off-licence around the corner and had seemed relatively upbeat and relaxed, the old easygoing charm coming out as he joked with Claire in the kitchen and helped to set the table. But at the first mention of the case, about the latest from the park and Liz Volpe—she could kick herself for having said anything—his mood had changed. It was as though a cloud had descended around him and he seemed unable to shake off the gloom.

'Why's he trying to rubbish our investigation?' Turner mumbled to himself. 'What's he up to? Is he playing politics, or something?'

'Stop being paranoid. Mark has no grudge against you that I know of. He's not point scoring or trying to get you or anyone else into trouble.'

'Pull the other one, it's got bells—'

'If he wants to review some aspects of the Watson case, it's because of the poem, because he really thinks something might have been overlooked, which didn't seem important at the time.'

'Like we cocked up, you mean,' Turner said bitterly.

'That's rubbish and you know it.'

'That's what he's getting at though, isn't it? You should have seen him tonight. He's a man on a mission.'

She shook her head in despair. 'He wants to find Rachel Tenison's murderer, that's all, and this could be a genuine lead. Just think how you'd feel in his position,' she added, although she realised as she said it that she was wasting her breath. In his current, inward-looking state of mind, Turner would find it difficult to empathise with anyone, particularly Tartaglia.

'Maybe we did focus too much on Broadbent and not enough on Jennings,' Turner said, with a dismissive grunt. 'Maybe mistakes were made. It's easy to say that now, looking back. But even if we had done things differently, the result would have been the same. We worked that case hard and there was no bloody evidence to bring even a whisper of a charge against either of them and make it stick.' He spoke quietly, but his face was red and tense with emotion.

'I'm sure you're right,' she said, noticing again his extraordinary colouring, highlighted by the rush of blood to his skin, and wondered if he had lost all perspective. 'But Simon, it's not about you and the Watson investigation. This is all about the Holland Park murder and that weird poem. That's what's worrying Mark. I just wish you could get it through your thick skull and stop taking everything personally.'

Turner shook his head disbelievingly. 'You're a sweetheart, Sam, but you're wrong. You've got a blind spot about Mark Tartaglia.'

'And you're your own worst enemy,' Donovan replied, exasperated, not knowing what else to say. The state of mind Turner was in, he wasn't seeing anything straight.

He looked over at her after a moment. 'Do you fancy him?' He mumbled the words and she almost missed them.

'No,' she said firmly, wondering why he had asked. Did everyone at work think she had the hots for Tartaglia? 'Mark's a good friend. That's all.'

He nodded and took a mouthful of whisky. 'I should never have let Wakefield talk me into getting involved in this. We had our chance when Alan was alive and it was over when the review team moved in.

No point trying to wake the dead.'

He grimaced and closed his eyes as though he was trying to block it all out.

She wondered what it would take to get him back to normal. How long to get over a short, misspent marriage? That was what was really eating him, not Tartaglia, though Turner would never admit it. Better to focus the anger on Tartaglia than lose face and admit the real cause: Nina. That woman had a lot to answer for.

She had seen her only the day before, having a sandwich with Karen Feeney in one of the cafés along Barnes High Street. They were sitting together at the counter in the window, so deep in conversation that Donovan had gone in and ordered her coffee without either of them looking up and noticing her. Nina had her elbow up on the counter, half-shielding her face with her hand. Her expression was tense and from what Donovan could see, she looked as though she had been crying. Donovan had tried listening in to what they were saying, but there was too much background noise to hear much, although she had definitely caught Turner's Christian name being mentioned several times. Wondering if Nina knew the state he was in, or if she cared, Donovan had half felt like going over and speaking to her. But what was the point? She wasn't close to Nina and it wasn't her place to get involved.

She had asked Karen about it afterwards and, although Karen was careful not to give too much away, she had said that Nina was very upset. When Donovan had asked why Nina should be upset when she was the one who had run off and apparently had someone else, Karen had replied that it wasn't true. That she had only left because he was making her miserable and she hoped it would bring him to his senses.

'She hasn't got anyone,' Karen had added. 'Simon's making it all up.'

'Why would he do that?' Donovan had asked.

'He's looking for sympathy, I suppose,' Karen said, with such a pointed look, that Donovan had stopped there. The last thing she needed was gossip going around the office about her and Simon Turner, although she would believe his version of events any day over Nina's.

Claire put her head around the sitting room door. She was wearing an apron patterned with small pink and red hearts and brandished a large wooden spoon in her hand as though she meant business.

'Right, you two, supper's ready.' Claire looked from Donovan to Turner. 'Feels like I've walked in on somebody's funeral. What's the matter?'

Turner looked embarrassed and mumbled something.

Donovan stood up. 'Just work, that's all.'

'Come on then, cheer up,' Claire said, smiling. 'Life's not that bad. It's Saturday night and we've got the most delicious lasagne to eat, with lemon steamed pudding and custard to follow. I've even got some music lined up so we can party.'

Turner got to his feet and gave her the ghost of a smile. 'Sorry. I'm not very good company tonight.'

'Don't worry,' Claire said, cheerily. 'You can come and have a laugh at my attempts at cooking. Most people do.'

23

Viktor Denisenko, Rachel Tenison's favourite barman, paced around his small bed-sit like a caged animal, making Karen Feeney feel unusually nervous. She stood watching him, her back to the closed door, waiting for him to calm down.

He turned to her with a look of helplessness, his big hands swinging uselessly at his sides. 'I didn't kill her, I tell you, I didn't kill her.'

'Let's not go through all that again,' she said, firmly. 'If your alibi checks out, you don't need to worry. Now, please sit down.'

He shook his head, as though he didn't believe her, and continued to pace, muttering to himself in what sounded like Russian. The room was cold, no sign of any heater, but he was sweating. Tall and powerfully built, his presence made the space seem even more cramped. Dressed in jeans, old trainers and a baggy sweatshirt, he was in his late twenties, with very short dyed-blonde hair and a shadow of dark stubble on his chin. He fitted the general description of the man seen by Liz Volpe in Holland Park a few hours before. However, according to Denisenko, he had only just come off his shift at the local pizzeria an hour before. Mineredes was busy checking with the restaurant, but for the moment she assumed Denisenko was telling the truth.

They had had difficulty tracking down Denisenko, eventually finding him through one of the other barmen where he used to work, who clearly bore him a grudge for some reason and seemed delighted that he might be in trouble. Judging from the almost total absence of any personal items—just a razor and toothbrush on the basin and a T-shirt thrown over the only chair—it didn't look as though he had been

living there long. Located in the no-man's-land of boardinghouses and
cheap hotels close to Paddington Station, it was like every bed-sit she
had ever been in, including the one she had first lived in only a few
streets away when she first moved to London. Once part of a grand
first floor room, the ceiling was high, with a view from the window of
a terrace of similar pillared, white-painted houses but the place was
cheerless, rendered impersonal by the endless stream of people passing through. The air reeked of damp and the wind rattled the sash like
a train passing.

'You want a cigarette?' she asked, taking a pack of Silk Cut from
her bag and wondering how she was going to get him to relax and talk.

'I don't smoke.'

'Well, please sit down. You're making me giddy.'

'Giddy?'

'Dizzy, you know,' she twirled her finger in the air to show him.
'My head's spinning, watching you.'

Denisenko hesitated and then nodded. He wiped his forehead
with the back of his sleeve and flopped down on the narrow divan,
which was covered with a sleeping bag.

'Right. I need you to tell me about the man you saw with Miss
Tenison.'

'You mean Stella,' Denisenko said insistently.

'Yes, Stella, if that's what you want to call her.' They had discovered that Rachel Tenison had used a variety of aliases with the men
she had picked up and taken home, all part of the role-playing game.
To Denisenko, she was Stella. 'You say she came into the bar where
you were working just over two weeks ago.'

'Wednesday. I work there Wednesday.'

'It's in Covent Garden, isn't it?'

'Yes. I am very happy to see her, but she have a man with her.
They do a lot of talking.'

'What did this man look like? How old? What colour hair?'

'I understand. He is older than Stella. Tall, like me. He has hair… a lot.'

'Your colour?'

'More dark. He look important man. Nice clothes. Expensive. I can tell.'

'Did you speak to her?'

He shrugged. 'I stay behind bar. She is busy with him. I don't want to embarrass her.'

'You said it was around eleven o'clock at night.'

'Yes.'

'Were they looking for something to eat?'

'No. They only have drinks. They have the red books for the opera—er…' He waved his hand in the air, struggling to find the word.

'Programmes, you mean?' Feeney said.

Denisenko nodded.

She knew the bar in question. It was opposite the Royal Opera House and only a few doors along from the former Bow Street police station, where she had worked when she had first started with the Met.

'Stella is beautiful,' Denisenko said, spreading his hands. 'Like always. So beautiful. So…so perfect. My friend Micky, he serve them. Stella, she does not see me. They have drink and they talk. Then she get angry and she hit him. Like this.' He slapped his cheek with his hand. 'Now he is very angry. He stand up. He come to bar and ask for the bill and they go.'

It sounded like a replay of what had happened in the restaurant in Kensington. 'Would you say they were just friends, or more?'

Denisenko frowned. 'Friends? The way she look at him, I see she love him. This man, he is her lover.'

'You say your relationship with Miss Tenison ended many months ago,' Feeney said. 'Why was that?'

'Stella she say she does not want me. She tell me to go away, like a piece of trash. So, I go away.' He sat up tall, palms on his knees, shoulders back and stared proudly at her. 'I still love her but I try to forget. It is better that way.'

'But you still care about her? Am I right?'

He nodded.

'Were you jealous when you saw her with this man? Were you angry?'

Denisenko met her gaze with fierce, watery eyes. 'Missus Detective Constable. You make mistake. I do not kill a woman because I am angry. In this country, I clean the streets, I empty the trash and I work in bars because I have no money. Everything I get, I send home to my mother. But where I come from, I am educated man. In Kiev, I study history and politics. I am not primitive. I am not animal. Yes, I am jealous when I see her with this man. But I do not kill her.'

'Is this the man you saw with her?' Feeney said, taking a copy of the identikit picture of the man seen at La Girolle out of her bag and passing it to him.

Denisenko glanced at it and nodded slowly. 'Maybe. Maybe it is him. If he kill Stella, you find him, yes?'

'How did he pay for the drinks?' Feeney asked.

'He use credit card.'

'We'll need to get the credit card details from the place where you work so that we can trace him.'

Denisenko gave her a weak smile. 'Not necessary. When they pay, I tell Micky I feel sick. That I must go home. I wait until they leave…' He paused and looked down at the floor.

'You were upset?'

Denisenko nodded and bit his lip hard. 'I want to know who is this man.'

'You followed them?'

'Yes. I follow them.'

'And?'

'I know this man's name. I know where he lives.'

24

'Do any of these faces look familiar to you?' Tartaglia asked. 'Are any of them the man you saw in Holland Park?'

Liz studied the four 10x8 colour photographs one by one, taking her time, hoping that something about one of them would leap out at her. Each man was attractive and young, certainly younger than Rachel, somewhere in his twenties or very early thirties. One was dark, three were varying degrees of fair, not that it made any difference. They had each been faceless as far as Rachel was concerned.

After a moment, she sighed and shook her head. 'I'm sorry. I don't recognise any of them.'

They were sitting opposite one another at a table in a bar on the corner of Portobello Road and Westbourne Grove, a block away from her brother's flat. The owner was Italian and the bar served exclusively Italian wine, along with a very small menu of good, simple things to eat. As neither she nor Tartaglia was particularly hungry, they had shared a plate of beef tagliata with rocket salad and were more than half way through a good bottle of Barolo, which Tartaglia had insisted on ordering. The bar was one of her favourite local haunts and she had suggested going there, hoping that it might appeal to Tartaglia and that maybe he would ease up a little and tell her more about the case. But so far he was giving nothing away.

She handed the photos back to him. 'Who are they?'

'Men who Rachel met at various times in the past year.'

She smiled, amused at his discretion. 'Slept with, you mean. Don't bother to spare my feelings. It doesn't shock me. Did she pick all of them up in a bar?'

He nodded. 'They have alibis which check out for the time of her murder but I just wanted to see if any of them might have been the man you saw in the park.'

She thought back to the bunch of deep red roses lying on the ground in the woodland enclosure, wondering at the possible emotions that had gone into that simple gesture. The flowers were now wilting in a police lab somewhere, being tested for God knows what. But at least it appeared that someone had cared. She wondered if Rachel had affected any of the men in the photographs that much, if she had mattered to them at all.

'It's funny but I can't get all the stuff you told me about Rachel out of my mind. I keep asking myself why I never twigged what was going on with her. It makes me feel like an idiot.' She looked at the wine in her glass, holding it up to the candle for a second, admiring the colour. Almost the same as the roses. 'I'm also beginning to feel that I didn't know Rachel at all.'

'If she's a mystery to you, she's certainly one to me,' he said, with a distant look that she didn't completely understand.

She gazed at him curiously, wondering why he was so fascinated. Perhaps detectives always tried to immerse themselves in their cases, involving themselves with the victims, but she sensed there was something more to it than that. He, too, had fallen under Rachel's spell. What could she say?

'Rachel was a mystery to a lot of people, Inspector. It was one of her main attractions.'

'Tell me about the man you saw,' he said abruptly, as though wanting to change the subject. 'Try and describe him to me. It's very important we find him.'

Liz sighed. 'I can sort of see him in my mind but the e-fit didn't look right, or at least not how I remember him.'

'But you'd never seen this man before?'

'Definitely not,' she said firmly, wondering now if he again thought she was hiding something.

He looked thoughtful, then nodded, as though accepting what she said. 'OK. Let's try something else. Close your eyes. Think back to when you first saw the man and tell me what you see.'

She didn't think it would do any good, but wanting to please him she shut her eyes. Blocking out the music and general background noise in the bar, she pictured the dark, damp, coldness of the woods, the quiet, the smell of the earth and the leaves. She pictured the bench where she had been sitting, smoking; the branches of the holly tree arching over it like a canopy.

'Do you see him?' Tartaglia asked softly.

In her head she heard the squawking of the rooks. 'Yes. He's running towards me. But it's getting dark and he's just a blur at this point. Before he gets to me, he stops by the fence.'

'What's he doing?'

'I'm not sure.'

'Is he searching for a way in?'

'Maybe. He walks up and down for a moment.'

'So, he's not exactly sure where it is.'

'No.'

'Describe him. How does he look, how does he move?'

'Athletic. He's wearing dark baggy clothes and an anorak or fleece with a hood. I'm about thirty yards away. He's tall...'

'Taller than me? I'm six feet.'

She opened her eyes and looked at him, trying to compare the two in her mind. Tartaglia was an inch or so taller than she was; the man in the park had been taller, bigger, or at least that's what she thought at the time. She felt suddenly confused, not trusting her memory. 'I don't know. It's difficult to tell at that sort of distance. I had the impression he's tall, certainly taller than I am. That's all I can say.'

'What did he do next?'

She screwed her eyes shut, forcing herself to think back, wishing that she could remember things more clearly. 'He looks around, as though he's making sure nobody's there. The way he behaved made me feel nervous, like he was up to no good, or something. After that, I kept very still.'

'But he doesn't see you?'

She shook her head. 'As I said, the light was poor. I was sitting on this bench underneath a holly tree.'

'Does he look in your direction at any point?'

'Yes. Briefly.'

'Stop there and tell me what you see. Try and freeze the image in your mind.'

'OK.' She frowned, struggling to picture it again. 'I think he looks the other way first. Yes. Then he turns towards me. I see a flash of his face. He's white, anywhere between twenty and forty. That's all I can say. He has this hood pulled down low over his head so I can't see his hair or forehead. His features don't stand out at all.' She tried to visualise him more clearly but nothing came. Frustrated, she opened her eyes and reached for her glass. 'I'm sorry. I make a lousy witness, don't I?'

'You weren't that close to him and it must have all happened very quickly.'

'Yes. One minute he was there, the next he was gone. I didn't really think about what it might mean until afterwards, after he'd run off, when I went into the woodland area and found the roses. The problem is, the more I try to remember what happened, what he looked like, the more it seems to go away from me.'

'Memory's a strange thing. Sometimes it's better not to think too hard about something. Let your unconscious mind do the work. You may find it'll come back to you more clearly later.'

She sighed, annoyed with herself for not being able to remember better. 'Perhaps you should hypnotise me.'

'Let's try something else,' he said, after a moment. 'I'm going to go outside and walk down the road over there just past that lamppost. It's about thirty yards away. When I turn around, I want you to look at me, then tell me what you see.'

She watched him go out of the bar and across the road. The area was always busy on a Saturday, the street and pavement thronged with street vendors and tourists visiting the bric-a-brac stalls which lined the Portobello Road and Westbourne Grove. But the shops and stalls had closed up hours before and there was nobody around. As Tartaglia walked a little way down Portobello Road, Liz noticed that it had just started to rain again, the heavy drizzle visible against the orange glow of the streetlamp. A little way down, he took off his pullover and put it over his head like a hood, covering his hair, then he turned around, facing her. The hood changed his face completely. It was funny, she thought, how here was one of the best-looking men she had seen for a long time, yet at a distance, with his hair covered, he might have been anyone. It showed her how pointless the whole e-fit exercise had been and she felt disappointed.

After a few seconds, Tartaglia started back up the street towards her.

'Christ, it's cold out there,' Tartaglia said, once back inside. His black hair glistened with moisture in the low light and he gave his jumper a good shake before putting it back on. 'Now, what could you tell about me? I know the light's not the same, but what was your impression? Try and compare me to the man you saw.'

She looked at him thoughtfully, wanting to be helpful. One thing was for sure: the man she had seen looked nothing like Tartaglia.

'Well, your colouring, for a start. Even with that jumper over your head, I could tell you're dark. It's your eyebrows; they stand out.

Thinking back, I realise now I can't make out this man's eyebrows or his eyes or lips; it's all a similar tone, and no shadows or lines.'

'So, he's fairish…'

'Yes. I'd say he was fair. Even at that distance, I could tell that your skin tone is darker.'

'Doesn't help that I need a shave,' he said ruefully, rubbing the thick shadow of stubble on his chin. 'Any other differences?'

She studied him, trying to be as objective as possible and not linger too long on any one feature, hoping he had no idea how much she was enjoying looking at him. 'Well, the general shape of your face is different,' she said, matter-of-factly. 'This man's was longer, less regular, maybe. I'd also say he's taller than you, bigger-built, although maybe it was just the anorak he was wearing.'

'That's very helpful. Is there anything else?'

She shook her head and sipped her wine. 'The wine's really nice,' she said after a moment, deciding it was time to change the subject and wanting to encourage him to stay awhile. 'Not that I'm an expert.'

'Me neither. My family imports wine from Italy, but according to my dad, I don't know the difference between the cheapest Chianti and a Sassicaia. That's rubbish, of course, not that he'd give me the opportunity of proving him wrong.'

'Well, I certainly can't tell the difference. And I hate all the fuss people make about wine.'

He looked suddenly thoughtful, as if his mind was elsewhere.

'What is it?' she asked. 'You're not still worrying about the park, are you?'

'Nothing like that. I was just thinking that you don't look very Italian.'

She smiled, relieved to talk about anything other than Rachel. 'Only half. My mother's English. My parents split up when I was very young and I was brought up over here. My Italian's lousy.'

'Do you still see your father?'

'Occasionally, when I go to Italy to visit family. He runs a restaurant in Siena. What about you? At least you look the part.'

'Fourth generation, usual story. My great-grandfather came over to Scotland in the 1890s from a little village in the Abruzzi hills. They eventually settled in Edinburgh and that's where most of them have stayed, apart from me and my sister.'

'Is she in the police too?'

'Christ, no,' he said, half-choking on his wine. 'What a thought. Nicoletta would never fit into anywhere as regimented and process-driven as the Met. Modern-day policing has no room for mavericks, and she's one hell of a maverick, in both the best and the worst senses. She teaches Italian at London University. In her spare time she runs a husband and two kids.'

'Does she look like you?'

'Apparently, although I think she looks a lot like Ronnie Ancona, without all the make-up and stuff, and I certainly don't.'

'No, you don't.' He seemed so normal and nice, but what a strange world he inhabited, dealing with violent death on a daily basis. It was a far cry from everything familiar to her and Italian blood was probably all they had in common. 'What about you? Do you have a family, I mean?'

'No. I'm not married, never even come close. That's a bit of a sore point, at least for my mother and my sister. Just because I'm in my late thirties and on my own, they think there's something wrong with me.'

Liz laughed. 'They sound just like my mother. She's also so bloody judgmental, as if she has an unblemished track record. She's currently on her third husband. It's enough to put anyone off. Wouldn't it be nice if they got on with their own stuff and left us all alone?'

'If only,' he said, with real feeling.

'Of course, I make a whole load of stupid mistakes, but at least they're mine. And maybe one day I'll learn. Maybe one day I'll get better at this whole thing.'

He smiled, his dark eyes creasing at the corners. It was the first time since they had arrived that he looked really at ease. 'I've done some pretty crazy things too,' he said. 'Really stupid. But if you don't take risks, you never get anywhere and it's what stops life from being dull. I just don't enjoy having my sister commenting on it all and analysing it. She fancies herself as an amateur psychologist, does Nicoletta.'

Liz wondered if he felt he was taking a risk being there with her, chatting about things as though they were two normal people and not involved in a murder case. Although he didn't seem at all awkward, she sensed he was treading carefully, something holding him back. Maybe he was worried about the lines getting blurred. Maybe in spite of what he said, he liked to play safe.

The image of the red roses still stuck her mind and she thought again of what had prompted the man to place them on the spot where Rachel had died. He had certainly taken a risk.

She drained her glass. 'Going back to the man in the park, do you think he murdered Rachel?'

'It's possible. Anything's possible.'

'But surely you don't put flowers on the place where someone died unless you cared very much about them.'

He shrugged as though it was pointless speculating, but she wasn't satisfied.

'But if he loved her, why did he kill her? And if he did kill her, isn't it taking a monumental risk going back there? Surely there's no place for sentiment if you've murdered someone.'

'You'd think if somebody was capable of murder, they'd think logically. But in my experience it's not often the case. Plus this man seemed to know exactly where her body had been found. The specific location was never mentioned in the press.'

'But surely anyone who runs in the park would have a pretty good idea of where it happened? Holland Park's not exactly huge.'

He frowned. 'You should stay well away from the park.'

'I can look after myself. I'm not a child, you know.'

'Nor was Rachel.'

The words made her pause for thought. She had assumed from everything that he had said before that what had happened to Rachel was a one-off. Now she wondered if he had told her the whole truth. 'You think it could happen again? You think there's some madman on the loose?' It was strangely more comforting than thinking that someone she knew might be responsible.

'At the moment we have no idea why she was killed. We don't know what the risks are.'

'But you seriously think there could be a repeat?'

'I'm not saying that. But if I were a woman, I wouldn't choose to go running on my own, particularly when there aren't a lot of people around.'

He said it in a way that made her feel foolish. 'Now you sound like my brother. I could get run over by a bus tomorrow but it doesn't stop me crossing the road.'

He compressed his lips, as though he didn't agree.

'What is it that you're not telling me?'

'I'm just concerned about you, that's all.'

'Nonsense.' She shook her head and folded her arms. How could he possibly expect her to help when he gave so little away? 'Why won't you tell me?'

'It's not appropriate for you to know. You're too close to everything.'

She wanted to say that that was the whole point, but looking at him she knew it would do no good.

He studied her for a moment in a way that made her feel quite uncomfortable, then he said: 'Why did the two of you quarrel? You and Rachel, I mean.' She was about to speak when he held up his hand. 'Before you answer, I don't want all that stuff you gave me the other night. I want the real reason.'

He wouldn't give up. Weary and worn down by his persistence, she took refuge in her wine, the image of what had happened filling her mind, the image of Rachel and *him* together in Rachel's big, dark bed. Perhaps it was time to end the charade and tell Tartaglia what Rachel was really like. It would feel good to shatter his illusions.

She met his gaze. 'What I told you was true, what she said to me, and the bit about the text at the table. I just left out one important part: Rachel stole somebody from me. Somebody I thought I loved very much. She did it deliberately and consciously because she wanted to break us apart. And more than anything, she did it because she could.'

'Stole? But I thought you two were good friends, that you loved her.'

She shook her head. 'For the last two months I've hated her. Although I didn't kill her, there were many times I wished her dead.'

He looked puzzled and opened his mouth to say something.

'I'm sorry to disillusion you,' she interrupted, before he had the chance. 'And you *will not* make me go into the details. As I said, I didn't kill her and what happened between us has nothing whatsoever to do with her murder. But I can tell you this. I will never forgive her for what she did. If I feel guilty for not being more charitable, it's the only guilt I feel about what's happened.'

For a moment he said nothing, then he reached out and touched her hand gently, with such a look of genuine understanding that it made her eyes tear. 'I'm sorry,' he said. 'Thank you for telling me.'

His phone started to ring and he sighed as he took it out of his jacket pocket, as if he didn't welcome the interruption. He listened to whoever was at the other end for a moment, then frowning, said a few words, which were lost against the noise of the bar, and snapped it shut. He stood up.

'Something's come up and I've got to go,' he said, quickly putting on his jacket. 'To do with the case. Can you see yourself home?'

'Of course. I'll stay and finish off the rest of the wine, if you don't mind. It's far too good to waste.' She tried not to sound too disappointed.

'I'm sorry. Really sorry. I wish I could stay.' He hesitated, as though there was something more he wanted to say.

'Don't worry about me,' she said briskly. 'I'm quite happy on my own and it's far too early to go to bed.'

He frowned. 'Sometimes I feel I'm married to the bloody job. There's no room for anything else.' He hesitated, then added, 'But I've enjoyed myself tonight. Maybe we can come back here another evening and pick up where we left off.'

'Nina wants to come back,' Turner said quietly, without any warning. He put the cigarette to his lips and inhaled deeply.

Donovan was silent, not knowing what to say other than that she didn't think it was a good idea, which was probably not what he wanted to hear.

They stood together just outside the kitchen door, sheltering from the rain under the overhang. Inside, Claire was busy heating up the sponge puddings and custard in the microwave and singing along with Snow Patrol.

'She's been ringing me for the last couple of days. Won't leave me alone. Wants to patch things up and make a go of it.'

Donovan had brought her wine glass outside and took a sip. She wondered whether she should tell him what Nina had said to Karen

Feeney, that she blamed him for the break-up. It would be wise not to say anything, she reminded herself. After all, it was none of her business and she barely knew Turner. In the end, curiosity got the better of her. 'What about the man Nina was with? What's happened to him?'

'You know, I don't think there ever was a man,' he said, draining his tumbler absentmindedly. 'At least not anyone important. I think she just said it to get a rise out of me. Thought maybe it would stir me up and make me see sense, or something, like I can turn my feelings on and off like a tap.'

'But I thought she walked out on you?'

'Yes. I thought it was because of this other man, but now I don't know. I don't know what she's been playing at.'

He looked so troubled, she was half tempted to put an arm around him, but was afraid he might take it the wrong way. 'What do you want?' she asked, looking up at him. 'Do you have any idea?'

He turned and gave her a wistful smile. 'What do *I* want? I'm not used to people asking me that.' He sucked in some more smoke and sighed. 'We should never have got married in the first place. It all happened too quickly. She got pregnant...I said I would marry her. What a stupid thing to do.'

'No,' she said, softly. 'Don't say that. You're being too hard on yourself.'

He shook his head and closed his eyes. 'Then everything went wrong. She lost the baby and she went down and down. She was out of control. I didn't know her anymore. She said I couldn't understand how she felt. She said I wasn't there for her and she blamed me for what had happened. Nothing I did made it any better. She was so bitter, so angry; I didn't know how to live with her and sometimes I thought she'd gone loopy. I realise now I can't put it right. It's too late for that and the best thing for both of us is to go our separate ways.'

She looked at him questioningly. 'You're sure?'

'Yes.'

'Have you told Nina how you feel?'

He nodded. 'She won't listen. Says she knows what's best for the both of us. Says she's going to move her stuff back in.'

She stared at him horrified. 'You can't let her—not if you don't want her to, I mean.'

'What am I supposed to do? Change the locks on my own wife? That doesn't seem right. I still care about her. Even after everything…' He closed his eyes again as though the thought was painful.

Donovan assumed he was referring once more to the baby they had lost. If anything, she would have thought such a thing would bring two people closer together, but instead it seemed to have driven a wedge between them.

'But what if she comes back? Will you just let her move in?'

'If she comes back, I'll have to go, although I've no idea where.'

He stared gloomily into the darkness. and for a moment all she could hear was the soft drumming of the rain on the kitchen extension roof.

'Well, if it's any help, temporarily I mean, we have a spare room. Or at least a spare bed in the study.'

He looked round at her, frowning. 'Oh, I wasn't asking…I wouldn't dream…'

'Honestly, Simon. It's OK. That's what it's there for. We're always having waifs and strays dossing down in between something or other. The last few were Claire's friends so it's well past being my turn. There's only a single bed and it's probably a bit short for you, but it's quite comfortable otherwise. Just think of it as an insurance policy, in case you need it.'

He smiled. 'Thanks. That's nice to know, although I hope it won't come to that.' He reached down to his feet and stubbed out his cigarette on the rim of an empty flowerpot, then looked round at her.

'You're a decent person, Sam, and I'm very fond of you. Always have been, if you must know. If only things had been different… Well, timing's everything, isn't it? Probably shouldn't be talking like this, in my current state. Maybe when I get things sorted…' He grimaced. 'God, I'm making heavy weather of this. What I'm trying to say is, would you come out with me? To dinner, I mean?' He frowned, searching her face for a reaction.

She didn't know what to reply. She hadn't been expecting anything like this. Naturally she was flattered. She did find Turner attractive, if she allowed herself to think about it for more than a second. But he had had too much to drink and "man on the rebound" was the caption that popped up cartoon-like in her mind, along with all the excellent advice about avoiding such men like the plague. Anyway, after what had happened so recently with the Bridegroom case, she felt she had lost her perspective on men completely.

He looked down at the glass in his hand and seemed surprised that it was empty. 'I'm sorry. I've had too much to drink. I've really overstepped the mark there. Let's pretend I never said it, OK?'

She smiled, amused by his awkwardness and touched by the fact that he didn't take her response for granted. It was one of the many nice things she was discovering about him.

'No, Simon. You haven't overstepped the mark. I just wasn't expecting you to say something like that, that's all.'

He gazed at her sadly. 'Stupid old Simon, always shoving his big foot in it. Put it down to the whisky and it having been one shit of a day.'

'No, I'm glad you said it. Honestly.' Resisting the impulse to reach up and ruffle his short, thick stubble of hair, she looked at him instead, liking what she saw, the pleasant, good-natured features, the extraordinary pale eyes that were hooded with sleepiness. She felt pleased that she had only had a moderate amount to drink and could manage to be sensible for them both.

'When this is all over, and you get your life back to normal, yes I'll have dinner with you.'

His face broke into a broad grin. It was the first time she had seen him really smile in days. He carefully put his glass down on the ground and took both her hands in his, kissing them each in turn. 'Good. That gives me something to look forward to.'

'Not until then, mind,' she said, gently pulling away.

'Sure,' he said, still smiling. 'You're just being kind, but I'll hold you to it, you know. There's no escape.'

Before she had a chance to reply, Claire rapped on the window just behind them and pushed open the kitchen door. 'Sorry to interrupt, Sam, but your phone was ringing, so I answered it. It's Mark. He says it's urgent.'

25

'I've been a silly boy, haven't I, Inspector?' Patrick Tenison said, with the resigned air of a pupil caught smoking by a teacher.

'This is a very serious matter, Mr Tenison,' Tartaglia replied firmly, holding his gaze.

Tenison sighed. 'Of course, and I said I was sorry.' As if that were the end of the matter.

Tartaglia and Donovan sat opposite Tenison in the confined space of interview room eight at Belgravia Police Station, tape machine running. Viktor Denisenko had led them to Tenison's flat a couple of hours before and they had then tracked Tenison down to a charity do in a hotel where he was one of the speakers. He was still in his dinner jacket and bow tie and looked a little tired and the worse for wear. There were no grounds yet to arrest him, but he was now being treated as a person of interest and he had insisted on having his lawyer, Geoffrey Mallinson, there too. Mallinson sat beside him, red-faced and puffed up like a fat bullfrog, ruffled and bleary-eyed from interrupted sleep.

Perhaps, as a politician, Tenison thought himself above the law, but if so he was mistaken. It was true that people lied all the time in investigations, often for the most silly and innocent of reasons. For some people, lying was an automatic reaction, not because they had anything specific to hide but because a lie was sometimes easier and less time-consuming than the truth: I wasn't there; I didn't see anything; I don't want to get involved. People also lied in murder cases because the stakes were higher. But if someone like Tenison lied about something as innocent as having dinner with his sister, it meant he was hiding something else, or so Tartaglia's instincts told him.

'At the very least, I can charge you with obstruction,' he said, still studying Tenison's broad, impassive face as though somehow it might give away a glimmer of the truth.

Tenison spread his hands. 'I've said I'm sorry. What more can I say?'

'What I don't understand is *why* you lied to us, Mr Tenison. Why didn't you just tell us right at the start that you had dinner with your sister on that Thursday night?'

Tenison frowned, as though it were obvious. 'It's none of your business, that's why.'

'Wrong. This is a murder investigation, Mr Tenison. Everything is our business.'

Tenison leaned back in his chair, took a deep breath and said, as if explaining an obvious fact to a very small child: 'What I meant was, Rachel was killed the following morning. I had nothing to do with that.'

'We only have your word for where you were. You have no alibi and you've lied to us once already. That calls into question everything that you've told us.' Tartaglia spoke slowly and deliberately, giving weight to each sentence.

Under the harsh glare of the strip lighting, Tenison looked visibly shocked, as if it hadn't occurred to him how his behaviour might be interpreted. There were dark shadows under his eyes and the few lines on his face seemed more deeply drawn. Perhaps events were taking their toll, or perhaps it was down to the formal clothes he was wearing, but he looked older and more worn than when Tartaglia had visited him at his flat.

'Right. Let's run through what happened that evening.'

Resignedly, Tenison ran a palm over his sleek, dark hair and gave Tartaglia a weary look. 'I had a quick drink with Rachel at her flat, then we went out to dinner.'

'Just for the record,' Donovan asked. 'What did you have to drink at the flat?'

Tenison glanced over at her, as if he'd only just noticed her there. 'I really can't remember, Sergeant. Why, is it important?'

'A number of dirty glasses were found in her flat from that night,' she replied. 'It would be useful if you could tell us which one was yours.'

'Well, I probably had a glass of wine. White, if I remember correctly. I *am* trying to help, you know.'

Tartaglia nodded. 'Please continue with your account, Mr Tenison.'

'We had a drink, then caught a cab to the restaurant, as we were running late. We were in the restaurant about an hour. Then we had an argument, as you probably already know, and Rachel left.'

'What was the argument about?' Donovan asked.

Tenison shrugged. 'Personal stuff, mainly.'

'I'm going to need the details, Mr Tenison,' Tartaglia said.

'Is this really necessary?'

'Yes. I need to understand everything that was affecting Miss Tenison in the run-up to her murder.'

Tenison looked away towards the small, barred window in the corner, drumming his fingers lightly on the table. 'If you must know, I'd been having some marital difficulties.' He spoke so quietly, Tartaglia almost missed what he said.

'Could you speak up, Mr Tenison. For the tape.'

Tenison turned around and glared at him. 'I said I was having some marital difficulties. Is that loud enough for you?'

'Yes. Thank you.'

Again Tenison looked away, avoiding eye contact. 'Rachel thought I was going to leave my wife and she was trying to stop me.'

'How did you react?' Donovan asked.

A flicker of embarrassment, or possibly pain, crossed Tenison's face. 'I told her it was none of her business. Rachel, being Rachel, wasn't satisfied with that. This wasn't the first time we'd spoken about it, but she wouldn't let it rest. When she had a bee in her bonnet about something, she just wouldn't give up. In the end, most people, including me, gave in to her.'

'Was your sister close to your wife?' Tartaglia asked, wondering what sort of grown man would allow his stepsister to dictate his life. It struck him again that Tenison was rather weak, certainly as far as his sister was concerned.

'Not especially. Although Rachel approved of Emma, they are—I should say were—very different types of women.'

It wasn't clear to Tartaglia if Tenison meant this as a criticism of his sister or of his wife, but he had the feeling it was the latter. 'So if Miss Tenison wasn't championing your wife's cause, why did she care so much about what you did?' Before he could answer, Tartaglia guessed the reason. 'There was another woman involved, wasn't there?'

Tenison winced as though he had tasted something bitter. 'Rachel didn't want me wrecking my life for what she saw as a fling.'

'Is that what it was?' Donovan asked.

'It's none of your bloody business what it was.'

'It is, where it concerns Miss Tenison,' Tartaglia said. 'You were telling us that she saw your relationship as something trivial?'

Tenison hesitated. 'Probably. She certainly thought I was being foolish.'

'Foolish?'

He spread his hands. 'Come on, Inspector. We've all done things on the spur of the moment without thinking them through properly, things we've lived to regret.'

Tenison didn't strike Tartaglia as the impulsive type and he wondered what had led him to take such a risk, both personally and professionally, and if he was trying to play down what had happened for their benefit. However, they were straying from what was important.

'Let's get back to the restaurant. What happened after Miss Teni-son left?'

'I left some money to cover the bill and got a taxi back to her flat. But she wouldn't let me in, so I went away.'

'You didn't persist?' Donovan asked.

'What was the point? It was late. I was tired. We'd had arguments before and it was nothing new.'

'What time did you give up and go away?'

'I really can't say. I guess it would have been about ten-thirty, or so. I didn't exactly look at my watch.'

'Where did you go?' Tartaglia asked.

'Back to my flat, of course.'

Tenison's tone was off-hand and dismissive and it struck a false chord.

'Nobody can corroborate that.'

Tenison gave the faintest shrug, as though it was of no concern.

'I think you're lying.'

Tenison's jaw set hard. He folded his arms and leaned back heav-ily in his chair. 'I don't give a damn what you think. That's what I did. You prove otherwise.'

Tartaglia shook his head slowly. 'What makes much more sense is this: you followed her home as you say. You were angry with her. Maybe your relationship was closer than you say it was…'

Tenison's face flushed with anger. 'What the hell are you imply-ing? I loved my sister, but not in *that* way, I can assure you.'

'Well, somebody slept in Rachel Tenison's bed that night,' Dono-van said. 'Are you saying it wasn't you?'

'God, you lot are twisted. Contrary to the squalid little stories you read in the gutter press, not everyone's into incest.'

'You went round to her flat and she wouldn't let you in,' Tartaglia continued. 'Then you find out she's got another bloke in there so you wait until the next morning when she goes out for her run and you kill her in a fit of jealous rage. You wouldn't be the first man to do it.'

'Hang on a minute,' Mallinson said, springing to life. 'This is all quite ridiculous. You have no proof and may I remind you that my client is here voluntarily. If you persist with this sort of questioning, he will leave.'

'You killed her, didn't you?' Tartaglia insisted, ignoring Mallinson.

Mallinson put a hand on Tenison's sleeve. 'They have nothing, Patrick. They're just fishing.'

Tenison shook his head. 'I'm fine, Geoffrey. You're letting your imagination run away with you, Inspector.'

'Really? I wonder how the press will see it. The gutter press, as you call them. As you say, they're used to things good and lurid, particularly where politicians are concerned.'

'It's trial by press now, is it?'

Although Tenison was trying to appear calm, Tartaglia had seen the split second flicker of horror on his face when the word "press" had been mentioned. It again confirmed what he had suspected: Tenison had something to hide. He had to keep running with it. It was his only lever.

'If you won't help us, Mr Tenison, well...' He opened his hands.

'That's blackmail.'

'Not at all. You lie to us about a simple matter of a dinner. We discover that you're the last person to see Miss Tenison alive, bar someone she sleeps with and someone who murders her. The simplest explanation is that you did all three things.'

'Stop right there, Inspector,' Mallinson interjected. 'My client has told you why he didn't come forward sooner. It doesn't make him guilty of anything.'

Still Tartaglia held Tenison's eye. 'Who knows what goes on between two people who appear to be close, what the real dynamics are? Contrary to what you say, it's not a huge stretch of the imagination to see you as either her lover or her killer.'

Tenison looked away and shook his head as though the whole thing were ridiculous.

Tartaglia wasn't sure what he believed, but if Tenison had murdered his sister it didn't explain the presence of the poem at the crime scene, let alone the other links with the Watson case.

Mallinson cleared his throat. 'This is a wild flight of fancy, Inspector, and you know it. Unless you have anything more constructive to say, I advise my client to leave now.'

'Your client has lied to us, Mr Mallinson. Therefore everything he says is open to question. We know they had an argument. Maybe it was about something more than Mr Tenison's little affair. Maybe he's still angry with her the next day. So he follows her into the park and she won't speak to him. He's really frustrated by now. They have another fight and he strangles her. At the very least, we're looking at a charge of manslaughter.'

Tenison scraped his chair back and got to his feet, his face contracted with anger. 'You're wasting my time. You've got no evidence and I'm going home. All I can say is that I loved my sister and I didn't kill her.' He turned to walk out of the room.

'Then what is it you're trying to hide?' Tartaglia called after him. 'We'll find out sooner or later whatever it is, as will the press. It's amazing how these things leak out. Is that what you really want?'

Tenison stopped just before the door and looked round.

'My client has done nothing wrong,' Mallinson repeated.

'In that case, why is he still lying?'

'Come back here for a moment, Patrick.' Mallinson patted the chair beside him. 'I'm sure we can sort this out amicably.'

'All I want is the truth,' Tartaglia said quietly.

'I am telling the truth, for God's sake!' Tenison shouted, his face red again. 'I didn't kill her.'

'All right, Mr Tenison. Please sit down and let's try and clear this up.'

Tenison stared at him for a moment, then shrugged. He came back over to the table and sank down grudgingly in his seat again, arms tightly folded.

'OK. Let's go back to the matter of your alibi. Once more, where were you between seven and eight a.m. the following day?'

'For the umpteenth time, I was at my flat.'

'What time did you leave the next morning?'

'About eight o'clock. I caught a train from Waterloo down to my constituency.'

'That's what, about a forty-five minute journey at most?'

Tenison nodded.

'But your PA says you arrived just before eleven and that you called ahead to cancel your first couple of meetings. Why were you late?'

Tenison gritted his teeth. 'Was I? I don't remember.'

'Look, it's very easy for us to check the CCTV footage to see what time you got to Waterloo. From what I can tell, you had ample time to kill Miss Tenison. If you didn't do it, you'd better give me a better reason for why were you late.'

'I overslept and couldn't get a taxi. OK?'

'Not good enough.'

Mallinson wrapped the table with his knuckles. 'Come, come, Inspector. Do you have any evidence to link my client with the crime scene?'

Tartaglia turned on Mallinson. 'I want the truth about where he was and either I get it out of him now, between these four walls, or I'll let the press do it for me. He can take his pick.'

Mallinson started to say something but Tenison wearily waved him away. 'All right, all right. I'll tell you where I was, although it's none of your business. I have an alibi for that night and the following morning. Before I say anything more, I need your word that this doesn't get into the papers.'

'Just tell us where you were,' Tartaglia said firmly. He wasn't going to make any deals with Tenison after the way he had lied.

Tenison fell silent and Tartaglia waited while he wrestled with private conflicts. After a moment, he cleared his throat. 'I stayed with a friend that night. A lady.'

'We'll need her name.'

He placed his hands down flat on the table and leaned across towards Tartaglia. 'Look, Inspector,' he said in a hoarse whisper. 'Please understand, I'm in a tricky situation, in terms of my career, I mean. Also, my wife doesn't know. I can't afford to have everything blow up in my face. Can you promise me that our names will be kept out of the papers?'

'You should have thought of that before. The name, Mr Tenison.'

Again Tenison hesitated, as though he was still deciding whether or not to cooperate.

'The name.'

Tenison sighed. 'I just hope to God all this doesn't get out. I was with Liz Volpe. Rachel's friend. She was the reason Rachel and I quarrelled.'

26

'It's true,' Liz said. 'Patrick stayed with me at my brother's flat that night.'

'Why didn't you say so before?' Tartaglia asked.

'Because Patrick told me not to.' Liz met his gaze with childlike innocence, as if things could be that simple.

They were in another meeting room, down the corridor from where Patrick Tenison had been interviewed. Pale, with eyes still puffy from sleep, Liz had been roused out of her bed and brought over to the Belgravia station. Wearing jeans, an old T-shirt and a voluminous black cardigan, which she wrapped around herself like a shawl, she had evidently dressed in a hurry, putting on the nearest things she could find.

'Do you always do what you're told?'

Liz looked away and shrugged. 'Of course not. But to be honest, it seemed the easy way out.'

'So you lied for him.' He struggled to understand what she saw in Patrick Tenison and why she would allow herself to be influenced by him. She seemed so independent, with her head firmly screwed on, and she certainly didn't seem to be the sort of woman to be impressed with status or power.

She frowned. 'And for myself. Don't blame poor Patrick for everything. I was just being practical. I'm looking for a job and the last thing I need is to have my name blasted all over the papers.' She hesitated, looking down at her hands, which were loosely clasped in front of her on the table. 'I'm not trying to make light of this, honestly I'm not. I don't like lying and I felt very uncomfortable about doing it when Patrick asked me to. But he's right. The newspapers love a nice, juicy bit of gossip and sleaze, particularly when someone's dead. Anyway, we've done nothing wrong. Neither of us had anything to do with Rachel's murder.'

She raised her eyes again and gave him such a direct look that he found himself believing her. He also had some sympathy with her view of what the press reaction would be, although he found himself feeling far less understanding where Tenison was concerned.

'You still should have said something before.'

'And risk it getting out?' She shook her head. 'It's not as though it makes any difference to your enquiry, does it? You still don't know who Rachel slept with that night. You still don't know who killed her.' Her tone was almost accusatory, as if she was trying to shift blame.

'That's not the point,' Tartaglia said sharply. 'I assume you knew about the argument in the restaurant between Rachel and her brother?'

'Yes. I gather it was about me. Reading between the lines, I think Rachel told him that he should give me up. She was worried that he was on the point of leaving Emma.'

'And was he?'

Liz pulled the cardigan even more tightly around herself, as though it gave her some comfort. 'In the early stages it was something he talked about. You know, in the way you talk about some nice, vague plan for the future. I didn't really believe him, although it was fun for a while to go along with it. I always thought that if push came to shove, he'd run home to little Emma. He's not very brave.'

'But Rachel believed that he was going to run off with you?'

'Yes. Things then came to a head and I suppose she thought he would do something rash. She had a blind spot where Patrick was concerned and she was convinced I was egging him on.'

'You weren't?'

Liz shook her head. 'I never had any idea of marrying Patrick, even if he were free. He'd make a lousy husband and you have to be a doormat to be married to a politician, or at least prepared to put them and their needs first all the time. That's just not my bag, at least where men are concerned.'

He nodded slowly, wondering what sort of man she saw herself with, or whether in fact she was one of those people who were quite happy on their own. 'Why was Miss Tenison so upset about your relationship?'

'She saw me as a threat.'

'A threat?'

'Surely you've guessed by now what she was really like?' She looked at him almost teasingly, half smiling. 'As Shakespeare said, beauty is a witch, and there were many who were caught up in her enchantment, although they had no idea what lay beneath. Even you were a little fascinated, weren't you?'

She was still smiling and he suddenly felt incredibly foolish. 'Intrigued, maybe, but then I never knew her,' he said, trying to make light of it, wondering how much she had guessed.

'No, you never knew her. Anyway, Rachel considered Patrick to be hers and only hers. I'm the only person who has ever threatened that.'

'But he's married.'

'That didn't matter. Rachel knew that she always came first where Patrick was concerned. He idolised her. He would do anything for her. Nice, sensible, down-to-earth, good-natured Emma never got a look in, although she's exactly the right sort of woman for him, if only the stupid idiot knew it. When Rachel found out about us, well...I can imagine what she must have felt.'

'You said she stole someone you loved,' he said, thinking back to their conversation earlier that evening. 'You meant Patrick Tenison?'

She nodded. 'She made sure that whatever we had together was well and truly poisoned.' A look of pain crossed her face and she folded her arms and turned away, focussing on a far corner of the room.

'What happened?'

'I told you about the night when we had dinner a couple of months ago.'

'Yes, I remember.'

'Well, all that was true,' she said distantly. 'We then went back to her flat afterwards for a drink. She seemed particularly keen that I come. Anyhow, she managed to turn the conversation around to the fact that she'd done something very stupid. Something she really regretted and she was feeling very bad about it. She wouldn't tell me what it was, but naturally I was intrigued. Then the phone rang. Looking back on it now, I think she must have told him to call. Anyway, she answered it and took it out into the hall as though it were private. When she came back, her eyes were alight and she was smiling. She told me that it was Patrick. She said that they'd slept together the night before and that he was coming over. She said she thought she was in love with him.'

Tartaglia stared at her astonished. 'Did she know...'

She looked directly at him. 'About me and Patrick, you mean? Of course she knew, although I didn't realise it at the time. Patrick had let something slip, the silly twit.'

'And you believed her?' he asked, thinking of the black and white photograph of Rachel Tenison which was now pinned up over his desk in Barnes. *Cold eyelids that hide like a jewel hard eyes that grow soft for an hour...the cruel red mouth like a venomous flower...*Beneath all the superficial loveliness, she was rotten to the core. It was odd how, even though he had never known her, he felt disillusioned, if not a little betrayed. He thought of Rachel as he had first seen her, kneeling down in the snow, with her head bowed and hands clasped and for the first time he saw her as someone punished. Punishment. Perhaps that was what it was all about. But if Liz were telling the truth, then she and Patrick Tenison both had alibis.

Liz gazed at him with large, watery blue eyes. 'Yes. I didn't need to speak to Patrick. I knew she'd never make up something like that.'

'Why on earth did you stay friends with her? You must have known what she was like.'

She shrugged. 'We'd more or less grown up together and we had a lot of very good shared experiences. The strains and differences started to appear as we grew older, but I let it go, tried to gloss over it. You know, she did something similar when we were at university. She seduced someone I was supposed to be going out with. I should have broken off with her then. But maybe I'm weak, like everyone else around her, or just so plain stupid and sentimental about the past that I didn't want to see her darker side. Does that make sense?'

He nodded. Some things were impossible to put into words and friendships, particularly ones that went back a long way, often defied logical analysis.

'I suppose we all made allowances for her,' Liz continued, 'because of what had happened in her past. She was damaged.'

'Damaged, yes. I see that now.' For a second, his thoughts turned to Viktor Denisenko and the man who had left the roses in the park. Rachel: lovely and damaged. It was a heady cocktail and he was grateful now that he had never met her. Who knew what might have happened and whether he would have emerged with his sanity intact.

'What did you do after that?' he asked, after a moment.

'I felt like hitting her, punching her hard, for starters. But I managed to control myself. I didn't want to give her the satisfaction of seeing how much she'd hurt me. So I left. It was all I could do until I got down to the street to stop myself being sick. I suppose I was in shock. My arms and legs were like jelly. I sat outside in my car for a while crying, thinking it all through, amazed at how much I hated her.

I was in no state to drive home. At one point I remember wondering if maybe she'd been lying, just to get a reaction out of me. Then I saw him...' Her voice tailed away.

'Did you speak to him?'

Liz nodded. 'I tooted the horn. He looked shocked when he saw me there. He knew instantly that Rachel had told me. Anyway, he came over. I rolled down the window and shouted at him, told him what I thought, then I drove off before he had a chance to say anything. I didn't want to hear his excuses. Nothing could make it better. He followed me back to my brother's flat but I wouldn't let him in. He then sent me a letter the next morning. He tried to explain it all away, as if it was a mere nothing, and he said that he loved me. But it was too late for that. I knew Rachel would always be able to get to him because of what he had done with her and that she would make him pay. And through him she would make *me* pay. It wasn't going to stop. In the end, I suppose I also realised what a spineless wretch he is.'

'Are you going to be OK?' Tartaglia asked, wanting to reach out in some way, but not knowing what to say or do.

Liz sighed and rubbed her face with her hands. 'Yes. I've had a lot of time to think. It still hurts when I picture them together, but I guess I'll get over it in time. For the moment, my emotional reserves are worn right out and I feel numb. If you told me I was going to die tomorrow, I probably wouldn't give a damn.'

'But you were in love with him?' Tartaglia asked doubtfully, still puzzled over what it was that Liz had found so attractive about Tenison. Then it dawned on him. She had told him earlier that Rachel had stolen something precious from her, but it was actually the other way around. Liz had taken something that Rachel prized, probably more than anything. Consciously or unconsciously, it was a way of getting back at Rachel, and if Liz had taken pleasure in it, he wasn't the man to blame her.

Liz frowned. 'Don't sit there judging me.'

'I wasn't.'

'However odd it seems now, there certainly was a moment when I thought I was in love with Patrick. Perhaps we should have got it out of our systems sooner, but timing's everything, isn't it?'

'But why did he come round to see you that night?'

She gave him a feeble smile. 'Like a lot of men, he won't take no for an answer. Of course he was full of guilt about what he'd done, but I was suddenly a challenge, something that had to be won back. Anyway, he'd had quite a bit to drink that evening. Plus Rachel had been saying all sorts of nasty, horrible things to him. I guess he was just looking for a bit of sympathy, as well as hoping I might let him back into my bed.'

He looked at her questioningly.

'I was having none of it,' she said emphatically. 'I made him sleep in my brother's room.'

'So he wasn't actually with you?'

'Not physically in my bed, no.'

'Are you sure he didn't leave the flat at some point without your knowing?'

'Positive. As you can imagine, I've got a lot of things on my mind at the moment and I'm having problems sleeping. That night was no different. I got up twice, once at about four in the morning and then at six. Both times I went into the kitchen to make a cup of tea and I looked in on him. He was fast asleep.'

'When did you see him awake?'

'He came into my room the next morning. My alarm had just gone off, so it would have been just before eight. He wasn't dressed.'

'He could have gone to the park without your knowing.'

She looked astonished. 'What, killed Rachel and come straight back to the flat, cool as a cucumber? I don't think so. He's not that cold-blooded. He really loved Rachel.'

'Some people kill the person they love most.'

'Why? What's his motive? There's never been a single moment when I thought him capable of murdering her, otherwise I promise you I would have said something to you before.'

'Maybe you're wrong about him.'

She shook her head decisively and folded her arms. 'No. If he had killed her, and come back to the flat, pretending that he'd been there all night, he wouldn't have been able to hide it. I would have known that something was badly wrong.'

'You saw nothing out of the ordinary in his behaviour?'

'Absolutely not. He was perfectly, healthily normal, albeit pretty hung over. He even tried again to persuade me to have sex with him. I really can't see him killing Rachel then wanting a shag, can you? Whatever you think of him, he's not that callous.'

Tartaglia smiled. Libido was a funny, wayward thing, with a mind of its own, but it would take a hardened psychopath to kill someone and show no emotional reaction whatsoever, particularly to someone who knew him well.

'What will you do?' he asked.

'I'm not going back to him, if that's what you mean. I'm probably going to return to the US for a while. I need a bit of distance from everything that's happened here.'

He nodded, understanding how she must feel. 'Well, thank you for being so honest.' He was tempted to add 'finally' but thought it would be cheap. 'Perhaps before you leave the country, we can finish our drink. I'm sorry we were interrupted earlier.'

She put her head to one side as if she hadn't expected him to say that and smiled. 'You know, I'd like that very much.'

'Good. I'll call you. In the meantime, I think that will do for now.'

He was about to stand up when he saw Liz hesitate. 'Is there anything else you want to tell me?'

Liz nodded slowly. 'There is something. Maybe it's just my silly suspicious mind...I don't think he killed Rachel...'

'You mean Patrick Tenison?'

'No.' Liz bit her lip, as though she had spoken out of turn.

'Please, I need to know everything, even if it's just a suspicion or a hunch.'

Liz sighed heavily. 'I don't think he had anything to do with her murder. In fact I'm sure of it. But I think Jonathan—'

'Jonathan Bourne?'

She inclined her head.

'Go on.'

'Well, I have no proof, but I'm pretty sure he slept with Rachel that night.'

27

Late Monday morning, Tartaglia was at his desk catching up on paperwork. With Gary Jones still on holiday and Turner out on the road somewhere, he had the cramped, low-ceilinged office to himself and he was appreciating the relative quiet. But try as he might to focus his energies on ploughing through the backlog, his mind kept wandering to the Holland Park case, wishing that somewhere a glimmer of light would creep through.

On the strength of what Liz Volpe had said, plus the two glasses in Rachel Tenison's flat with the same fingerprint, they had hauled Jonathan Bourne out of bed early on Sunday morning and grilled him hard. He had finally admitted that he had gone back to Rachel Tenison's flat the night before she was killed, and had slept with her. It explained the phone call she had made to him around eleven o'clock that night when, according to him, she had asked him to come over. It also explained the two glasses with the same set of prints. But however much pressure they exerted, he stuck to his story: he had left her flat at about five the next morning and had gone straight home. He denied point blank having killed her. He had no alibi, but, as with Patrick Tenison, if Jonathan Bourne had killed Rachel Tenison, there was no explanation for the definite links to Catherine Watson's murder.

Meanwhile, Broadbent had also been re-interviewed, but nothing interesting or new had emerged. Although every effort had been made to treat him with kid gloves and it had been impressed upon him that he was not under suspicion, he had no recollection, two years on, of having seen Catherine Watson in the company of any man. Everywhere they tried seemed to lead to a dead-end; nothing was giving.

Tartaglia looked up at the photograph of Rachel pinned to the board above his desk, and then at the one next to it of Catherine Watson. They seemed so different in every way, one exploited by men right up until the end, the other exploiting mercilessly. What could they possibly have had in common?

Feeling tired from being closeted all morning, he got up and stretched, flexing his shoulders and neck to get rid of the stiffness. His eye fell on the miserable sight of three half-drunk mugs of cold coffee huddled together on his desk, one for each hour he had been sitting there. Deciding to stretch his legs, if nothing else, he gathered up the mugs and walked along the corridor to the office kitchen. The room was small and windowless, having once been a storage room, and even though it was generally kept clean and tidy, it had a permanently stale, unappetising smell. He avoided it whenever he could, but short of going out to one of the many local shops, there was no alternative.

He put his mugs in the dishwasher and almost without thinking switched on the kettle, spooning another helping of instant coffee into a fresh mug from the cupboard. As he waited for the water to boil, he wondered if he should make the effort and go out to get a proper cappucino instead. He had been brought up with good Italian coffee at home and had never managed to acclimatise his taste buds to instant, but he still had a lot of work to finish and it would have to do for the moment.

As the kettle pinged, Dave Wightman put his head around the door.

'Ready when you are, Sir,' he said brightly. 'Shall I set it up in your office?'

Wightman looked unusually fresh for someone who had had little sleep. He had managed to locate and retrieve from store the original disc copies of Broadbent's entire photo collection, made at the time of

Gifford's investigation. The files comprised thousands and thousands of jpegs, going back over two years up to and including the time of Watson's murder. Having loaded them all onto a laptop, Wightman had been busy for most of the previous twenty-four hours sorting them into date order.

'Use Gary's desk,' Tartaglia said, filling the mug with hot water. 'I'll catch up with you in a moment.'

Wightman disappeared from view and Tartaglia added an extra measure of coffee to make the brew stronger, followed by a few drops of milk. Satisfied with the colour, he carried the mug back down the corridor to his office, where Wightman was now sitting at Gary Jones's empty desk next to the window, the laptop open in front of him.

Tartaglia pulled up his chair and sat down, peering at the screen, which was filled top to bottom with photographic thumbnails, eight per line, just big enough to make out a basic image but nothing more.

'These were all taken by Broadbent?' Tartaglia asked.

'Yes. There are a few crappy shots taken with a mobile, but he's mostly using two cameras throughout: a serious piece of Nikon kit with a big telephoto and a Canon Ixus 55.'

'What's that?'

'It's a small pocket camera. The zoom's nowhere near as powerful as the Nikon's, but it's a heck of a lot more discreet and portable. I've removed everything after the time of Watson's murder to make it easier and I've re-ordered them into separate folders according to date.'

'I can't tell what's going on,' Tartaglia said, still unable to see anything recognisable.

'I'll make them bigger in a minute. What time frame do you want to look at?'

'Let's start as close as possible to the date of Catherine Watson's murder and work back.'

'OK.' Wightman scrolled to the top of the screen. The folders ran down the left-hand side of the screen and as Wightman opened one of them, a series of images sprang up. 'These were taken the day Watson died,' he said. 'The first lot are in Oxford Street. He spent a good few hours there, judging by the times on the pictures. Then there's another batch on a bus, then some more in another street, somewhere a bit more suburban, although I couldn't see a post code or street name anywhere.'

He clicked on the top-left picture and enlarged it, showing a view of a crowded pavement, people bundled up in overcoats and scarves, carrying shopping bags, some walking, some gazing at a large, expensive-looking window display. It was a bright, sunny winter's day and the quality of the pictures was good. Tartaglia scanned the faces but nobody looked familiar.

'This lot's outside Selfridge's,' Wightman said, tabbing forwards, showing an apparently endless stream of similar views. 'After that we get John Lewis and Top Shop.'

As Tartaglia looked closer, he realised that the camera was tracking the progress of a pleasant-looking woman with shoulder-length, curly dark hair. She was in the company of another woman who was shorter and plumper with layered, streaky blonde hair. The two walked together along the road, chatting and stopping to look in shop windows. A perfectly normal Saturday, apart from the fact that they were being followed and photographed.

'Is there a lot of this sort of stuff in there?' Tartaglia asked, pointing at the laptop.

'Yeah. It's pretty representative, from what I've seen. He's out with his camera most Saturdays. Seems it's his big day out. He took over three hundred shots in total on this day alone.'

'How many did he take of that particular woman?'

'At least fifty. He only stops when she and her friend go down into Bond Street tube. After that, he follows another woman, and then another. It seems to be quite random, although they all look rather similar.'

'They all look like Catherine Watson, you mean. He's obviously got a physical type he likes. Are all the other photos like this?' he asked, thinking back to what Turner had said about the majority being of unknown women walking around in the street, and wondering if they were wasting their time looking through them.

'More or less, although he's also got a thing about architecture, mainly churches. Some of the shots are quite artistic. He also likes schools.'

'Schools?'

'Never any kids. Just the buildings. And the women.'

'Weird.'

'Takes all sorts, Sir,' Wightman said, as if he'd seen it all in his short life. He tabbed backwards in time.

'Is there any pattern to it? I seem to remember he had some sort of part-time job during the week.'

'Yes. Saturday and Sunday are the busiest, followed by Monday and Thursday. I imagine he works the other three days. The little Canon seems to go with him everywhere.'

Wightman tabbed slowly through the rest of the file, image by image. Almost all of the pictures taken that Saturday were of women, none of them aware of being photographed. As Turner had said, there was nothing illegal in any of it, nothing hinting at a darker, more violent side, but it was still very bizarre and Tartaglia wondered what sort of peculiar mind found satisfaction in doing such a thing.

'Right. That's Saturday over and done with,' Wightman said, once they had looked at every frame. 'The next lot were taken on the Thursday before Catherine Watson died.' He looked down at his notes. 'Yes. Somewhere along the Finchley Road, close to where Broadbent lives, judging by the postcode.'

A series of photos followed of a busy road, lined on one side with fruit and vegetable stalls. Cars and buses passed, people thronged the pavement and it was like a thousand other thoroughfares outside the city centre with its halal butchers, fast-food outlets and endless cheap clothing shops. Apart from the backs of people's heads, it wasn't clear what Broadbent was photographing. Tartaglia's head was already beginning to swim and he wondered how much more he could endure when he suddenly he spotted a familiar face.

'That's her, that's Catherine Watson,' he said, almost rising in his chair. The shot was of a café window, with a woman sitting inside. He recognised her even though she was half obscured by the blurred images of people passing in front of the camera. It looked as though Broadbent had been standing on the opposite side of the road with his telephoto. She had a cup of something on the table in front of her and had turned her head to look out of the window at the street. 'Are there any more in the sequence?' he asked impatiently.

Wightman tabbed forwards and they saw her now in profile, her chin resting on her hand as she looked in front of her. He could tell instantly from her body language that there was someone opposite her.

'Can you enlarge it? She's not on her own.'

'Sure. Give me a minute.'

Wightman clicked a few buttons and zoomed in on the table. Tartaglia thought he could just make out the shadowed profile of a face.

'The light's reflecting off the window and I can't see inside clearly. Go forwards and let's see if we can get a better image.'

Wightman tabbed through the shots until finally he found a number taken from a different angle. Maybe Broadbent had been asked to move or couldn't see what was going on inside the café.

'Look there.' Tartaglia pointed at the screen. Watson was no longer at the table but there was someone else on the other side. 'Can you enlarge that bit?'

He watched as Wightman enlarged the image, zooming in on a khaki-coloured sleeve and a pair of masculine hands cupped around a mug of something. Wightman tried the next image and then the next until a triangle of face and blonde hair were visible as whoever it was bent forwards to sip from the mug.

'I wonder if that's Michael Jennings,' Tartaglia said, remembering the head and shoulders he had seen of Jennings in the file and trying to contain his excitement. 'Can you enlarge it a bit more, see if you can get a better image?'

Wightman fiddled with the keyboard and mouse until the picture gradually became clearer.

'I'm sure that's Jennings,' Tartaglia said. 'Go back to the beginning of the sequence. I want to see all of them now.'

The first twenty frames in the series showed Catherine Watson walking along the road. Now that they knew what they were looking for, they could pick her out in the crowd. She was simply dressed in a long beige mac and was carrying a large leather bag and an umbrella. The camera followed her along the street, snapped her going in through the door of the café and sitting down.

'Is Jennings already there?'

'It's not clear,' Wightman said, clicking through the images.

'I'm sure he was there before her,' Tartaglia said emphatically. 'Look at that one. Even though he's not in the picture, you can tell from the angle of her face as she sits down that she's looking at someone opposite. And she's smiling.'

'Looks like he was waiting for her. No chance meeting.'

'Yes. Which means Jennings lied. He said that the last time he saw her was a week before her death, at college. He also denied ever meeting her anywhere else. Are you sure about the date these were taken?

'It was the Thursday before her murder.'

'Can you make double sure?'

Wightman clicked on the image, drew down a menu and clicked again. A pop up box appeared. 'There you go. All the info you need. Number of pixels, date and time of photo, date and time it was imported and modified, name of jpeg, size and even the make of camera. Pretty neat, isn't it?'

Wishing he had such fluency with the technology, Tartaglia checked the date and time. The picture had been taken at 15:37 on the Thursday before Watson's murder. 'Thank God for digital. What happens next? You have Watson coming out on her own, don't you?

'Yes.'

'I want to see where she goes.'

The pictures showed Watson emerging from the café and walking down the street. The angle changed as Broadbent crossed the road and followed behind her. The pavement was crowded but in most of the shots they could see the back of her head and shoulders as she walked along.

'There's Jennings,' Tartaglia said, nudging Wightman's sleeve. He pointed at the screen. 'Look, there, the bloke in the green anorak.'

Wightman frowned. 'It's him, isn't it? With the blonde hair?'

'Yes. He's right behind her.'

'He's definitely following her. Why didn't Broadbent mention this at the time?'

Tartaglia shrugged, thinking back to what Angela Harper had said. 'Any number of reasons. By all accounts he was very upset and confused when he was first questioned. Maybe he wasn't even aware of what he had caught on film. He's watching Watson. She's his focus. He may not even have noticed Jennings at all.'

As the camera followed Watson down the busy street, Jennings's head was just visible amongst the crowd of people. Watson turned into what Tartaglia recognised as her road, rushing between the traffic across the street, a shopping bag and satchel in her hand. The last few close-up shots showed her climbing the steps to the front door and fumbling in her bag for her keys. As she went inside, Broadbent zoomed out to a panoramic view of the street.

'Can you see Jennings anywhere?

'No. I don't think so.'

'Isn't that him over there, by the bus stop?'

Wightman selected the area and enlarged it.

'Certainly looks like him. He's got his back to the camera. He's staring at Watson's house.'

Tartaglia pushed back his chair and got to his feet. He had seen enough. 'I want you to go through the rest of the photos with a fine-tooth comb and I want a printout of anything that looks remotely interesting, along with a log of the date and time it was taken.'

'It will take a while, Sir.'

'Take as long as you need,' Tartaglia said. Steele would just have to wear the overtime expense. 'If it helps, I could ask Nick to give you a hand...'

Wightman's boyish face cracked into a wide grin. 'I'm better off on my own, Sir. Nick doesn't know his arse from his elbow when it comes to computers.'

'Point taken. When you're done, send the files and a list of the ones we're interested in to the anoraks at Newlands Park. Let's see what they can get out of them.' A good computer-graphics technician could work the most amazing wizardry with a jpeg.

Feeling almost high from the tension, Tartaglia went over to his own desk and dialled Turner's mobile. But there was no answer and he was diverted to voicemail. He slammed the phone down hard in its cradle, causing Wightman to look up questioningly. They had to find Jennings, but there was nothing to be done until he got hold of Turner.

Needing to fill in the time until he heard back from Turner and take his mind off things, Tartaglia said, 'I'm going to get a coffee and stretch my legs. Can I get you something?'

'A large latte would be nice, if you're going out.'

Tartaglia put on his leather jacket and marched down the corridor to Turner's old office on the other side of the building, wondering if he had taken refuge in there. But it was empty, as was the large, open-plan office outside, most of the detectives being either at lunch or out on the road somewhere. Eventually he tracked down a young constable on Turner's team microwaving some soup in the office kitchen and asked her to page Turner immediately and have him call him on his mobile.

Outside the air was cold and damp, the sky heavy with cloud. He walked through the small, crowded car park at the rear of the building and out through the front gate, zipping his jacket up and shoving his hands in his pockets for warmth. Excitement still bubbling, mixed with frustration and irritation at not being able to reach Turner, he strode briskly down Station Road towards the village, wondering just how long it would take for Turner to call him back.

Whilst the photographs showed a previously unknown meeting between Watson and Jennings, somewhere close to where she lived and far from the university where she had taught, they didn't add up to much more than that. To his eyes, it didn't look like a chance meeting, but such things were open to interpretation. There was no record in the files of Jennings calling Watson's phone at any time, although it was possible he had used a payphone. Maybe the meeting in the café wasn't the first; maybe she had invited him over for dinner on the Saturday and he had murdered her. But it was pointless speculating. What they had was barely enough to arrest him, let alone take to the CPS. Having coffee with a woman and following her home didn't add up to a watertight charge of murder. He felt as though they were clutching at straws, but it was all they had. Somehow, they had to find proof.

He caught the smell of wood smoke on the air, someone nearby enjoying a proper open fire in contravention of council regulations. A fire was one of the things he liked most about winter, taking him straight back to his childhood home in Edinburgh where his father had insisted on making a log fire every Sunday, in spite of the fact that they had central heating. As he approached the Green, he heard a shriek of high-pitched laughter together with a sudden clamour of quacking and looked across the road. The grass under the trees was almost entirely covered by a thick, sodden brown carpet of leaves, brought down by the recent wind and rain. A woman with a pushchair and a couple of small children about the same age as his nephew and niece stood on the path by the pond. Wrapped up in bright yellow macs and Wellingtons, the children were scattering bread to a crowd of ducks, geese and pigeons. Each scrap was being loudly fought over and a couple of geese were trying to steal a march on the others by trying to grab the bread straight from the children's fingers. Judging by the children's laughter, they didn't seem to mind. Looking at them, they seemed so carefree, with all the time in the world, and Tartaglia envied them.

He turned left into the High Street and walked the last few yards to the Food Gallery, a recently opened café and delicatessen which served the best sandwiches and coffee for miles around. The morning trade was always brisk and the stools at the counter in the window and to one side of the door were all taken, the occupants busy reading the magazines and daily newspapers provided, as they drank their tea or coffee. Tartaglia edged his way through and joined the back of the small queue, behind a broad-shouldered middle-aged woman in a green tweed coat. Her basket was full to brimming with jars of jam, chutney and mustard from the large dresser display at the back, along with a couple of packs of Thai fishcakes from the freezer. The sight made him feel suddenly hungry. As he studied the blackboard of daily specials, wondering what to have, he heard another woman loudly proclaiming to the owner, Nikki, how the shop's homemade brownies were the best she had ever eaten. He had just decided on bacon, avocado and watercress on rye, with mayonnaise, together with an espresso for himself and a latte for Wightman, when his phone rang. Turner at last.

'Got your message. You'll be pleased to hear I've finally found Jennings.'

'Good. Are you with him now?'

'No. He's been kipping at a flat on Camberwell New Road. He's due back in a couple of hours. You said it was urgent. What's up?'

'We've got enough to arrest him.' Tartaglia briefly told Turner what they had found amongst Broadbent's photographs. 'Where are you?'

'Still at the flat. The girl who has the flat said I could stay until he gets back. But if I'm going to arrest him, I'll need some backup.'

'I'll be there as quick as I can and I'll bring Nick with me.' Although Turner had at last come up trumps in finding Jennings, Tartaglia decided it wasn't wise to leave anything to chance, or to Turner.

'Make sure you keep a low profile,' Turner said, after giving him the address. 'Jennings knows we're looking for him and I don't want him to sniff us out and do a runner.'

28

Jennings's address was in the middle of a dilapidated terrace of eighteenth-century houses on the Camberwell New Road, south of the Thames. The tall, five-storey building was set back from the heavy traffic behind corroding iron railings and a strip of untidy concreted front garden. The brickwork was almost black and grimy net curtains stretched across most of the windows, with satellite dishes sprouting from every floor.

Minderedes parked the car around the corner and he and Tartaglia walked along the main road and in through the rickety wrought iron gate. Rap music thudded from somewhere above, almost drowning out the cries of a small child on the ground floor.

'This way,' Tartaglia said, noticing a large black arrow painted alongside the number 34a, pointing down towards the basement. They skirted around a collection of overflowing bins and bags of rubbish and descended a set of steep, slippery, moss-covered steps to the basement front door.

Minderedes turned up his nose. 'God, it stinks.'

'Cats and drains,' Tartaglia replied knowledgably.

He knocked and Turner opened the door almost immediately.

'Come in, guys,' he said, with a grandiose sweep of his hand. 'Make yourselves at home.' The temperature was cellar-like and the air was rank with damp; still the powerful, retch-making smell of drains.

'What's the layout?' Tartaglia asked, trying to hold his breath as he glanced around the narrow mustard-yellow hall.

'Bathroom in there,' Turner said, pointing to a door immediately behind them. 'There's bars on the window.'

''Scuse me. Gotta have a pee,' Minderedes said, disappearing inside and switching on the light.

'What's in there?' Tartaglia asked Turner, gesturing towards another half-closed door on their right.

'Bedroom. Again, bars on the window. The lounge is this way.'

Tartaglia followed Turner down the narrow passage to the sitting room at the back where the curtains were tightly drawn as though it were still night.

'I didn't want to open the curtains or a window,' Turner said. 'Jennings is a clever sod; he'd know something's up.'

The only source of light was a naked pink bulb in the centre of the low ceiling, which Turner knocked with his head, sending the pool of soft light spinning around over the mottled, greyish-green walls. The room was littered with empty beer cans, takeaway cartons and overflowing ashtrays, and the centre of the floor was covered with a rug in an indeterminate shade of brown that would hide most stains. The only furnishings were a sofa, an armchair, an old TV, and a makeshift coffee table that had been assembled from piles of bricks and an old door. It all looked as though it had been hauled off a skip.

'What a shithole,' Minderedes exclaimed, coming into the room behind Tartaglia and looking around. 'God, I hope I don't catch something just standing here.' He dug deep into the pockets of his coat and put on a pair of new-looking black leather gloves.

'Is this his flat?' Tartaglia asked, surveying the debris.

'Belongs to his girlfriend,' Turner replied. 'She's a smackhead; doesn't seem to be into using a Hoover.'

'But he's staying here?'

'According to her, he's been dossing down here for the last three months. Beggars can't be choosers, I guess.'

'Where is she?'

'Soon as I paid her off she was out the door like greased lightning to score some skag. She's in the bedroom now, sleeping it off.'

'She knows you're here?'

'Yeah. She told me I could stay.'

'Good. What about Jennings?'

'He's got some kind of a job in a restaurant or pub kitchen. She wasn't sure where. Says he usually comes back sometime after three.'

Tartaglia looked at his watch. There was a good hour to go. 'Is there a back exit?'

Turner pointed. 'In the kitchen through there, but I'll cover it. He's not getting past me, I promise.'

Minderedes walked over to take a look. 'Jesus,' he said, swiftly ducking out again. 'This fucking place is alive. There are cockroaches everywhere.'

'All in the line of duty, Nick,' Tartaglia said. 'We're here for poor Catherine Watson.'

'She won't be paying the bloody dry-cleaning bill, will she?' Minderedes replied crossly, brushing something invisible off his sleeve and scraping the heel of his shoe on the edge of the rug.

'Go outside and wait across the road by the bus stop. Text us when you see him coming.'

'Where will you be?' Turner asked Tartaglia, as Minderedes left the room.

'I'll cover the front from the bedroom. What about the girl?'

'She's in la-la land; she won't give you any trouble.'

'Well, I just hope we don't have long to wait. This place gives me the creeps.'

'I've got all the time in the world for Michael Jennings,' Turner said, sweeping an empty pizza box off the armchair and sitting down. 'This one's for Alan Gifford and I'm going to enjoy every minute of it.

I just hope we can make something stick. It would kill me if we have to let him go again.'

'How did you find Jennings? Did you get a tip-off?'

Turner nodded. 'I told you I put the word out with all his old mates. The girlfriend, or whatever she is—her name's Heather—she heard we were looking for him. She called me this morning as soon as he'd gone out. She shopped him for the princely sum of two hundred quid. I paid her a hundred up front, and told her there's another hundred to follow if we get Jennings, plus fifty for good behaviour if she cooperates.'

'How does she come to know Jennings?'

'They were at uni together, although you'd never know she's that young, or had it in her to study something. Poor thing looks wrecked. I'll bet she's on the game to finance her little habit.'

'Did she tell you anything useful about Jennings?'

Turner nodded. 'Said he's real strange. He likes to dress up in army stuff, combat gear, like he's a para or something. When I asked her about his sexual preferences, if he did anything weird with her, she clammed up like she was the Virgin Mary.'

'Maybe's she's embarrassed.'

'She's a bloody tom, for Christ's sake. No point in her being embarrassed, is there?'

Tartaglia wanted to say that even someone who sold their body could have a sense of dignity, but Turner wasn't in the mood for subtleties. 'Anything else?'

'Yes. She's got some interesting marks on her wrists, like rope burns, and bruising on her arms and neck, and it's not just from the needle.'

'Really?' Tartaglia said, now interested. 'And you think Jennings is responsible?'

'Has to be. I asked her if he hurt her, but again she wouldn't say anything, although she didn't actually deny it. Gave me the big-eye treatment and sucked her finger. I don't know what he's been doing to her, what games he's been playing, but she's scared shitless.'

'Poor girl,' he said with feeling. He thought back to what Angela Harper had said about Michael Jennings fitting the profile and how the killer would be keeping his urges and fantasies in check. Harper had been right all along and he looked forward to telling her. 'Do you think Heather will talk?'

'Maybe. If she feels safe. But we'll have to lock Jennings up first, so he can't get to her in any way.'

'Why's she decided to turn him in?'

'She was also one of Catherine Watson's students and she knows what happened to her. Maybe what Jennings has been doing to hurt her has made her join up the dots. As I said, she's real scared. She told me he knows we're looking for him and he's threatened her. Said he'd kill her if she told anyone where he was.'

'Well, she's certainly brave. Thank God we're here now. I just hope we'll be able to find something to put him away. Have you had a chance to look around?'

Turner nodded. 'I had a good scout about once she'd gone out. Of course, I put it all back the way I found it, so Jennings won't know anyone's been nosing around. But either it's well hidden, and we'll have to pull the place apart to find it once we've nabbed him, or he's got it stashed somewhere else.'

Tartaglia glanced around the room, thinking that there weren't many obvious hiding places. 'You're sure he's staying here?'

'That's what Heather said. He got kicked out of the place he was in before and moved in with her. I found some clothes of his in a chest of drawers in the bedroom, and there's a rucksack and a bag of books in the cupboard. But apart from that, nothing interesting.'

Tartaglia thought back again to what Harper had said. 'He has to be keeping his rape kit somewhere else, then. He'll want to have access to it, have it all close to him.'

'She said he's got a big bunch of keys which he never lets out of his sight. Said he practically brained her when she took them once to go to the shops while he was asleep. Maybe he's got a lockup somewhere.'

'If he has, we've got to find it.'

Tartaglia left Turner and went down the hall to the front room. As he opened the door, he was greeted by a wave of sweet, musky incense, which was so strong it masked the general odour of the flat for a moment. A pair of dirty red patterned curtains were drawn against the day, but there was enough light coming from the passage for him to make out Heather, lying flat on her back in the middle of a mattress on the floor, a sheet half twisted around her middle. He had seen more than his fair share of junkies in his time on the beat, often after they had OD'd, but he was not judgmental. It was impossible to understand another person's hell and looking at the outline of the young girl on the bed he felt a deep sadness.

He moved into the room, and as his eyes adjusted to the dim light he noticed how pale she looked, her skin almost luminously white. Dressed in tight jeans and a T-shirt that stopped well above her midriff, she looked like a doll, one scrawny arm flung across the pillow, her bare feet poking out awkwardly over the end of the mattress, not quite touching the floor. A syringe, spoon, lighter and other bits and pieces of addict paraphernalia lay scattered beside her, along with a tattered old teddy bear, its glassy eyes staring up at the ceiling.

He bent down and looked at Heather more closely, taking in her short, ragged brown hair and her neat-featured face, with its small, upturned nose and pretty little mouth. He thought he could see the bruises and burn marks at her wrists and ankles that Turner had described and some sort of bruising or shadowing on her neck. He instantly thought of the similar marks on Rachel Tenison's body. Maybe she had picked Jennings up in a bar somewhere. Maybe that

was the connection. Catherine. Rachel. Heather. At least Heather was
still alive. But Turner was wrong about one thing: in her self-induced
torpor she appeared hardly more than a child.

It also struck him suddenly that she looked like Sam Donovan, although the idea instantly made him uncomfortable. Perhaps it was a
trick of the light, or the lack of light but, gazing at Heather, it was as
though he had glimpsed Donovan in another life, or in a nightmare,
and the thought brought him up sharp, making him instantly want to
see her, warm, hearty and healthy, and put his arms around her.
Maybe it was just the echoes from the Bridegroom case again coming
back to haunt him. He wondered if Turner had noticed the physical
resemblance, just as he wondered yet again what Turner had been
doing at Donovan's house the other night.

Heather lay motionless and silent. Concerned, he knelt down on
the mattress and listened hard until he finally picked up her faint,
slow, shallow breathing. Reassured, he parked himself on a corner beside her, content with the steady drone of the traffic outside and the
beat of the music from up above, and settled down to wait.

It wasn't long before he felt the vibration of his phone in his
pocket—a text from Minderedes, as arranged, sent simultaneously to
him and Turner:

Jennings coming. Will follow.

He looked at his watch. Jennings was home early. He stood up
and moved into the shadow behind the bedroom door. Within seconds, he heard the thud of feet on the basement stairs outside the
window, then the sound of a key in the lock. The front door banged
behind him and Jennings marched straight past the bedroom door and
down the hall into the sitting room. As Tartaglia came out from behind the door and followed him down the hall, he heard shouts,

followed by the drone of Turner reading Jennings his rights.

Jennings stood just inside the doorway facing Turner, arms tense by his sides as if ready to make a move, the muscles in the back of his neck rigid.

'Shut up, will you?' Jennings shouted, over Turner's voice. 'You're crazy. I've done nothing wrong.' He seemed unaware that Tartaglia had come in behind him.

Although Jennings couldn't have been more than about five eight or nine, he was muscular and thickset, as though he worked out regularly. He had thick, layered, streaky blonde hair and was wearing jeans, trainers, and a navy blue fleece with a hood. Tartaglia instantly thought back to the description of the man Liz Volpe had seen in Holland Park, wondering if she might have been wrong about his height. At a distance of thirty yards, in poor light, it would be easy to make a mistake.

'You've got no right to be here. Get out!'

'We've got every right,' Turner said. 'Haven't you been listening?'

'You can't arrest me. I've done nothing wrong and you know it. This is persecution.' His voice was a high-pitched whine.

'Tell him how it is, Mark,' Turner said flatly, glancing over at Tartaglia.

Suddenly aware that there was someone else in the room, Jennings swung around, looking first at Tartaglia, then back at Turner again. 'I've done nothing wrong, do you hear me? You know I had nothing to do with Doctor Watson's murder. Why are you persecuting me?'

Turner shook his head. 'Don't give me that self-righteous crap, Michael.'

'You're trying to stitch me up, like last time.'

'Shut it, Michael. Got new evidence. This time you won't get away.'

As Turner moved towards Jennings, Tartaglia saw a flash of steel. 'Look out!' he shouted.

'Hey, steady, Michael,' Turner said, jumping back and raising his big hands. 'Put the knife away. You don't want to do anything silly, now.'

Breaths coming in short, sharp bursts, Jennings shifted from foot to foot, the blade of what looked like a Commando knife glinting in the light. He held it out in front of him confidently, as though he knew how to use it, his eyes flicking from Turner to Tartaglia and back again.

Tartaglia wondered if Jennings was high on something, although his speech and coordination seemed normal. 'Put the knife down and we can talk. That's all we want to do. Just talk.'

Jennings stabbed the air with the knife. 'No. Get away from me. You can't arrest me.'

'Don't be a plonker, Michael,' Turner said. 'It won't do you any good. You're coming with us.'

'You're not taking me. I'm innocent, I tell you.'

'Then put the bloody knife down.'

'No. Let me out.'

His voice was shrill and desperate. It was an extreme reaction given that he had been through this before and Tartaglia wondered if there was something more than a bit of alcohol or dope behind it. He needed to be handled very carefully and Turner's heavy-handed approach was not helping matters.

'Look, if you're innocent, you've got nothing to worry about,' Tartaglia said, trying to calm him.

'Yeah, that's right, Michael. Give it up, for Christ's sake.' Turner took another step forwards.

'No,' Jennings shouted, shifting around towards Tartaglia, as if about to make a run for it.

Tartaglia raised both palms to him in an appeasing gesture. 'Whoa, Michael. Put the knife down.'

Jennings was sweating, face bright pink in the light, and he was panting loudly. He looked anything but rational. Turner started to edge forwards again behind him.

'Back off, Simon,' Tartaglia shouted, not taking his eyes off Jennings. 'Let me handle it.' He lowered his voice. 'I'm going to ask you one more time, Michael. Put the knife down.'

Jennings held his ground. 'Get outta the way or I'll fuckin' kill you.'

Hands still up, Tartaglia clenched his fists and positioned himself, ready. 'Can't do that, Michael. I really don't want to hurt you, but you've got to come with us.'

Out of the corner of his eye, Tartaglia saw Turner move forwards again.

'Fucking get back, Simon,' Tartaglia shouted.

Without warning, Jennings lunged at Tartaglia, thrusting the knife towards his chest. Moving fast, Tartaglia turned with a scissor movement, grabbing hold of Jennings's knife hand and slicing his other arm down hard on Jennings's elbow. He heard the snap of bone. Jennings screamed and the knife clattered to the ground as Tartaglia forced him down onto his face on the floor.

'Cuff him, will you, Simon?' Tartaglia said, still holding Jennings down as he kicked the knife away into a far corner.

Before Turner had a chance, Minderedes appeared through the doorway, ready with a set of cuffs, and bent over Jennings.

'I'll have you for this,' Jennings yelled at Tartaglia. 'I'll fucking have you for this.'

'Shut it or I'll hurt you even more,' Minderedes growled. Securing Jennings, he pulled him to his feet, still yelping with pain, and turned to Tartaglia. 'There's a couple of uniforms waiting outside, Sir. We'll take him to the local nick and get him a doctor.'

'His arm's broken. You'd better get him straight over to A&E. But whatever you do, don't take off the cuffs. He's desperate to get away for some reason.'

'Jeez, Mark. You're lethal,' Turner said, wiping the sweat from his brow with his hand as Minderedes propelled Jennings out of the room. 'Didn't know we had fucking Steven Seagal on the team.'

'It's Ju-Jitsu, not Aikido,' Tartaglia replied sharply, wanting to put him in his place. Maybe it was nerves on Turner's part and the release of tension, but it didn't feel right to make light of things. He wasn't proud of what he had done, but it was either that or take a knife in the chest and, in his view, Turner had provoked the whole situation unnecessarily.

'Bloody useful, whatever it was,' Turner said, nodding slowly as though it meant something to him. 'You a black belt, or something? Maybe you can teach me a few moves.'

Tartaglia said nothing.

'When did you learn all that stuff?' Turner asked, trailing him out of the room.

'At school. I don't practise it now.' It was over fifteen years since he had last set foot in a dojo, but it was one of those things, like riding a bike, which you never forgot, instincts and reactions still as natural and automatic as breathing. Luckily, he rarely ever had cause to use it.

'You like the tough guy stuff?'

'Quite the opposite. I was being bullied.'

'What, you?'

'It can happen to anyone. My dad thought martial arts would give me confidence.'

'Is that what did it?' Turner said with a half smile. 'There was I thinking it was the Latin blood.'

Resisting the urge to wipe the silly expression off Turner's face, he stopped outside the bedroom door. 'I just want to check on Heather.'

He pushed open the door and went inside. She hadn't moved. He knelt down beside her and listened again for the sound of her breathing. He could barely hear anything now. She was cold to the touch and for a moment he couldn't find her pulse. He put his face close to hers again. There was no smell of alcohol on her breath as far as he could tell, which was good, although it was possible she had taken a cocktail of something else with the heroin. Maybe she would be OK; maybe she would wake up on her own. But instinct told him she was slipping away. Apart from the human cost of a girl he had never spoken to, to whom he felt some peculiar bond due to her resemblance to Donovan, they could not afford to lose her. She was the only person alive that they knew of who could bear witness to the perverted character of Michael Jennings.

'Tur-ner!' he shouted urgently, not taking his eyes off Heather.

Turner put his head around the door. 'She OK?'

'No. Get a fucking ambulance.'

29

'I didn't do it. I had nothing to do with Dr Watson's murder. How many times do I have to say it for you to believe me?' Eyes tearing, hands clasped in front of him, Michael Jennings looked imploringly across the table, first at Donovan and then at DS Jason Pindar, next to her.

Donovan shook her head slowly from side to side as though she had seen it all before and didn't believe a word of it.

They were in a room at Camberwell Police Station. It was nearly eight in the evening and the tape and camera had been running for almost two hours. Tartaglia, Steele and Turner were sitting in another room nearby, following the proceedings on video link. Tartaglia was watching Jennings's every reaction to the questions put to him, but his boyish face remained a picture of unwavering innocence, the heavy-duty plaster on his arm and the sling an additional, theatrical touch of helplessness. With his mop of blonde hair, snub nose and blue eyes, he appeared incapable of doing anything nasty—more likely to be rescuing a cat stuck up a tree or helping old ladies across the road than committing violent acts of rape, torture and murder. Hunched low in his chair, with his torn, paint-spattered jeans, fleece and dirty trainers, Jennings looked like any young student. It was almost impossible to imagine that this man had pulled a knife on Tartaglia and Turner several hours earlier.

Jennings's brief, Andrew Harrison, was a tall, angular man in an ill-fitting suit, with a shock of greasy black hair and heavy-framed glasses. He sat beside Jennings, fiddling with the top of his pen and, for the most part, he let Jennings deal with the questions on his own. Jennings was doing well without him, and Donovan and Pindar were finding it impossible to make any headway. Whatever they threw at him, he just hit it straight back. He was innocent of Watson's murder and nothing would make him say anything different.

It looked as though they were in for a long night and Tartaglia wondered how he was going to endure it. The small room was stiflingly hot and airless, the atmosphere so dry his throat felt raw. He and Turner had taken off their jackets and ties and rolled up their sleeves, but it made no difference. The sweat was running down his neck and his shirt felt constrictingly tight across his chest and shoulders as though it had suddenly shrunk. He could smell Steele's faint lemony perfume, though it was almost smothered by the acrid odour of cigarette smoke that hung around Turner like a cloud. Turner had already nipped out once on some pretext and had come back reeking of it. Tartaglia was surprised Steele hadn't noticed, but her nose was blocked, judging by her thick nasal tone. She sat next to him, even paler than usual and shivering, her overcoat wrapped tightly around her shoulders like a blanket and an ice blue woollen scarf wound several times around her neck. She had a large bottle of mineral water beside her, which she sipped from sporadically, and had insisted that the window remain closed.

'Jennings is good, isn't he?' Turner said, glancing round at Tartaglia and Steele. 'This is exactly the sort of stuff he gave us last time round. You'd think butter wouldn't melt. We went over and over everything but he kept singing the same effing tune.'

'I guess if the wheel ain't broke, why fix it?' Tartaglia said, thinking back again to the very different Jennings he had faced earlier, the one with real madness in his eyes. If only that had been captured on film, to replay to a jury or whoever was going to be investigating Jennings's complaint about the way he had been arrested and the injury he had received.

'He's a real little Boy Scout,' Turner replied acidly. 'Put him in a suit and tie and tidy him up a bit, and any female member of a jury's either going to want to mother him or shag him.'

'It's never going to get that far, at this rate,' Steele said with feeling, turning bleary, red-rimmed eyes briefly on Tartaglia and Turner. She gave a dry hacking cough, took a pack of tissues from her bag and blew her nose loudly. 'I don't see Jennings confessing to anything. We're going to have to find something else.'

'I 'ave your signed statement here, from when you was last interviewed,' Pindar continued, in his deep, flat tone. 'You *said* you never met Catherine Watson outside university. You *said* you had never been near her home. Yet we turn up these photos of the pair of you, taken two days before she died. There's you and Watson, in a caff five minutes from her house. You're even sitting at the same table.'

'I tell you, I didn't know where she lived,' Jennings said, his voice rising. 'I must have bumped into her. That's what must have happened.'

'Doesn't look that way to me. You're waiting for her when she comes in. She goes right over to where you are and sits down, like she's expecting to see you. What do you make of that?'

'I just happened to be there. It was an accident.'

'But you didn't live anywhere near there,' Donovan said insistently. 'Why did you go to that particular cafe?'

'I don't remember.'

'You had an arrangement to meet there, didn't you?'

'No.'

'Then why go there? Why choose that café?'

Jennings shrugged. 'Maybe someone had told me about it. Maybe it was Dr Watson, but I just don't remember. I'm really sorry.'

'That's a lie and you know it.'

'No!' Jennings shouted, gripping the edge of the table with his good hand. 'I'm not lying. It's God's truth.'

'You're full of shit,' Donovan said, with a dismissive shake of her head.

'Why won't you believe me?'

'OK, Mr Jennings,' Pindar continued, more quietly. 'Let's say for a minute, we believe your little story. Why didn't you tell us about it before?'

Tartaglia saw a flicker of relief on Jennings's face, or possibly a glimmer of hope as though Pindar had offered him a lifeline.

'I'm sorry I forgot to mention it,' Jennings said. 'Honest I am. It must have slipped my mind.'

'Slipped your mind?' Donovan's tone was incredulous. 'You are joking.'

'Look. I was upset when I heard what had happened to Dr Watson. Incredibly upset. I just plain forgot.' He looked at her beseechingly, willing her to believe him. 'I'm telling the truth. Please will you listen.'

Donovan shook her head. 'I don't buy that, Michael. It was just two days before she was murdered. How could you forget such a thing so easily?'

'I told you, I was very upset. Anyway, we just had a coffee, that's all. No big deal. I didn't think any more about it.'

'So you met by chance? You really expect us to believe that?'

'But it's the truth. What more can I say?'

'How do you explain following her home?' Pindar shoved a sheaf of photographs across the table. 'For the benefit of the tape, I am showing Mr Jennings photographs taken in the Finchley Road and West End Lane, on Thursday, ninth of February 2006, between three twenty-four p.m. and four thirty-seven p.m.'

As Pindar laid the photographs out in sequence on the table, Donovan leaned forwards across the table towards Jennings. 'They show *you*, Mr Jennings, following Catherine Watson out of the café and along the road.'

With a cursory glance at them, Andrew Harrison gave a small cough. 'With all due respect, they don't show that at all.'

'You then follow her home,' Donovan said, ignoring the solicitor.

Jennings squinted short-sightedly at the photographs and shook his head. 'Is that really me?'

'The fact that my client and Dr Watson appear in the same photographs means absolutely nothing,' Harrison said, with a shrug of his narrow shoulders.

'Are you sure that's me?' Jennings was still studying the photographs with a look of deep puzzlement that Tartaglia found disturbingly convincing.

Jennings was playing his part to perfection, as good as any seasoned actor from the Royal Shakespeare Company. He thought back to the Jennings he had seen in Heather's flat and the raw panic and anger in his eyes. He hadn't been faking then. That was the real Jennings.

'You saying it's not?' Donovan asked.

'If it is, it was a coincidence. I mean, I may have been going the same way, but I wasn't following her.'

'That's rubbish and you know it.'

Harrison shook his head. 'These are busy streets, Sergeant. We're hardly in the back of beyond. The fact that my client appears to be taking the same route as the victim can be interpreted many ways. There are lots of other people in the photographs.'

'But they didn't all know Catherine Watson, did they?' Donovan replied.

Pindar cleared his throat. 'The last few photographs show Mr Jennings at the bus stop outside Catherine Watson's house.'

'You followed her home because you were obsessed with her,' Donovan said, locking eyes with Jennings. 'Isn't that right?'

'No. I liked her, of course. She was my tutor and she was a nice woman. But it wasn't anything more than that. I wasn't obsessed with her.'

'What were you doing at the bus stop outside her house?'

'Catching a bus, I imagine.'

'Where were you going?'

'I have no idea. Home probably.'

'You were living where at the time?'

'Kennington, I think. Or maybe Clapham. I can't remember.'

'According to your statement, it was Clapham.'

'If you say so. I moved around a lot. Couldn't find anywhere decent that I could afford.'

'None of the buses from her street go anywhere near Clapham.'

'Maybe I thought I could change or catch a tube. I honestly don't remember. I mean, can you remember what you were doing on a particular day two years ago? Can you?'

'We're the ones asking the questions, Mr Jennings.'

'But it's a fair question, isn't it?' Jennings turned to Harrison. 'I'll bet they can't.'

'Yes,' Harrison said. 'It's a very fair question. I'm sure a lot of people will agree with you.'

'Going back to the photographs—'

'Excuse me, Sergeant, but all you've come up with so far is a set of old photographs that don't add up to anything. Unless you've got something else up your sleeve, I suggest we call it a day right now.'

'We'll sit here all night if need be.'

'You'll be wasting your time. Based on what you've got here,' he said, tapping the table, 'you haven't got any prospect whatsoever of charging my client with murder and you know it.'

'Your client is going nowhere, Mr Harrison. We know he murdered Catherine Watson.'

Jennings cleared his throat. 'Excuse me, but if you're going to keep me, please can we take a break?' He put his hands on the arms of his chair and half rose. 'I'm really sorry but I need the toilet.'

With a glance at Pindar, Donovan nodded. 'OK. Let's take a ten-minute break here. Interview suspended at eight-fifty p.m.'

'I think I'll follow suit,' Turner said, getting to his feet and cracking his knuckles loudly one by one. He had the edgy look of a man wanting a cigarette rather than a pee, but Tartaglia said nothing. He felt deflated. If Jennings carried on with this show, and there was no reason to think he would crack, they had nothing.

'One minute, Simon,' Steele said, making an effort to push back her chair so that she could see both him and Tartaglia. 'If Jennings killed Catherine Watson, he's the best bloody actor I've come across in years. Am I missing something? We're sure he's our man?'

'He's a clever sod,' Turner said wearily, wiping the sweat from his brow with his hand, as he loomed large over both of them. 'In the absence of anyone else, I suppose he's our best bet.'

Shaking his head, Tartaglia stood up. 'He's more than that. Much more than that. I'm convinced now that he murdered Catherine Watson. When I saw what he'd done to Heather, his girlfriend, any doubts I had went out the window. The marks were almost identical to the ones on Catherine Watson's body. He also threatened to kill Heather if she gave him away and I believe he meant it. You said she was really terrified.' He looked at Turner. 'Simon?'

'Yeah, from what I saw, they look similar,' Turner said grudgingly. 'Although I didn't get a good look.'

'She's obviously not doing it to herself,' Tartaglia said sharply. 'And you told me she was shit scared. But whether Jennings had anything to do with the Holland Park murder's another question. He denies ever having met Rachel Tenison and we have nothing to say that he's lying.' He glanced over at Turner, half-expecting to be contradicted, but Turner's face was without expression, as though his thoughts were elsewhere.

'Let's leave the Holland Park murder out of it for now,' Steele said, blowing her nose loudly again. 'We haven't got even a whiff of anything against him there.' She took a crumpled pack of Day Nurse out of her bag, popped a couple of capsules in her mouth and washed them down with water. 'Any news from Jennings's flat?'

'The search team is finishing up now,' Tartaglia said. 'But no joy.'

'What about the papers from Catherine Watson's flat?'

'We're waiting on the lab. Tomorrow's the earliest we can expect to hear back.'

Steele shivered and pulled her coat even more tightly around her shoulders. 'Well, unless I ask for an extension, and I'm not sure how the powers that be will like that, we've got twenty-four hours from the time he was brought in here. That gives us until roughly six p.m. tomorrow. Then Jennings walks. We've got to come up with something else fast. Any ideas?'

Tartaglia nodded slowly. 'Watching Jennings just now, I kept thinking of how he behaved when we arrested him. His reaction was quite extraordinary.'

Turner raised his eyebrows. 'Violent, you mean. Shows he's guilty.'

'I'm inclined to agree,' Steele said. 'An innocent man doesn't usually pull a knife unless he's crazy.'

'Sure, but that wasn't what I meant,' Tartaglia said. 'Even if Jennings is as guilty as hell, it still doesn't make sense to react like that. He's been arrested before and never shown any signs of violence.'

'That's right,' Turner added, with a nod. 'He was gentle as a lamb.'

'But this time's different. I keep asking myself why. He's not stupid. Why did he panic?'

Steele looked at Tartaglia questioningly. 'So, how do you read it?'

'Jennings knows we're looking for him, but he thinks he's safe in that flat. He comes home as usual and finds me and Simon there. He freaks out and gives us all that stuff about being innocent. Then for no reason he pulls the knife. I remember the look in his eyes. He wasn't scared, he was angry. Like someone who's been...' He searched for the right word.

'Trapped?' Turner suggested.

'No,' Tartaglia replied. 'Not trapped in the physical sense. He looked like someone who's worried about being found out. But if he knows there's nothing to find in his flat, why risk everything? He should have been relaxed, let us take him in without a fight, like last time.'

'You're right,' Turner said, nodding again. 'He was desperate. He would've done anything to get out of there.'

'My guess is he's got something really hot, something that's worth trying to stab me to protect. We know it's not in the flat otherwise we would have found it. Again, if he felt secure about the hiding place, he wouldn't have been so worried.'

'Where else have you tried?' Steele asked.

'I sent a team over to his parents' place in Tulse Hill,' Turner said, 'but nothing's turned up. According to his mother, he hasn't been home for at least six months.'

'We should check his keys,' Tartaglia replied. 'You remember what the girlfriend told you, that he didn't like her touching them?'

'I'll take a look,' Turner said. 'The duty sergeant should have them.'

Steele looked at Tartaglia. 'What are you expecting to find?'

'His rape kit, for starters. If he's been using it on the girlfriend, it's got to be somewhere handy. But I'd also put money on his having Watson's photograph. It was never found. It's very likely he took it as a souvenir, so that he could keep the memory fresh and relive the whole experience when he wanted.'

Steele nodded and got to her feet. 'That makes sense. I want every-

one who's available to check with Jennings's friends and known as-
sociates. Find out if he's asked anyone to keep something for him.'

'I'll also talk to Heather as soon as she comes round,' Tartaglia
said.

'*If* she comes round,' Turner added. 'She looked on her way out,
to me.'

Steele gave a loud sniff and picked up her bag. 'What's the latest?'

'She's alive but on the critical list,' Tartaglia replied. 'I sent Jane
over to A&E earlier.' Jane Downes was one of two family liaison officers on the murder investigation team and had previously worked for
several years for a specialist unit dealing with the victims of rape and
domestic violence. 'Jane and Karen will take it in turns at the hospital. They'll call me if there's any news.'

'Good,' Steele said. 'Let's just hope, for all our sakes, that the girl
lasts the night.'

'If she comes to, perhaps we can get her to press charges for rape,'
Turner said. 'At least that should buy us some more time.'

'No, Simon,' Tartaglia said, firmly. 'That's not good enough. Even
if she survives, who knows if she'll be prepared to do that. You said
she's terrified of him. I want the bastard charged with murder. I'm
banking on finding that photograph.'

30

Just after eight a.m. the next morning, Tartaglia stepped out of the lift onto the tenth floor of the north wing of St Thomas's Hospital. After consulting the large directions board, he followed a series of arrows down a long right-angled corridor towards reception. Pushing open the last set of heavy swing doors, he spotted the short, dumpy figure of Detective Constable Jane Downes. Dressed in a baggy, beige-checked trouser suit, with chin-length straight blonde hair and a heavy fringe, she stood, hand on hip, beside the coffee machine, engrossed in conversation with an Asian nurse sitting behind the reception desk.

'There you are, Jane,' he said, coming up behind her.

She swung round. 'Ooh, you gave me such a fright, Sir. I didn't know you were there.' She looked up at him with large, tired, owlish blue eyes and made a bad job of stifling a yawn.

'You been here all night?' he asked, wondering how her husband and three kids felt about it.

She nodded. 'She's been out for the count for most of it. You got here quicker than I expected.'

'Came straight over when I got your message. Where is she?'

'In a private room on this floor. I sweet-talked them into putting her in there temporarily. Luckily the woman in charge was sympathetic when I gave her the bare bones of what had happened and told her we needed to talk to Heather. It's this way.'

With a quick smile over her shoulder at the nurse, she steered Tartaglia past the reception desk towards another set of doors.

'How is she?' he asked, holding one side open for her.

'She'll be fine. Don't know what they gave her, but she only woke up an hour or so ago. That's when I called you.'

He walked with her along the corridor, slowing his pace so she could keep up. 'Have you spoken to her yet?'

'Only for a few minutes. She's still pretty drowsy and knowing what she's been through and that you were coming over, I didn't want to push it straight away.'

'But you think she'll talk?'

'I don't know. She wasn't very interested in me.'

'You've told her what happened at the flat? That we've arrested Jennings?'

'She certainly heard what I said, although there wasn't much of a reaction.'

'You said they'll discharge her later today. We haven't got much time.'

She sighed. 'I know. I'll see about getting her permission for some photos of her injuries, but she's a long way from pressing charges against him for rape and GBH, if that's what you're hoping for.'

'Well, keep on at her. If we don't turn up anything, we're going to have to let him go.'

'I'll do my best, but when you see her, tread carefully. You're a big, strong-looking man, and particularly intimidating in those leathers.'

'I came on the bike. Shall I go back and change?'

'No. Just be extra gentle. Remember that it was a man who did this to her. And to put up with this sort of abuse, she's probably had a background of male violence in her life. It usually starts early on.' Downes stopped outside a door near the end of the corridor. 'She's in here,' she said, and knocked on the door before pushing it open. Tartaglia followed her inside.

Heather lay propped up in bed attached to a drip. Headphones were clamped to her ears and she was watching GMTV on the television on the opposite wall. Her eyes flicked to Tartaglia and Downes as they came in, then back to the screen. Apart from the areas of bruising around her neck and at her wrists, which had deepened into a violent shade of blackish purple, she still looked incredibly pale. But at least she was alive to tell the story, if only she would trust them.

There being only one chair in the room, Downes went outside to find another while Tartaglia took off his jacket, pulled up the chair beside the bed and sat down. Heather carried on watching the television as though he didn't exist. Looking at her closely, he noticed that her eyes were a light hazel, not grey like Donovan's, and her face was considerably thinner and more angular. The superficial illusion of resemblance receded and he felt strangely relieved. He could see clear thumb-mark bruises on the front of her neck and finger marks on the side; it looked as though Jennings had half-strangled her. They appeared recent, maybe only a couple of days old. The rope marks around her neck and wrists were even clearer now and she had the beginnings of a black eye, which he hadn't noticed before in her bedroom. Even if a good defence brief might try to discredit her, the wounds would speak for themselves. He just hoped she would allow them to take photographs.

After a minute or so of being ignored, he stood up, reached over and gently removed the headphones from her head, as though dealing with a child. She put up no resistance. He used the remote to switch off the TV, then sat back down. For a moment she continued to stare at the screen; then she folded her arms across her bony chest and slowly turned her gaze to him, looking at him questioningly in a half-focussed way.

'My name's Mark,' Tartaglia said. 'Mark Tartaglia. I need your help, Heather.'

She said nothing, still gazing blearily at him.

'I'm here about Michael Jennings.' He spoke slowly and deliberately, letting the words sink in. 'He's done something very bad, very bad indeed. We believe he killed a woman you knew called Catherine Watson.'

'Catherine Watson,' she repeated slowly, as though taking it in. Her voice was sleepy and strangely girlish and nasal.

'Yes. He murdered her. As I said, I need your help.'

'You police?'

He nodded. 'We're holding him somewhere secure, but we need to find out where he keeps his things.'

She looked at him blankly, as though she didn't understand what he meant.

'I've got his keys here.' He pulled the clear plastic bag containing Jennings's bunch of keys out of his zip pocket and held it up for her to see. A chunky silver metal fob dangled from the bunch with some sort of Chinese symbol and he hoped she would recognise it and that it would reassure her that they had Jennings. 'There's one for your flat and one for the front door upstairs, one for his parents' house, one for a padlock...'

'His bike. He has a bike.' She spoke faintly, as though it were an effort.

He smiled, pleased that she had responded. 'That's right. We found it in the coalhole, outside your flat. But there are two others on here.' He shook the bag, trying to hold her attention. 'They look like some sort of padlock keys, too, but we don't know where they're for. Do you have any ideas?'

She sighed and closed her eyes, as if it was all too much for her.

'Please, Heather. I'm sorry to bother you, but it's very important. We've got to find where he keeps his things.' After a minute or so of silence, he asked, 'Did Michael ever show you a photograph of Catherine Watson? It was in a wooden frame.'

'No,' she said, in a half-whisper, eyes still closed.

'You're sure?' She didn't reply. 'I know what he does to you, Heather,' he said softly. 'I know what he puts you through. I'm not going to ask you to talk about it if you don't want to. But he's a very dangerous man. A sick man. He shouldn't have made you do those things. He needs to be locked away so he can't do it again.'

He waited for a response, but there was none. Maybe, in spite of everything, she still cared for Jennings, although she had been desperate enough for money to turn him in. Perhaps she was so inured to what had happened to her, so numb, that the horror of what he had done to her didn't really register.

'He has a knife—more than one. Am I right?'

She opened her eyes and looked down at her hands, rubbing the edge of the sheet gently between her fingers.

'He has a collection of knives; he likes to take them out. They make him feel powerful. He uses them to frighten you, doesn't he? Doesn't he, Heather?'

He waited patiently for some sort of response. A few seconds later, Heather gave an almost imperceptible nod of her head.

Encouraged, he continued, 'I know about the things he uses to secure you—the handcuffs, the plastic ties, the gags and stuff.'

He paused, scanning her gaunt face for some sort of a reaction, but there was none. There was no point asking her why she had put up with it. Jennings had chosen his victim well. She had sunk so low, she would have put up with anything. It was probably the only thing that had saved her, although at some point Jennings would have tired of her and Tartaglia knew what would have happened. He felt a sudden rush of anger on her behalf. He would nail Jennings, as much for Heather as for Catherine Watson.

'Please talk to me, Heather. We need to find these things. They're proof of what he does. And we must have that proof so we can put him away for good. He's got to be keeping them somewhere. We didn't find anything in your flat. Does he bring them home with him?'

Tears had started to roll down her face but she made no sound. Instead, she looked away, eyes focussing back on the dead TV screen.

'He must have a bag, or something. You must have noticed.'

Still she said nothing and he wondered if she were frightened that Jennings would know that she had talked and would come to find her.

'You know, Michael tried to use one of his knives on me when we came to arrest him.' He raised his voice a little, hoping to get her attention. Maybe if she knew that he had been in the flat with her it would make a difference. 'Michael attacked me. Tried to stab me in the heart. If I didn't know how to defend myself, he would probably have killed me.' He hit his fist against his chest for emphasis.

Slowly she turned her head and looked at him, surprised, her mouth slightly open. 'You?'

Tartaglia nodded. 'Yes. I was there, with DI Simon Turner. He's the tall blonde man you let into the flat. We arrested Michael and I had you brought here. I was very worried about you, Heather.'

She was still looking at him, as though she was struggling to remember. 'They told me...you saved my life. Thank you.' Her voice was so very small and faint, he nearly missed her words. She said it simply, as if she was thanking him for doing something trivial.

He smiled again. 'It's OK. I'm just glad I was there. Look, Heather, we've got nothing to hold Michael. Unless we find something to put him in Catherine Watson's flat, we're going to have to let him go later today.'

She tensed and he saw fear in her eyes.

'You don't want that, do you?'

'No. Please...' She gasped, swallowing hard.

'I don't want that either. Before he killed Catherine Watson, he tied her up and did the same things to her that he's been doing to you.

She suffered as you've suffered, but she died. You're lucky he didn't kill you too.' He let the words sink in before adding, 'It's possible he may have killed another woman, just two weeks ago. We've got to put him away. For good. So he can't come back and do it again. Please, please will you think?'

She wiped her eyes and face with the corner of the sheet and stared at him helplessly as though it was beyond her power to remember anything.

He had to keep trying. 'I think one of the reasons he was so desperate to get away and why he attacked me is because he's got something which might incriminate him. He's afraid that if we look before he has a chance to hide whatever it is, we might find it. Is this making sense? Where could he be keeping his stuff, the things he uses on you? Who does he see? Where does he go, when you're not with him?'

After a moment, she nodded. 'Mike has a bag. I know what it means, when he brings it home. What he's going to do.' She bit her lip hard, her fingers clamping so tightly around the sheet that he saw the white of her knuckles.

He wanted to reach out and touch her to comfort her but he didn't want to frighten her.

'So he brings this bag to your flat sometimes?'

'When he comes in with it, he's whistling…happy. "I've got a surprise for you," he says.'

'But it's not a surprise.'

'No. It's…' Her voice trailed into nothing.

'What does it look like?'

'It's small. Black. Like a doctor's bag.'

'Where has he been when he brings this bag home with him? Has he been out at work?'

She shook her head, studying her short, bitten fingernails. 'Not when he comes back from work. Never.'

'So when do you see it?'

Her eyes again fixed for a moment on the blank TV screen. 'After he goes to the gym. Always after the gym.'

'What gym?'

'He works out,' she said quietly, as though she hadn't heard him, her thoughts still on Jennings. 'His friend, Daz, he's on reception. Gets Mike in for free. Mike covers for Daz...when Daz's sick...or too wrecked.'

'Where is the gym?'

She sighed heavily and closed her eyes as if it was all too much of an effort. 'Under the arches, near Waterloo Station.'

'Do you know what it's called?'

'Waterloo Green? Waterloo Place? Something like that. He took me there once...wasn't my sort of thing.'

'Thank you, Heather,' Tartaglia said, standing up, already feeling in his pocket for his mobile phone. 'Thank you very much. I've got to go now.'

'Go?' She looked alarmed and flailing, reached out for his hand. 'Will you come back?'

He caught her hand and gave it a gentle squeeze before placing it back on top of the covers. 'You're safe here for the moment. He has no idea where you are or what happened to you. When they discharge you, Constable Downes, who was with me just now, will find somewhere safe for you to go. We will look after you, I swear.' As he spoke, he looked deep into her eyes, willing her to believe him.

Tears started to stream again and she clenched her fists. 'He'll find me...'

'No. I'll make sure he can't.'

As he spoke, a red-faced Downes shouldered her way into the room carrying an armchair that was almost as big as she was.

'You can't imagine the bureaucracy in this place, just to get a flip-ping chair,' she said, panting and dropping the chair down beside the other one. 'I practically had to fight someone for it.' Dabbing at her face with a tissue, Downes flopped down heavily on the chair and smiled at Heather.

'I've got to go,' Tartaglia said. 'Heather's ready to talk now. Call me with an update.'

'Wait.' The small, breathless squeak came from the bed.

He looked over at Heather. 'I must go now.'

Not taking her eyes off Tartaglia, Heather said, 'Mike's sick. He's evil. You've got to stop him.'

Tartaglia nodded. 'I promise you I'll do everything I can to lock Michael Jennings up for good.'

31

'Do you recognise either of these keys?' Tartaglia shouted over the throb of piped dance music coming from overhead speakers, holding out the two keys in his palm.

Ryan Phillips, the assistant manager of Waterloo Place gym, looked at them and shook his head. 'Members supply their own padlocks for the lockers. That way, there's no comeback if something goes missing from one of them.'

Dressed in a suit and tie, with thinning sandy hair, he was a large-necked, red-faced South African and had only just come on duty. He had initially resisted the police coming into the club until Tartaglia had explained exactly what a search warrant entitled them to do.

Tartaglia handed the keys back to Donovan, who was standing with Minderedes and Wightman and two uniformed officers in the entrance lobby. A tall, blonde girl, in a tight-fitting grey tracksuit, watched open-mouthed from behind the reception desk. Several phones were ringing on the counter in front of her but she ignored them all.

'What I want to know is, how was Michael Jennings able to come and go without being a member?' Tartaglia asked Ryan.

'It's possible he could borrow someone's swipe card. Or someone on the desk could buzz him in.'

'A member of staff, you mean?'

Ryan nodded.

'So much for security,' Tartaglia said, casting his eye around the expensive glass-and-chrome interior, wondering how much an annual membership cost. 'Why don't you clamp down on it?'

'If we catch them, we do. I'm just saying it happens. You wanted to know.'

Tartaglia nodded. 'Thank you for being honest. So, say someone let Jennings into the club, where would he have had access to?'

'The usual guest facilities.'

'Not staff quarters?'

'Unlikely. Someone would spot him and he'd be asked to leave.'

'So if he's got something hidden here, it will be in one of the changing rooms?'

'Can't think of anywhere else it would be.'

Tartaglia turned to Minderedes. 'You heard that?'

'Loud and clear.'

'Start with the members' areas, the men's first. Try every locker and padlock you find.'

'What if the keys don't fit?' Minderedes asked.

'Listen, Cinderella, open them anyway. I want you to go through everything here, no matter who it belongs to. I want this place turned inside out.'

'Is that necessary?' Ryan asked, turning a bright pink. 'There are members in the club.' His collar and tie were already very tight and he looked as though he was about to choke.

'Yes it is, Mr Phillips. The members will just have to put up with it. And I can't have anyone leaving until we're finished.'

As he spoke, the glass entrance doors parted, and a couple of heavily made-up women in padded jackets and jeans, carrying sports bags, walked into the foyer. One of the uniformed PCs stepped forward and shepherded them back outside.

'Make sure nobody goes in or out,' Tartaglia said to the other PC. 'The rest of you can start searching.'

Armed with several copies of the keys, they disappeared through a pair of shiny wooden doors into the club beyond.

Tartaglia turned back to Ryan. 'Do you have someone called Daz working here?'

'Daz Manzara, you mean? What's he done?'

'Nothing, so far. I need to see him. Where is he?'

Ryan looked over at the blonde girl. 'Where's Daz?'

'On his break. I think he's in the café with Mitch.'

The phones were still ringing. Ryan reached behind the desk, picked each one up in turn, then slammed it back in its receiver. 'Get hold of him. Tell him I want to see him now.'

'In your office,' Tartaglia prompted.

'In my office,' Ryan repeated to the girl.

Tartaglia smiled at her. 'Don't say why. OK?'

She gave him a hesitant smile and nodded.

Ryan frowned. 'Has Daz done something wrong?'

'Not so far. Now, let's go to your office.'

With a heavy sigh, Ryan led the way through a door marked MANAGER at the back of the reception area, and into a small, windowless, brightly lit room. It was furnished with a series of filing cabinets, a couple of chairs and a bank of two desks, facing one another, both empty.

'Have a seat,' Ryan said, flopping down behind the nearest one. 'If he's in the café, he won't be long.'

'I'm fine standing.'

Within minutes, a short, stocky, dark-haired man put his head around the door. 'You wanted to see me?'

'Come in and close the door,' Tartaglia said, before Ryan had a chance to reply.

Daz turned to Ryan, bewildered.

'Do as he says,' Ryan said gruffly. 'He's a detective.'

Daz closed the door behind him and stood facing Tartaglia, looking nervous. He was wearing an identical tracksuit to the one worn by the girl behind the desk, only his fitted less well. He was a similar build to Jennings, but possibly a few years older, with swarthy skin, an earring and a small goatee.

Daz spread his hands and looked at Tartaglia questioningly. 'What's it about? I haven't done anything wrong I know of.' He had an Australian accent, although it might have been New Zealand. Tartaglia found it impossible to tell the difference.

'Sit down, please,' Tartaglia said, gesturing towards the chair opposite Ryan. 'You're Daz?'

'Yes. What do you want?'

'I understand you know Michael Jennings.'

Daz nodded. 'We're mates. Why? What's he done?'

'I need to ask you some questions and it's very important that you answer them truthfully. I may need a statement from you.'

Daz shrugged. 'Sure. Whatever. But what's this all about?'

'I'm investigating a murder, Mr Manzara.'

Daz's small brown eyes stretched wide. 'Murder?' He looked at Ryan for confirmation and Ryan nodded. 'What's it got to do with Mike? Is he OK?'

'I can't go into that now,' Tartaglia said, 'but you let him use the club from time to time, am I right?' Seeing Daz hesitate, he added, 'I need the truth.'

'Go on, tell him,' Ryan said, sharply.

Glancing at Ryan, Daz shrugged again. 'I may have done, from time to time.'

'When was he last here? I need to know precisely.'

Still looking uncomfortable, Daz grimaced. 'Maybe Friday, maybe Saturday. Can't remember. What's Mike done?'

'You were on reception? You let him in?'

With another look in Ryan's direction, Daz nodded.

'What did he usually do?'

'What he always does. Used the gym.'

'So he hadn't come to see you?'

'That too.'

'Did you spend any time with him when he was here?'

'Yeah, we had a quick bevy in the bar. Mike had a beer, I had a juice.' He glanced over at Ryan. 'It was on my break.'

Ryan looked away, as though it was nothing to him.

'What did you talk about?'

Daz's eyes swivelled back to Tartaglia and he gulped.

'You're not in trouble,' Tartaglia said, seeing his confusion. 'Not at the moment, at any rate. Just answer the question.'

'OK. Mike talked about some club he wanted to go to. He was always going to clubs, trying to pick up girls. And...' Daz hesitated.

'Well?'

'He wanted to borrow some money...wanted to score some stuff. But I'd just paid my rent so I was skint.' With another glance at Ryan, he clasped his small, stubby-fingered hands in front of him.

'Anything else?'

'He's looking for somewhere to live. Wanted to move out from where he is.'

'So he's thinking about leaving his girlfriend Heather?'

Daz frowned. 'Yeah, but she's not his girl. Not according to him, at any rate. He's just stopping with her till he finds somewhere else.'

'Are you aware he beats Heather up?'

Daz gripped the arms of his chair. 'What, Mike? You gotta be joking. He wouldn't hurt a fly. Is she dead? Is that what this is all about?'

'No.'

'She's a junkie. If she's topped herself, you can't blame Mike.'

'This doesn't concern Heather, or at least not for the moment. Going back to what you were saying, you and Michael Jennings had a drink. What happened next?'

'That was about it. I had to go and help clean up one of the WCs. Some stupid cow had been sick all over the floor. Stuck her finger down her own throat, no doubt. That's what they do around here.'

'Did you see Michael Jennings when he left the club?'

'Yeah. I was back on reception by then.'

'Do you remember if he was carrying anything? A rucksack or a bag or something?'

'Yeah, I think he had a bag of some sort.'

'Can you describe it, please?'

'It's a bag, a sports bag, nothing special.'

'What's it look like? Any distinguishing features?'

'It's navy blue and white, with some kind of logo. Nike, I think.'

'So it's not made of leather?'

'No.'

'Have you ever seen him with any other bag?'

Daz shook his head.

'Are you sure?'

Daz knitted his brows again, thinking hard. 'Come to think of it, maybe he did have another bag with him when he went out. He was carrying something else, but honestly I didn't pay it much attention.'

'This was when, Friday?'

'Maybe Saturday. Now I think about it, I don't think he came in Friday.'

'And you haven't seen him since?'

Daz shook his head.

'Could he have come back here on his own after that?'

Daz shifted in his chair and looked sheepish. 'Well, he asked if he could borrow my swipe card. Said he wanted to come into the gym on Sunday,' again he looked over at Ryan. 'Just to leave some gear, that's all. I wouldn't let him use the club unless I'm here.'

'One last question. Has Michael Jennings ever asked you to keep anything for him? A box, maybe, or another bag?'

'Well...yeah, now you mention it. He gave me a small suitcase to look after, one of those cabin-bag type things. Told me to keep it safe. It's got his valuables in it.'

'Valuables?' Tartaglia tried to stifle his excitement.

Daz scratched his head. 'Personal stuff, things he'd hate to lose or get nicked, I suppose. I guess he didn't trust Heather.'

'Have you opened it?'

Daz looked affronted. 'I wouldn't do anything like that. Anyways, it's got a whacking great padlock on it. Couldn't open it even if I wanted to.'

One of the phones on Ryan's desk started to ring. 'Answer that, will you please?' Tartaglia said to Ryan. As the noise stopped, he turned back to Daz. 'Where do you live?'

'Not far from here. I share a flat with a couple of the other blokes from the club.'

Tartaglia stood up. 'Right. I need you to take me there. I want to see the bag.'

'What, now?' Daz looked over at Ryan, who was talking, hand cupped over the phone. It sounded as though he was explaining what was happening to his superior.

'Yes. We won't be long. I'm sure Ryan here will look after things while you're gone.'

With a final hesitant look in Ryan's direction, Daz slid to his feet and followed Tartaglia to the door. Tartaglia was about to open it when there was a knock and Donovan put her head around the door.

She was smiling. 'Can I have a word?'

Tartaglia turned to Daz. 'Stay right there. I'll be back in a minute.'

Shutting the door behind him, he went out into the lobby with Donovan.

'We've got it,' she said, turning her back on reception, where a young man with a shaved head was leaning on the counter, talking to the girl. 'Dave found it in one of the lockers in the men's changing rooms. You should see the stuff in it; it's a real bag of horrors. Handcuffs, gags, knives, the lot. Makes the stuff we found in Rachel Tenison's flat look like a load of children's toys.'

'Well done,' he said, wanting to punch the air. 'What about the photograph?'

She shook her head.

'OK. Tell Dave to take the bag over to the lab right away. Then I want you and Nick to come with me. Bring the keys and ask Nick to bring his tools, although I hope we won't need them. We're going to look at another bag belonging to Michael Jennings.'

'This is the one,' Daz said, hauling a small, black suitcase down from off the top of his bedroom wardrobe. The zips were padlocked together. 'It's pretty heavy,' he said, testing the weight with his hand. 'Feels like he's got rocks in here.' He blew wads of dust off the edges and top and set it down on the divan, where Minderedes had spread a plastic sheet.

'So, nobody's touched this since Michael Jennings gave this to you three months ago?' Tartaglia asked.

Daz shook his head. 'I'd totally forgotten about it till you mentioned it.'

Tartaglia turned to Minderedes. 'Will you do the honours, Nick?'

'My pleasure.' Minderedes stepped forward with a copy of Jennings's key. Putting on a pair of latex gloves, he tried the key in the padlock. It clicked open immediately. He unzipped the case and flipped open the lid. A handful of hardcore S&M porn magazines lay on the top, along with a couple of DVDs in the same sort of vein.

'Crikey,' Daz said, looking over Minderedes's shoulder. 'Didn't know Mike was into that sort of thing.'

'Please step back,' Minderedes said, pulling out a large plastic shopping bag, the ends tied in a tight knot. He looked over at Tartaglia. 'Shall I open it? Or shall we get it straight down to forensics?'

'I want to see what's inside first,' Tartaglia said. 'But don't take anything out. Just look and tell me what's there and if there's a photograph.'

'Who's the photo of?' Daz said, craning to see.

'If you don't keep quiet, Mr Manzara, I'm going to have to ask you to leave.'

'Feels like clothing or material in here.' Minderedes wrinkled his beaky nose as he felt around inside the bag. 'Jesus, it stinks.' He sniffed again. 'Like dried blood. Sure enough...' He held up the remains of a woman's pale pink blouse and a pair of cream lacy knickers. Both had been slashed into ribbons with something sharp. Both covered in dark brown bloodstains and spatters.

'Fuck me,' Daz said, folding his arms and shaking his head slowly as though he couldn't believe what he was seeing. 'To think that's been sitting up there on my cupboard all this time. Is it for real?'

'I'm afraid so,' Tartaglia said.

'Do you think it's Catherine Watson's?' Donovan asked. 'Her clothing from that evening was never found, but Rachel Tenison's is also missing.'

'Well, there's quite a lot of stuff in here,' Minderedes said, still feeling around in the bag.

'Leave it where it is,' Tartaglia said. 'It will have to go off to the lab. Just tell me if there's a photograph in there.'

'I think I have it, Sir.' Minderedes pulled out a small, framed photograph and held it up for Tartaglia to see. 'Is this it?'

Catherine Watson's smiling face gazed back at him.

'Yes,' he said quietly. 'That's the one.' He closed his eyes for a second, feeling the light-headed near nausea that follows tension. His mind was racing, but he needed to keep himself in check. 'Tie it all up again,' he said, taking a deep breath to calm himself. 'And get it straight over to forensics. We'll need you to make a formal statement, Mr Manzara.'

Still looking shocked, Daz nodded.

As they went downstairs, Tartaglia's phone rang. It was Turner.

'I've just spoken to the lab. They've found a partial print belonging to Jennings on one of the sheets of paper from Watson's flat.'

'What?'

'And get this, there's semen on it. Looks like the scumbag had a wank, then touched the papers.'

'Does the DNA match?'

'I've told them to step on it, but it will be another twenty-four hours before we know. But it explains why a couple of the pages were missing. Jennings thought he'd removed all the evidence of what he'd done in the flat, but he thought wrong. Tell Sam, will you? This is down to her.'

32

Donovan didn't know what she felt more—exhausted or elated. It had been a long and intense day, but a very good one. As she walked up the path to her front door and put her key in the lock, for the first time in a while she felt a sense of fulfilment. Days like today made the job worth doing.

She let herself in, took off her coat and hung it up on the hook by the door. Dropping her handbag on the hall table beside a pile of un-opened post, she carried the bag of groceries she had bought at Tesco's into the kitchen and took out the bottle of Australian shiraz. It had a pretty label with a green and gold dragonfly, which said 14.5 % proof. She unscrewed the cap, poured herself a generous glass and took a large sip. It was full-bodied and tasted good. Just what she needed and she felt instantly more relaxed.

Claire was out at some sort of business event and Donovan had the house to herself. She put Amy Winehouse's *Back to Black* on the kitchen CD player and started to unpack the groceries. She paused to decide what to leave out for her supper and her thoughts turned to Michael Jennings. In the face of all the evidence, he was still in-sisting that he was innocent, and was now trying to shift the blame onto Daz Manzara. He was so convincing, if she hadn't seen the con-tents of the suitcase, or heard about Heather Williams, she would almost have been prepared to believe him. But he could lie all he wanted. The fingerprint, and hopefully his DNA, placed him firmly in Catherine Watson's flat, along with the photograph and Catherine Watson's blood-spattered underwear. The only thread left untied was the Holland Park murder.

She put the last few items away in the cupboard and was about to sit down to enjoy her glass of wine when she heard the sound of her mobile ringing. She ran into the hall and dug around in her handbag to find it, answering just before the call diverted to voicemail.

'Glad I caught you,' Feeney said. 'Someone's passed on a message that was supposed to be for Nick, but he's tied up with Mark at the moment and I can't speak to him. I wouldn't have bothered you but it sounds quite important.'

'Who is it?'

'The woman who used to work at the Greville Tenison gallery. She called in about an hour ago. Her name's Amanda Wade. Apparently Nick spoke to her parents and they then got in touch with her and told her we wanted to speak to her.'

'Where is she?'

'She's helping out at some art fair in New York for the next week or so. Do you want to call her or shall I?'

'I'll deal with it,' Donovan replied. 'Does she know what's happened to Rachel Tenison?'

'She's only just heard, apparently. Sounded quite upset.' Feeney gave Donovan the number, which she scribbled down on the back of one of the envelopes lying on the hall table.

'I'll try it now.'

Donovan hung up and dialled the number, but when she got through a man answered and said that Amanda was somewhere else in the exhibition hall. She left a message, with her mobile number, asking Amanda to call, then went back into the kitchen with the unopened post and phone, sat down at the table and started to leaf through the various envelopes. Amongst the usual bills and fliers, she spotted an envelope with just her name written on the front. It seemed to have been delivered by hand, as there was no stamp or address. She opened it and took out a postcard:

> Dear Sam, thanks for a lovely dinner on Saturday—please
> thank Claire as well—and for putting up with me and all my
> troubles. Things *will* get better! Just to let you know, I'll be
> holding you to your promise, whether you like it or not!
> Love Simon xx
> P.S. I remembered you grew up near Richmond and thought
> you might like this card.

The picture on the front looked vaguely familiar and she saw from
the inscription on the back that it was a picture of the Thames, from
Richmond Hill, painted by Turner; the view had barely changed in
two centuries. She looked at the lovely, peaceful, sunny landscape,
cows grazing in the foreground, the river snaking its way lazily into
the hazy distance. Something nagged at the back of her mind. Simon
certainly was thoughtful, although she had no recollection of telling
him where she had grown up. Maybe Claire had said something. At
least the tone was upbeat and more cheerful than the other evening.
She had barely seen him since and she had been so busy that she had
hardly given their conversation a moment's thought, but she wondered now if she had been rash to say she would have dinner with
him. She had no desire to encourage him.

She was wondering whether she ought to say something to him
when she heard the sound of the doorbell. Reluctantly, she got up to answer it, expecting to find someone collecting for charity on the doorstep,
or a child wanting sponsorship for something, those being the only
callers at that time of night. Instead she found Simon Turner on the top
step, brandishing a bottle of champagne in his hand like a trophy.

'Simon. What are you doing here?' she asked, trying not to sound
too surprised or unfriendly.

He gave her his usual, easygoing, lop-sided smile. 'Hey, Sam. How you doing? Hope you don't mind my coming over, but I thought we should celebrate.'

'That's a nice idea,' she replied a little hesitantly.

'If you're busy, I can come back another time.'

'No. No, I'm not. Come on in.'

He seemed suddenly so huge, towering over her as he stepped into the small, low-ceilinged hall and bending down to give her a peck on the cheek. In spite of the temperature outside, he was coatless and, judging from the suit and tie, had come straight from work via an off-licence.

'Thought you only drank whisky,' she said, eying the expensive-looking bottle.

'And champagne, when there's something to celebrate.'

'Well, make yourself comfortable in there.' She gestured towards the sitting room. 'I'll go and get us a couple of glasses.'

She went into the kitchen and hunted around in the back of the cupboard until she found a couple of flutes. They hadn't been used for a long while and looked rather grimy. She wiped them hurriedly on a tea towel, hoping Turner wouldn't notice, and carried them back into the sitting room, just in time to hear the soft pop of the cork.

'Whoops,' Turner said, quickly grabbing a glass from her hand and holding it under the overflowing bottle. He shook the excess from his hand and licked his fingers, suddenly noticing the small wet patch on the carpet. 'Lucky it doesn't stain. Shall I get a cloth?'

'Don't worry about that. This floor's seen a lot worse.'

Little by little, he filled the glasses and then passed her one, which she took over to the armchair by the window. He sat down with his glass in the middle of the sofa opposite and sank back heavily against the cushions with a sigh, stretching his long legs out in front of him under the coffee table.

'What a day.' He smiled as he raised his glass. 'Cheers, Sam. Here's to you.'

'And to you. It must feel fantastic to have finally nailed Catherine Watson's murderer.'

He nodded and took a gulp of champagne. 'Never thought I'd see the day. I just hope Alan Gifford's watching from wherever he is, poor sod. He'd be real chuffed.' There was a pause, then he said, 'I suppose Mark's all full of himself now—Carolyn Steele's golden boy and Superintendent Cornish's too, no doubt.'

Donovan gave him a weary look. 'Now don't go ruining the moment. You know he deserves most of the credit. He's the one who thought to look at Broadbent's photos, which gave us enough to arrest Jennings. He's also the one who worked out that Jennings was hiding something and he got Heather Williams to tell him about the gym and Jennings's friend, Daz.'

'Suppose so,' Turner said sullenly.

'Come on, Simon. You did your bit too. You found Jennings. Without him, there was nothing.'

He shook his head. 'Of course Mark would have found him in the blink of an eye, given half a chance.'

'Stop being bitter. It doesn't suit you. We're here to celebrate.' She raised her glass. 'Here's to you, Simon. And I mean that.'

He said nothing. Perhaps he felt he didn't deserve any praise.

'Anyway, the last thing Mark's doing is dancing around with glee. He's still fretting about the Holland Park murder. We still have no idea how Rachel Tenison and Jennings met, assuming he's the one responsible.'

Turner shrugged as if it didn't interest him and took another large mouthful of champagne.

'They must have come across one another in one of the bars she visited,' Donovan went on. 'But our only way of proving the link is to splash Jennings's photo all over the media and hope someone comes forward to say they saw them together.'

Turner was staring down at his glass as though mesmerised.

'Do you think Jennings is guilty?' Still no response. 'Simon?'

He looked up and frowned, as though she had interrupted his train of thought. 'Sorry, you lost me. What were you saying?'

'I asked if you honestly think that Jennings is responsible for the Holland Park murder.'

'He's the obvious candidate, isn't he?' he said without enthusiasm. 'But I don't see him owning up to it in a million years. I'm afraid Mark may have to learn to live without a conviction.'

Deciding it was time to steer him off anything to do with Tartaglia, she was about to ask him if he felt like something to eat when she heard the distant ringing of her mobile coming from the kitchen.

'Back in a sec,' she said, putting down her glass and racing along the corridor. She grabbed the phone from the table and flipped it open.

'Hello?'

'This is Amanda Wade. Is that Detective Sergeant Donovan?'

'Yes. Thanks for calling back.'

Getting a paper and pen from her bag in the hall, Donovan sat down at the kitchen table and explained the background to why they wanted to talk to her.

'How long did you work at the gallery?'

'Just four months, up until last Christmas. Then I went off on my travels.'

She had a girlish, breathy Home Counties voice, as though she had just walked straight off the hockey pitch. Donovan pictured a clone of the current gallery assistant, Selina, all silky blonde hair, short skirt and endless toned legs.

'Why such a short time?'

'I was temping. I was only supposed to be there for a month or so while they looked for someone permanent, but I ended up staying longer than expected. I liked working there and they were having problems finding the right person.' She sighed heavily. Donovan was about to ask another question when she added, 'I liked Rachel. She was nice to work for. I'm very, very sorry she's dead.'

'I know this must be upsetting for you, Miss Wade. Would you rather I call back another time?'

'Really, I'm OK. I'll be fine. Please carry on.'

'We're trying to find out about Miss Tenison's friends, particularly male friends, and anyone who she may have been involved with romantically. Unfortunately, at the moment we're drawing a bit of a blank. Can you remember anyone she might have seen or talked to?'

There was a pause at the other end before Amanda spoke. 'Men used to call her, of course. But apart from her brother, there wasn't anybody in particular.'

'There must have been someone else.'

'Well, there was a journalist, Jonathan something.'

'Bourne?'

'Maybe. He used to ring from time to time. She *said* he was a friend.'

Donovan heard the doubt in her tone. 'We know about him,' she replied.

Bourne was still a suspect without an alibi, but if he had killed Rachel Tenison there were no means of knowing how he had found out the details of the Watson case. 'Is there anybody else you can think of? Even someone she didn't seem to know that well? Anyone hanging around?'

There was another pause. 'Well, there was someone. Again she said he was just a friend. She made quite a point of it, in fact, although anyone could see that he couldn't take his eyes off her. He came into the gallery a couple of times when I was there.'

'Do you mean a client?'

'Goodness no. You can tell. And she didn't seem that pleased to see him. Each time she whisked him off somewhere quite quickly, like she wasn't comfortable with him there, although he seemed perfectly nice to me.'

Wondering if the man was Jennings, Donovan asked, 'Was he bothering her?'

'Not then, not actually bothering her. But there was another time. There's a café right opposite the gallery—'

'I know it,' Donovan said. It was where she and Minderedes had bought coffee.

'Well, I saw him sitting outside at one of the tables on the pavement one day. He was just staring into the gallery, bold as brass. I could see him from my desk and it was very odd indeed. Really quite unnerving.'

'Did she know he was there?'

'I watched him for a while and when he didn't leave, I went downstairs to her office and told her. She came up and took a look. When she saw who it was she just said, "Don't worry about him; he'll go away." The way she said it, I got the feeling it had happened before.'

'And did he go away?'

'No. Half an hour later he was still sitting there, still watching. It was freezing but he didn't seem to mind. He had a cup of coffee or something in front of him but I never saw him drink it. It must have been stone cold but he wouldn't let them take it away. I went downstairs again and told her. I thought it was quite creepy.'

'Why didn't you speak to Richard Greville? Or call the police?'

'Richard wasn't there, I'm sure. I suggested calling the police but Rachel wouldn't let me. Said she'd deal with it. She put on her coat and went out to speak to him.'

'Did you see what happened?'

There was another hesitation, followed by a sigh. 'Well, I couldn't help being curious, could I? And I was worried for her, so I kept an eye on him. But nothing happened. She just went across the street and said something to him. Then she came back into the gallery and went downstairs.'

'What did the man do?'

'He sat there for a moment then he got up and left.'

'He didn't come back?'

'Not that I know of.'

'When was this?'

'Just before I left. Early December, I think.'

'Can you describe him?'

'Yes. Yes, I can. He was very tall. I'm about five nine in my heels but he towered over me. He had very short, very blonde hair and the most extraordinary eyes. They were the most striking thing about him.'

'In what way?'

'They were pale blue, like one of those dogs. You know, huskies.'

'Was there anything else?'

'Well, I think she said he was a policeman, although maybe I've got that bit wrong.'

As Amanda spoke, Donovan's eyes fell on the postcard from Simon Turner. She knew what had been bothering her before. It was his handwriting: the same, distinctive, backwards-sloping writing she had seen before on the card sent to Rachel Tenison. Only the colour of the ink was different. That's what had muddled her. She remembered the words and the obsessive, plaintive tone. It was as if someone had moved the tuner on the radio and in place of the hiss of static, everything was sharp and clear.

Her breath caught in her throat. 'A policeman?' She barely heard herself say it.

'Yes. Or a detective,' Amanda babbled away in the background. 'When I said I was going to call the police, Rachel laughed and said there wasn't any point. She said it would be like taking coals to New-castle. Maybe she meant he was a *private* detective and he was keeping watch on her.'

'Do you remember his name?' Simon. Simon Turner. As she waited for Amanda to say it, she thought of him sitting only a few feet away in the other room, knocking back his champagne. What the hell was she going to do? Her hand was trembling as she held the phone to her ear and she leaned back against the wall for support. She must try and keep calm until she could end the call.

'No. I'm sure she never mentioned it.'

'But you'd be able to identify him if you saw him?'

'I think so, although put him in a room with a load of Scandina-vians and I'm not so sure.'

'Do you have any idea how they met?'

'No. Hang on a sec.' Donovan heard a man's voice in the back-ground at the other end, then Amanda came back on the line. 'I'm sorry, but some clients have just arrived and I've got to go. Is there anything else you wanted to know?'

'I think we've covered everything for now. We'll need you to put this in writing. I'll get one of my colleagues to call you tomorrow.'

Trying to focus on the task in hand, she thanked Amanda for her time and ended the call.

As she snapped her phone shut, she heard Turner's voice right behind her.

'Came to give you a top up.'

She wheeled around and stared at him.

He was carrying the bottle and his glass, which he had refilled.

'Sorry. Didn't mean to give you a fright,' he said, putting the bottle down on the table. He peered at her.

'You OK, Sam? You look like you've seen a ghost.'

Feeling as though all the breath had been kicked out of her, Donovan
stared at Turner without focussing. She couldn't think straight. Could-
n't see straight. Images of Holland Park and Rachel Tenison's body
kneeling down in the snow flashed through her mind, followed by the
photographs she had seen from the Watson case file; Turner's case.

'Talk to me, Sam. What's wrong?'

His voice jolted her back to the present. She examined the genial,
familiar features, taking in the look of genuine warmth and concern.
Simon Turner, a murderer? Was it possible? There had to be another
explanation.

'Tell me what's wrong?' he repeated.

'I know about you and Rachel Tenison.' She saw the colour rise in
his face, the tightening of the muscles, the narrowing of his strange,
pale eyes.

'I see.' He took a mouthful of champagne and put down his glass.
He took a pack of cigarettes out of his breast pocket and lit one, gazing at her thoughtfully. 'You're a very clever lady, Miss Donovan. Still
can't work out how you know. Won't you tell me?'

His tone was almost blasé and it shook her. At least he hadn't tried
to deny it. She remembered what he had written on the postcard to
Rachel Tenison only two months before, and the desperate hopelessness of his tone. *I see your face everywhere and I can't stop thinking about
you. Why won't you answer my calls?*

'You were in love with her, weren't you?'

He blew a stream of smoke into the air. 'Yes. Very much. Why?

Does it matter?'

'Jesus, Simon,' she shouted. 'Of course it bloody matters. What happened?'

He sighed and pulled out a chair from the table, straddling it and resting his arms along the back. 'It's pretty straightforward. Things weren't good at home. I don't want to go into the details, but you can probably imagine…' He looked at her for some sort of confirmation, but she just stared back at him. He gave another deep sigh. 'Well, I was interviewing someone in Notting Hill one evening, to do with a case I was working on. By the time I'd finished, it was late and I was dog-tired. Like most nights, I didn't feel like going straight home— couldn't face seeing Nina, if I'm honest. So I went for a drink. There was a place on the way back to the tube and I went in and ordered myself a drink. Rachel was sitting at the bar and we got chatting and had a few more drinks together.'

He frowned as he puffed at his cigarette, as though the memory was painful. 'It's amazing how easy it is to talk to a total stranger,' he continued after a moment. 'Particularly when you're down and a bit the worse for wear. Everyone seems so much more approachable and she was pretty. Very pretty, in fact. She was wearing this tight-fitting black top…well, she looked real good. And she smelled so good too, always wore the same perfume. Something sweet, some sort of flower. Used to smell it afterwards on my clothes. Anyway, she listened. I guess I was lonely and she seemed lonely too. You can fill in the rest.'

'Christ, you make it sound so simple.'

He shrugged. 'Not really. As usual, I wasn't thinking things through. To start with, I suppose I was just looking for something to take my mind off what was going on at home. A diversion, if you like. Something to brighten up the day.'

'Was that all it was?'

He shook his head. 'You know, it was the first bit of excitement and attention I'd had in a long time. Wasn't expecting to get involved. Took me by surprise. Before I knew it, I was in deep, way out of control. She had me hooked, real hooked. I'd have done anything for her. But the more I wanted her, the less she wanted me. That's how it is, sometimes.' He gazed at her through a haze of smoke.

She could just picture him, swept away on a tide of emotion, caught up in everything and under the spell, oblivious to all the signs, desperate, idealistically persistent where others would have given up.

'Is that why Nina left you?'

'No. She doesn't know about Rachel. She went away to sort herself out, or at least that's what she said. As I told you, I thought she had someone else.'

She thought back to what Karen Feeney had said: "Nina hasn't got anyone. Simon's making it all up." She wondered now if Turner had lied to her all along about what had happened between him and Nina and if he was lying now.

Turner took another long drag of the cigarette and stood up. Moving the chair to one side, he came towards her. 'Look, I'm not proud of what I did. I know it was wrong, but I've been paying for it ever since. Christ, she made me pay. She was never out of my mind and I thought I'd go mad with the wanting. I tried to see her, but she wouldn't take my calls, wouldn't even speak to me. She treated me like a piece of shit that she had to scrape off her shoe.'

She pictured him sitting at the table outside the café, hopeless and desperate, waiting for a glimpse of Rachel; saw her going out to speak to him, saying something cruel and cutting that sent him away. She wouldn't have spared him. She would have been brutal. There was no row, no fight. He just accepted his punishment as though he deserved no better.

'What about the laptop and phone? You went to her flat and took them.'

He shook his head. 'No. No, I didn't.'

'Don't lie to me, Simon. Of course you did. You were trying to cover your tracks.'

'Not me, I swear. Sure, I used to send Rachel texts and call her. I even bought a phone specially, so Nina wouldn't know. But I never emailed her. She didn't want me to, and I didn't want anyone in the office snooping and finding out.'

Maybe he had been watching Rachel Tenison's flat. He must have known she had someone with her that night and maybe he had seen Bourne leave early the next morning. He must have been waiting for Rachel when she came out of the building for her run and followed her into the snowy park. Maybe he had just wanted to talk to her, have it out with her, and she hadn't wanted to listen. Perhaps she had provoked him, made him so angry or jealous that he had tried to hold on to her to stop her going. Or maybe he just couldn't bear the idea of anyone else having her.

'It was you that Liz Volpe saw in the park, wasn't it?'

Turner didn't appear to hear. He inhaled some more smoke and seemed to lose himself in his thoughts. He picked up his glass from the table and took another slug of champagne, staring at the bubbles fizzing in the glass, as if looking into another world.

'Answer me, Simon. The roses were from you, weren't they?'

He looked up. 'A crass, sentimental gesture, I know. But it made me feel a bit better.'

'A bit better? Surely you felt guilt? Remorse?'

'No. I've no regrets. I still love her, stupid fool that I am. Bloody fool for love.'

He had smoked the cigarette down to the butt and he went over to the sink and ran it under the tap before throwing it away in the bin. He turned around.

'I'm sorry, Sam. I know I should have told you about Rachel, but

I thought it was better not to. I knew you wouldn't lie for me and I didn't want everyone to find out. I need to get over this on my own somehow. Do you understand?'

She stared at him, horrified, still struggling to take in his extraordinary lack of concern and the terrible thing he had done. He was out of control. Unstable. It had to have been an accident, something spur of the moment, as always his emotions getting the better of him. She couldn't imagine him murdering anyone in cold blood, least of all a woman he had loved.

'If you think you can deal with this on your own, or hope that Jennings will carry the can for you, you're mad,' she shouted. 'I'm going to call Mark now.'

Her phone was on the table behind her and she reached for it.

'Put it down,' he said sharply, moving towards her. 'Please, Sam. Wait. Let's talk about this first. Why does Mark need to know? It doesn't change anything.'

Phone in hand, she hesitated, picturing again in flashes what must have happened. Yes, it had to have been an accident.

'Please put the phone down, Sam,' he repeated, fiercer and louder.

The words penetrated and for the first time, she felt afraid. He wasn't going to let her make the call. How could she have been so wrong about him? Still holding the phone, she let her hand drop to her side and swallowed hard. 'If you think I'm going to cover for you...if you think I'm going to lie for you, you're out of your mind.' She struggled to find the right words. 'I'm sure you didn't *mean* to kill her...'

'Kill her? Me?' He frowned, his mouth dropping open. 'You think I *killed* Rachel?' He reached out.

'Don't touch me,' she said, backing away from him and knocking against the table.

'Christ, you're serious, aren't you? You think I did it! You think I fucking killed her! Sam, you've got to be joking.'

Shaking his head in disbelief, he stretched for his glass and tipped the rest of the champagne into his mouth. He slammed the glass down. 'How could you possibly think I killed Rachel?'

'But it all makes sense.'

He rubbed his face with his hands. 'Shit, nothing's making sense, Sam. Believe me.'

'Stop lying.'

He moved towards her, hands held out. 'Look,' he said, his expression softening momentarily. 'I wouldn't lie to you. I didn't kill her. However much I hated her for the way she treated me, I still loved her.'

The gentleness of his tone threw her and she started to doubt herself. 'If you didn't kill her, why did you keep it all a secret? Why didn't you tell someone you had been her lover?'

'Because of Nina. After everything she's been through, I didn't want her to know. I didn't think she could take it. I also thought there was a chance that we could patch things up, try and start over again.'

'That's bullshit.'

'I may be a fucking idiot, but it's the truth.'

'You must have been over the moon when Steele brought you in on the case, or did you manage to wangle it somehow?'

'No way! How can you say that? It was the last thing I wanted, being involved with anything to do with Rachel's murder. It was torture, hearing about what had happened, reading the files, looking at the photographs of her. Just imagine.'

'I can't.'

He moved closer. 'Jesus Christ, Sam. How can you believe I killed Rachel?' His eyes bored into her.

She didn't reply. She didn't know what to do, what to say. Surely he wouldn't harm her.

'Think, Sam. You know me. Why would I kill her? What earthly purpose would it serve?'

'You were jealous, obsessed,' she said, edging away from him sideways. 'You didn't want anyone else to have her.' There was no point trying to run for it; she wouldn't stand a chance. The only hope was that Claire would come home.

'No. It wasn't like that.'

Without warning he reached over and grabbed her wrists, yanking her towards him and pinning her with his weight against the table. The phone clattered from her hand to the floor.

'Look at me, will you? Honest to God, Sam, you've got to trust me. Please.' He practically lifted her into the air as he spoke.

'You're hurting me,' she shouted. 'Let go.'

His face was slick with sweat and he was so close, she caught the sour reek of champagne and cigarettes on his breath. Could he smell her fear? she wondered. Would he hit her? Would he try and kill her, too, to stop her talking? She tried to wrench herself free but he was far too big and strong.

'You've got to believe me,' he said, still gripping hard. 'I had nothing to do with it.'

She thought of the poem. A love poem was what Professor Spicer had called it. He had first seen it in Catherine Watson's flat. Maybe what Rachel Tenison had made him do to her had reminded him of it. Maybe he had even enjoyed it. That must have been what had given him the idea of linking the murder to the unsolved Watson case.

'Tell me about the poem,' she said, hoping to buy some time. 'Did it strike a chord? Did it mean something to you?'

'Christ, I don't believe I'm hearing this,' he shouted, his face inches away from hers. 'I told you I don't even remember the bloody thing from Catherine Watson's flat. I wasn't lying about that. For fuck's sake, listen to me. I—didn't—kill—Rachel—Tenison.' With each word, he shook her.

She screwed her eyes shut, waiting for the blow.

'Will you just listen, you silly, bloody woman? I have an alibi. Do you hear? I have an alibi.'

It took a moment for the words to penetrate. Stunned, she slowly opened her eyes. Tears streamed down her cheeks as she stared at him. His face was bright red and he looked almost unhinged.

'Yes. I have a fucking watertight, cast-iron alibi.'

He let go of her hands and thrust her away from him. She lost her balance and fell against the table. He picked up the bottle and started to drink from it as though he was incredibly thirsty, the champagne running down his chin and neck.

She struggled to her feet and retreated into the corner of the room, rubbing her wrists, unable to take her eyes off of him. 'I don't believe you.'

He looked up. 'Well, you'll bloody have to,' he said, holding the bottle in one hand and wiping his mouth with the back of the other. 'Just don't think badly of me.'

'What do you mean?'

'Don't judge me, right? I was in a bad, bad way. I'd been back to that bar the night before Rachel died, hoping to see her, wanting to have it out with her. I'd been there most days that week and the week before. I barely went home, except to sleep. As I said, she wouldn't take my calls, wouldn't speak to me. I knew it was over, but I just wanted to tell her how I felt, how much she'd hurt me, how it's wrong to treat someone that way. Anyway, I went back there again, but she wasn't there. I had a few jars, probably a few too many, got talking to this woman at the bar. Well, I ended up going home with her, didn't I?' He shrugged as though such things were inevitable. 'Piece of bloody luck, that, eh?'

'Luck?'

'She'll give me an alibi.'

Was it another lie? 'You sure about that?'

There was a glimmer of a smile. 'Yeah, she'll remember. We had a good time together.'

She wanted to slap him hard, wipe the bragging smirk off his face, the doubts still swilling in her head.

He put the bottle down, moved over to her again and took hold of her limp hands. Beads of perspiration were rolling down his cheeks. 'Sam, please listen. Once and for all, I didn't kill Rachel. You don't know what it's been like, having to keep this all in, having nobody to talk to. Whatever stupid, stupid things I've done, I'm not a murderer. You've got to believe me.'

She wasn't sure, but if he really did have an alibi…but maybe he was lying. Her head was spinning. It was impossible to see clearly.

He was still looking at her, watching her, trying to gauge her reaction. Seeing her falter, he gently pulled her towards him. 'Please believe me, Sam. I could never kill anybody.'

He stared down at her with a look of such hopelessness, that it was impossible not to feel for him, even if she still wasn't sure if he was telling the truth.

'Do you believe me?'

'I don't know what to believe.'

'Believe this.' Without warning, he bent down and tried to kiss her.

'Simon, stop it,' she shouted, jerking her head away and pushing her fists against his chest. 'That won't make it any better and you know it.'

'It might make *me* feel better.'

'That's not the point,' she said, disgusted. In his desperate state, he seemed driven by the moment, incapable of thinking anything through properly, centred only on himself. He was like a child.

He shrugged and turned away, grabbing the tea towel off the rail of the cooker and wiping his face with it.

'Well, thanks for listening.' He spoke as though that ended the matter. 'I suppose I'd better be going.'

'You've got to tell Mark.'

'No. It's none of his fucking business.'

'You've got to, Simon.'

'No fucking way. I'll be crucified.'

'You have no choice.'

'Yes, I have. And I've made it. He's got Jennings. He's the killer. They don't need to know about me and my sordid little affair.'

'You've got to tell the truth.'

'No. It'll ruin me. Is that what you want?' He stared at her angrily.

'Why will it ruin you? All you've done is withhold information. As you say, it doesn't affect the investigation. We know who the killer is. If you explain about wanting to protect your marriage, maybe they'll understand.'

He shook his head vigorously and started to pace up and down the room, hands in his pockets. 'Maybe it won't be a disciplinary matter, but I'll be off the murder squad. Who'll want me then? Tell me that? Do you really see me back in uniform behind a desk? I don't think so.'

'Whatever happens, it's what you've got to do.'

'No.'

'I'll take you to see Mark now. After what you've drunk, you're not fit to drive.'

He glared at her. 'Why? Why must I?'

'You don't need me to explain. You bloody well know why. And if you don't want to talk to him, you should go and see Carolyn Steele. You've got to come clean.'

He shook his head. 'No. I tell you, I'm not going.'

'If you're innocent, if you had nothing to do with Rachel Tenison's murder, that's what you'll do.'

'No. It's too late for that. Thanks for your hospitality and stuff. You'd probably like to see the back of me, so I'll be off now. I need another drink.'

Before she could stop him, he turned on his heel and walked out into the corridor. She ran after him, catching hold of him as he paused to open the front door. She grabbed his arm but he shrugged her away as though she were nothing more than an irritating fly. He yanked open the door and marched outside and down the path.

'Simon, stop. Please come back.'

He was already at the gate. As she ran up to him, he banged the gate shut in front of her, holding it closed so she couldn't pass.

'I'd do anything for you, Sam. But not this.'

She folded her arms about herself, shivering. 'You know it's wrong. You know it.'

'Maybe. But it's what I want to do.'

'I can't believe this! You're putting me in a terrible position.'

'Can't help that, Sam. I told you, I'm very fond of you and I'm real grateful for all you've done. But I'm on my own with this. That's how it's got to be.'

Before she could reply, he leaned over the gate and kissed her full on the mouth.

'Thank you for everything.' Then he turned and strode off down the street.

'If I don't hear from you in half an hour, I'm calling Mark,' she shouted after him. 'Half an hour. Do you hear me?'

She thought she saw him shrug but he kept on going and he didn't look back.

When he disappeared around the corner, Donovan reluctantly went back inside and closed the front door. Her arms and legs felt like

jelly and she needed to sit down. She also needed a drink. With Simon
Turner's words streaming through her mind, still not sure what to believe, she went into the sitting room.

 Her half-drunk glass of red wine was still sitting on the coffee
table, but she didn't feel like it any longer. She needed something
stronger. She went over to the small drinks tray on top of the cupboard in the corner and studied the array of odd-shaped bottles full of
garishly coloured substances. Most of them had been picked up on a
whim by Claire when on holiday. None of them were appetising, unless you were desperate or actually liked things very sweet and syrupy,
which she didn't. The only other option was the bottle of whisky that
Turner had brought when he came to dinner, which still, surprisingly,
had several inches left. She wasn't that fond of whisky, but it was better than nothing.

 Wondering how long she should give him before calling Tartaglia,
she fetched a large tumbler full of ice from the kitchen and poured
herself a generous measure. As she raised the glass to her lips, inhal-
ing the pungent, peaty smell, she heard the sound of the doorbell.

 Thank God he had had the sense to come back, although she suddenly felt wary of seeing him again. She put down her glass and went
to open it, but it wasn't Simon Turner on the doorstep.

34

Nina stood framed in the doorway, the overhead light casting a shadow on her face.

'Nina.'

'Yes. May I come in? I think we need to talk.'

She was still dressed in her work clothes, and with her long hair pulled tightly back in a ponytail she looked tense and strangely pale, her dark eyes deep smudges in her face. Something was wrong.

'I was about to go to bed,' Donovan replied, failing to mask her surprise. 'What do you want?'

'I need to talk to you about Simon.'

'Simon?' She studied the taut, hard lines of Nina's face, wondering what was the matter. 'Can't we do this another time? I'm really tired.'

'No, Sam. It can't wait. Please may I come in?'

Now curious to know why Nina should want to talk to her so urgently, Donovan stepped aside to let her pass and followed her into the sitting room.

'His favourite brand, I see,' Nina said sharply, as she put her handbag down on the coffee table next to Turner's bottle of whisky.

Donovan folded her arms, hoping this wasn't going to take long. 'What do you want to talk about?'

'How much has he told you?'

'About what?'

'About us. About our marriage.'

'Not a great deal,' she said surprised, not knowing what to say or what answer Nina was expecting.

Nina nodded. 'That's typical. It's why I came here. I thought maybe you didn't know what was going on. Did he tell you I'm moving back in?'

Donovan put her hands on her hips and sighed. 'Look, I don't understand why you want to talk to me about this. It's between you and him and it's none of my business.'

Nina flushed and took a deep breath, as though making a great effort. 'Please don't lie, Sam. I saw the two of you together just now. And he was over here the other evening. I know what's going on.'

Donovan shook her head wearily. So that's what it was all about. Nina was jealous. But how on earth did she know where Turner had been? They were supposed to be living apart. Maybe he had said something, not realising how it would be misinterpreted.

'Nothing's going on,' she said calmly. 'You really don't have to worry.'

'I thought you'd say that. Do you mind if I sit down? I've been on my feet all day.'

'I don't think you should be here.'

'I haven't finished,' Nina said, sitting down on the edge of the sofa and smoothing down her skirt. 'You know, it's funny,' she added, pointing an accusatorial finger. 'You're the last person I'd expect him to chase after.'

'Look. I can see you're upset, but he's not chasing after me. He was here to do with work.'

'He arrived with a bottle of champagne and I saw him kiss you just now. And don't try and tell me it was a friendly peck on the cheek because I saw, and I saw the look in his eyes.'

Donovan felt the colour rise to her cheeks. 'You're wrong, I promise you. It doesn't mean anything.'

'Maybe not to you, but how do you think I feel? I'm married to him.' Nina's voice was a shrill whine and Donovan caught the look of bitterness in her eyes.

'What were you doing here? Were you spying on him?'

'I need to know what he's up to. I want to move back in with him and give it another go, but if he's carrying on with you, there's not much point.' She studied her long red nails for a moment, then looked back at Donovan. 'You're a decent person, Sam. I've always liked you. I came here to ask you to give him up.'

There were tears in her eyes and Donovan felt for her. It must have taken a great deal of courage to swallow her pride and come. 'He's not mine to give up. But if you feel that way about him, why did you leave him in the first place? I hear you had someone else.'

Nina looked at her amazed. 'Me? No. Is that what Simon's been saying?' She shook her head as though she couldn't believe it. 'You know, he'll say anything to get what he wants. Sometimes I don't think he even knows what the truth is. He's the one who abandoned me.'

'But you left.'

'Yes, but ask yourself why. After I lost our baby, I had never felt more alone. He was hardly ever home. I barely saw him from day to day. Of course, there were the usual excuses about work and stuff. But he preferred to be in the pub with his mates than come home to me. It was as though he didn't want to have anything to do with me any-more.'

Donovan couldn't imagine Turner being so callous. He was impulsive, unthinking maybe, but not cruel. She remembered what he had said about Nina's depression, about everything spiralling out of control, about his feeling shut out. There were always two sides to a story. As she looked at Nina, with her staring dark eyes and tense, thin-lipped mouth, hands clasped tightly in her lap, she had the impression of someone on the edge, about to break.

'I'm sorry, I—'

'I don't need your sympathy,' Nina cut in sharply. 'I'm telling you because you should know what he's like.'

'Really, Nina. This isn't doing either of us any good. Please will you go?' She walked over to the door and held it open, but Nina didn't move.

'Don't you want to hear why I moved out?' Holding Donovan's gaze, she gave a feeble smile. 'He was having an affair. I knew the signs, you see. I'd been through this before with someone else. When I saw Simon, when he bothered to come home that is, his mind was elsewhere. He was obsessed with her. Sometimes I could smell her perfume on him and once I found strands of her hair twisted around one of his buttons. He was so careless, almost as though he wanted me to find out. It was like I wasn't there anymore, like I was invisible. That's why I decided to leave. It was the only thing I could think of to make him come to his senses.'

Donovan shook her head sadly, thinking of the two of them and what Turner had said earlier about Rachel Tenison: "I still love her, stupid fool that I am. Bloody fool for love." What a horrible situation. Her heart went out to Nina, although she was clearly misguided. There was nothing that would make Turner come to his senses in the way she wanted. He was lost to her.

'You shouldn't be telling me this,' she said quietly, feeling like an intruder, caught in the middle.

'Maybe, but I love him very much. I'm prepared to forgive him and I want him back. So I'm asking you, please leave him alone. He doesn't mean anything to you. You can find someone else.'

'I'm really not in your way, Nina. Honestly.'

'But it has to be you. I know he hasn't been seeing anyone else. The other woman's out of the picture now but he's saying he wants a divorce.'

'So you know about Rachel Tenison. You knew who she was,

about his relationship with her. Did he tell you?' She studied Nina's dark eyes for a reaction.

Nina gave a bitter laugh. 'He didn't tell me, but yes, I knew. Rachel. Rachel. He used to say her name over and over again in his sleep. It wasn't hard to find out where he went and who he was seeing. But it wasn't a real relationship. It was just sex. Simon's like that, like so many men. He never really cared about her.'

'For Christ's sake, you were the crime-scene manager,' Donovan said, picturing Nina walking towards her that morning through the snowy car park in Holland Park. She had seemed perfectly normal. 'Why the hell didn't you say something at the time?'

'I couldn't. It was Sunday. Tracy had just phoned in sick and I was the only other CSM on call. What was I supposed to do? Turn it down? Leave her lying there for all to see? It didn't influence the way I did my job.'

'You still should have said something. Someone else should have been called, however long it took.'

'And air my dirty washing in public? Have everyone laugh at me because my sodding husband can't keep his hands off other women?'

'Nobody would laugh at you,' Donovan replied, struck by the weirdness of the situation. 'But you dealt with her body in the park, you went all over her flat. You were there for days. How…'

'How did I cope?' Nina said with a toss of her head. 'How could I carry on with it all, imagining him there in the flat with her, the two of them in that great big bed of hers, doing stuff together with all those nasty, disgusting things in the trunk? Well, I just put it out of my mind and got on with my job. It didn't matter to me who she was. She was dead. No point worrying about her anymore.'

The way she described it was almost voyeuristic and Donovan felt sickened. 'Don't you care what happened to Rachel Tenison?'

'No. She deserved what she got. She tried to steal my husband.

And if he killed her, I don't care.'

Donovan bit her lip, surprised, not sure if Nina was joking. 'You honestly think Simon killed her?'

'Yes,' Nina said quietly. 'Maybe it was an accident. As I said, I don't care.'

'But Simon has an alibi. He was with someone.'

'With you?'

'No.'

Nina shook her head wearily. 'He's lying again. He was with her. I know. I wanted to speak to him and I went back to the flat, but he was out, as usual. I waited all night but he never came home. When I saw him the next day, he looked wrecked and he stank of booze. Of course he was with her.'

Donovan took a deep breath, her mind whizzing through everything that Turner had said earlier. She thought of him suddenly wanting to leave; he couldn't get out of the house fast enough and he had refused to talk to Tartaglia. Maybe she had been a fool to believe him, but Nina was wrong about one thing. Jonathan Bourne had been at Rachel Tenison's flat that night, not Turner. If Nina was telling the truth and Turner was out all night, where had he gone? He couldn't have been hanging around outside all that time. Even in a car, he would have frozen to death. He had to have stayed somewhere. She had believed him, believed the way he had described picking up the other woman in the bar and going home with her, even down to the smug, laddish little grin that had accompanied 'We had a good time together'. It rang true.

Nina was watching her intently. She saw the sharp, knowing, spiteful look in Nina's eyes and frowned. 'I believe him,' she said firmly, but, starting to puzzle over the situation.

If it wasn't Turner, if her instincts were right about him, who else might have wanted Rachel Tenison dead? Who else might have known about the Catherine Watson case? Not Simon. Nina.

What colour there was had drained from Nina's face and she stood up, slightly unsteady on her heels. Donovan heard the sound of her phone ringing in the kitchen. Maybe it was Turner. Maybe it was Tartaglia. She must speak to someone. Had to get out of there.

'My phone,' she muttered, turning to go. 'I'll just...'

She heard a sudden movement behind her and felt a sharp pain at the back of her head. Her legs crumpled and she fell forwards, hitting the floor with her face. The room was swimming. She felt sick. She closed her eyes, but it made things worse. Somewhere through the fog she heard the faint sound of a bell, then a distant banging noise and voices. Someone was calling her name. The voice grew louder but sounded as if it were underwater. She tried to call out. Tried to say something. Then she felt another splitting pain on the back of her head and everything went dark.

35

It was nearly thirty-six hours before Donovan was allowed visitors in the small ward at St Mary's Hospital, Paddington. She lay deep against the pillows in bed, her head heavily bandaged, feeling a little groggy having only just woken after several hours of sleep. But Tartaglia was relieved to see that, in spite of her injuries, there was some colour in her cheeks and she had managed a faint smile on seeing him.

'How do you feel?' he asked, drawing the curtains around her bed as tightly as possible.

Even though the sky was thick with cloud, the grey wintry morning light coming in from the strip of windows near her bed was still too bright for her. He also wanted to shut out the watchful eyes of the elderly woman lying in the bed opposite, who seemed to have nothing better to do than stare, head cocked, mouth half open, as though she was hoping to join in the conversation.

'Could be worse, I suppose,' Donovan replied, as Tartaglia pulled up a chair and sat down beside her. 'It's like I've got the most massive hangover. I just haven't had the fun of getting it. If I move, my head spins and I feel incredibly nauseous. I've also lost my sense of smell.'

'I hope it's not permanent.'

'Apparently it's quite common if you have a blow to the back of the head. The doctor says it's impossible to tell at this point if I'll get it back.'

'Otherwise you feel OK?' he asked anxiously, searching her face.

'Yes, at least mentally. Certainly a lot better than the last time I was in hospital, if that's what you're getting at.'

He smiled too, relieved that she could refer to the Bridegroom case in such a normal way. He had worried that finding herself back in hospital only a few months later would awaken unpleasant memories from that time. 'Do you remember anything about what happened?'

'No. Nothing. One minute I'm talking to Simon out in the street, then I'm back in the house. I have some sort of vague impression Nina was there, but that's all. Blank. Fast-forward, and I'm waking up here with a nurse staring down at me, feeling my pulse or something. It was quite a shock.'

'I can imagine.' It would have been good to know exactly what had happened and what Nina might have said, but it was a mercy Donovan knew nothing about it. You couldn't have nightmares about something you didn't remember.

'Again, the doctor says my memory will probably come back, but he can't be sure when. To be honest, I don't really care.'

He reached over and gave her small hand a squeeze, hoping she wasn't just putting on a brave face for his sake. 'By the way, when I spoke to Trevor this morning, he sent his love. He wants to come and see you.'

'That's kind, although it'd be easier if he came when I'm back home. They're letting me out tomorrow, if my scan's OK. If not, it will be the next day.'

'I'll tell him. Nice flowers,' he said, glancing at the huge, brimming vase of dusky pink roses and stargazer lilies by the bed, wondering who had brought them and wishing that he had had time to get her some on the way. Even over the general medicinal hospital smell, the perfume was headily sweet and overpowering. She was lucky she couldn't smell it.

'They're from Simon, according to the card, which the nurse read out to me. I was asleep when he came earlier.'

'He came to see you?' he asked, amazed that Turner had dared show his face and unaccountably irritated that he had given her flowers.

'Yes.'

'I suppose it's the least he could do. Are the chocolates from him as well?'

'No. They're from Karen. She came in just before you.'

'There was I, thinking I was going to be the first to see you.'

'You'll just have to be quicker next time,' she said, a little sharply. 'So tell me what happened. I know Nina...'

'She's been charged, although she's admitting nothing. She's trying to put the blame on Simon.'

'Simon's alibi...did I dream it?'

'No, you didn't. Assuming the woman's telling the truth, and we have no reason to doubt her, it checks out. So he's in the clear, at least as far as any murder charge is concerned, although I don't know what will happen to him as far as work goes.'

'But there's evidence against Nina?'

'Yes. It turns out she was one of the SOCOs on the Catherine Watson case. It's apparently where she and Simon first met. She knew about the poem and the way Catherine Watson's body was displayed. We couldn't find Rachel Tenison's laptop and phone, but we did turn up the missing photograph. It was wrapped in a pair of knickers in one of Nina's suitcases at her mother's house. Even though there's nothing to actually put her at the crime scene, the CPS say it's enough to go to trial, along with motive and other circumstantial stuff.'

She gave a deep, contented sigh. 'Do you think she planned it all?'

Tartaglia puckered his lips. 'Difficult to tell, although I think probably not. If nothing else, given her background, you'd think she'd have done things differently, more perfectly and less spur of the moment.'

'But the snow...it *was* perfect. The best way to get rid of any evidence, if there was any. If the body hadn't been found until after it had melted...'

He shrugged. 'Who knows. Reading between the lines, based on the little she's said and what we've turned up so far, I think she'd been watching Simon and Rachel for a while. She probably knew Rachel went running most mornings. Nina thought Simon was with her that night, although we know otherwise, and when Rachel came out for her morning run, I think Nina just saw the opportunity and seized it. I'll bet she killed her right there on the path. I'd guess that trying to make it look like the Watson murder only occurred to her later, when she'd had time to think about it.'

Donovan sighed again, then closed her eyes.

He imagined Nina panicking, possibly horrified at what she had done. As he pictured her standing there on the dimly-lit, snowy path looking down at Rachel Tenison's body, part of him refused to see her as a cold-blooded killer, even though she had been thinking clearly enough to try and hide the body. Somehow she had managed to drag or pull it off the path and into the woodland area, leaving it out of sight in the bushes, probably under one of the large holly trees close to where it was found two days later. There it had lain, undisturbed, until Nina had come back later, either that night or early Saturday morning.

'Maybe she tried to confront Rachel,' he continued, still trying to work out in his mind what had happened. 'Maybe she hadn't intended to kill her. Rachel tried to get away and she felt she had to stop her, make her listen or something. Whatever the truth, she was sufficiently calculating afterwards to go to the flat to get the laptop and phone.'

'She would have wanted to see what they wrote to each other, to understand what was really going on between them. That's what I would have wanted…in her place.' She spoke softly and her voice drifted away.

'Maybe, when she went to the flat, she had a look around and saw the photographs and the things in the trunk. Maybe they made her think of the Catherine Watson case and the poem. It certainly fitted the bill with Rachel. Then she went back to the park and shifted the body and made it look the way Catherine's body had been found.'

'It must have been hell for her going to the flat and finding all those things, imagining Simon...'

He reached over and touched her hand again. 'Don't worry yourself about it now.'

'I can't help it. I can't stop thinking about it. Do you feel any sympathy for her?'

'Do *I*?' He was surprised at the question, wondering why it all seemed to matter so much to her. Yet again she was accusing him of being unsympathetic and it made him doubt himself for a moment. Strangely, he felt some sympathy for Turner, understanding easily how he had fallen under the spell of a woman like Rachel Tenison and knowing how cruelly she would have treated him. But he felt nothing for Nina. 'I might have done, given everything, but she nearly killed you. She meant to kill you, I'm sure.'

For a moment, Donovan said nothing. Then she nodded slowly. 'Maybe you're right. Maybe I'm being soft. So what happened? Karen said Simon found me, that he came back to my house for some reason.'

'Yes. You told him to, or so he says. Apparently you had given him some sort of ultimatum.' He looked at her questioningly, wondering what exactly had gone on between the two of them, and if it was more than just friendship, at least on Donovan's side. How she could find a man like Turner attractive was beyond him, but he knew better than to say so. Whatever had happened, it had been a stroke of luck, Turner going back there, seeing Nina's car in the street. 'When you didn't answer the doorbell, he became worried.'

'Why didn't she kill me?'

'Simon got there first. He looked through the window and apparently he could just see your feet poking out from behind a chair. So he broke down the door.'

'I see. What happened to Nina?'

'She got away out the back, or at least that's what he says.' Again he wondered what had really gone on in that house, whether Turner and Nina had spoken and if he had let Nina get away.

'But you caught her?'

'She gave herself up. You know, I think maybe Simon had an idea Nina would be there. Maybe he had seen her earlier.'

'No,' she said, with a small shake of her head that made her wince and close her eyes. 'He couldn't know, otherwise he wouldn't have…' She paused and peered up at him, frowning, as though struggling to make sense of it all. 'If he knew she was there, why did he go away? I'm sure he hadn't seen her. He can't have done.'

'I'm sure you're right,' he said, wanting to calm her.

'And why would he be worrying about me when he saw her car—unless he knew…' Again her voice trailed away.

'Don't think about it now,' Tartaglia said firmly, concerned that Donovan seemed more preoccupied with Turner than anything else.

In the back of his mind, he was sure that Turner had either known all along, or suspected, that Nina had murdered Rachel. However, he had no proof, and Turner had repeatedly denied it in the many interviews with his superiors that followed Nina's arrest. The official view seemed to be heading in the direction of accepting Turner's word, but it still didn't add up. Who else had a link to both the Watson murder and Rachel Tenison? Surely Turner must have wondered about it. His saying nothing about his affair to protect his marriage also didn't hold water. The marriage was over, at least as far as he was concerned. There was nothing to risk. The only explanation that made sense was that he was protecting Nina out of some vestige of love, or a mixture of shame and guilt. His obsession had destroyed three lives and it must have weighed heavily on him, although

Tartaglia wasn't sure if he was the sort of man to have a conscience. But the last thing he wanted to do at this point was openly to voice what were only suspicions to Donovan. The less she thought about Turner, the better. She needed to recover, and hopefully that recovery wouldn't involve him.

'No. It doesn't make sense,' she continued emphatically, as though she had thought it all through. 'There's no way Simon knew that Nina had killed Rachel. You remember what he was like? He was in a desperate state, just getting through the day and the night. I don't believe he was thinking about anything logically or clearly. I'm sure if he had suspected anything, he would have said something. He really loved Rachel Tenison.'

'I hope you're right,' he said, although he didn't think so. 'Anyway, it seems as though Nina had been stalking both Simon and Rachel Tenison for a while. When we showed a photograph of her to the assistant at the Greville Tenison gallery and to the porter in Rachel's block, they both remembered her. She had gone into the gallery a couple of times, pretending to be a potential client. The porter also remembers her asking questions, claiming to be an old school friend. As she was a woman and wasn't behaving at all suspiciously, neither thought to mention it.'

'Poor Nina. She killed a woman and all for bloody nothing. Simon would never have gone back to her.'

He gazed at her for a moment, wondering what to say. Her normal common sense seemed to have deserted her; she was unable to accept that Turner had played any part in what had happened.

'Who knows what goes on between two people and what drove her to it?' he said pointedly, refusing to let Turner off the hook.

'Quite.' He could tell from the sharpness of her tone that she didn't want to talk about it anymore.

A sudden babble of voices penetrated through the curtains from across the room, where one of the other women in the ward was greeting some visitors. 'I hope I don't have to stay here longer than one more night,' Donovan said. 'One of the women snores really loudly and another talks in her sleep. I'm going to go stir crazy. Apart from my head, there's nothing wrong with me.'

'Well, if you are sent home, maybe you'll feel up to going out somewhere at the weekend?'

'Go out? Like this?' She raised a hand to her bandaged head.

'Yes. You don't look that bad.'

'*That* bad? Thanks.'

'I just thought you might like to get out. One of my cousins has a band...'

'Which cousin is that? You have so many, I lose track.'

'This one's called Alessandro. He runs a very successful broking business in Milan, but in his spare time he plays in a band. They're really good. They do cover versions of everything from the Beatles to U2. Anyway, they're playing in a charity gig for one of his clients...'

'And you wanted me to come with you?'

'Yes. Thought you might enjoy it. If you haven't any other plans.'

'Is Nicoletta going to be there?'

'Probably.'

'Any of her girlfriends?'

'She mentioned she might bring Sarah along.'

'Sarah?'

'The latest one of her friends she's trying to set me up with. I think I told you.'

'I see.' Her face cracked into a smile and she closed her eyes for a moment. He wondered what she found so funny. 'If I feel up to it, that would be very nice, thanks,' she said, after a moment. 'But I don't want to be your bodyguard. And I don't need looking after, you know, if that's what you're thinking.'

He cursed himself for saying the wrong thing, although sometimes there was no pleasing her. 'I wasn't. That wasn't what I meant. I just thought—'

'Knock, knock,' said a cheery female voice on the other side of the curtain. Before Tartaglia could finish what he was going to say, Claire poked her head through the gap.

'Hi, Mark. Hi, Sam. Hope I'm not interrupting anything. I can always come back later.'

'No, don't go,' Donovan said. 'We're done, for now. Unless there's anything else?' She looked over at Tartaglia inquiringly, still smiling. 'Alessandro? I've always liked that name. Let me know when and where.'